# THE SEXTANT

## By
## Lynn Clay Byrne

Published by New Generation Publishing in 2013

Copyright © Lynn Clay Byrne 2013

First Edition

**www.newgeneration-publishing.com**

 **New Generation Publishing**

This story
is in memory of
Patrick Clay Byrne
My first born
My first editor
My songbird

# FOREWORD

I would just like to introduce you to the origin of this family saga before you leap into it. It encompasses more than sixty years, from 1880 to 1947. It veers from the Long Island Sound in post-WWII America to the Turkish occupation of Crete, travels around the world on a steamship and back again to Long Island, a couple of times. It is navigated by Greek shipping captains at the height of Greek shipping dominance. The story is riddled with mythological symbols and characters derived from the gods themselves. But the heart of the story is a simple coming-of-age tale of a lonesome, yearning boy trying to find the hero path.

I chose the hero path, or monomyth, as described by my own hero, acclaimed mythologist Joseph Campbell. His compilation of similarities in traditions across all cultures and religions throughout history is astonishing, and forms the basis of his own philosophy that is soulfully steeped in universal lore. The hero theme as he describes it, and as depicted in many well-known stories throughout time, includes such stages as The Call to Adventure, The Crossing of the Threshold, The Belly of the Whale, Atonement with the Father and Bringing the Elixir. In my version of these stages, the characters strive as the gods strived; passionate, flawed, vulnerable.

In order to match the breadth of a god's desires, the hero must have within him a boldness and vitality that allows him to overcome weakness, and to embrace triumph; rarer still, the courage of choosing the hero path and aspiring for the privilege of following it.

"Find a place inside where there's joy,
and the joy will burn out the pain."

~Joseph Campbell

# THE SEXTANT

## List of Characters

CRETE

Chiron, born 1862
Corinna, born 1862
Kristof Karras, married to
    Maria of Chios


BEECHWOOD

Karras Family
    Kristof, ship captain, born 1862
    Maria, born 1870
    Nick, their son, born 1912

Bayard Family
    Hephron, born 1902, married to
        Adrianne, born 1907, parents of
            Herman
            Iris, twins, born 1937

Maggie McGinley, housekeeper, born 1888

Clement and Clarisse, staff

Thea, born 1913, cook, granddaughter of Corinna

Chiron, ship captain, estate keeper

LOWER EAST SIDE

Anna, born 1884, daughter of Corinna, married to
        Jasen Nikandros, parents of
                Alexsy, born 1910, married to
                Adicia, parents of
                        Perry, born 1932
                        Todd, born 1933
    Thea

# CHAPTER 1

## 1946

Adrianne was indisposed.

The sun had risen above the copper beech outside her window. The dew had succumbed on the most far-flung peonies. Downstairs, a shaft of light reposed across a Norman Rockwell magazine cover, set at the perfect angle on the drawing room table.

The kitchen was quiet as well, abandoned for the morning and left to its echoes of bustle and clang. Thea was abed, but that was to be expected as she spent much of her time there these days. The hallway leading from the kitchen to her room was dim and cool, alluring to any who might approach her door. But none did that morning.

It was left to Maggie to contain the children, or the little pirates, as she called them. Her housekeeper's cap was already askew, making it impossible to take her seriously. She insisted on wearing it, a habit left over from the first family she had served here over twenty years ago, claiming it protected her hair from furry (or was it fairy?) dust mites. The little pirates often speculated about the whereabouts of such battle-worthy scoundrels, but the possibilities were endless and invariably resulted in a round of giggles and shaking of heads, in sympathy for plights experienced only by Maggie McGinley.

At the moment, she was flapping her apron at the puppy, trying to keep him away from her laundry basket. He had already succeeded in dragging a pillowcase half-way down the pine needle path leading from the clothes lines on the far side of the house toward the veranda behind. The twins, Iris and Herman, were hooting at his antics and Todd was bowled over with delight. The puppy was intently advancing toward his next victim, a lacy white table cloth, creeping along on stealthy foot pads, convinced his prey was unsuspecting.

Maggie heaved her broad bosom in his direction, apron unfurled, and unleashed a burst of epithets that few had heard from her before and which gave pause even to Herman, who was normally immune to all reprimands. The puppy, though thrown off course, was undaunted. His eye caught Iris' canvas rag doll, lying on the grass, abandoned at the onset of the caper. The little rogue pounced on it and ran off down the path, vanishing around the corner and into the garden.

The small crowd scampered quickly in pursuit, Maggie lumbering behind in her heavy work brogues. The tone was changing rapidly, as everyone knew of Iris' attachment to that doll, and no one wanted to face the consequences of its demise, or even the effects of any new teeth marks upon her otherwise battered, faded and beloved personage.

Three years older than the twins, long-legged and strong, Todd rounded the last stand of scrub pines along the north edge of the property in time to see the puppy race across the beach and leap from the edge of the surf straight into an oncoming wave. Todd skidded to a stop in surprise, and in frank admiration, at the dog's athletic grace and bold escape. By the time Herman arrived, he lurched to a stop as well, scanning the shore line left to right, realizing the puppy had disappeared. Iris ran by them, and unleashed a wail when she saw the deserted landscape. A raven caught her eye as it cawed and shook out its oily wings, clinging to its perch on the nearest dock post, intently eying the water where the puppy was last seen.

In a sudden fountain of spray, the puppy rose above the surface like a geyser, seemingly delighted with his swim, his very first, and paddled until his paws touched sand. His jaws were plainly empty. He loped across the receding shoreline, his back feet getting ahead of his front a couple of times and tumbling his muzzle into soft sand. He ran wide of the human dragnet, came ashore farther down the beach and turned to look again at the waves, tail wagging as if in anticipation of another assault.

Maggie staggered onto the scene, minus a couple of loose hairpins, including those holding her cap to her head. She waved her wadded cap at the gathering before her, presumably as a substitute for the words she could not formulate while heaving so. The first person she saw as she stood clutching her knees was Hephron Bayard, standing a few feet closer to the shore than his companion, Chiron. Both were intently watching the water, uncertain yet apparently amused by what they saw. She followed their gaze.

Gasps escaped all around, joined by a fresh wail from Iris, when the puppy leapt directly back into the surf and disappeared once more. The twins ran to Hephron, unwilling to take their eyes off the empty waves, yet anxious to throw their arms around him for comfort. "Daddy, Daddy," Iris cried. "My doll is drowning! The puppy!" She choked and pointed. "The puppy—he disappeared with my baby doll!"

At that moment, the puppy's head shot above the surface again but was instantly submerged by an oncoming wave. Everyone moved forward as one, leaning in to get a better view into the dark sea froth. The ones who squinted could swear they saw eyes coming toward them just under the surface, eyes propelled swiftly through the foam and tumble of the wave. Eyes and a nose and floppy ears approached at a terrific pace. "Oh my, my," Daddy breathed.

The wave receded and the puppy emerged ahead of the surf and paddled back serenely to the shore, where he gently deposited the sodden doll and looked up at Iris, wagging his tail in pride at having rescued her treasure.

The raven flew off.

As Iris swooned in turn over her doll and the puppy, the two boys rolled in the wet sand in a tumult of gritty, salty puppy kisses and whoops of delight. Daddy watched for a moment, coming to a decision. He made the announcement there on the spot that he had chosen the name for their new little sea-dog. "Poseidon," he boomed, as if it had been decreed by the sea god himself, as if this were the propitious baptism. As in fact, they would discover, it was.

Hephron, or Heph as he was known, looked over at Chiron, eyes gently gleaming. Chiron nodded formally and stated, "I believe you have chosen a Chesapeake Bay Retriever worthy of its name, Sir." And so it was settled.

"Daddy," Iris pulled on Heph's sleeve. "She wasn't really drowning." She stood on tip-toes to get closer to his ear. "I knew she couldn't really drown," she whispered. "It just felt to me like she was drowning." Heph looked down sympathetically into his nine-year-old daughter's beseeching blue eyes. He could tell that despite her relief that the episode was over, she was worried that she had acted a little babyish in front of her father. He and she both knew for a fact she had opened herself up to ridicule at the boys' first opportunity.

"I know how it felt," he said. "I felt that way, too." Iris smiled shyly, and the pain evaporated from her eyes. She could take on the boys later. She had plenty of practice with that.

As they started back toward the house, Heph scooped up Poseidon and began vigorously brushing the sand off his wet fur, which even at ten weeks was showing signs of future curls along his rust-colored flanks. Heph seemed unaware of the ruinous effect on his summer-weight suit, or the blood in Maggie's eye at the sight of him. The doll was receiving similar grooming from Iris and the boys were trying out nicknames for Poseidon, then solemnly agreeing no substitute could be worthy, when the first fat drops of rain began to fall. No one had noticed the clouds forming above the shoreline or the sky beginning to darken. Their attention had been riveted exclusively on the sea and its occupants.

The distended raindrops fell in slow motion at first, bursting upon contact into cascades of tiny droplets. One by one each person looked up, ducked their head reflexively into their shoulders and began to scurry for cover. Chiron had left them back at the shore for the path leading to his rooms in the gatehouse. Maggie, clucking, threw out her arms in a wide circle to herd her young charges toward the back entrance of the house by the drive, into the cloak room near the kitchen. Heph turned off toward the greenhouse, where he planned to wash down the pup in the garden shed, dry him and get him settled for a well-earned nap. The pace of the raindrops picked up and began to pelt.

The noisy excitement of the dripping, bubbling children spilled across the kitchen, where Thea stood by the counter. Leaning against the edge of the sink as if for support, she turned with effort in response to the commotion. She smiled with quiet enjoyment at their bedraggled appearance, their laughter, their exuberance, their inescapable life force. Her glance may have rested a little longer on Todd, assessing any signs of damage. Finding none, she allowed herself a chuckle when Maggie exclaimed, "Oh, no you don't, you little pirate-girl," as her quick fingers grabbed the tail of Iris' blouse and yanked her back from the brink of the clean wooden floor. Her motion was accompanied by a flash and a crack of thunder so close to the house they all jumped and shrieks of alarm escaped from every mouth. The lights flickered, hesitated, came back on. The two women glanced at each other. The kids became consumed by their own squeals and had to be hushed several times before they realized it was themselves making all the racket. By that time another thunderclap struck and the lightning that produced it was enough to finish off the electricity for the rest of the day.

Thea provided the children lunch in the kitchen, but had soon cleaned up and disappeared into her bedroom while they ate, leaving Maggie to direct proper napkin use and general comportment. The room was charged with speculation and dramatic predictions about the storm, raising the hair on their arms and the tenor of their voices. But the excitement began to wear off with the continued drumming of the rain overhead, first in sheets and then steadily, showing no signs of abatement. As Maggie directed them to place their dishes in the sink and push in their chairs properly, the "what if" questions began.

"What if it never stops raining?" asked Herman.

"What if the ocean rises so high it covers the whole house and we have to climb up to the roof to get air?" speculated Iris.

"What if I throw your precious doll back in the water, then, from the top of the roof?" asked Todd archly. "Do you think Poseidon"—here he stopped to listen to the sound of that name as it lingered in the air—"do you think Poseidon would save her for you again? Before she drowns?"

"Maggieeee!"

Another lightning flash, followed more slowly this time by another clap of thunder. Maggie raised her eyes to the ceiling, or the heavens, grateful for the first indication that the storm may be passing. "Maggie, what if the house was struck by lightning and caught on fire? Would we all burn up like that fried chicken you made last week?" demanded Herman, also regarding the ceiling. Maggie squinted at him and scowled. That was a night when Thea, the family cook, hadn't been up to making supper.

"Fire?" asked Maggie, raising an eyebrow at Herman as if he had no idea of the meaning of the word. She was formulating an idea. "I'll tell you about fires, young buccaneer. The Equitable Life Assurance Fire of 1912. Fried chicken my eye." With that one eye on the hallway leading to Thea's room, she motioned, "Let's go on out by the veranda and see if we can sit ourselves under the awning where there's at least a little bit of air to breathe. I wonder who closed all those windows before the storm came?" She was speaking to herself now, frankly perplexed as neither Thea nor Adrianne was likely to have performed the duty and everyone else had been down by the water. Maybe it was Chiron's assistant, she considered. He was probably around here somewhere.

She reached up to adjust her cap, only to be reminded it was no longer protecting her damp, exposed head. She grabbed a tuft of hair and pulled in frustration and quickly shooed the children out of the kitchen into the back hall. Then she returned to the cloak room, rummaging among the discarded shoes and tracks of mud and sand for the wadded, wrinkled, essential housekeeper's cap. No good, it was missing. She must have dropped it outside in all the confusion.

Her mouth formed a perfect O. She stood stock still. The rain! Outside! Her laundry! "Oh Lordy!" she cried, forgetting the pirates and the tale of fires and even the lightning. She charged out the back door, straight into the deluge. It took little time for her clothes to be soaked through as she lunged around the back of the house, past the veranda where the children, dry under the awning, watched her with wide-eyed curiosity. She hurried past them, unseeing, across the top of the garden, onto the pine needle path and around the corner toward the far side of the yard, to face the reproving clothesline.

"What's she trying to save wet clothes from, anyway?" mused Herman.

It was just as well the children did not hear Maggie's tale of the Equitable Life Assurance Fire of 1912 that day. It was going to give them nightmares when they did hear it and Maggie sometimes lost sight of which lessons were best left for another age and time.

They chose to visit Chiron instead. Confident that there were no chaperones on duty at the moment, they ran out from under the awning on the veranda, across the patio and towards the gatehouse, their favorite destination. They stopped to wipe their feet with care, knocked politely and awaited the habitual "Enter!" from the caretaker's salty, deep-throated voice. There was a hint of an ancient accent in that voice, a cultured accent that the children took for granted.

They entered one by one, dripping from every strand of hair and clothing seam. They waited by the doorway while their eyes adjusted to the smoky semi-darkness of the room that served as Chiron's parlor. They noted the hand-wave beckoning them into its recesses, and each one smiled with anticipation at the sign of welcome. They approached the table where

Chiron was seated, where the space around him was lit by the glow from a high window whose single shaft of light slanted sharply, piercing the floating dust particles to focus on his workspace below. As they gathered around the table, they felt bathed in his circle of nimbus. Despite the humidity of the June thunderstorm, the soggy clothing and bare feet puddling on the cold stone floor, they were content.

Chiron's eyes showed no sign of dismay at their appearance. Though he said nothing, he leaned forward to regard the effects of dripping rain water on his floor.

"Oh, sorry!"

"Sorry, Chiron!"

"Oh gee, look at the floor, wow!" the three exclaimed at once. They all turned and ran back to the door, swung it open wide and stepped back out onto the doormat. They began wiping their feet again vigorously, wringing out their shirttails, shaking the water from their hair and smoothing it down for a more sober, plastered look of presentability. A couple more quick squeezes to their shorts cuffs and they were satisfied. They peered back into the dim light to see if Chiron concurred. He nodded once. They scampered in, forgetting their formal demeanor of a few minutes ago at their delight to be so easily reconciled. The twins shouldered by each other trying to reach the desk first. Todd turned right toward the gatehouse storeroom and came back with an old towel, which he used to wipe up the last of the water, aware that Chiron watched his progress.

The gatehouse, which also served as Chiron's home, was a museum of seafaring relics. The walls behind the table were covered with large maps of the oceans of the world, two dating from the mid 1800s, one from 1893 and one, the largest and the only one displayed behind glass, was bought by Chiron in London in 1913, the year Thea was born and sixteen years before he left the sea for good.

His footlocker stood by the wall next to his desk. The rounded top boasted wide brass bands, burnished from countless rubbings, and leather straps at each end, black from regular oiling. The plain wood box had been kept in perfect condition, despite the years of sea salt and battering storms. To Iris, the trunk was imposing and mysterious, as long as she was tall, as deep as four of her footsteps and a little too high to sit on without climbing. Not that she would ever do that again, after Chiron found her there pretending it was Queen Persephone's throne. Persephone never should have leaned against the map behind the trunk, either.

Her favorite article, however, the object she always ran to immediately when she entered Chiron's home, was the "Little Midshipman" on his desk. It was a miniature statue from a London instrument maker of the last century, dressed gaily in a sailor's outfit, painted in bright blues and deep reds. He held a tiny sextant in his raised arm. This time as ever, she checked to see that the sextant's directional mechanism still moved freely on its hinge and then adjusted the angle at which the midshipman stood, facing between Chiron's chair and her own position at the desk, just so. She was satisfied.

She was then free to turn her eye toward the other object of her regular assessment, the bottle of Remy Martin cognac on the shelf behind the desk that served as a bookend as well as a loyal companion to the seaman an arm's length away. She carefully noted the level of golden liquid against the height of the centaur on its proud label, mentally charting the ebb and flow of Chiron's days. She could not know the incongruity of this particular staple in a household with a caretaker's salary. But when she asked him once why he liked it so much, he answered that it aged better than any other fruit of God's labor and he therefore wished to remain closely associated as such. She tucked that explanation away the same as she did most of Chiron's philosophy, convinced she would make more out of its wisdom by examining it at a later date.

Herman always checked in with Chiron immediately upon arrival, to ensure that Chiron did not inadvertently omit him from any share of attention. But once he had registered plainly on Chiron's consciousness, he couldn't resist the lure of the alcove at the far end of the living room. If there were not any immediate business that required his attendance, he would dash off.

The main charm of the gatehouse, in the view of some, was the mechanism built strategically into the inside wall adjoining the gate without. At the back of the alcove there was a small, shoulder-height window through which approaching vehicles could be inspected. The gate keeper, upon being notified by a buzzer that a visitor was requesting entry, could manipulate the operation of the gate by use of a lever located under the window. Thus, the gate keeper was protected from both the weather and any unwanted interviews. Otherwise, he could always open the window. The wieldy apparatus and window arrangement were strikingly similar to the pilothouse of a ship, lacking only a captain to steer the vessel, or at least a sturdy first mate.

A wooden box lying nearby, when employed as a step, made Herman the perfect height to peer over the ledge of the window and man the lever. He was strict about whom he would let pass through his gate, especially as he was not allowed, under any circumstances, to unlatch the safety hook from the device. There were signs lately that temptation was overtaking prudence and skeptics might be forgiven for questioning Chiron's trust.

Hanging next to the window, within reach of the pilot, was a clipboard displaying a list of names, with the date and estimated time of arrival neatly filled in across each row. Some lines had been crossed off with the attached pencil. Herman leaned in closer to the wall and read the first un-crossed-off name. He saw that it spelled clearly: Nick Karras – June 10 – 5:00pm. He read it again, and sneaked a look over his shoulder at Chiron. He verified the name and gave a low whistle. Then he scurried off the box and shoved it back against the wall, before anyone noticed his exclamation.

Iris and Todd were about finished with their recounting of Poseidon's adventures in the morning sea. Iris tended to report things with great detail, even if the listener had been present for the event. She needed to go on record. Most times, Herman was right next to her, interrupting, mentioning tidbits she hadn't had a chance to address and ruining the whole story. She was delighted with her free rein today, knowing Todd rarely embellished.

Todd was most interested in Chiron's assessment of the new puppy's performance and anticipated voicing a corresponding endorsement once he had heard Chiron's. Oftentimes, though, Chiron elicited more comment than he offered. It had come to pass over the course of countless interviews, and especially now that Todd was twelve years old, that rather than trying his hardest to give Chiron the answer he thought he wanted, Todd knew to give his own best interpretation, even if flawed. He knew Chiron would rather hear a misguided answer than a borrowed one. But it was always tempting to agree with him. He couldn't think of a time when Chiron turned out to be wrong.

As her comments wound down, Todd noted a change in Iris' tone. It reminded him of her mother's occasionally imperious style. She placed both hands on the edge of the desk, pulled herself up to her full height, shoulders back and began speaking slowly, emphasizing the pertinent words.

"Now Chiron, we have to make sure Poseidon never takes my doll again. He must be strick-ly trained to know the difference between precious possessions," she paused dramatically, "belonging to people in his family, and everything else, such as pirate booty. And such." She lowered her chin and raised her eyes at him meaningfully.

She was so exasperating.

"On the other hand, Iris, that doll would be the perfect training toy in this case, since the puppy is already so attached. Just think. It'd be heroic of you to sacrifice one sappy doll for a true and noble purpose. And we could buy you any other foolish dolls in any store in the world with our pirate booty."

"Chiron!"

When Chiron spoke, all discussion was suspended. All eyes turned toward the desk. "Have you heard the story of the Turkish garrison of Athens?" he asked softly. Todd knew this was not an unrelated response. He knew Chiron was not changing the subject.

In a flash, three sets of still damp elbows converged on the front of the desk, jostling for position. Each pair of hands supported the chin of an eager face, each face containing only eyes and ears, all eyes and ears concentrating wholly on the person of The Storyteller.

Chiron settled back in his chair, and braided his fingers together over his midsection. Allowing a few seconds for quiet anticipation, he began. "By the time of the Greek Revolution in 1821, the Turks occupied most of Greece. Their power in Greece was so strong, in fact, that the Turkish army had a garrison stationed in Athens right at the Acropolis, using that ancient consecrated site as a fortress. It was such a colossal insult to the citizenry that it wasn't long before the Turkish regiment came under siege by the Greek revolutionary army.

"After several days of fending off the bombardment, the Turks had begun to run short of ammunition. Being cut off as they were, they had no way to replenish their stores. The Greeks were watching closely from their vantage point and noticed that the Turks began to pull down the marble columns of the Acropolis. As you may imagine, this was greatly upsetting to the sentimental Greek soldiers.

"The columns had been designed by the ancient builders to be as strong as possible. They would need to be able to stand up under the effects of frequent minor earthquakes, inevitable in that part of the world. Therefore, the columns had been constructed with hollow centers that had been filled with lead. Upon closer observation, the Greek soldiers realized the Turks were taking out the lead from these priceless artifacts in order to restock their supply of ammunition.

"After conferring among themselves, it wasn't long before the Greeks sent an envoy to inquire of the Turks exactly how much lead they expected to extract if they took down every single column of the Parthenon. Once the amount had been determined and agreed upon, the Greeks delivered a shipment of precisely that much lead to the hands of the enemy, with the understanding that in exchange, the remainder of their temple would be left untouched.

"Mind you, these are the same Greeks soldiers, most of whom could not read or write, who had torn up virtually the entire ancient library of the Kaisariani Monastery in order to use the paper as cartridges! But their temple, their Parthenon, was so precious to them that they were willing to risk their own demise to preserve it. It was their Greek heritage, it was their history, it had a value they placed above all other values. It was theirs. Others may not understand it or appreciate it and might be able to make a good case against what they did, but none could question their right to such devotion."

The children ruminated. Herman and Iris wondered if that were the end of the story. But Todd's eye went to the chair where the doll had been casually deposited upon arrival. He was quite convinced that Iris would have helped tear up that old Greek library willingly, with zeal. He sighed and smiled ruefully, shaking his head in resignation.

Chiron pushed his chair back from the desk and stood up slowly, as if mentally commanding each set of muscles as they performed their portion of the rising process. He walked over to the back wall of the house and opened a small drawer in his cabinet-of-a-thousand-drawers. He withdrew a diaphanous piece of paper folded neatly to protect the contents within. He motioned Iris over and said, "I understand Adrianne is not well today. Here, little one, give this to your mother. It will help to settle her stomach."

She made a move to open the packet. "Ah-ah. Don't touch," Chiron admonished.

"But it looks just like the medicine you send over to Thea," she said, trying to see more clearly through the wrapper.

He looked down at her appraisingly. "It is similar, you are right, my girl. They both contain the substance mastic, from pistacia lentiscus, as the base. But as you know, Thea's ailment has nothing to do with her stomach."

"Yes I know, but..."

"Hurry along, now, all of you. The rain has all but stopped."

The boys bounded out the door, knowing they otherwise risked being told twice, but Iris stood by the armchair juggling her options for transporting her doll while safely carrying the packet of medicine. She eventually decided to put the tablets in her breast pocket, then covered it with her hand as insurance against the menace of lingering raindrops. She picked up the doll with her other hand, and proceeded to the entryway. There she paused to contemplate the heavy, smoke-streaked oaken door, observing how firmly closed it was. After the shortest hesitation, she efficiently snapped the doll under her opposite armpit, pulled back on the latch with the full consequence of her body weight, and dragged the portal wide. Intent on her mission, she shifted the doll once again to her free hand and marched out, leaving the door agape.

Chiron watched, but did not comment.

# CHAPTER 2

## 1946

The house, officially named Beechwood, occupied a slight rise about 300 feet from the shoreline that provided an exceptional view of the Long Island Sound from one angle, north by northwest, while gaining privacy from its specimen and fir trees off to the east where the working part of the estate, and Maggie, presided. The house sat closer to the shoreline than the public road. The driveway wound gently from southwest to northeast about a quarter of a mile before it arrived at the gatehouse, where it paused in front of the imposing edifice straddling the gate itself. Built in 1911 like the rest of the buildings on the estate, the gatehouse appeared to be a fanciful interpretation of a guard house, with half the building to the left of the drive and half the building to the right, connected by a second story that passed above the wrought iron gate. The center crossing was capped by a decorative arch, a keystone prominently displayed at its peak.

Once past the gate, a visitor would catch a glimpse of the greenhouse and the back corner of the mansion before they were obscured by tall hedges, carefully pruned and neatly bedded, curving along the driveway and around to the front of the house. There the landscape opened up for the circular drive, the handsome fountain inside it, the full expanse of the home's wide facade and the rolling lawn beyond. Three-quarter circular steps led up to the front door, which was framed lyrically by vines of ivy that had progressed unfettered from the fully encased turret on the left side of the building, across the lower portion of the front, up the side of the door frame and were now reaching doggedly for new heights beyond the entryway.

The first hint that this house had been imagined by a seaman was the row of windows along the second story, all circular in shape. Portholes were not the first thing that came to mind but upon reflection, fit the description. The other unusual effect for a house of its vintage was that its stucco and stone walls were all painted bright white, no shutters or other breaks in the expanse, other than the ivy. As for the proportions of the house, they were graceful and pleasing, though often houses of this size were a story higher, and perhaps not quite as wide. Emphasizing the appearance of extended length was the stand of mature evergreens obscuring the right corner of the house, making it difficult to see where the building ended.

Several yards beyond, standing alone and commanding the attention of any visitor was the copper beech, over a hundred years old, grand, lush and imposing. It exuded wisdom and beckoned intimacy. It balanced the house against the weight of the rest of the world. It stood as sentry, protector and confessor. Each occupant of Beechwood felt a private attachment and spent many an hour under its canopy of purple intimacy. It was a faithful proprietor and kept its secrets well.

It was in that direction, around the corner and just before the garages, that Maggie was retrieving unleashed table napkins, a puddled bath towel and various hand-washed undergarments. One embroidered blouse of Adrianne's, sodden, was swinging from a single clothes pin and flapping ominously with each gust of wind. Today was white day for the wash.

There was no hint now that sometime between the puppy thievery and the storm, just a couple of hours earlier when the laundry was still freshly clean and partially hung to dry and the remaining items in the large wicker basket awaited Maggie's return, an interloper had slipped through here without appreciating or even noticing the pristine articles of clothing on display.

It was only his first of two visits that day, and quite unintended.

Nick Karras had been back on Long Island for more than a month, though it seemed much longer. He had arranged to buy a small, neglected stone cottage a few miles east of here, its main attraction being its site, a low bluff overlooking the sound, and its proximity to Beechwood. Besides the view, which was paramount, it provided him a few acres of privacy and room enough for expansion. For now renovation was the main goal, no small undertaking, yet so far proving to be inadequately distracting for its new owner.

The importance of its proximity to the house his father had built and what was left behind there Nick did not acknowledge at all, except with every attenuated nerve ending in his body, sporadically throughout the day and most acutely at night.

Before he bought the little house, he hadn't been closer to Beechwood than the Merchant Marine Academy at Kings Point, over 30 miles to the west. Ever since 1932, barely 20 years old, he had stayed away.

That was long before the war unleashed its cataclysm; before it claimed its victims of the spirit as well as the flesh in its upheaval of world complacency. Healing for the survivors had hardly begun, even now, he knew. But Nick's world had been much smaller and so it wasn't foremost the war or death or fear that exacted its greatest toll on him. It was the five years of banishment before he enlisted that had changed him first, indelibly. It had tempered the man who throughout the war would serve his country criss-crossing the North Atlantic, blindly following orders, ever vulnerable, unarmed and exposed as all merchant ships were. There, his existence pared to the immediacy of duty and survival had perfectly suited his disposition.

It had been an ingenious form of self-imposed exile, from which he never hoped to escape. Nonetheless, he now found himself alive and back in home territory. Feeling like an unmoored civilian since early spring, he had deftly managed to remain isolated. He was free to be morose, with no superior officer or official duty to deter him. He knew his judgment these days was open to scrutiny and suspected some permanency in that condition, but he had no friend to cajole him with an honest sense of humor or the counterweight of an objective viewpoint for balance. On the contrary, the overriding incentive to indulge his self-pity was the fact that he now had the freedom to do so. He swam at night. He drank at noon. He slept for a day and a half, then hardly at all for a week. He found perverse pleasure in self-indulgence, discovering that action itself, any action, served to diminish the torment of contemplating his infinite choices of possible action. Oh hell, he couldn't explain it. He just found himself on the road to Beechwood and was surprised it hadn't happened sooner.

He noted with some satisfaction, nearing completion of his mission, that he had accomplished exactly what he had set out to do, veering not at all from the plan and providing himself a nice demonstration of willpower: he had passed right by the entrance to the property, hardly even slowing down to gaze between its stately stone columns. He had held tightly to the steering wheel, lest his hand reach for the door handle (or something else he couldn't predict), forcing him to stop the car before the door swung open, for example, offering the rest of his body the chance to get out of the car and be free to walk right up the driveway unchallenged. The hands were the weakest link, the first component most susceptible to rebellion against the discipline of the whole. It wasn't about his mind; his mind was set and practical, and had only allowed this brief car ride past his childhood home because of its strict parameters. It was his hands that could betray him. He knew that, as they were shaking when not fiercely clenched around the column.

His forehead was prickled with sweat by the time he passed the driveway. The tension began to subside then and he congratulated himself that it had been that simple. He was slightly disappointed at how little gratification he got, however, from the glimpse down the avenue, that first turn toward the main house so quickly obscuring the view beyond the entrance. He had just let down his guard and felt his pulse beginning to compose when a fresh pain lurched between his ribs, coinciding with his recognition of the dirt road just ahead. It led to the back end of the property, back by the barns and garages. He had completely forgotten about that entrance. It was seldom used for anything but service vehicles and was nearly invisible to the casual passerby, overgrown as it was.

The very privateness of the access crushed any remaining resolve he had. He was one of a handful of people who knew that winding path, where it led, its connection to Beechwood. It was a lure he hadn't anticipated, a pitfall he hadn't pre-avoided in his game plan. His resolve was so thoroughly deflated that he sat for a moment, engine off, a few yards in, resting his head on the steering column and recognizing true relief, accepting the fact that he would see the house after all, and possibly venture a fleeting glimpse of his most guarded memories.

He could have blindly walked this track on the blackest of nights, which in fact he had done more than once, yet was still surprised at how familiar every crook of the path felt to him considering the lifetime, the deathtime, that had passed in between. It wasn't long before his car had disappeared from view behind him and the familiar windings of the narrow road had drawn him into a wondering awareness of nature's disregard for progress. He walked slowly, glancing keenly every which way, and began to perceive a fecund transformation from present to past. He recognized the gnarly tree root that cut angularly across the path in front of him as he left the dirt road for the cut-through to the house and the wide rut, maybe a little deeper now, that dipped just beyond. Overrun by briars, he came upon the neglected gate that always caught on the uneven ground whenever someone tried to open it. A few yards beyond the gate, he saw the red-berry bush that he had never learned the real name for but would forever associate with poison, still growing and bearing fruit there by the old plow shed. It was the berries from that bush he had eaten as a child, then been force-fed syrup of ipecac in order to be divulged of.

He impulsively plucked a berry from the nearest branch and crushed it between his thumb and forefinger, held it briefly to his nose and then dropped it without looking at it, absently sticking his hand in his pocket where he kept his handkerchief. He walked on.

By the time he came upon the waiting clothesline he was so enraptured by childhood sensations he had to close his eyes, pause. It was all in his mind's eye, anyway. It was all the same and he was the same, he was who he used to be and hadn't been since, even in his most fervent prayers. He was immersed in a profusion of memories that were mercifully barren of everything that came later and were as palpably sweet as those long ago summers he jealously cherished.

It was a fleeting sensation, that state of transcendence which is a trance of gossamer embrace. It dissolves at the slightest earthly interruption and is impervious to the most fervent resistance to its dissolving. He held on with all his childish might, that this feeling might prove sustainable.

He glided past the clothesline, skirted the dense shadow of the evergreens at the corner and stopped, startled by the appearance of the imposing old beech tree, its reach wider than ever, casting its cool embrace in his direction, drawing him close, welcoming him. Standing before it gazing, his eye was caught by the impossibly bright façade of the house, the looming presence of the building that reinforced his own smallness. The reality struck him that his home, which had become a fantasy over the years and lost its hold on time and space, reflected so concretely his memory. It was a shock to discover it still stood, exactly as he fancied, as if the dream created the reality and not the reverse. He could hear nothing but the whooshing of blood in his ears. He did not know how long he stood regarding the house, smelling, savoring, touching its rough textures with his imaginary fingertips.

He was leaning against the old beech, eyes closed, feeling the familiar protection of its rustling leaves. The might of the trunk, many times his own girth, supported his body the same way he remembered, imprinting its sympathy across his back and shoulders, providing well-worn footholds for his shoes between its roots.

An animal rustled between the bushes, a rabbit, a cat, something. His head jerked sharply in its direction.

He straightened up, paused, then slowly took a deep breath, letting it out silently, carefully. He stepped out briskly from under the tree's low branches, suddenly detached and composed. He looked around and verified efficiently, as if checklist were in hand and he a mere inspector, every detail of the prevailing surroundings. The ponderous concrete benches along the far side of the circular drive had acquired the tiniest creep of lichen. The shrubs between them had been recently shorn, maintaining their expected decorum. The stone frog that he had regularly stroked for luck, however, seemed neglected, crowded by untrimmed tufts of grass.

He pursed his lips. There were plainly cracks in the risers on the front steps, how could Chiron miss those? The fountain's majestic dolphin had been replaced with four smaller fish. Their scales were glistening under gentle cascades of water, tails rakishly supporting a new waterspout. The gravel was different somehow, too, maybe whiter, maybe chunkier, he didn't know but his feet marched purposefully across it toward the kitchen door on the opposite side of the house, his intended destination. All that remained of his rapture was a fluttering in his chest.

It didn't occur to him to avoid being seen until he turned the corner. He realized he was not invited or expected and most likely not even welcome by some. His ears strained for sounds of activity from the house or nearby. He started when his foot kicked a stone against a copper downspout, ringing loudly against the emptiness of the yard. He began to tip-toe with exaggerated movements, like an actor in a dark comedy. He did not knock. He clasped the handle of the screen door and pulled slowly, prolonging the squeal of aluminum on its hinges. He cringed. He entered.

He nearly forgot his purpose as a waft of childhood swept through his nostrils. He stood motionless, a little stunned, but he did not resist. By mistake he cleared his throat. As if breaking the silence presented an opening, he stepped in farther. His battle instincts were still trigger-happy; he felt a heightened awareness of his surroundings, the tension of impending confrontation, indecision.

It seemed a long time before he began to wonder: if she wasn't in the kitchen, where was she? This time of day she would be in the kitchen. Was he mistaken? Was she no longer living here? The dreadful sinking feeling of doubt in his stomach was more alarming than any fear of being caught sneaking around. He had not considered the possibility that she would not be here. He almost laughed at the realization. How naïve, how wishful, how one-tracked he had been. He thought for a moment. There should be lots of activity in the kitchen at this hour. What if something is wrong? He looked toward the hallway at the back of the kitchen, knowing it led to her room, knowing this time his approach would be actual, not fantasized.

He crept along the passage, saw the door to her room closed and forbidding, knew he was forewarned and dismissed the thought. He breathed for a minute by the door, or held his breath, he could not say. He grasped the knob and turned. There was mercifully no squeak and the door gently unclosed, revealing a chair, the foot of the bed, the bed itself. He looked.

She lay on top of the coverlet, feet angled, legs bent, arms limp, bared neck vulnerable, lips parted, eyes fluttering momentarily in a dream, breath lifting her breasts lightly, barely. Her fragile beauty was a shock, her translucent skin a wound to his heart, her untamed hair an assault upon his senses. He withstood the sight for as long as he could, overcome with longing.

She stirred. He instinctively pulled the door shut, barely preventing it from slamming. His body throbbed as he hesitated long enough to listen for sounds of disturbance. He retreated.

He found himself back in the kitchen in a whirlwind of confusion, lungs filling up, thoughts floundering, a flood of lost opportunities and aching regrets rising before his clouded eyes. His arms hung limply by his sides, hands slack, palms facing forward beseeching the kitchen gods for strength.

He was convinced something was wrong. After all the years of heightened awareness and imminent danger, he instinctively grasped the indications. It seemed surprising now that he had not known it before he saw her. Sadness sapped his energy. He closed his eyes. He was defenseless against this kind of enemy.

The windows were darkening, the first raindrops beginning to strike as the firmament signaled the coming siege. Suddenly Nick felt compelled to act. Noting the open windows he rushed to shut off their vulnerability. In a flurry of decisive action he departed, just ahead of the deluge.

His movements had disturbed Thea after all and she emerged from her room seconds after the screen door closed behind him. She was there, getting a drink of water by the sink, when the children blew in.

By the time he found himself back at home, Nick was irrational with fear and foreboding. He had second-guessed his impressions a dozen times within the last half-hour and was as sure she was just resting from a slight headache as he was positive that she was dying from an incurable affliction. He couldn't tell! Why had he been so convinced there was something terribly wrong with a woman whom he hadn't set eyes on in thirteen years? Was he just overreacting to the emotion of seeing her again? Wasn't it more likely a

34

desperate man's guilt of abandonment? Was he so arrogant as to think she could not survive without him all this time, long after she had probably forgotten his existence? Why had he turned tail and run away without being seen? He was afraid she would recognize him for the coward he knew himself to be, that's why. His judgment was skewed. His judgment was screwy, that's what. This was not to be borne. No sane man could withstand this agony of not knowing.

In truth, there were few indications of serious illness. No one could be that beautiful and be dying. She hadn't lost that much weight, just some of the plump rosiness of youth, hardly at all. She was dressed for a work day and she wasn't even under the covers. How silly he was. How like him these days, to seek evidence of suffering, preferably his own, at every turn. This was maddening. This was torture.

He paced for a few minutes before becoming distracted by the banging of a loose shutter, freed in a sudden gust of wind. He looked up as it creaked, sagged and then thudded onto the porch to its final resting place, shattering the clay pot beneath it. He went over to inspect the damage. By the time he had assessed the broken pieces, he knew absolutely that Thea was seriously ill and that he had probably discovered it too late to be of any help. There was no logic involved, no dissection of the evidence required. It was a fact, and he was weak in the knees as he accepted it. He sat in the rocker next to the shutter at his feet.

Heph had just finished bathing and settling Poseidon on a clean blanket in a corner of the greenhouse when the phone rang. He had answered the extension quickly, hoping to stop the ringing before it disturbed his wife. He was quite taken by surprise at the caller's identity and the request for a visit. For one thing, the

Bayards had not heard that Nick was back in town and certainly not that he had purchased a home in the vicinity. Secondly, it was only yesterday that he and Adrianne had discussed the scandal that forced the Karras family to sell this estate and return to Philadelphia back in '32.

It was a passing remark that Maggie made last night that started the subject. Heph and Adrianne had been sitting together on the sofa with their cocktails, listening to a radio broadcast about soldiers who were still making their way back home all these months after the fighting had ended. Maggie was passing through, worrying the pillows and smoothing the doilies. She said the strangest thing.

"I wonder if Mr. Nick's lifeboats came for him after the war."

"I beg your pardon, Maggie dear?" asked Adrianne.

"Hmmm?" She acted as though she hadn't realized they were listening. "Oh, it's just something his daddy always promised him is all. Ever since he was a tiny babe too young to make out the words. I still think about it sometimes, especially now that the war is over and most everyone else in the neighborhood is back home. I surely would like to know about those lifeboats. I don't even know what home Mr. Nick would have to go back to these days. If he made it back." With that thought she lowered her eyes and stood quite still for a moment.

She passed out of the room without further explanation. The couple looked at each other, used to Maggie's declarations and abrupt exits, and turned back to the radio.

They had both speculated about the likely whereabouts of Nick after the war, having heard no word concerning his circumstances and with no one to ask. The family had cut all ties with The Harbor when they moved away and any information Heph had been able to gather about them since was through his own connections in the ship-building industry. The rest, what they heard from the neighbors, was conjecture. And even though Captain and Mrs. Karras had formed few close social ties in the nearly twenty years they lived here, there was a strong loyalty in town to Nick that seemed to catch hold of most tongues before they began to wag.

It had all died down long ago.

Herman wasn't involved in the Karras family mystery until after dinner. He had come into the study to report what Maggie had said to the refrigerator repairman about planning to ask his mother for a clothes dryer, the latest model she had just heard about at church from Mrs. Devine. It comes with a timer on it! She was just waiting for the right occasion to mention it and wanted to know what the repairman thought about the new General Electric machine. He said it was very expensive. Maggie didn't have so much to say to him after that.

His parents had their backs to him as he entered.

"Sometimes I forget that Maggie was here for all of it. It hadn't occurred to me that she would know the details of what happened, that the Karrases would have included her in their family secrets," Adrianne was saying. When Herman heard the word secrets, he quickly slipped to his left and disappeared behind the leather armchair next to the reading lamp.

Herman was something of a snoop and was in fact one half of the set his parents called "the Messengers," as his vessel of knowledge could only hold whatever information it acquired for as long as it took him to find somewhere to spill it. It was a trait the twins shared and could occasionally devolve into a competitive sport. Blood had been shed more than once. But Iris

37

had recently acquired the skill of withholding portions of her information, at least from him, which had given her the upper hand on several recent occasions. Tonight, however, Iris was nowhere around and Herman could tell from the furtive tones of his parents' voices that this was going to be good. He brought the full force of his talents to bear. His hearing was excellent.

"Well, it says a lot for her character that she has never mentioned a word of it to us, not once in thirteen years. I think of her as our family, funny isn't it?" Heph replied.

"Did you realize she was here from the time Nick was a baby? That would have been right when the house was built. They came here just before the baby was born, if I remember."

"I knew she was the nanny before she was the housekeeper. She told me that quite indignantly one day when I suggested she tend to her cleaning and refrain from pointing out my parental shortcomings."

Adrianne chuckled. "Was that the day you asked Herman to fetch your inkwell and bring it to you in the breakfast room, which involved crossing the Persian rug in the hallway? The Persian rug with the corner that turned up just a little bit and lay there waiting for a little boy's distracted foot? Or perhaps it was the day you swatted Iris with your newspaper after she screamed at a mouse and you jumped so high you overturned your own coffee cup? Or—"

"That's quite enough. I am a model father and no one would argue that except you and Maggie, just for the chance to gang up. No. It was neither of those times. It was one of the times when I had behaved quite fatherly and authoritatively and all she witnessed were the tears of regret on the part of the perpetrator, whoever that was."

"I see." She patted his knee. "Well. I'm certain she overstepped her bounds, Sugar. But be careful, Heph, she's well over fifty and I fear for her heart, too. Now. What did she tell you? How did she end up working here, an Irish girl in a Greek household?" Adrianne loved speculation and intrigue after a couple of cocktails.

"I really don't know. Why haven't we ever asked her? But I did overhear her saying to someone in the house, I can't imagine who, one day early on that she was much relieved that the days of scandal were over and she could live in peace again. As I recall, that was a day when the twins squalled from morning to night and again to morning while the two of us and the baby nurse (Mrs. Danforth, wasn't it?) were pacing the floor until our knees buckled. 'Live in peace again.' Maggie's sense of timing has always impressed me."

Adrianne pulled her feet up onto the sofa and turned sideways to face her husband, settling in for a cozy chat. "You know, when we moved here, being new to The Harbor, I thought the people we met at first seemed to be wary, like we might have brought a contagious city-dwellers' disease with us from Manhattan. Or maybe that was just the way people from the North Shore were with newcomers. But since then I have wondered if it weren't Beechwood that they were reacting to. No one would really say but it was clear they associated the Karras family with something shameful. Kristofer Karras' financial collapse never seemed to justify the kind of silence the mention of their name always triggered. We used to talk about that all the time, remember? Were those rumors true about his swindling his partners? I thought you told me they were false accusations. Did you ever talk to that new partner at Huntington Shipyard who knew the family?"

"I didn't tell you, did I? I forgot. He said something astonishing to me when I spoke to him about Karras' Moonstar Line. It was a few weeks ago, when I stayed overnight in the city after my meeting with him and James. He, Randolph I mean, the new partner, said, 'For as long as I live, I will not speak a word about the circumstances surrounding the Moonstar Line's demise as long as someone so closely involved is still alive to be protected.'"

"To be protected? From what? Who needs to be protected? What was he talking about?"

"That's the strange part. It completely slipped my mind, I don't know why. He was talking about Chiron."

Adrianne drank two or three more old fashions that evening. She wasn't aware of the count until the next morning when she awakened and guessed it.

Most of what his parents discussed was lost on Herman. The part about Chiron needing protection seemed silly and he dismissed it, convinced as usual that his parents were pitifully unaware of what really went on at Beechwood. But the fact that there were family secrets from long ago, right here in this house and Maggie was in on them, intrigued the little sleuth. The mystery man named Nick was new to him and would be to Iris as well, he was sure. He almost chirped with glee, but caught himself in time. He could tell he was becoming more expert in his spying methodology. He congratulated himself, as spying was his future career and required some real-life experience if he wanted to be a real-life agent. Wait till the feds got a load of him. He wondered if he should consider turning this Nick character in. Once he figured out how to escape from behind the armchair, that is.

But that was last night. The next afternoon at five o'clock precisely, when the only remnant of the rainstorm was oppressive humidity, Nick rang the front doorbell. He had been admitted through the gate by Clement, the assistant on duty at the time, in accordance with the Visitor's Sheet hanging in the gatehouse alcove, the same sheet that listed his name, and earlier had evoked Herman's furtive whistle.

Chiron was down at the boat house checking out the effects of the storm on the sailboats and fishing craft, and possibly giving Nick a chance to avoid seeing him. Nick stood, shoulders back, hands in the pockets of his new trousers, cinched tightly by his new Italian-made belt. He wore an ivory shirt with maroon pin-stripes and a coordinated, conservative tie. They set off his dark blue eyes, accentuating his bronze skin which blended nicely with his deep brown hair, swept back casually. It was too hot for a jacket and he felt confident he would be forgiven the omission.

Adrianne answered the door herself. She smiled with pleasure and a bit of surprise at the handsome young man before her. Except for the intensity in his eyes, he looked like a fresh, modern man-about-town quite at his ease. As for herself, other than a slight blue cast under her eyes, she showed no signs of her day spent in bed, or why. Her dark blond hair, cut bluntly just below the chin, curved smartly along her cheekbones and shone quite gloriously against the dim background of the hall behind. Her carriage was elegant and athletic, her broad shoulders a hanger for her slender body and long legs, her stance casual yet well aware of its effect. She wore a sleeveless, belted sheath of blue-green silk cinched tightly at the waist, the neck cowled, the leather flats matching the belt, both reflecting bits of silver. She stood appraising him for a few seconds, head tilted toward her hand resting protectively against the door frame. Satisfied, she gracefully extended her arm in welcome.

"Mr. Karras, we are so honored to have you as a guest in the home your father built. I am Adrianne Bayard and I am so pleased that you have come for a visit."

The door swung wide and Heph filled the vacant space with his burly frame and his deep voice. "Hephron Bayard, you can call me Heph," he boomed as he vigorously shook the hand of his quiet visitor. "Welcome home, son. You must have some mixed emotions about being here and I don't blame you at all. I'm not sure if we've kept up the old place to your father's standards! Please come in and have a look around."

Nick was immediately taken with Heph's enthusiastic welcome and his casual approach to this awkward reunion of sorts. Heph was a little larger than life, barrel-chested, several inches taller than Nick (who was six feet tall himself), ruddy-faced, with waves of unruly copper hair that swept across his forehead with each toss of the head. His clothes were obviously tailored from expensive cloth, yet simple and light. His linen shirt was open-collared and his loafers were sockless. He exuded fresh air and enthusiasm. Nick clasped his hand firmly and smiled sincerely, feeling welcome. It wasn't until they turned to enter the foyer that he noticed the slight limp in Heph's stride, favoring his right leg. It appeared more like part of his rhythm of motion than an affliction. It fit him, like his charming demeanor, and was forgotten.

This morning's surreptitious visit helped Nick manage the flood of old memories he encountered while under the scrutiny of the Bayards. He followed them into the library with composure, where refreshments were already laid out, and a fully-stocked bar awaited. He focused on the bar rather than the haunting familiarity of the surroundings. He heard the ice tinkle softly as it melted and rearranged itself in the sweat-glistened bucket. Then he turned to smile at the Bayards' expectant faces.

This arrangement was extraordinarily disappointing to one member of the family, the one concealed behind dank, humid velvet curtains in the living room, where his expertise had assumed was the obvious place his parents would bring a formal guest. He had been standing there for many, many long minutes and had just decided to quickly rearrange himself into a sitting position for the long haul, and to cough the frog out of his dry throat before it became an issue, when he heard the objects of his attention turn into another room altogether. He was nonplussed. He waited, thinking they would realize this error of bad manners and soon escort their guest out of the library, over here to his lair. He heard voices murmuring pleasantly, a burst of laughter from his dad, something that may have been a good-natured slap on the back, probably also from his dad, but nothing he could make out clearly. Excellent hearing was of no use at this distance, professional spying could not succeed under such insulting disregard for protocol. He stomped his professional foot, somewhat hampered by his cross-legged position.

Heph and Adrianne were politely asking Nick about his recent return from duty, his new home and his intentions for remaining on The Harbor. Had he seen any of his old gang since he had been back? Would he like another gin and tonic? For his part, Nick was politely responding to their inquiries with the same light tone of voice he noted in them, hoping his answers were cohesive and on subject. He risked a glance around the room, familiar in its rich scents of tobacco, old leather, slightly musty books and polished wood. The diffused light from the stained glass windows could not soften the blow of the homesickness this room evoked. This is where his father spent most of his time and where Nick, his only son, was always welcome.

Heph noticed his wandering eye and interjected, "Nick, we brought you here to the library hoping you would take some time to look at the books your father left behind. You may recall that your parents had some valuable artifacts from the old country, I believe, in the attic and an impressive collection of beautiful books here in the library. There are some priceless first edition volumes of poetry from the last century that should be returned to you. Here, come over to this shelf in particular." He gestured and reached up to a high row of books, gingerly pulling down a thick tome that Nick did not recognize.

As he and his host pored over the rare pages, Adrianne heard scuffling along the hallway and turned her attention towards the door. Hair mussed from the draperies' caress, shirt untucked and signs of snot wiped across his flushed cheeks, Herman trudged down the hall and scowled when he saw his mother's face peer out of the library door. He didn't answer when she exclaimed at his appearance, but continued past her, head down, too miffed to try to catch a glimpse of his quarry. "Go straight upstairs, young man, wash your face and tell Iris and Todd to come down to meet Mr. Karras. Right now. Do as I say," she hissed. He didn't alter his pace or turn to her voice. But he did as he was told and within a few minutes, the men still ensconced in their volume, the three children arrived and were introduced.

Iris stepped forward first, delighted to meet the handsome stranger with the sad eyes. She curtsied, to show she knew how. Nick was amused by her effervescence and impressed by her resemblance to her mother, including the long legs that threatened to

44

outpace the appropriate length of her sundress. Like her mother, that is, except for one noted feature. She was head-to-toe covered in freckles. Her small nose, wide cheekbones, the tips of her ears, which showed daintily on either side of the thick blonde braid pulled loosely behind, her bony shoulders, her graceful arms, even her lips and eyelids as they smiled up at him in open friendliness were generously sprinkled with light reddish freckles.

"Did you have beavers living in the T'Iris and You're Afraidies when you were a little boy, Mr. Karras?" She nodded her head at him in encouragement and waited expectantly. He smiled quizzically and started to formulate a response when Herman, who had arrived determined not to say one word to the slippery suspect, jumped forward and said, "Iris, we've told you over and over the T'Iris and You're Afraidies is too little for beavers to build a dam in!" He stood, fists on hips, toe to toe with his twin sister, the huskier, more coppery version without the freckles but exactly matching the flashing green eyes, glare for glare.

While they stood facing off, Todd quietly stepped forward and held out his hand to the visitor. "I'm Todd, Mr. Karras. Pleased to meet you."

"Todd is the nephew of our cook, Thea. Her brother's son. He stays with us for most of the summer," Heph explained. Nick, clasping Todd's outstretched hand, looked up at Heph when he heard Thea's name. He then regarded Todd anew, searching for a resemblance to her and fancying he could see something in Todd's reserved smile.

"How do you do, Todd? I am very happy to make your acquaintance. I remember your mother from when I lived here myself a long, long time ago."

Heph laughed good-naturedly. "Of course you do, forgive me for being so self-centered about this place. You know way more about Beechwood than any of us, maybe even more than Chiron, although that's hard to imagine."

"Heph, my father told me when I was younger than these kids here never to question Chiron's memory about anything, and by now I suspect you know that as well as I do!" It was pleasant to share history with someone outside the world of a war ship, even if the history were linear rather than concurrent. "Now, tell me about this 'Tigress and Afraidy Cat' you were talking about. Did you discover something on this property I never found?" He addressed Todd, Iris and the back of Herman.

"Come on, come on, let's go show you!" Iris exclaimed. Nick looked over at her mother. Adrianne, eyeing the tension between Iris and Herman and knowing its unpredictability, was quick to agree to the outing. No one noticed as Nick craned his neck down the hallway towards the kitchen as they passed out the rear of the house onto the patio.

They were a jovial party, even Nick being caught up in the kids' enthusiasm and the simple pleasure of walking the grounds with chatty companions to keep his dreadful misgivings at bay. They were soon in the cool of the woods that ran along the edge of the water past the boathouse and beyond the end of the sand, where rocks lined the shore and took the beating on behalf of the private inlet.

Herman guffawed and doubled over with laughter when Nick stepped in a swampy hole up to his ankle. The effects of the rain had hardly receded and they were not far from the twin brooks which had overflowed prodigiously in the storm. Nick shook out his pants leg, took off his new leather deck shoe and turned it over. A trickle of water spilled out, eliciting giggles from every onlooker gathered round. He smiled sheepishly and said, "I'm fairly sure that hole was not here when I was your age. Herman, have you been digging? This is a pretty good trap you set, I'd say. And I fell right into it."

Herman smiled like a sphinx, and thawed a little towards his quarry.

Nick pulled out his handkerchief and began to wipe the mud off his shoe and then his hands. By the time he was through he had smeared it everywhere, removing little yet spreading it widely, leaving the handkerchief caked. He held it up with two fingers, wondering what to do with it. Herman volunteered, "I think you ruined that handkerchief you got there."

Nick brandished it a little in Herman's direction. "Oh, it's no problem. I have hundreds of them. You see, my father insisted I have a handkerchief for every possible occasion. Every time I left the house he would say, 'Have you got your white handkerchief, Nick? You never know when you might need it.' And what do you know, it looks as if he was right." He shook it a little. "I just wish he had told me what to do after I was finished needing it." He looked at Herman and laughed freely. Then he shoved the thing in his pocket.

"This is it! This is it!" Iris jumped up and down, then bounded over the scattered rocks to avoid the boggy undergrowth along the banks of the two meandering brooks. They were following a familiar trail that Nick had explored countless times back in the days when barefoot was his preferred mode of transportation.

Todd pointed ahead and said, "See where they criss-cross up there? The two brooks come together and then switch over to the opposite sides of each other. We were building a dam right where they meet. Looks like it's all gone now though, I guess the storm washed it away."

"We're going to make a pond behind the dammed-up part so we can ice skate this winter!" crowed Herman. Heph smiled, impressed by their ingenuity and unconcerned about the chances of its eventual completion or any impact on the water's ultimate course. Adrianne didn't quite hear the plan because she was standing stock still, surrounded by soft ground on all sides and inches from ruined sandals, remaining several yards behind the tour group.

"I wish I had thought of that," Nick commented sincerely, envisioning the skating rink. He was amused to realize he almost hoped they would ask him to help them. Funny how easily he slid into the children's perspective, catching their enthusiasm like a contagion he had no immunity for.

"Well, I'm going back to the house to scare up my ice skates! They need sharpening and I plan to be the first one to test the ice!" promised Heph. "Let's get out of this quagmire, I'm for another drink—what do you say, Nick?" He gingerly took giant steps back towards Adrianne on her island, figuring to rescue her.

Todd stood regarding the area surrounding the imaginary dam. There wasn't the slightest evidence that there had been any construction site at all except for some debris caught up against various rocks and crooks down stream. They had worked on it for three days.

"How jackleg," he thought, disgusted.

"Wait a minute!" Nick exclaimed. "I came out here to see the Tigers and Fraidy Cats! We can't go back yet!" He looked around as if the wild cats might jump out at any second.

Iris giggled. "This is it, silly. The T'Iris and You're Afraidies rivers! Right in front of you." She gestured to indicate the obvious.

Todd turned to Nick. "It's the name of the twin brooks, you see? I named them after the twins. These twins here." He pointed at Iris and Herman standing soberly before him, demonstrating appropriate twinness. Nick did not understand.

"Chiron told us the story about the Tigris and Euphrates rivers from Mesopotamia, see. Then when we came here it seemed natural—"

Herman interrupted him. "Todd always called me a baby because he said I was afraid of everything, which I wasn't, but one day when we were scouting for robin's eggs a fox jumped out at me and I got really scared, wouldn't you? And Todd called me a fraidy cat and then he decided on the name of the streams to match the rivers Chiron told us about. Only it wasn't fair and besides I was just a little kid."

"It was a squirrel and you know it!" laughed Todd raucously.

"The 'T'Iris and You're Afraidies,'" Nick enunciated the words with concentration. "Now I get it." He shook his head in admiration. He was having fun.

"Aw, come on Herman," Heph pounded his son on the back, "you've outlived the name of your own river, son. You should be proud. Now let's get out of here before someone gets swallowed up in this quicksand."

"Where? Quicksand?" Herman turned left and right, lifting his feet high one after the other to prove he still could, and then double-checking to make sure. Heph's booming laugh could be heard all the way back to the house, and everyone joined in, even Iris, who then surreptitiously checked her own footing.

Once back in the library, the Bayards invited Nick to join them for dinner, explaining it would be picnic-style as the electricity was still off, and that Clement's wife, Clarisse, would be the cook this evening. Nick started to inquire about Thea then, knowing this was his opportunity, but choked on the peanut he was munching and gave in to a coughing fit that precluded any questions, or the desire to ask them. He demurred politely. He thanked them sincerely for the tour of the property, the chance to examine his father's books, the opportunity to meet those charming children and to enjoy the hospitality they had all generously proffered. He asked if they would mind if he stepped over to the gatehouse to see if Chiron were in. They thought he would be, and encouraged the visit. Nick left through the patio door once again, cutting across the U-shaped back of the house and around the west side toward the driveway. His heart began pounding before he saw Chiron's door. He was flooded with emotions he could not name. In that short distance, his shirt clung to his back with sweat and ringed his underarms. He was approaching the point of no return. Confirmation of his fears.

With every step he took that evening he was aware that he might be observed, discovered, avoided. He knew the door to the gatehouse was visible from the kitchen windows, even from her bedroom window. He felt the heat of her gaze, but lacked the courage to verify his intuition by looking over his shoulder. He wanted to avoid her yet he wished his presence known to her with a thrill of dread and longing.

Chiron opened the door before Nick had a chance to knock. He seemed to fill the doorway with his presence, his dark eyes riveting, his hair the color of steel, his accustomed white shirt luminous and his black pants tucked into his boots as ever.

"Nicholas," he said.

A chill passed along the back of his neck, down his spine. "Chiron."

They stood a few seconds regarding each other. Then Nick reached out and clasped his arms fiercely around his old mentor, pressing them tightly across Chiron's back and feeling the answering embrace like a poultice for his wounds. Now he was back home. This is what it felt like to have family; he had forgotten. They stood unabashed, hugging each other and remembering for as long as it took to be convinced of each other's physical reality, then pushed back, hands on each other's shoulders, grinning, laughing, misty-eyed with unvoiced emotion. "Come in, come in, my boy!" Chiron opened the door fully and swept his free arm in a wide, welcoming arc to include the whole of his living quarters. He did not take his eyes off Nick's face.

Nick's eyes strained to adjust to the dim light. He looked up, as he always did, to the clerestory window that was the main source of light and struck a beam of focused brightness on the flagstone directly in front of the desk, piercingly brilliant to any under its scrutiny but softened now by the lateness of the day. The smell of the fireplace imbued every absorbent pore of the living space, and lay placidly on top of things impervious. Nick breathed it in mightily. He and Chiron crossed over to the sitting area and found their seats deep in the cushions of the two overstuffed chairs, each with a quilted blanket across its back and another one lying on the accompanying foot stools below. Each was stained by time, none like the others in any way except through the hand-sewn details of the expertly, lovingly crafted patterns. The colors were faded, the folded creases permanent, the soft fabric rubbed to a sheen in several patches. Nick sighed with contentment and rested his head against the softness.

As Nick relinquished his burdens to the ambiance of his childhood and the embrace of the chair's yielding comfort, Chiron sat regarding him. When Nick opened his eyes, sensing his gaze, Chiron clasped the arms of his chair with his strong, knotty fingers and hoisted himself up to a standing position in order to go pour a couple of mugs of ale, not bothering to consult his guest. He soon stood before the son of his old master and friend, offering the drink with his extended arm and smiling down at Nick, seeing every detail of their mutual history and more in Nick's tormented eyes.

Accepting his drink, Nick self-consciously glanced around the room, pausing at the table in front of the fireplace. "The chess set," he stated.

"Yes."

"I played some on the ship. It reminded me of you." He regarded the old boxwood and ebony chessmen who dated back to the 1860s, gracefully carved and imposing. He recalled that the smoothly burnished pieces were unweighted and felted. He admired the familiar bishops' miters, wide and almost vertical, their tops somewhat bulbous. He leaned forward to get a better view of his favorites, the horses. Each was virilely carved with a strong muzzle and prominent nostrils and sported startling blue and white porcelain eyes, offset just enough that he'd always imagined they looked a little skittish. Carved into the neck of each horse he could still make out the insignia "B&C, London." While leaning forward, Nick took note of the chessboard he would have recognized anywhere among a thousand like boards. It was fitted with squares of birdseye maple and ebony, bordered by rosewood parquetry inlay. There was a small chip on one corner, from the time he himself had raced through the room and knocked against the delicate table. He didn't have to see the chip from this distance to relive the incident as fresh as yesterday. He flushed with remorse, even now. He heard Chiron chuckle and looking over at him, realized he had read the memory plainly on his face. Nick laughed softly, knowing better than to deny the truth of it.

The exquisite chess box reposed on a side table, next to one of the two high-backed, gold velvet chairs that faced each other across the chess board, occupying the place of honor in front of the fireplace. The box was made of polished rosewood with birdseye maple corners and a matching circular inlay surrounding the keyhole in front. Nick remembered where Chiron kept the key. His heart skipped a beat, as it was reminded of hidden things in this room. His eyes went involuntarily to the left side of the fireplace, at the bricks just inside the left corner. Chiron saw the sudden change in tension, noticed the glance and followed it.

The fireplace was big enough for Todd to stand up straight in. The high mantel was simply a roughly squared-off log from a chestnut tree on the estate. It extended past the ends of the fireplace almost to the edges of the wall and displayed several iron hooks dangling at various distances along its underside. The blackened fireplace itself was almost as wide as the wall it was built into, and nearly deep enough to roast a suckling pig.

Feeling foolish at having his thoughts so easily read, Nick lowered his glance to the rug filling the space between the two men and the chess set, the braided rag rug he remembered so well, of jeweled hues that warmed the room even when the stone floor was so cold it sent a chill up the sides of every traveling ankle. The burgundies, deep greens, cerulean blues, golds and more golds blended into an unpretentious carpet of rich color. That was, perhaps, in deliberate contrast to the elaborate tapestry directly above it to their left, nearly covering the large side wall across the room from Chiron's desk. Some past visitors here, among the more worldly of the gatehouse guests, had noticed nothing else about the room but the tapestry. In fact, it dominated the room in every way except in the children's eyes, who took it for granted and couldn't appreciate the workmanship, considering how muted the colors were, how subdued the design. Nick's view stemmed from his own childhood, so much so that he was almost surprised to see it hanging there. He cocked his head and was just beginning to scrutinize the delicate figures when Chiron spoke.

"Your father didn't speak to me for a week after I bought this wall hanging," he said lightly. "He could hardly look at me, he was so infuriated."

Nick raised his eyebrows. He looked back at the tapestry with renewed respect. "What's wrong with it?"

"I don't know that it was so much what was wrong with it as what was wrong with me. I was twenty-six years old and it cost me half a year's wages to pay for it."

Nick whistled. He studied it. "I have never known you to make a foolish decision, Chiron," he said matter-of-factly.

"Well, not this one, anyway," he nodded. "I have been repaid the price of this tapestry many times over in the joy of seeing it hanging before me every day since. No, I'd say it was a bargain and your father would probably admit that himself, if he were here today."

Nick contemplated the wall hanging. Chiron explained it was a 17th century French verdure tapestry, 6'2" by 12'1". Its fine wool and silk were predominately in shades of green, all faded and inclining with age toward their blue tones, combined with golds and browns and rusts. There were threads of real gold woven throughout, as in the bodice of the woman's gown and on her young lover's shoe buckles. Gold leaves among the millefleurs, the background of countless small flowers, were also ribbed in real gold thread. There was a story to be told in this design and Nick attempted to construe it. The border itself was plain, dark and unadorned. The entire left side of the tapestry was dominated by a tree in full foliage, gently blowing and reaching over the foot bridge that crossed the main part of the tapestry. As balance to the weight of the tree, on the right side there was a beautiful young woman stepping lightly onto the bridge, followed by the young man who was plainly enamored of her. She was looking over her shoulder at him and motioning with her arms as if to say, "You cannot follow me here." He was looking at her imploringly and seemed to be hesitating at the base of the bridge. Below the bridge was a flowing brook inhabited by three large birds, indistinguishable as to species, but the one closest to the bridge was in the process of taking flight toward the couple, and appeared somewhat menacing, forbidding. The overall effect was compelling yet haunting, a little unsettling. Nick looked over at Chiron, who was also studying his tapestry. It appeared the story held no mystery for him, instead providing a customary appreciation and maybe a hint of resignation.

Chiron turned away from the hanging and looked at Nick. "You're back," he stated.

Unprepared, Nick jumped a little. "I," he licked his lips, "I think so."

"You have bought a house. You have lived in it for several months. You are back." Chiron had his own sources. No one here had told him of Nick's recent whereabouts.

"I am. I'm not sure why, exactly. It wasn't until you opened the door that I even realized it was partly because of you that I came back. I didn't even think—" He looked off, speaking to himself. "I didn't even think."

"One of your less admirable traits, as I recall," Chiron commented. Nick laughed, but Chiron was not smiling. Their eyes met.

"Tell me about Thea," Nick said softly.

# CHAPTER 3

## 1880

Chiron sat back on his haunches and nearly lost his balance, barely catching himself before sprawling onto the packed dirt floor of his father's smithy. He had been experimenting with a volatile mixture of ingredients he had acquired from a questionable source and was already on edge. He had especially chosen this time when he expected to be alone for a couple of hours at least to perform another one of his chemistry experiments in the name of medical research. The voice of his cousin, shrill at any time and piercing when excited, took him quite off guard. He was rattled well before he comprehended the import of the sharp words.

"Mother of God, why do you creep up on people and then squeal at them like a cursed screech-owl, you half-wit!"

That was not the reaction his cousin expected. He looked affronted and disappointed, both. "I'm not a screech-owl, you...cuckold!" There, that was more like it. Chiron was usually the one throwing around fancy words, well here was one for him. He looked down from behind his colossal nose at Chiron, still squatting there on the floor.

Jorrin realized if he wanted to make an impression, he would have to repeat himself. He had apparently lost the element of shock. Chiron, displaying no curiosity at all, was simply waiting for him to leave. A glint of cruelty grew in Jorrin's eyes as he began again. This news carried its own shock value.

"Corinna is engaged to be married to Felipe Ballos. The wedding will take place in a fortnight!" No response. "Her father is in the tavern celebrating with a round of drinks for everyone even now!" He had been leaning forward during his announcement and now, slightly breathless, let his weight fall back on his heels. He smiled with satisfaction. The color had drained from Chiron's face.

"Get out," was all Chiron said, but he said it while rising and Jorrin thought better of overstaying his triumph. He retreated with alacrity.

He left behind a universe of silent, swirling dust. There was an echo of laughter somewhere in the distance and a slap of leather on a passing harness, then nothing.

Chiron did not know how much time had passed. He hadn't moved since his threatening shift towards Jorrin, had hardly even blinked. He was stunned and had lost his faculties of motion. He would have disbelieved it, as the very idea was insupportable. But he knew Jorrin for the coward he was. He would only display such open triumph if he were absolutely confident in his source. His head began to pound. He leaned over and heaved, retching up his insides again and again, trying to disgorge his own consciousness in an effort to unknow what Jorrin had told him. Unknowing, unbeing, untruth. He slipped to his knees, sagging heavily. Head in his hands, he shook with a palsy. Occasionally, he took deep gulps of air. Nothing else, nothing at all.

By the time his father returned, it was dusk and Chiron was gone. He left behind the forgotten vessel, the spilled concoction, the vomit. It was as his father expected.

Corinna Stephanos' family had fallen on difficult times. It wasn't an easy period for any Greeks as Crete was still, in 1880, under Turkish occupation. The thumb of their oppressors left everyone to scrape by, rising resentment growing at a much steadier pace than the hopes for their future or the stability of their incomes. Another revolution was just months away, but not a one of them believed in it. They had been subjected to such dogma for generations, to little avail.

Sabastian Stephanos was a fisherman by trade, hard-working and honest. But he had no sons. His three daughters required dowries that he could not sufficiently provide. Under such circumstances, a Cretan family negotiating a marriage would suffer philótimo, a loss of honor, and was therefore extremely limited in its options. Even though Chiron was hopeful his father would accept a lesser dowry from Corinna's family, he knew his parents could not afford to waive it any more than any other family in the little southern village near Lerapetra. He was not aware of any family who would relinquish a source of income considered its right and privilege. And Corinna's father would be in the same position again when it came time for his two younger daughters to be betrothed, with no forgiving father-in-law likely offering concessions for them. It was Stephanos' obligation to make the best use of his assets when arranging a marriage and he believed he had but one option in that regard.

Filipe Ballos' father was the general merchant in the village and was indebted to Stephanos for a great service rendered, one that had saved his business from prolonged disruption and possible ruin. The episode stemmed from the great storm of '78, during which half of the village was washed away and extensive damage was sustained by the pandopoleon, the general store, which had flooded and whose inventory was almost entirely spoiled or lost. With bills due, no goods to sell and damage to the port leaving him isolated from his vendors, his friend Stephanos had offered to make the risky trip by sea to resupply his stock until regular ferry service was reestablished. Stephanos forwent his own income from the fish he may have caught over the extended period his voyage required, but insisted to his wife the trip was justified. "O kalos filos, stin anangi fenete." A true friend proves himself when needed, he said to her. It was clear to him in those volatile times that every man must by necessity be able to rely on his neighbor. As well, he felt confident the favor would be remembered. He was a good man, and prudent.

Now two years later it occurred to Stephanos that Ballos' son, Felipe, was of marriageable age. Felipe was a sturdy young man, if not stout-hearted; forthright in his actions and temperament, and not unkind. He had a future in his father's store and seemed a responsible sort. Corinna, beautiful and spirited, would be well cared for, never mistreated, and would, frankly, be moving up in stature by marrying into the Ballos family. More to the point the príka, the dowry, might be forgiven, in payment for past services rendered.

The arrangement was a relief, in fact, to Ballos as well, who knew it was entirely possible Stephanos' generous actions had saved him from ruin and who had dreaded a higher price expected as repayment of his obligation. Not only would his shy son be overjoyed at the prospect of marriage to the beguiling Corinna, this agreement was finite and terminated all sense of obligation. Debt weighed on Ballos and germinated resentment, something he had grown more and more aware of over the months and years as Stephanos had not named a favor in return, not even breathed a reminder of the event.

After an evening at the local ouzerie toasting their friendship with shots of the house specialty, ouzo served neat, and sharing platters of mezedes, traditional Greek appetizers, both men were well satisfied with themselves and had shaken hands on the agreement.

When she heard of it, Corinna had fainted.

There was nothing to be done. There was no arguing with a father's decision, not a Cretan father's decision. Even the sympathy her mother felt for her disappointment was mitigated by the benefits of the arrangement. In fact, her mother was proud to say her daughter would be joining the household of the successful merchant Ballos.

There was no solace to be found anywhere, and no word of Chiron in over a week. Corinna's heart was a heavy weight in her breast, with no relief or expectation of relief. Almost overnight her blue eyes became dull within their hollow sockets, her skin ghastly pale. Her hair lay in lank sections across her suddenly frail shoulders, her shoulders closing in on each other in their attempt to protect her ailing heart. She fussed and fidgeted all the day through, her hands unable to keep still, her mind unable to relax or concentrate or focus on the flurry of wedding preparations around her. She passed from room to room, unresponsive.

She did little more than rumple her sheets at night, twisting them in the turmoil of her disrupted dreams, drenching them in the fevers of her helplessness. The relief that came with daybreak was short-lived, but at least allowed her to escape the confines of her bed, where only her mind was free to roam, the one part of her body she wished to still. At the first glimmer of light, she flailed her arms and pedaled her legs free of the covers, like a sea nymph tangled in seaweed and afraid of suffocating. Then she would lie there, sprawled, staring, knowing any thought of escape was illusory.

Anyone who had not seen her recently was alarmed at the sight of the ebullient Corinna, radiant beauty and gregarious companion, suddenly brought low. Not a single friend took pleasure in her decline, despite any envy they may have felt in the past. The pain was too

61

deeply etched across her brow, too severely evident on her colorless lips and in her liquid eyes bereft of hope. While normally disdainful of an eligible young lady who failed to appreciate such a lucky match, the matriarchs of the village and their eligible daughters were inclined to sympathy, whatever romance yet remaining in their hearts being sparked by the compassion they felt when they saw her forlorn resignation. They seemed to understand: a person jumping off a small incline onto the stony shore does not know the cruelty of the jagged rocks below the same as one who must plummet from the bluff.

Her mother would pat her on the back of the hand when she found Corinna sitting by a window, or she might attempt to tame a lock of her daughter's hair when she came upon her lingering vacantly in a doorway, but she knew Corinna was unaware of her ministrations. For the most part, she left her to deal with her grief in her own way. After all, there was nothing to be done. Acceptance was a matter of time and there wasn't much of that. Better to face it now and be done.

There was feverish activity surrounding the wedding celebration, her mother overseeing the proper preparation of the foods to be served to the whole village after the ceremony. There were the honey and nuts, of course, and the rice in wild goat soup or gamopilafo, traditional at any wedding, plus the wild goat, the herb pie, the legumes, vegetables and lamb with cheese. All would be served using olive oil as a base and oh yes, accompanied by the lilting music of the pear-shaped, three-stringed lyre. The lyre, in fact, had yet to be arranged. Corinna's mother raised a finger, making a mental note of that. Her preoccupation left little time for worry, her wedding duties consuming her attention. Her domineering tendencies, being given free rein, quite suited her.

Her two younger sisters could not meet Corinna's unreproaching gaze. They spent their energies smothering her with their false cheer, babbling to cover her absent behavior in front of visitors, fervently attempting to smooth with overindulgence the approach of the inevitable wedding day. They soothed her and encouraged her and attempted to bolster her up, but they could do nothing to stop the progress of time or the arrival of the day of days.

A sob escaped her only once. She was sitting outside, behind her family's cottage facing the distant view of the sea beyond the cliffs, and a memory bubbled irrepressively across her closely guarded thoughts, catching her off guard. It was a day the two of them had reminisced over, time and again, comparing thoughts and impressions, bestirred by the secrecy of shared intimacies.

They had been fifteen, she and Chiron, and had just recently begun to suspect that the ardor each had privately felt for the other was mutual. It started in the usual way, but they did not know that. She caught him staring at her. He saw her blush. His hand brushed against her fingers when he went to take the heavy water bucket from her grasp in a sudden attempt at gallantry. He did not look at her then, but she glanced sideways at him and saw his embarrassment. They each had thrilled at that barest touch of flesh and desperately yearned for more.

She had shocked herself and nearly felled him outright after he handed her back the bucket (foolishly careful not to touch her this time). She stood contemplating him for a moment. As if of its own accord, her arm extended itself toward him and she placed her hand on his chest gently, tentatively. She let it drop slowly, grazing his abdomen with her fingertips, following a timid path clear to his navel. She heard herself saying, "You are a gentleman, my Chiron." She looked him straight in the eye and he knew for a fact his feelings belied her statement. He had turned to marmalade in the exact places she had touched and was struck breathless. His mouth, he thought, was perhaps hanging open, he couldn't tell nor do anything about it. She smiled and the jelly turned to molten lava and his knees began to give way, but he bucked up, stood straight and managed to clear his throat. "So are you," he said. She laughed with delight, eyes dancing in mischief and she learned at that moment what it means to be a coquette. She turned her back on him and sauntered away, bucket swinging. He realized what he had said and was mortified.

For two-and-a-half weeks he scrupulously avoided her. But every time he thought of her hand on his belly he experienced the identical electrifying arousal of that moment, as if she were doing it again and that memory, at least, was some solace for his sufferings, except that it did seem to exacerbate the problem. In truth, he gloried in his misery. Meanwhile, as he was avoiding her, he looked for her with every step, as much as the constraints of a small town, her mother's close supervision and his own obligations would allow. He was willing to forgo food and sleep, that had more or less taken care of itself, but he could not bear not seeing her. A glimpse was enough; anything more was dreaded, after all.

She was quite miffed at his absence, having been confident that her actions had worked a spell on him and furious to realize she had imagined his enchantment and worse, that her ardent longing was one-sided. She hated him, passionately. She would not acknowledge him ever again, not as long as she lived.

She escaped a few days later, trying to climb out of her skin and unable to do so while pent up at home among the confines of thick walls, duties, bickering voices and cloying femininity. She nearly flew down the path of the steep slope leading to the sea. Three quarters of the way down she stopped at an outcropping to catch her breath and think for a minute, searching for relief in the rolling waves beyond. Something made her turn and look up to where she had been and she saw him. The wind blew her skirt and he could see the light passing through it. He could see the shape of her legs beneath. Her collarbone formed a shadow above the vee of her open collar when she turned her head to look at him.

He was standing perilously close to the edge of the bank, holding her motionless within his gaze.

Her heart, which must have stopped beating altogether, dropped when he disappeared from view. She did not move, not so much as a shiver, for as long as it took. Finally, he rounded the bend a few yards away, and she turned. He was slightly out of breath and slowed his steps to a measured pace, approaching, nearing, searching her face intently.

They stood face to face, awed by the intimacy of this illicit encounter.

"You have taken away my equanimity, Corinna," he said quietly. "With one flashing glance and one," he paused as he envisioned it, "stroke of your fingertips, I am untethered." He looked off to his right, out over the ledge to the horizon in the distance, then back at her. "My will is turned to dust and you are the wind that scatters it." He never dared imagine he would give voice to such thoughts, yet remained unaware of how remarkable such words would sound to her susceptible female ear. He reached up to catch a lock of her hair as it blew free, caught up in a gust. Then he stroked her hair, gently, trembling at her closeness.

This time it was her mouth that was open, achingly vulnerable. He contemplated it, then tenderly leaned in. He pressed his lips against hers with all the yearning of his fifteen years. A small groan of exquisite shock escaped from her throat. He reached his arms around her and she responded to his embrace.

They were tentative and awed at first. The sensation of pressing his body against her body, the idea of his touching her skin with his hands was overwhelming to them both. He kissed her gently and then thrice more in quick succession and they giggled, shyly glancing in each other's eyes, then closing them for the first passionate kiss, the first inkling of love, the first moment of sharing rather than reacting, when they began to relinquish their timidity and to submit to the greedy pangs of desire.

She started, at one point, at the caw of a gull and pulled away, looking anxiously up the path, realizing how exposed they were. He laughed, and took her chin in his hand, tenderly turning her head back to face him, forcing her to look directly at him, to see the laughter in his eyes, the reassurance in his gaze. As she studied him, the anxious crease on her brow evaporated. Slowly she gave him a knowing, womanly smile as she melted into his captivating allure, enchanted.

Heedless of their precarious position at the ridge of the slope, they unwittingly drifted from the path and were caught off guard as they felt themselves slip sideways, tipping over the edge of the landing, finally falling heavily upon the receding ground. They clung tightly to each other instinctively, picking up speed, entwined and rolling down the bank as one. They tumbled over and over again, bracing, laughing, giddy as children, wanton as the budding lovers they had suddenly become.    As the slope leveled out, they slowed to a stop.  Chiron found himself positioned on top of her, his legs spread on either side of her hips, his knees digging into the stony grass, his torso impressing itself against her, her form arching up to meet his.  His elbows closely hugged her shoulders, his hands cradled her head, gingerly protecting it from the ground.  She beheld then in one long moment his capacity for happiness, his deep intelligence, even his willingness to expose his vulnerability to her, freely reflected there in his gaze.  And she knew that her own destiny would forever be tied to his unspoken declaration.

This is what she remembered, that day on the eve of her wedding.  She remembered the intensity of his dark eyes, the way he seemed to be trying to pierce her heart with the force of his will.  She recalled the mixture of the smells of the earth and of his desire.  She felt the scratches from the passing briars, the bruises from the hard, uneven ground as they rolled over it and each other, the dizziness that encompassed him, too, both swirling together in joy and mutual longing.

He did.  He did pierce her heart.  And his eyes; his eyes seared his promise on her consciousness indelibly.

*      *      *

The wedding approached at an alarming rate.  The candied almonds had been prepared, the rings had been blessed and the mothers of the bride and groom had made their rounds of the houses in the village, sprinkling their neighbors with rosewater and handing out white candles for them to bring to the church on the wedding day.

Corinna's parents, concerned about her health, had requested an early date for the ceremony.  They heard no complaint from the bride.  Her sisters' frowns deepened, but no word of concern was voiced by either of them.

The wedding day dawned fresh and clear. As she leaned against the window sill, in wonder at God's contempt for her happiness, Corinna's eye followed a lone crow as it flew across the blue expanse, cawing out its concurring disdain. Her wedding dress lay across the bed. Two wedding crowns, stéphana, woven with white flowers and joined together by a ribbon, were lying expectantly beside it. "O, Lord our God, crown them with honor and glory," the priest would say as the groom's godfather would ceremoniously exchange the crowns over their heads three times. Three times the couple, wearing the crowns, would circle a small table displaying the book of Gospels, the wedding rings, a cup of wine and two white candles. In this way God, through the rituals of the marriage ceremony, would bestow His love on them, that they may live their lives in peace and harmony.

She tasted the bitterness of such irony and her throat closed against it. "Dear God, do not sentence me to Your merciless false pretentions," she said. From habit, she searched the landscape once more to see if there were any sign of her lover's approach, then closed her eyes in resignation and turned from the window. It was the last time she ever prayed.

Three days later, while the newlyweds tackled the installation of the stephaníki, the glass box containing the two wedding crowns, above their bed as was the custom, Chiron strode purposefully into his family home and stood facing his parents, who were quite startled by his sudden reappearance.

"Babá, Mamá, I have returned," he pronounced needlessly. "And I have brought with me a proposition that I hope will prove satisfactory to all parties." He allowed himself the hint of a smile, a glint of hope in his tired eyes. He regarded his parents, who were afraid to speak.

"First, I went to Dr. Poulus, who as you know has overseen my medical training these three years. He agreed to write a letter of introduction for me as a student of medicine with sufficient experience to serve as ship's doctor." This news caused his father's eyebrows to move upwards half an inch, while his mother tentatively caught her breath. She shifted a little in her chair, adjusting her head scarf, cautiously open to hearing what he might say next. Despite all the implications, it was a good sign if her son were making plans that indicated acceptance of, well, unalterable circumstances, even if the plans so far seemed alarming. She had feared worse. She had feared for his self-possession.

"I had the most astounding meeting in the port of Agios Nikolaos!" Now his father sat up straighter and clasped the carved claws at the ends of his armchair, his knuckles blanching. Chiron had been to the northern border of Lassithi Province and back in the last ten days. "I was in a café on my third night in port when I saw Kristofer Karras! He was well met, Babá! He was just the man to help me in my plans and there he was before me drinking raki with half a dozen of his cousins from Chios! I will tell you I felt relieved and cheered when I shook his hand!"

Chiron's black shirt was dusty, his pants largely untucked from his carelessly-wiped boots. The bandana he wore with its knotted fringe, similar to the one his father had on and probably made by the same hand, was in need of a washing. His color was high and his eyes artificially bright. His voice had a rasp and he brushed his hand across his forehead, wearily, more than once as he spoke. His sense of false-cheer betrayed his nervousness. Something in the way his parents looked at him divulged an apprehension greater than their concern for his whereabouts. He tried to ignore the warning he felt. The skin across the back of his shoulders prickled. He spoke louder.

"I have procured a place on Kristof's ship!" Kristofer Karras was the schoolmate whose mother was from one of the powerful shipping families of the island of Chios. He had gone to sea before he turned sixteen and had fared well. The family had accepted him, even though his father was not a Chiot, and he had proven he deserved their faith. Loyalty was paramount among Chiots and in that way, Kristof's blood flowed true. With little urging, he had proffered a billet on his ship for his old friend, Chiron.

"It is his first voyage as captain, what good fortune, no? And he has offered me the title of ship's doctor"— he felt he could not afford to pause at this juncture, "as long as I am willing to pull my weight as a sailor as well! I was hardly in a position to argue, as I am barely more qualified to be a physician than I am a seaman." Here he did pause to grin sheepishly, conspiratorially at his father, trying to keep the report jovial and inclusive. His parents looked a little stunned. Well, that was natural enough, he had given them a shock by his sudden return and had made no effort to prepare them for this dramatic change in his circumstances. He thought of what to say next. He took a breath and then stopped. They were regarding him as if the ship's parrot were already on his shoulder and they weren't sure whether or not he knew it. Both had leaned back and to their right, parallel to one another, as if they themselves were on the ship, listing starboard. Now he did pause. He lost his train of thought, and his head of steam.

"I leave immediately for London," he finally managed. "I will be back in a few months' time, whereupon I will have earned enough money to invest in Kristof's next voyage, to America. After that," his voice had gotten progressively softer, more serious, "I will have earned enough money for the dowry that Corinna's father cannot afford and I will offer my hand in marriage." He wound to a stop. He stiffened, as if to prepare for a blow. His mother raised her apron to cover her mouth, resisting a sob. His father said, "Son." That was all. He looked from one of them to the other. The sadness he saw in their eyes was a stab in a fragile part of his heart. He looked, trying to construe a different meaning from their puckered eyebrows, their drawn cheeks, their pain that was more wrenching for being on his behalf.

"How?" was all he said. No one moved. No one looked away.

"Is she all right?" Panic rising in his throat. His mother saw it and quickly nodded, still holding the clenched apron to her mouth.

"I am too late, then." Someone had to say it. A tear slipped down his mother's cheek, smiting him in its conviction.

A minute ago he feared his backbone would snap from the tension. Now it felt as if a valve had been opened that let drain every last ounce of strength from his body. He looked down, as if to see evidence of it on the floor around him. He turned and walked toward his room, stumbling only slightly.

Two days later he emerged, a bulging rucksack across his shoulder containing all he meant to take with him. In his hands he carried the dishes of food his mother had slipped into his room at hopeful intervals. He entered the kitchen and placed them carefully in the basin, then turned to face his parents. He took a step purposefully toward his mother, who was standing with her hands entwined before her, searching for any sign of peace in his features. He made a good effort at a smile, gave her a heartfelt, warm hug, patted her sagging shoulders, inhaled once more the scent of nutmeg and cloves that had always comforted him, savoring it a moment with closed eyes. He turned then to his father.

"Son." Babá didn't realize he was picking up just where he had left off two days ago. He was not a verbose man and rarely emotional, yet trying hard to guess what a proper father would say at such a moment. There was too little to express and too much in his heart for him to separate the meaningful from the obvious and his respect for his son prevented his taking the chance of getting it wrong. He grasped his son's outstretched hand, held it long, and reached out with his other hand to clasp Chiron's shoulder, where he conveyed as much feeling as any words he might have chosen.

"Babá." He looked from his father to his mother and back, as if trying to imprint in his mind this picture of the three of them here in the kitchen of his childhood, the way they would always appear to him, the unchanging way they had always seemed to a son's eye, to be savored time and again for perhaps longer than any of them anticipated. "I will write. Do not worry. Mamá," he repeated, "do not worry."

"God speed," his parents said almost at the same time, like an echo. Their words repeated in his ears for the first few miles of his journey, lulling him into a distracted preoccupation, a kindly fog.

The port of Agios Nikolaos was bustling, sparks of tension practically visible to the discerning eye as a result of reports of the latest skirmish with the Turks. Vendors were skittish, yet galvanized by the brisk business surrounding the flurry of activity that often accompanied political unrest, intensified at any port, naturally, where opposing sentiments were most likely to run amok. There was evidence of the beginning of the end of the Turkish occupation of Crete, though few Cretans or Turks as yet recognized the signs. Still, frustration among the Greeks was growing. Tensions were high and isolated brawls broke out with little provocation across the city, threatening to spill over into something meaningful. Aware of the tenuous peace and unprepared to be caught up in the turmoil, Kristofer Karras had rushed his crew to make ready, arranging departure on the morrow's tide and sending word that all men on leave were to report for duty. Kristof himself was a short block away at the Church of St. Nicholas, praying to that patron saint of the seas for a safe voyage, the same as all dutiful captains did since time immemorial.

Chiron strode with wooden determination down the wharf toward the aging brig that would bear him away from this island that was all he knew and that held captive every last thing he held dear. He fought the impulse to turn round and retrace each step, nearly succumbing to the desire to look upon Corinna one last time; the opportunity having been wasted when he departed his parent's home and he hadn't enough wits about him to find her then, when he still might. He even turned back yesterday, or was it the day before, when he had lurched from a tavern just east of here, bound or be damned for his village and a glimpse of his beloved. He lost his way among the infernal alleyways of the crowded fishmongers' neighborhood and spent a cold night sobering up, more or less unmolested. He would have been halfway home by now if he hadn't backed himself into a broken cistern, mercifully drained, and spent the wee hours trying to claw his way out. Even then, he was lucky not to be arriving at his post this evening stripped of every possession he had, including his boots. The headache helped and he relished it. But it couldn't override the pain that assaulted his battered heart and threatened the grip on his reason. He longed for her with such acute pain that it felt as if his very skin had been stripped from his flesh, exposing his senses eternally to the playful depravity of the gods.

Glassy-eyed, his heavy feet barely lifting off the ground, he slowed to a stop part way along the quay. He felt dizzy from the swirling reek of snails and sea urchins overflowing from barrels arrayed along the pier, accompanied by the unwashed bodies of proprietary hawkers. He was assaulted by the mobocracy of rough language, bawdy laughter, pressing elbows and swaggering shoulders. He felt the hungry lapping of dirty harbor water butt along the dock's undersides, sucking at the anchored vessels, promising adventure, escape, escape. He set down his load long enough to press his palms against his temples, shutting his eyes tightly for the space of a dozen heartbeats. Then he slowly lowered his arms, flexed his fingers unconsciously, and opened his eyes. The ground did not sway under his feet, the bile in his stomach did not heave, the roiling darkness around him was not so menacing. He picked up his belongings, raised his eyes and recognized the ship's masthead before him. Regarding it, he humbly acknowledged the vessel's majesty, its undeniable allure. He set his jaw, lowered his chin and forged irrevocably forward, knowing this moment was his greatest test; his only possible reward, survival.

Later, he stood at the deck's railing scanning the farthest horizon, defined at this hour by faint stars seeping into the inky depths. As he contemplated what the gods prepared for him in that vast vacuum of undreamt loneliness, the words of Tristan and Isolde came to him unbidden.

"Love is bigger than pain or death or everlasting hell."[1]

He thought about this for a long time. He heaved one great sigh and prayed this conviction might sustain him.

He turned to glance at the man next to him, his youthful companion who was his last connection to home, and took solace. Gradually he became aware of the energy emanating from his friend, gleaning that it was the pent up thrill of the journey, the excitement and intrigue of the unknown. Chiron, defenseless, found it irresistible.

Kristof exuded confidence standing there, shoulders back, chin raised, feet planted wide and firmly in the habitual sailor's stance, absorbed in his own thoughts, his gaze at the watery landscape by habit a professional assessment and a familiar seduction as well. There was no moon tonight and the sea was calm. The two friends stood silently side by side, surrendering to the introspection that afflicts seamen before every voyage. Kristof felt the anticipation of the adventure ahead as well as the sweet connection of his shared childhood with Chiron, truly glad to have his old friend with him on this, his first commission as master. The moment held poignancy for these two young men so inexperienced in buffeting life's storms, and they were still capable of succumbing to its enchantment.

At parting, they exchanged hearty slaps on the back and a few raucous chidings that drowned out any personal concerns and bid each other good night as Chiron retired to his berth. Kristof remained alone on deck a few minutes longer as was his custom the last night in port, and reflected on the night sky. This would be a successful voyage and he would prove he deserved the faith his Chiot family had placed in him, he was sure of it.

Just after sunrise next morning, the Leonardas glided gracefully along the harbor, guided by a pilot as far as the breakers, where a waiting gust of wind filled her sails and she launched her might into the vast seascape that beckoned. The mood among the crew was high, the provisions plentiful and the old brig sound. It was an auspicious day and Chiron found the atmosphere and the salt spray infectious. He set about to find his place here, and to earn it.

Kristof commanded the wheelhouse in his familiar stance, looking back once at the rocky hills of Crete that caught the sun and magnified its reflected brilliance, burning it evermore on every observer's memory. He thought he glimpsed the cross of St. Nicholas Church rising amid the jumble of harbor buildings, its golden angles glinting in the morning light, winking farewell and safe travels. As he turned his eyes back to his task, he pictured the icon he had visited the day before in the vestibule of the church whose patron saint his own father had been named for. He was familiar with the icons of every church he had attended in every port where he had moored, but this was the one he always envisioned when he was at sea. Instead of a simple portrait of the church's namesake like most icons, this one depicts a story and it felt like his story. The inspired mosaic consists of thousands of tiny tiles, the background of lustrous gold covering an entire wall, depicting several men at the start of their journey in a boat with billowing white sails. The devil is in the water below them trying to gain passage, trying to pull himself out of the water and up the side of the boat. Standing alongside the craft, somewhat larger than life, is Saint Nicholas in his fine ceremonial vesture, holding the gospel in one hand and raising his other hand to the devil, forbidding him entry. When evil is shaking the boat, St. Nicholas serves as protector.[2]

As he steered a course to the north and prayed once more for safe passage on his maiden voyage as master, Kristof impulsively vowed to name his first-born son after the saint. He would in truth merely be following the tradition of naming his child after its paternal grandfather. Nonetheless, it was a fervid act of faith and it bolstered his confidence. He smiled into the shimmering sun and his smooth, broad forehead was unclouded.

There were ten seamen on this 232-ton brig built thirteen years earlier in 1867. That was just slightly more than the average number of sailors on any given sailing ship and slightly older than the average tempest-battered vessel. Chiron discovered his first night that the accommodations were surprisingly generous, including a bathroom in his cabin, but he soon realized he would have to get used to living with the inevitable bugs in his bedding. When he was introduced to the cook, he was informed he was meeting "the most important man on board" and before long understood the truth of that distinction. A Greek ship was generously stocked with an abundance of varied foodstuffs including chickens, beans, eggs, fresh fruit, salt, caviar, vegetables, pigs (two in this case), bread, biscuits, watermelons, smoked fish, preserved tomatoes, lemons, olive oil, rice, onions and parmesan cheese. The only supply noticeably absent was alcohol. As he soon learned from crew members who had experienced life on British and other European-owned ships, the differences were vast and pointed. Treatment of sailors under those flags was abysmal, the provisions bland sustenance at best, the atmosphere distrustful, the officers surly and the crew disgruntled. No self-respecting, capable Greek seaman stayed long on a foreign ship.

Most captains on Greek ships were self-taught and often co-owners with other merchants and shipping agents. Kristof had lived for more than a year on the island of Chios, where he was introduced to the clan theory of commerce, the basis of the success and ultimate domination of the Greek shipping industry. During that time he lived in the house of his "patron" merchant, his mother's brother, participating in daily family life and being exposed to a formal commercial education while learning the cultural traditions of his clan. This proven method of preparing future members of the clan for membership instilled frugality, piety, discretion and honesty, along with obedience to elders and the love of hard work. Kristof learned his lessons eagerly, despite the fact that he never overcame his fierce sense of independence, a fault attributed to his Cretan background and ultimately, perhaps, his Achilles heel.

In those days a sailing ship would complete an average of three voyages a year, each voyage lasting about four months. But steamships were beginning to make their way into the sea lanes and were showing signs of achieving supremacy at quite a pace. The traditional philosophy of the Greeks was to buy old ships at discounted prices and maintain them well for as long as they were viable. The practice had always paid off for them. By 1880, however, being that steamships were still relatively rare, in order to invest in them a buyer would have only new, high-priced vessels to choose from. The difference in productivity was so marked, however, it often rendered the decision clear-cut: the average steamer was over 1,000 tons, completed eight voyages a year of six weeks' duration each, and the potential for increased profits was unprecedented.

At this turning point in shipping history, the Greek maritime network was a model of efficiency and breadth. There were Greek agents stationed in nearly all ports of call who could handle any master's requests. There was a substantial concentration of Greek shipping owners in London and they belonged to the world's biggest freight market, the Baltic Exchange. The Greeks operated on the philosophy "buy when everybody sells, sell when everybody buys" known as the "anticyclical method" attributed to them. Simple as it sounded, it worked. A model student, Kristofer Karras took note; he had been well taught by the Chiot clan.

The clan itself was the key to Greek supremacy on the seas. The close-knit group of essentially extended family members worked together effectively in a clearly defined hierarchy to bring business opportunities to each other's attention, sharing exclusive information that any member may not have access to individually, but pooled together, increased each member's growth potential substantially. Trust was the key, and patience. If a member of the clan was not awarded new business by the leaders at any given point, he must have faith that his turn would come. In order for the clan model to work, each member had to protect the whole above the individual. The rewards were impressive. The clan's ability to support each other in rough times, in essence to be able to spread risk, was invaluable in the shipping industry, which suffered volatility of demand, causing huge fluctuations in prices over the years. They also invested in each other's ships, allowing members to finance their own vessels, pay expenses and earn profits with little risk of losing their investment. Greeks from the island of

Chios especially were known for their capital liquidity, often acting as guarantors for their members. All of these things Kristof knew, as well as the other incentive for loyalty: the ability of the group to ostracize any member who behaved contrary to the unwritten rules of the clan. It was their only power against actions of self-interest and it depended upon self-restraint by all members for its supremacy.

Kristof's prediction of a successful voyage proved true. When they got to London, he was offered the opportunity to oversee the building of a steamship, then became its master. He was young for the position, but it was not unheard of for a merchant to invest in an energetic, well-liked captain who could be cultivated within his growing fleet. Kristof knew to jump at the chance, and convinced Chiron to stay in London with him while the ship was under construction. Chiron, feeling little ambition and less desire to break off on his own, used this opportunity for self-education and circumspection. He became a voracious reader and developed his keen eye for art as he prowled the streets of the city, the antique houses and museums, although he did not have the funds yet for acquisition. All of his money was invested in the new steamship, along with Kristof's.

Kristof used this time to carefully attend his finances, investing more of his savings not only in this new venture, but in becoming further attached to the clan infrastructure, and familiarizing himself with other promising enterprises within the Chiot organization. His elders took note of his ambition and encouraged it. They had taken a chance on this Cretan outsider and were heartened by the signs of commitment Kristof enthusiastically exhibited. These were giddy days for shipping, prices were good and there was plenty of business for all. The Baltic Exchange was flourishing and Greek agencies were flexing their muscle.

By 1883 Kristof's and Chiron's ports of call included Philadelphia, London, Sierra Leone and Marseilles with a trip to the Island of Chios soon after that resulted in two life-altering events.

Kristof offered his hand in marriage to his aunt's young cousin, cementing his ties within the clan and trumping his aspirations for good fortune with happiness. Her name was Maria. She was dark-haired, shy, sweet and lovely. She adored her wayfaring betrothed and accepted his absences with quiet forbearance. Captain Karras had by now amassed enough savings to invest in his own ship, a 1,120-ton steamer that he christened the Nichola. Her maiden voyage was to Philadelphia, where he contracted one of the first transatlantic shipments of oil bound from the United States to London. She also carried grain, coal and lumber. She did not carry Chiron.

When the steamship docked in Chios, Chiron had taken a leave of absence and departed on a large fishing boat bound for Crete.

# CHAPTER 4

## 1946

It was to become known as the Shadow Hunt. It would grow into something more sinister, but the day of its inception started out uneventfully enough. The only other thing that stuck out in Herman's memory that day, before he discovered what he termed The Shadow and everyone else called his Imagination, was his discussion with Maggie at lunch. He was ruminating over liverwurst and mayonnaise on Sunbeam, when he turned to her and asked, "Maggie, did you come to Beechwood when Mr. Nick was born? Are you his mother?" He was fairly sure his own mother had said something to that effect the other night while she was under his surveillance. His memory was excellent, as long as he was listening.

"Oh for gracious sakes, rascal, where did you come up with such a question!" She hooted. She did look at him out of the side of her eyes, however, having heard that Nick had been here last night and she had missed the whole thing, nursing her poor, half-drowned old body over a hot toddy in her room. She had retired before he arrived, but Adrianne had been full of the news this morning, remembering the concern Maggie had expressed about his whereabouts "and here he was all this time just down the road a piece! I'm sure he would have loved to have seen you, Maggie," she had added, noticing Maggie's stricken face as she spoke. She did not suspect that Maggie's reaction was not over missing the chance to see Nick, but over the chance that she might have had to face him, and just barely escaped it.

The relief of knowing he was safe was tremendous, still. She had prayed for him nightly for years and recently begun to despair of ever knowing his fate but certainly she did not want to speak to him. The end was still fresh in her mind, how badly the family behaved as they practically flew away overnight, barely taking a civil leave of her or the others. Nick had behaved abominably, so angry he was at his father for whatever forced their departure. Her wounded pride had not recovered yet, after all those years when she was his nursemaid and practically raised him single-handed.

He had been the apple of her eye, the baby she never had, and then to discover he did not care a fig for her anymore and had left with barely a wave, not even noticing her tears, much less her broken heart. And not a word since, not a word. She wrote the family for years, until Mrs. Maria had passed, but never received a note from him, or an inquiry as to her well-being. How bitterly she remembered those days of reassuring herself he was young and unmindful, and sooner or later would feel the weight of her absence in his life. She expected him to show up at her door one day, knocking the secret knock he had contrived as a boy when he wanted a cuddle and a chat before bed. Oh how she had doted on him, secretly happy that his mother was detached, spending her time tending her garden instead of her child.

Mrs. Maria had seemed awkward around Nick, as if she might handle him incorrectly, as if he might reject her advances at mothering. She was a quiet one, never comfortable on this big estate and never quite belonging in the local social spheres. She clearly adored her husband, but her shyness prevented her from commanding much of his attention, and little of his concern. She never complained, you could say that about her. And she was a prolific gardener, in this way letting her passions bloom radiantly season to season, all across the back of the house, flowers bursting into riots of color and glory in great swaths, changing week to week and surprising passing strollers with a profusion of blossoms in unexpected patterns. Maggie recognized her expressions of ardor in these labors, and encouraged Mr. Karras to appreciate his wife's handiwork; it was Maggie's attempt at making up for the guilt she felt in monopolizing Nick's affection, although to little effect.

Thinking of these things, she glanced out the window at the peonies closest to the patio, slightly past their peak yet still audacious in their burgeoning majesty. They had been Mrs. Maria's favorites and this her happiest time of year. Lost in thought, Maggie jumped at Iris' shriek, turning just in time to see the glass of sweet tea tumble over and spill its contents across the oil cloth, reach the edge of the table and cascade onto the unsuspecting snout of Poseidon, who blinked and shook his head in confusion. The children lurched from their chairs in a flash, the spell was broken and Herman's question about Nick's babyhood was left unanswered. But as she stood watching the boisterous scene, she hugged her arms to herself, remembering her boy.

Her reverie was broken not by the ruckus of the lunch bunch, but the arrival of Thea, coming to see what deviltry was taking place in her kitchen. She looked rested today, if pale, but alert and amused by the scene she stepped into. She quickly had the mess under control and wondered aloud how much of the spill was tea and how much might be excited-puppy accident. The children acted indignant at the suggestion, but guffawed despite themselves and scampered out the screen door, shooing him along with them. Maggie breathed a sigh of relief, then remembered the afternoon's schedule and without a word to her darling

Thea, scooted off after her marauders, flapping her arms at them from behind.

They encountered Adrianne coming up the drive, who, when she spotted them, rolled down the window of her new Packard, a two-tone Custom Long WD Sedan, and asked them pointedly where they thought they were going without their bathing suits and towels and to hurry up now or they would be late again for their lessons at the club. She parked the car, set the emergency brake and opened the door to emerge into the dappled shade of the beech tree, looking like summer itself in her yellow, leaf-pattern sundress with the smart halter top, nicely set off by her bright yellow sandals. She held white sunglasses in one hand, her straw clutch, which perfectly matched her floppy-brimmed hat, in the other and was quite defenseless when Poseidon jumped up exuberantly to greet her, damp paws and all. Maggie had just come around the corner, was practically whirled about in a circle by the retreating herd of arms and legs, just in time to observe the dog's big welcome. She stopped, put her fists on her hips and tsked, shaking her head reprovingly, while barely suppressing a smile. Adrianne caught her twinkling eye, raised her shoulders in resignation and laughed. Maggie chuckled, deciding not to mention the nature of the wet prints, then called the dog to her, motioning vigorously and chiding him for all his shortcomings. As they turned back to the house Adrianne called after them, "Make sure Iris has an extra shirt to put on after her swim lesson, her shoulders are peeling already!"

The Yacht Club in nearby Lloyd Harbor was bustling as usual, the thwop of tennis balls ever-present, the slap of waves against the docks forcefully rhythmic, the sharp breeze invigorating and welcome, if somewhat pushy at times. The children, marginally restrained by ancient rules of club decorum were nonetheless buoyant, criss-crossing the grounds all day long, never still, confidently purposeful. Glimpsed from the road above, they bobbed like colorful balloons dancing on someone's invisible strings.

The twins took daily swim and tennis lessons, while Todd spent his afternoons in the harbor learning to race the catboat designed for him at Hephron's shipyard. He was a natural sailor and was more at home on his forward-mounted, single-sail novice craft than on shore among the members of the club. He loved the demands of the open water, the banter between the wind and the sea, the struggle to conquer the untamable whims of the ocean, the vast infinite allure of its depth and breadth. He felt his strength, his promise and even his destiny rise in his chest when he braced against the current, when he anticipated and rode its swells. The wind was his messenger, his duty to read it well and respect its temperament, to become its artful servant. He cherished this solitude, this test of self-reliance and skill. He brought to bear everything Chiron had taught him, combined with the rigorous training of his instructors, including Hephron himself, each time he cast off and faced the inscrutable surface of the dark waters. He let go of his other life here, only out here.

His biggest challenge in sailboat racing was the turns. He became tense and anxious at the crucial point where he could lose his usual advantage. He became distracted by the maneuvers of his competitors and would try to cut them off, sacrificing control of his own vessel, a penalty flag the invariable result. He practiced again and again, and performed well enough when no one else was nearby. But when there was a challenger who may crowd him or out-strategize him he overreacted, sometimes even got dumped and his pride drenched accordingly. He was particularly feeling the frustration today, having attempted his instructor's advice for the third time in an hour and still losing ground among the other vessels, again swept wide at the last moment trying to avoid an overlap.

In a rebellious expression of futility, he allowed his sail to luff, his boat to glide farther out to sea, out of earshot. He turned his back to the shore. He was drifting, his mind blank, his lassitude putting him in danger of alarming the staff on shore.

Something made him look over his shoulder for signs of fog, the dread as palpable as ever, the prickling at the back of his neck a reminder of that day last summer, the last day of his time on The Harbor for the year before he returned to his mother, his flat on the Lower East Side, school, his world apart, his real home.

It was the first time he'd contemplated an alternative to the ritual allotment of the Beechwood season, fleeting and finite, when he was abruptly barred after a certain date that did not vary. He was hurtfully aware he was the only person subject to this calendar of temporariness and realized it hung over him from the moment he arrived, its inevitable end looming even from its beginning. Not only did he lament his inability to forestall its end, but felt suddenly enveloped in dread of the hollow winter ahead.

Before long that one afternoon he had found himself at the water's edge, with a tote filled with such essentials as he had hurriedly gathered, scrutinizing the boats in dock. He chose the Zealander, a twelve-and-a-half-foot Kauri clinker dinghy with a modest outboard motor; manageable, reliable, known more for stability than speed. He untied it and shoved off, deftly pulling the cord to start the motor, easing away from the shoreline without arousing attention. He was a speck on the water in no time. They couldn't send him away if they couldn't find him.

The day had been breezy, with lofty clouds that took on the perfect embodiment of his imagination and played across the sky writ large, the paintbrush of the wind transforming each one before long into a clever new image, leaving him just a little wistful for the original shape casually dissolving, escaped. The sky had told her tales for quite a while by the time the clouds began to cluster and merge, when Todd glimpsed what looked like fog off in the distance.

He was not concerned, particularly, because it was still sunshine ahead, with his vessel facing southeast. Nor did it appear to be advancing as it hovered on shore far to the west. He turned his back and continued across the harbor toward the inlet.

When the first wisps of fog flirted alongside his boat, he didn't notice. His mind had been churning with schemes of hiding out. Though he was doing his best to romanticize his escape, his strategy was beginning to feel like its own ban from Beechwood. He was confused and becoming less indignant by the minute, more circumspect. Cloudy. Foggy. Oh.

Before long, he was encased. His visibility was about three feet. He was afraid to move the tiller because he couldn't tell which direction he was heading anymore. He squinted, desperately searching for the Huntington Harbor lighthouse. In an instant he was screaming with a convulsion of terror in concert with the horn of a great cabin cruiser that suddenly materialized a few yards port. Its headlight diffused across the fog, it heaved into sight, loomed, passed soundlessly then rocked his dinghy in its mighty wake. He was flotsam; less. He was invisible.

He whimpered, shivered and resorted to prayer. The waves that rolled his boat were no longer from the passing vessel. The wind whipped across the bow, scattering jets of water across his chest, his thighs, his floppy hair. His feet were soon in standing water. He bowed his head to keep the salt spray out of his eyes. The motor, his only comfort, surged and hummed, surged and hummed.

He pictured a day last October less than a year before. Up until then the procedure had been the same every October. His mother took them on their outing every year, as long as he could remember. It was the anniversary of the day his father, his and Perry's, was beaten and arrested. Or maybe it was the anniversary of when, a few days later, he died in jail of his wounds; he was never sure. As they stood on the quay regarding the scene of black, oily water floating with debris, slapping erratically against the cement pier, emitting a foul odor with each lap, she pressed them ever closer to the edge and hovered over them, whispering what they already knew.

"The same thing will happen to you, mark my words, if you don't take heed. Mark my words."

He would picture his little body floating in the scum, his mother's face hanging over the side above him, her eyes glinting with the proof of her prophecy. He would rock back and forth in time with the smack of the waves as he contemplated his fate from above. He felt queasy, seasick, like he never did in a boat.

What made her prediction most convincing was that this pier was not where his father had been waylaid; that location was a few blocks inland. This spot here was where his grandfather, his father's father, had washed up a couple of decades earlier, the predecessor-victim of murder himself. The first in the series.

His own imagined young face, floating below, would dissolve before his eyes into the bloated face of an old man, evil, rotting, the very source of the putrid smell surrounding them. He had no doubt of the culpability of this corpse. He felt the evil creep up the side of the quay and claw at his feet, even when he squeezed his eyes tightly and banned the image from his mind. He would usually turn then, to hide his head in his mother's coat, and wrap his arms around her to keep from falling in. She would always pat him then, satisfied, and repeat the importance of taking heed.

When they would get back home, Adicia would invariably remove their clothes for washing and scrub them raw in a hot tub, a ritual cleansing that seemed to satiate her, and placate her demons. That was what it seemed like to him.

Last October, though, it was different.

The tradition began as it always did, and progressed as expected. The boys were getting older, however, and had found ways to disengage their thoughts from the scene at least part of the time and maybe their mother sensed that, he didn't know. But this time, when they got home, she removed their clothes, wadded them up and flung them into the stove, clanging shut the door just as the flames began to surge. Then she left him standing in the kitchen, shivering, while she took Perry upstairs. How long later he didn't know, but he heard the faucet creak, the water pipes thunk into action, and the flow of water into the bathtub ricochet off the old porcelain. She returned without Perry and motioned him to follow her. Upstairs she performed an enema on him, though he did not know what that was. He only knew how it felt and the mortification of it.

After the ritual bath she made them brush their teeth until their gums bled, then she cut their fingernails and toenails to the quick. Finally, she took a long-handled razorblade from the cabinet, soaped their hair and shaved their heads. They stood on the bathroom floor surrounded by wet chunks of dark hair, like featherless chicks in a haphazard nest. Then she went downstairs to make dinner.

She was cheerful after that. She made them pastitsio, their favorite, and Kataifi rolls for dessert. They called them wooly worms, because they looked hairy with their coating of crushed almonds and honey. He couldn't remember eating them, though.

When next he looked up into the fog, he imagined he saw a brightness off to port almost astern, then it was gone. There. That was it again. No. Gone. Yes, surely, it's a light for sure; the lighthouse must be there, blinking, rotating, guiding wayward sailors and foolish boys. He had almost passed it and abruptly over-reacted, thrusting the tiller away to turn the boat, which promptly took on a foot of new water and swayed sidelong to near submersion until he leaned hard, righting it but taking on almost as much water starboard before he could settle the rocking with his bodyweight, spread-eagled. As he caught his breath and gauged again the angle of the faintly pulsing light, he felt his limbs turn heavy and resistant to his commands. A chill was creeping up from his feet, an ache criss-crossed his shoulder blades, a weight lay upon his eyelids. A desire to take a little rest was tempting and sweet.

With more luck than skill he located a rock outcropping on the far side of the lighthouse and sat shivering upon it, where he hoped to escape notice from the keeper, a reasonable expectation as the fog remained perverse and amorphous for some time. Contemplation came easily then, with no distractions beyond the rock ledge other than his physical discomfort and the sounds of the sea. He jumped when a seagull complained a few yards off. He recovered his nerves and quickly resettled into his pose; chest bent closely over his legs, his arms wrapped around his knees, his face pressed to his thighs, his ears protected by his hunched shoulders. His fingers were stiff, his toes numb. He had been wet for hours. His lower back was exposed where his shirt pulled away from his shorts, beaded and glistening with drops of condensation.

He sat up to blow on his fingers and looked around. Off to his right he noted a brightening, a glow of pink and gold that signaled, possibly, sunset. The fog had thinned. A cat emerged from around the bend and he nearly leapt into the water aghast. Its back went up, tail frizzled, eyes brighter than the setting sun. He laughed uneasily with relief and let it brush against his legs, wondering at its acceptance of the dampness all around. He patted it awhile, taking a broad view of life alone and the comforts of companionship.

The distant shrill of a whistle penetrated his trace, finally, and he was once again in the waters off the yacht club, where the buoy marking the turning point in the course was his most formidable threat. He found himself drenched in sweat and trembling.

Floundering, he suddenly heard Chiron's deep voice rush through his mind. It was borne on the breeze and quickened his pulse with its message.

"Whenever man is in conflict with others," he had said one day as they studied, "he is in danger of defeating himself. If he wants to resolve his conflict he must be in accord with the truth as it exists in nature. In order to be in accord with nature, he must transcend fear and desire."[1] Todd contemplated that theory for a moment, working out why it came to him now, so removed here from both the musty books of Chiron's study and the murky, murderous quay. He understood fighting fear and desire. He understood being in accord with nature; he drew from its energy often enough. It was the reason he felt so at home, content, on his little boat. His vessel provided him a connection to nature that both soothed and excited him.

It seemed different, though, when other forces were involved, when it wasn't just him and the sea. It was different when he felt compelled to prove himself; he was never sure to whom.

The only way to be in accord with fear and desire, he reasoned, was to rise above them. Not to fight them. Could that be what Chiron meant? He furrowed his brow. He squinted into the sun. He looked archly over his shoulder and considered the final buoy brazenly buffeting the swells, laughing, luring him into its watery turf.

He waited patiently for one of the older boys to make a run for the mark. With precise timing, he came about and swiftly approached his target. This time, however, he concentrated on the water instead of the other vessel or the flag, and read its rhythm, followed its flow and used its power as his own. He felt instinctively the other catboat would not be a factor. He felt calm, natural. He watched the bow of his skiff peripherally as it rose and fell gracefully, keeping his sheet taut, feeling its pull through the line controlled by his left hand, ready to ease the tension as needed. He approached his target as if drawn by a magnetic force. It was intoxicating, that synergy of the water, the boat and his will. He timed the rudder's shift to the roll and thrust of the current, crouching to avoid the beam as it came across, his tack perfectly executed to accommodate the modulating breeze. His turn clean, his momentum barely checked, his boat carried flawlessly through the momentary, ever-changing path of least resistance. He was only marginally aware the other boat had given way.

His body and mind had synchronized, he thought, with all the tidal forces of all the oceans deep and wide in all the history of time. He had done it! He leapt to his feet in triumph and raised his arms above his head in utter joy, a cheer erupting across the bay to the clubhouse beyond. He barely held his footing before lurching to grab the rudder once again, ducking the boom and narrowly correcting his course in time to avoid being swamped. But the elation he felt was unbounded, his triumph a victory over his greatest challenger, his fear of conflict, and he knew no future competitor would likely provide the same thrill of conquest as the one he faced today. He steered straight to the docks, his grin as wide as the horizon, to apologize to his superiors for sailing outside the boundaries, and to bask in his accomplishment.

Yet he decided not to mention his achievement to the Bayards, or even Chiron. He wanted to savor it for awhile. He wanted it to be private.

"How was your sail today, son?" Heph asked Todd at dinner. "How were you loaded?" he smiled.

"To the Plimsoll line, sir." Todd responded, as was his custom in this, their daily exchange.

"That's fine, son, keep it up." Heph had explained to him once that a ship loaded to its Plimsoll line was a ship loaded to safe levels. This was short-hand banter for checking on his young charge's progress, Todd guessed. He liked it. It felt good to be checked on.

That night the children chased the season's first fireflies around the garden while Adrianne and Heph sat on the patio with their cocktails, enjoying the action. It was a cool evening for June, even the kids wore sweaters and Adrianne had wrapped herself in a woolen shawl, sporting pants and heavy socks with her soft Italian loafers that she propped casually on the chair next to her, long legs crossed at the ankles. Heph smoked a cigar, allowing it to roll unattended across the wrought iron table when he jumped up to rescue escaping fireflies. Iris had tripped, launching her jar across the lawn, where the lid popped free. She was so impressed by her father's swift response and his agility at recovering her quarry that she didn't even whimper, but joined forces with him and together they achieved a fairly high percentage of recapture in no time. Todd did not have a jar himself, instead choosing to catch his lightning bugs on behalf of the twins, depositing them alternately in one jar or the other. Quantity being the priority for Herman, he was quite satisfied with the arrangement and counted all the bugs in his jar as his own plunder.

Adrianne shivered, announcing she longed for a nice, hot bath, and Heph returned to pull back her chair as she rose. The kids begged to be allowed to show Chiron their booty and were indulged. They ran off to the gatehouse.

They barreled inside after a cursory knock and imagined "Enter." They stopped in confusion when Chiron wasn't at his usual post behind his desk. They peered into the semi-darkness for clues to his whereabouts. They didn't call out, the hushed atmosphere precluded that boldness, but they separated, creeping lightly into the room. Todd saw four empty glasses, two tall, two short, on the table between the armchairs; a rare example of neglectful housekeeping in Chiron's home. Iris, going through her checklist, noted the Remy Martin bottle was full, when yesterday the level was two inches lower. Herman did not notice anything but said, "Let's go upstairs to the guardroom lookout, maybe we will see him coming!" They bounded up the stairs, where they were met by the familiar pungent, sharp smells of the upper floor, and the underlying acrid odor of something recently burned. They jostled for the best vantage point at the windows of the landing. They each glanced at the closed door to

Chiron's room, where none of them had ever been or even glimpsed. If Chiron had been in there at this hour, he would have heard them by now and made his presence known. Todd was sure there was a laboratory inside, and held out hope that he would someday receive an invitation to see for himself. If the landing were any indication, the private room must be a treasure trove.

The wide, disorderly hallway was a jumble of equipment, mementos, artwork, picture frames, a cracked, stained mortar and pestle, a pair of binoculars hanging from a nail, a telescope on its tripod (which was strictly invitation-only as they well knew), as well as unidentifiable objects shoved against the walls, piled on a table in the corner, lying on the window seat haphazardly, neglected, disused, intriguing. It always reminded Todd of the old plow shed, minus the rust and cobwebs. "Look!" he exclaimed, speaking of the plow shed, "That's Ole Webster flying up over the fountain! Did you see him? I think he had something in his talons!" Ole Webster was the Eastern Screech Owl who lived in the rafters of the plow shed and was spotted occasionally soon after dusk making his rounds.

"Where, where?" demanded Herman, weaving and bobbing to get a better view. "Aw, gee, I missed him. Wait, wait," he grabbed Todd's arm and tugged. "I see something. I see someone in the shadows by the edge of the trees! Did you see that? Is it Chiron?"

Todd and Iris made the same skeptical face, pursing their lips to one side, looking at him from under their lashes. "Just because you never see Ole Webster doesn't mean you have to make up something in the shadows, Herman," Iris scoffed.

"No, really, I did!" he insisted half-heartedly, knowing they would never believe him. "Aw come on, I really did. Chiron will be here any second, you'll see." But Todd was pressing his right cheek to the windowpane, peering out as far as he could to his left, toward the cove, from where Chiron was more likely to approach. He disappeared from time to time on his cutter, sometimes staying away for days and never offering any explanation when he returned, a little wan, perhaps, but picking up right where he left off without missing a beat. No one, not even Heph, inquired about his absences. After all this time, Chiron maintained his independence and their respect for him precluded suspicion or prying. Thinking of the whiff of liquor in the glasses left downstairs, Todd wondered if it might be an indicator of such a trip.

All three of them noticed Hephron as he emerged from the edge of the garden, Poseidon bounding around his legs, nearly tripping his master with his brash overtures. The glowing tip of Heph's cigar jerked up, across, sideways and back, describing a scarlet trail as it eluded ignition of the pup's nose, tail and flopping ears. "Come on, let's go, your dad's probably wondering what happened to us by now," Todd said as they leapt off the window seat, clamored down the stairs and raced across the main room out the open door, which someone ran back to close.

As Herman scuffled down the back hall in his pajamas to his bedroom that evening, he paused to look out the window one more time for any sign of Chiron. It was a patchy night, the moon a sliver emerging every few minutes from behind a misty cloud, lethargic in its night-watchman's duties, encouraging the boldness of shadows and shifty nocturnal pursuits. Herman's scalp tingled and he shivered. He imagined he heard Ole Webster hoot, hoot. Suddenly, he straightened and tensed as he remembered where he left his Ba. It was in his shorts pocket, which he had carelessly thrown with his other clothes down the laundry chute! It was in the basement! "Oh, no!" He gasped and turned back towards his parents' room. "Mom! Mommy! Where are you!" His Ba was his greatest embarrassment and his dearest possession. He always, invariably, kept it with him in his pocket except when he went to bed, where he slept with it clenched in his fist, even at his age. ("Even at your age!" Maggie would say whenever she washed it, ironed it and returned it to him not ungently). Hardly more than a frazzled strip of faded baby quilt, it was a life-long companion, an indescribable source of comfort and courage. And now it was alone, by itself, way down in the basement.

By the time the Ba was retrieved, tempers were short all around and terse goodnights exchanged as each member of the search party turned towards his or her own bed. "No tucking in tonight," Herman thought. He heaved a sigh that lifted his shoulders clear up to his ears and then dropped them with a huff, as he glanced once more through the passing window. There. Something moved in the garden. He peered more closely. What was it? Where did it go? "It's nothing. A cat," Todd would have sneered.

"But I saw it," he whispered softly to the sentinel moon, and slipped off to bed.

# CHAPTER 5

## 1946

The next morning was overcast and drizzly. The kids stirred soggy Toasted Corn Flakes around their bowls, bickering over each other's unignorable shortcomings like slurping and staring and being a spaz. Herman kicked rhythmically against his chair legs while Iris offered spoonfuls of cereal under the table for Poseidon to lick. Todd lapsed into a reverie and the kitchen eventually became quiet except for the lapping tongue and rapping foot. Herman's legs finally relaxed as he followed the progress of a stealthy blond spider dropping fitfully by its invisible thread from the top of the window frame behind the sink. He wondered what would happen if he put it in the jar with his lightening bugs. No one had told him Heph had left the jars open by the greenhouse door before going inside last night.

Thea fairly ejected them from the room as she swept through on her way to the back door, where she was accepting a delivery from the butcher. The children raised their eyebrows at each other, noting this unusual burst of energy from Thea, the Old Thea. Iris thought about the medicine, the mastic Chiron had been sending over. Well, things were looking up, and a ray of sunshine broke across the linoleum floor momentarily to punctuate the fact. They were fond of their cook, Todd's aunt, and her failing health might have weighed on them more than they realized. Their spoons clattered to the table and their chair legs scraped the floor stridently as they called their cheerful goodbyes and ran off through the hall in search of the next diversion.

Maggie was approaching them, hind part first, pumping a wet mop as she progressed. The mop handle provided an excellent hurdle, which she observed up close once, twice, thrice, then spied the dog aiming next. She dropped the mop, turned hard in his direction and exclaimed, "Whoa, little bandit, don't you dare come into my front hall!" She caught him in her ample arms mid-leap and unceremoniously marched to the rear hall door, pushed it open with a shove of her surprisingly supple hip and dumped him onto the stoop. "One more false move from you and I'll throw you back in the sea!" she warned as the screen slammed shut behind his retreating tail end.

The kids crept back, sidestepping the bucket and wet floor marks, to witness the outcast's retreat. It began to rain in earnest then and they spied him scratching at the greenhouse door, whimpering. Someone let him in, probably Clarence. When they turned around they faced a stern-mouthed Maggie, fists on hips, cap pulled low over glowering eyes.

"Maggie, Maggie, Maggie," said Todd with a disarming grin, "How's about one of your wonderful stories on this gloomy-rainy day?" She thought he might have winked at her and her eyes widened at the cheeky nerve.

"I know!" proclaimed Herman, "You can tell us about how Mr. Nick was your baby and all!"

"No, no, I have a much better idea," stated Iris definitively. "We want to hear the Equable Fire Story, the one you were going to tell us the other day, about the terrible fire, remember?"

"Yeah! Yeah!" both boys agreed. "That's the one!"

"Equitable," Maggie said, thawing reluctantly. "The Equitable Life Assurance Company fire of 1912." She regarded them, considering. "Oh, all right, you go on now and do your summer reading for your mother and let me finish this floor. Then I'll tell you all about the second worst disaster in the history of New York City.

"How do you know it was the second worst disaster in the history of New York City?" asked Herman when they'd settled into the cushions of the summer furniture out on the screen porch, lemonades and sugar cookies in hand.

"Well no, pirate boy, for me it was the worst possible disaster of all time. I was there." She paused. "But the history books say the very worst calamity was The Shirtwaist Fire of 1911. You've heard about that."

"Everybody's heard about that. They teach it in school," confirmed Todd. The twins looked at each other. They were a little young for that history lesson, but they nodded just the same, used to being left out of what everybody else knew.

"Well, I'm sure that was true, but this," she slowly shook her head back and forth, picturing that day, "this was a bad one, a tragedy for sure, as well as a miracle of sorts, too, at the end." Goose flesh appeared on Iris' arms at Maggie's tone.

Maggie looked up, remembering her audience and gathering herself, sitting up straighter and clearing her throat. One quick adjustment to her cap and she knew where to start.

"It was, in fact, on the day Nick Karras was born," she began.

"I knew it! I told you he was Maggie's baby!"

"Herman, I insist you sit there with your interruptions locked up tight as a sunken treasure, you hear? We will never get a fraction of the way through this story if you don't keep still."

He was unabashed. "Nothin' to it, Maggie. Don't worry about a thing. I know when to keep my trap shut. I promise, really, you can count on me."

Maggie glared. He started to reassure her but she held up her hand. He sat back in his cushions, slightly deflated but mute.

"It was January ninth. It was a cold, frigid, blustery, gray day when no one in the city of New York would choose to be outside who didn't have to be. That morning, about seven in the morning, my friend Anna stopped by." Maggie looked over at Todd.

"Todd, did you ever hear the story about how your Aunt Thea came to work here?"

"Aunt Thea?" He looked confused. What could the big fire in 1912 have to do with Aunt Thea?

"Yes, Thea. Not then, but later. How she got to be employed here by the Karras family." Todd shook his head. Maggie was prone to going off on tangents and he suspected this was one of those times.

"Well, let's see how this story turns out and then we'll worry about that. You pay attention, now. Anna was stopping by to tell me my new job was about to begin, any day now. We didn't know at the time it was to be that very day, or that we would not get another chance to chat for quite some time, but then who could imagine any of the things that happened that awful day of the Equitable Life Assurance Fire.

"You see, Anna was coming here, to Beechwood, to be the baby nurse for the Karras' new baby. The baby who would be Mr. Nick." She looked at Herman, who opened his mouth to speak, then closed it again. "She needed the job, you see, to help support her family. She was married to that no good pig-in-a-poke Jasen— well, never mind about him"— she looked back at Todd. "And she had a little boy name of Alexsy, sweet little thing, who she would have to leave behind so she asked me if I would watch over him. Well, that was a job I could not turn down. We were always short of money in those days, being as my papa had debts that never seemed to get cleared up and being as he always sent whatever money he could back to the Old Country. And I was out of work for the winter, being as I was a

102

fresh fruit vendor up on the corner of Thirteenth and Third, but I sure wasn't selling any fresh fruit in the middle of January, I can tell you that. So I took the job and thank you ma'am.

"That morning I was planning to get my errands out of the way, so I would be all caught up and prepared to mind Alexsy." She was still eyeing Todd, he was sure of it. "Ready to get him nice and settled in our little apartment where Papa and I lived over on Ludlow Street. Over on the Lower East Side. Along about eight thirty that morning, though, just about the time I finished washing the kitchen floor, my neighbor Mrs. Connelly came bursting in the front door when usually she knocked. 'Did you hear about the big fire over on Broadway down by the Stock Exchange?' she said. Her husband was a fire fighter, too, the same as my papa. 'It's a Borough Alarm!' she cried and then I knew why she was so worked up. A borough alarm was the call which meant there was a catastrophe. It meant every engine company in Manhattan below Fifty-ninth Street was called to the scene. All the companies above Fifty-ninth Street had to spread out and move down to take the others' places, that's how serious a Borough Alarm was. Most every engine from Brooklyn raced across the Brooklyn Bridge that day, too. The building, you see, the Equitable Building, was the first skyscraper ever built. Well, it was called a skyscraper, even though it was only nine stories high. But it had an elevator. It had the first ever elevator, made by the Otis Company, I remember that, and the elevator itself turned out to be a big part of the tragedy."

Maggie began to appear agitated. Her hands alternately clutched her neckline, her apron, each other, fidgeting anxiously, itching to take flight. The boys did not notice; what they saw before them was taking place downtown, long ago, in wild heat and icy temperatures. Firelight practically danced in their eyes. Maggie saw this and tried to focus on her listeners.

She made her hands into two fists and placed them one on each knee, upright, thumbs facing each other, as if she were holding her knees in place that way. She kept them like that until the very end of the story, until after the story was over. That was the part Iris would always remember; the way she held her fists tightly like that, not moving them.

"By the time Mrs. Connelly and I got to the scene of the fire, Papa was already dead, only I didn't know it yet. Somewhere near the back of the building, where there was a restaurant called the Café Savarin, several bakers had been at work baking since five o'clock that morning. The fire started back there somehow and two or three of those men were killed right off the bat. That's when the fire spread to the elevator shaft. You see, the way elevators were built, straight up through the building to the top without stopping, they acted like a chimney, pulling the fire and smoke right along, sucking it all the way up through every floor right to the roof. The fire chief, Chief Walsh, he was leading his men up the stairs about that time, trying to get to the Lawyers' Club rooms, they say. Papa was right there, right behind him. All the most important law papers were stored in that Lawyer's Club, a whole library full, and maybe Chief Walsh thought they could master the flames before they consumed all those important papers, I don't know. You see, The Equitable was an important building. Besides the irreplaceable books and records, there were more than one billion dollars' worth of stocks and bonds and jewelry and what-all in the vaults of that building. At least, that's what the newspapers said, and the firemen who survived, the ones who told about the horror they witnessed that day.

104

Some of them didn't want to talk about it, not around me. None of them talked about it at the funeral, I can tell you that.

"One of the big problems was the low water pressure, you know, like when I do the wash and you try to take a shower at the same time, right after you get back home from your swim lessons at the club. There were so many engines hooked up to every single hydrant around the building that there wasn't enough pressure to keep them pumping.

"Unbeknownst to the firemen inside, like Papa, there were three other men in the building who had raced up to the roof after the smoke and fire escaped out of the elevator shaft. I didn't see this part myself, but we were told they stood out on the roof next to a cupola near the edge facing Cedar Street, calling out for help. The firemen on the street below begged them to wait, not to jump and they tried their best to listen. The firemen grabbed scaling ladders and climbed toward the three men when flames began shooting out of the windows halfway up and the firemen, they had to back down. Right then, it was right then, that the back of the building collapsed behind those men." Maggie's voice was now no more than a whisper. "Right then is when my papa and the chief were killed by the collapsing floors above them. They never stood a chance, those poor brave fire fighters, Papa and Chief Walsh, risking everything, trying everything, and still, the walls collapsing in on them, trapping them, killing them…" She took a deep breath, not willing even now to linger on that part of the story. Her eyes focused on the children. "The others were spared. The other firemen escaped."

"But by that time, the heat was so horrific on the roof, like a furnace, the three men could not stand it. Two of them knelt at the edge, prayed for a moment, and jumped." Herman gasped. "The third man fell backwards into the inferno." Both boys fell back into their chair cushions. "Like I said, I didn't see it, though I surely feel like I did.

"I didn't know about any of that part, though, not yet," Maggie did not pause, but pushed on to tell her story, heedless now of her listeners, lost in the memories that rarely found voice, rarely found release, yet remaining careful not to dwell too closely on her loss.

"The part I remember, the part I saw, was just unfolding when we arrived, me and Mrs. Connelly.

"Nick's papa, Mr. Kristofer Karras, he was there too, that day. I had never laid eyes on him before but later, when I met him, I knew just who he was. I could picture him as I saw him that day plain as anything standing a few yards farther down Broadway, watching the same square patch of grating on the front corner of the building as I was, like he was made of stone and not capable of moving, not even blinking. Staring. Horrified. Everything else that day was in fast motion around us; chaos and whistles, shouting, running feet, the whoosh and hiss and whoosh of water from the fire hoses forming freezing and frozen waterfalls, covering everything it sprayed, turning everything thick white, stiff, onlookers pushing, craning, crying, like a moving picture film. All except for Mr. Karras and me. We were frozen stock still. We were watching the grate from two different angles, while the view was blocked for most of the folks, who wouldn't see what we could see until it was all over. I glimpsed him just once, but I could feel him nearby like we were partners at an execution, watching, helpless, not able to look away and the next time I looked up, afterwards, he was gone."

The three children were used to Maggie's scary stories. They had thrilled to her pirate tales and ghost stories for as long as they could remember. But this story was something different. It was different because Maggie was different while she was telling it. Her voice was soft and calm but her body was tense, practically vibrating, and her eyes were seeing what her words could not convey, seeing it, hearing it, reliving it. Iris rubbed her own arms, watching Maggie, feeling the chill herself on this humid day thirty-some years removed.

"Now one of the bigwigs, a man named Mr. Giblin, president of some kind of bank or other, he was in the Breslin Hotel tending his sick wife when a clerk came to tell him about the fire. He hopped in a taxicab and arrived at the Equitable when it was still early. He grabbed a watchman, a man called Sheehan, and together the two of them went in the building on the Cedar Street side. His company's vault was on the ground floor, which was a couple of steps lower than the street and kind of dark at that hour. He used a set of keys to open the big steel door by the sidewalk. Just when they got inside, a falling piece of debris hit against the door and slammed it shut on them with the keys still left hanging in the lock outside.

"On account of it was a spring lock, the two men were stuck, no way to get out and no one to tell. But they made their way in the dark to the front of the building, not knowing how close the fire was getting. That Mr. Giblin stepped into his big vault and started searching for whatever papers he thought he needed to save. Back in that vault he had no idea how much smoke was starting to fill the area. As soon as he stepped out of there, though, he realized how serious the situation was, and that they were prisoners down there in the smoke and darkness. Well, it was about an hour after those men had entered the building that someone outside the front of the building, and to this day I believe it was Mr. Karras, noticed something between the bars of the grate near the Broadway entrance and notified the fire department's chaplain. He couldn't get near the building himself, the police were keeping everyone back, away from the falling arches and lintels. So he went and found the chaplain and told him what he saw.

"It was a white handkerchief he saw, and it was Mr. Giblin waving it for all he was worth, trying to get someone's attention, to let someone know there were live people down there. See, he had found Mr. Sheehan but Mr. Sheehan was in a bad way. He had also made it over by the bars of the grate, he had gone there when he saw the other man, the other watchman who was down there, a man name of William Campion, I will never forget that man's name. See, Mr. Campion had grabbed onto the bars like this, see," here Maggie shook her fists back and forth across the top of her knees "and tried pulling on them," she tried pulling on the imaginary bars, to no avail, "when he was hit by timbers from the ceiling and was killed. But, but, he didn't let go of the bars. He was dead but his hands were gripped to those bars and they froze there, just like that, they froze solid to those bars. Meanwhile, both he and the timbers fell against Mr. Sheehan and pinned the poor man against the wall. Mr. Sheehan couldn't get his arm free and had to stand there helpless. So there the three of them were, one of them dead, one of them pinned down and one of them waving that white handkerchief desperately out from between those bars, sunken down like I said lower than the sidewalk.

"This was about the time me and Mrs. Connelly arrived. The first thing that attracted my attention to

the corner where those men were was a decorative stone from above the doorway that come crashing down right there near that grate. A fireman, Fireman James Dunn, was running across the street, dodging the falling debris, holding a couple of saws. He handed one to Mr. Giblin and they both started sawing at those bars, trying to cut enough space for someone to be able to pull those men out from between them. Smoke was coming out the window and another fireman began aiming his hose into it, trying to keep the flames at bay but what happened was everything turned to ice. Every inch of the wall outside was frozen a foot thick with layers of ice like the devil's own wedding cake, Mr. Sheehan was coated in ice, Mr. Giblin had to give up sawing his hands were that numb, and the hands of William Campion, still holding onto those bars, were encased, like they were wearing a pair of giant white gloves, and still refusing to give up on those bars."

The telephone rang in the hallway and all four of them jumped. Herman had taken his Ba out of his pocket and was kneading it between his fingers, holding it close to his face.

"I was praying with all my might, I can promise you that. I was praying out loud and wishing like the dickens I had my rosary with me. Finally Mr. Jim Dunn cut through the iron bar and they pried it to the side with a chain. Someone blocked my view and by the time I could see again, I realized there still wasn't a wide enough space to fit the men through. Oh Lordy, murmurs ran through the crowd then, word spreading that the men were doomed. It took more than an hour longer to cut through the second bar, pry it apart and start pulling. But they did it, they sure did. Those two poor souls were carried off to the boiler room of the Trinity Building, where doctors from The Gouverneur Hospital were waiting for them. But all the rest of that day and into the evening, those two white hands stood sentry at the grate, frozen for all time in the minds of us who saw them."

Maggie looked down, then, seeming to notice her own hands for the first time. She slowly unclenched them, working them stiffly, awkwardly, back into circulation. She massaged them, first one and then the other, concentrating, a new crease forming across her forehead, hard to say from which pain. Suddenly looking up she commented, "Why, I don't think I've ever seen you scoundrels sit so still for so long. What's gotten into you? You wouldn't let a little tall tale bother you, now. Would you?" Herman hiccupped and when everyone looked at him, he swiftly stuffed the Ba back into his pocket. Then they all turned back to look at Maggie, expectantly. It made her uncomfortable, their watching her like that.

"All right now, go on. Shoo." She motioned them off as she stood up. They followed her with their eyes. "What? What is it?" She plopped herself back down into her chair. "All right, let's not get all worked up about it. It was just a story is all. Most of it was hardly even true. I trumped it up, decked it out and put a big bow on it just to entertain you and keep you out of trouble on such a rainy day. Now don't make me sorry I gave up my morning's duties for your personal entertainment, you hear? Iris, you hear? Herman? Todd?"

Todd swallowed. "How did Aunt Thea come to work here, like you said before?"

"Oh dear me, this day is never going to end," Maggie sighed. She looked down at her hands, then stuck them under her thighs, in an attempt to keep some part of herself out of trouble. "Let me see if I can answer that for you." She stalled for time to think.

"Now let me see. Anna. I mentioned Anna before, didn't I? Anna was a young woman, a beautiful young woman who used to come by my fruit stand every day to see what I had on display. Sometimes she would buy, sometimes she would just look and we would chat a little bit. Cherries were her favorite, I remember that, she did love cherries, the darker and sweeter the better. She could hardly resist those and sometimes I gave her a handful even when she wasn't buying. She was always so polite and she was company. It got lonely sometimes standing on that corner all day, trying to keep my produce in the shade, trying to keep the hands of little rapscallions way more sinister than you three out of my fruit boxes. I don't miss those days, not for a minute I don't.

"Anna had her little boy, Alexsy, with her, of course. He was a sturdy little fellow, had chunky fat legs sticking out of his short pants, scuffed shoes and all. He was a serious little thing, but sweet as could be and I would play with him sometimes when it was slow. Well, one day after Anna had been by every day for two weeks without buying a thing, I asked her if everything was all right. She seemed kind of shy about it but she said she was doing pretty good, in fact she was going to have to say goodbye before long because she just got a new job. Well, I was right surprised to hear that, considering she had her little boy to take care of and a husband and all. But she said no, no, it was a real good job with a friend of her godfather's, and she was happy about it. The problem was, she would be staying out on Long Island all week long and didn't have a place yet to leave Alexsy, she hadn't worked that out yet. Her godfather promised he would help, though. She wasn't worried.

"Well, that was at the end of the fall, when my fruit stand was winding down, apples, bananas and pears, a few tomatoes were about all I had left, and I started to thinking. Maybe I could take care of Alexsy for the winter, why not? Well Anna jumped on that idea like a June bug on clover and we planned out the whole thing.

"See, it turns out Chiron was her godfather." Maggie paused to wait for the children's reaction. They had no reaction at all, this part of the story being something of a denouement and somewhat hard to follow. "It turns out Chiron had been looking out for her all these years but things were getting difficult with her husband Jasen and it was Chiron's idea to get her out of that household, somewhere where he could make sure that she was all right. So he arranged for her to be the baby nurse for the Karras family's new baby. Simple as that! And I got the job of minding Alexsy and the whole schedule was worked out for January, when the baby would arrive." It seemed so simple then, so deceptively simple. Maggie smiled sadly at the two young girls who thought things do work out for the best, for the girls who were excited about their futures and contently bound to each other's happiness like the sisters neither had. It had seemed like an adventure to Maggie, and she had embraced it.

The children regarded her quizzically. All of a sudden Chiron was part of the story. And Anna had something to do with Todd, at least it sounded like Maggie had said that. Now she was off in her own world again and this was getting confusing. Was she really making up stories today, like she tried to tell them she was?

Adrianne's clicking heels made their way down the hall toward the staircase, pausing to deposit her keys in the basket on the telephone table. She did not come through the living room, but mounted the stairs purposefully, footsteps muffled and eventually extinguished by the carpet above. The children sensed

112

their time was limited and urged Maggie to get to the point.

"Maggie, I thought you were Nick's baby nurse," admonished Herman.

"Oh, well, yes I was, my desperado. But not yet. Not at first. Anna had the job that first year of Mr. Nick's life, but then she found out she was having another baby and so she had to leave the job and go on back home to take care of Alexsy and her husband. Chiron, he was not happy about that at all but what could he do, there was a new baby coming after all. So he provided for Anna and the children, he made sure they wouldn't want for anything this time, and he allowed that good for nothing Jasen to take them back. Oh, he warned him good, he did, if he ever lifted—he warned him he better be a proper husband and father or he would have Chiron to answer to, make no mistake about it. Chiron himself cleared out every bottle in the flat and made it known he would have someone checking in regular-like.

"Now I spent that year in a bad way. I had my papa's affairs to tend to and I didn't know much about how to go about it, neither. It was a rough time in that little apartment looking at Papa's empty place at the table, with the smell of his tobacco lingering for months in the living room by his easy chair," she absently rubbed the fabric of the cushion she was sitting on "and his things that needed to be cleared out, sold or given away more like. Oh Lordy, his finances were such a jumble I don't think I ever would have untangled them if it weren't for one or two friends from his engine company who collected all the miscellaneous scraps of paper, paid off his debts and got me squared away. Some of them made sure a collection was taken up for the fallen men's families, plus they demanded a fund from City Hall itself, which

I lived on that whole year, what was left after the debts were paid, that plus the money Anna gave me for tending her little boy.

"But that's how I got to be the baby nurse after all, when Anna saw what a state I was in and now I wouldn't even have Alexsy for company any more, now he had his mama back. He was about all the comfort I had that first year and considered myself lucky to have him. So Anna, she spoke on my behalf to Chiron, her godfather like I said, and he agreed, though I think it was because he was distracted by the dilemma with Jasen and all, more than because he approved. After all, I am not a Greek and that's a fact. Greeks are very clannish folks and they were even more so back then. Mrs. Karras herself didn't hardly have a single acquaintance who was not a member of her Orthodox church over in Roselandale. So I considered myself right lucky to get the position, and I moved in quick as I could." Maggie slapped her knees and began to rise. "Now you know everything, you little sleuths, you pried it all out of me and I am whipped. This time I'm done and I mean it. Off you go."

"Wait, Maggie. Just one more thing!" Todd raised his hand to her, palm first. "You asked me if I knew about Thea. You never even mentioned Aunt Thea. Where does she fit into this story?"

Maggie's whole baggage deflated with a whoosh as she fell back into the indentation her behind had left in the chair cushion. She blew a stray strand of hair off her face through one side of her mouth. "This is it, rascal. The end of the tale so help me, amen. Anna's new baby was Thea. Thea was Alexsy's baby sister. Thea's big brother Alexsy was your papa. Alexander Nikandros." She rose, with dignity, and marched off.

# CHAPTER 6

**1912**

Kristof did not remember the trip home. He never would, in fact, because once his car pulled into the circular drive, he saw the doctor's vehicle and all thoughts of the fire evaporated in the new crisis of the premature arrival of Nicholas Karras, namesake of the patron saint of the seas.

Clarisse, the housekeeper, rushed past in the direction of the kitchen, hardly acknowledging him as he made his way up the stairs to his wife's bedroom. There, the doctor presided, leaning over attentively at the side of Maria's bed. Kristof stood a few seconds, blinking at the scene, trying to piece together the meaning of the positions of the actors and their implications. Lumps of bedclothes shifted restlessly. The bedstead seemed to tremble. The open medical bag, the rolled up sleeves, the towels, the bowls, the air of anticipation hanging over the room, a sweet earthy smell that was vaguely familiar if not quite pleasant, all seemed reasonable enough. He gave a sigh of understanding and ventured a step into the room.

He instantly found himself back in the hallway alone with his pounding heart, following the bestial cry that could not have emanated from his wife, let alone any other natural being. Yet his last glimpse was of her distorted features, her arched back and her white fingers as they clutched and reclutched the bruised coverlet. The doctor reacted by shifting position, mercifully obstructing the view but not the reverberation of her moans. Kristof reached out swiftly and closed the door.

He stood outside the room with his head leaning against the door frame, eyes to the ceiling. His hands were clenched behind his back, his thoughts scattered willy-nilly.

A picture came to mind, he could not imagine why, of his mother admonishing him from the open kitchen window as he scurried about the small dirt pen out back. He was six years old. "Come now, Kristofer, just one chicken, you must catch for me a chicken!" But they had all scattered and whichever way he turned they eluded his grasp one after the other, squawking riotously in canny evasion, a centimeter from capture with every grab, flapping their wings and wagging their tail feathers mockingly. He had been tormented by those chickens for years. He could neither catch them nor save them from their fate. He blinked and shook his head. He listened again at the door.

The thoughts that he had kept at bay for the last seven or eight months could not be escaped today. He and Maria had prayed for a child for all the years of their marriage. Maria, even though she was a decade younger than her husband, had passed the age when most women were fertile. They had each despaired, separately, and privately mourned their failure. Silence had crept over their roof, growing year by year, belying their kind treatment of each other and their protracted avoidance of sensitive topics of any kind.

When they found she was expecting, their joy was boundless. It took a sobering conference with the doctor to understand that the outcome of the gestation was far from guaranteed. Maria was so intimidated by his warnings she took to her bed at first, as a precaution. But almost before the doctor's words had faded in his ears, Kristof dismissed them. He blustered jovially through the weeks and months, determined by force of will to ensure the healthy outcome of childbirth by refusing to accept any alternative.

Maria was startled every time he entered the room or barked out words of encouragement. She became nervous and could not concentrate even on her knitting, while he studied her sideways by the hour. But she was tenacious. She was careful in all things and she was hopeful. She was already in love with her baby. She dreamt all day about her future happiness with her adoring child and doting husband. She was happiest when left alone to fantasize over their future domestic tranquility.

Finally, this side of the birthing chamber, Kristof realized the extent of the danger she faced and he felt the shame of his calculated ignorance.

It was hard to say how long he stood there, muscles tense and ears straining, anticipating each violent outcry, then agonizing over the meaning of the quiet in between. Once, his eyes were drawn to the window by the scratching of a twig on the pane, whipped by the capricious January wind. Later, a small beam of light caught his attention and he looked out, seeing the edge of the moon crossing the window, framed in its luminous ascent. He regarded it for a long time, taking comfort from its intimacy.

The next cry described its torment and Kristof was riveted once more to the picture in his mind's eye and his prayers for mercy.

He did not know that the doctor had offered Maria the relief of "twilight sleep," an injection of morphine and scopolamine that induced a sleepy state during labor, and no memory of the painful event itself. She had heard it was becoming popular among young mothers fortunate enough to have a doctor attend their births. She refused it emphatically, not trusting the effect it may have on her baby. Try as he might, she would not be convinced of its safety. She would not risk the outcome in hopes of escaping some of the discomfort. Kristof had been confounded by her stubbornness, no more than the doctor was himself. But she prevailed and she won his grudging respect for it.

With all of his focus in the room behind him, Kristof did not hear Clarisse's approach. She, seeing his anxiety and feeling her own, impulsively reached out and patted him on the arm. He jumped and looked at her in alarm, wondering at her sudden appearance and what dire development may have provoked it. She had never touched him before. He assumed the worst and drew back, bracing for her news, then watched in confusion as she passed by wordlessly, entered the room and closed the door behind her.

He saw that she felt sorry for him, but he realized he was of little consequence at the moment and no use at all. Mortified, he began to recount his deficiencies. He had made so many blunders. He knew he was disappointing as a husband. He knew he was not prepared to be a father. Just as he had been helpless this morning as he watched men scream in desperation for their lives and he had not been able to help them, here he stood cowering behind a closed door, incapable of safeguarding his wife and even now refraining from action. He wondered if the lowest form of manhood was the coward. He looked mournfully at the door; not that it barred him, but that it mocked him.

He turned in search of the moon to implore, but it was sequestered behind a cloud and would not reappear. He kicked the baseboard rhythmically and found that if it did not quell the cries behind the wall, it at least muffled them. He focused on his shoes, wet through still and chalky from snow melt. Funny, he thought as he wiggled his toes, he could not feel the cold. He coughed a few times and wiped his mouth with his sleeve. He was surprised to see he still had on

his overcoat and the woolen fibers as yet glistened with tiny drops of water. He should take it off. He should shake it over the mat downstairs and hang it to dry on the coat rack. Where was his hat? He reached up to check if it were still on his head. No. Hmph. It could be anywhere: hung properly downstairs, lying on the car seat, buried under a foot of ice on Wall Street, or there in the bedroom behind him with the actors in this nightmare.

He asked himself what kind of a god would subject his children to torture as the price of love. He doubted the ability of anyone to recover from the anguish of this unending day.

Beads of sweat on his brow, his breathing becoming labored, he had just decided to pace the hallway when another cry pierced the walls and his instincts were rent between charging in or running off. While his mind tried to gain the upper hand over his terror, he heard another sound; a mew, a whimper, a murmur of new life announcing its arrival.

He closed his eyes in gratitude. Unbidden, a torrent of tears spilled along his fevered cheeks. His arms and legs went limp as he slid to the floor, the sobs rising in his chest unchecked. His exaltation bordered on madness, this joy and relief beyond his capacity. He did not know how long he squatted there, he may be sitting there still if Clarisse had not opened the door to beckon him in. Expecting him to be where she left him, she was surprised at the empty space by the door until her eye was drawn to the pile of humanity huddled on the floor, shaking with emotion.

"Captain Karras, you may come in now," she offered gently. He slowly uncovered his eyes, looked up at her as if trying to discern what she had just said. Then he leapt up like the young man he no longer was and threw his arms around her in happiness,

119

exclaiming, "Thank you, thank you, Clarisse!" And rushed past her into the bedroom. Clarisse's eyes followed him, softly gleaming.

A few gossamer hours later, peace reigned in the nursery. Anna had arrived and was asleep, or resting her eyes, in the rocker across the room. Kristof knelt beside the cradle, gazing at his son, engulfed in the universe of tiny sighs, sucking motions, clenched fists under double chins and sublime contentment, all emanating from the tender fulcrum upon which his whole world now turned. He gently wiped away the last missed patch of creamy white vernix that the doctor explained often coats the skin of a baby born two or three weeks early. Nicholas opened his eyes for a moment and looked up at his father, trying to focus, peering quizzically into his face as if wondering where he had seen him before. Kristof reached across and cupped the palm of his beefy hand around the wee head and watched as his son drifted serenely back into slumber.

Early the next morning Anna was confounded by the discovery of a handkerchief, white, with a simple K embroidered in one corner, folded and tucked neatly inside the baby's swaddling clothes.

Daily the new father knelt by the cradle for a session of confidential patter, delighted by his receptive audience, duly impressed by the whole-body response; arms and legs pumping in unison with furious grunts of agreement. They were of the same mind on every subject and because he was convinced his son looked forward to these regular tête-a-têtes, Kristof refused to leave town for even a day in the months following the birth.

The last in this unbroken string of meetings occurred on the night of April 15, when Nick was four months old. That evening his father arrived home well after midnight, disheveled and wild-eyed. He might have been inebriated, yet his agitation was startlingly focused, his madness deliberate in its fury. He might have been mistaken for a calculating inmate from the local asylum, and that would have been closer to the mark.

Something had shifted inside his mind the day of the Equitable Fire, not enough for anyone to notice, but the chink that resulted became a little more vulnerable with the sudden, savage desire to protect his offspring. Perhaps the one set off the other, the fire and the birth coming so closely in succession that day and fear ultimately overriding joy. Regardless, his viewpoint veered off course a little, and would tax his emotional compass from that day on.

What had resonated within him the morning of the fire, as he stood vigil outside in the frozen street, was the total dependence of the imprisoned men upon their rescuers. He himself had a small fortune within the vaults of the Mercantile Safe Deposit. It was the reason he happened to be present that morning, and although he was aware of the serious hazard to his holdings, that was of little concern in the context of the unfolding scene. He, a commander of the seas, strained against the conventions that held him of his own free will across the street as a spectator, rather than a participant.

Yet, the same feeling overwhelmed him again that evening in his self-imposed quarantine from his wife's labor, his own son's birth. He was shaken by the memory of how powerless he felt that day and vowed he would never again stand aside watching, leaving fate in the hands of others. Being a vow that could prove beyond his limits, it held a danger of costing too much.

The chink widened on the fateful day of April 15, 1912. Kristof had been dismayed when he first learned about the ship that was considered unsinkable. Now he

121

was horrified to hear that intrinsic safety rules had been ignored in the owners' vainglorious disregard for the basic tenets of ocean travel. He was sickened by the fact that there were insufficient life boats provided on the voyage. He was murderous at the arrogance of the fatal decision he had heard on the docks that day; that the few lifeboats on board were provided specifically for the rescue of survivors of other sinking ships. He was haunted by the utter helplessness of the trusting passengers on the Titanic who had perished in the freezing waters of the North Atlantic. He was tortured by his own sense of impotence as a mere reader of the newspapers announcing the disaster. He had little experience with passenger liners, but he knew the responsibilities of a master and ship owner to the lives entrusted to their professional judgment. This disaster was criminal in nature; it was a moral black mark on the shipping industry and the surviving perpetrators deserved the stiffest retribution. The depths of his indignation could not be measured.

He stood over his son's crib that night, the rails vibrating from his convulsive grip on them, and he recited the words he was to repeat to Nick countless times in the course of his young son's life. They were invariably invoked whenever a potential for danger arose over the years, real or imagined. Nick would always take the pronouncement very seriously, though it alarmed him and felt more like a threat than a comfort.

"I promise, before God and Saint Nicholas, that you, my son, will always be provided with enough lifeboats." Its very earnestness betrayed him. That first night, he proclaimed it out loud and stood for a few moments, hearing the words reverberate in his mind as terms of a covenant; symbolic and sacred. Finally, somewhat mollified, he thrust back his weight from the railing of the crib, pushing so hard it woke the sleeping child, who began to wail in fright.

*     *     *

Kristof had taken a chance on oil. He wasn't the only Greek to do so; in fact, the Greeks were among the first to become independent oil carriers. It was a risky business. Leakage could cost from 5% to 12% of the cargo and vapors could turn the ship into a bomb. Nonetheless, Kristof saw it as an opportunity to be at the forefront of a new industry that he sensed was destined for world prominence. America was the new frontier for oil, so he headed to Philadelphia.

It was not long before he encountered the widespread theory that businessmen do not make money from Greeks. The theory was not unique to Americans, but Kristof was something of a rogue in the U.S. and had to prove himself as an individual, not as an affiliate to some far-flung conglomerate. He learned to be direct, iron-fisted and reliable. He learned to use his clan association for his benefit, and to give the clan loyalty in return, but only so far as overtly required. He was inching away from his Chiot connections year by year yet unwilling, even fearful, of causing a rift within the membership.

Shipping was a volatile business at best and Kristof rode the shifting fortunes along with everyone else in the international shipping community. It wasn't long after his first voyage on the Nichola in the late 1880s that freight rates fell to a sharp low, the result of the recent economic crisis which was exacerbated by the cheaper cost of new steamships. He had spent 110 days in Sierra Leone with no cargo to transport. He had to let his crew go. The clan covered his expenses during that time despite the fact that they were all suffering from slack times, and he accepted their support gratefully.

In 1893 ten steamers were sold off when the Greek Steamship Co. went bankrupt. Kristof bought his second steamer then, at a bargain price. It wasn't until 1908 that he added to his fleet again, when rates plummeted and he followed the clan adage to buy when everyone else sells. By 1909 shipping rates reached their bottom and he began to think about building his flagship.

Kristof's fleet consisted of tramp ships. In essence, he rented out his ships' holds to merchants for transport. He did not own the cargo. The client paid one half the cost of the shipment in advance. The other half was paid by the clan's agent in the London office of The Baltic Exchange. Therefore, the ship was chartered by the agency, insured and fueled, so all Kristof had to do was to supply the crew and maintenance. This in turn reduced his overhead enough to cover payments on borrowed capital and commissions.

His record was good, his losses minimal. His crews were healthy and loyal in their own right. There were few serious injuries. His leadership style was based on clear rules and goals, then trusted to the decisions carried out by his competent crews. Soon after he bought his fourth ship, in 1909, he received a report from the first mate saying they had grounded on a bank three miles north of Taganrog. He succinctly yet scrupulously described the toll: they had jettisoned sixty tons of bunkers and eighty tons of cargo; they were aground for 7.5 hours; when they reached London, Lloyd's was called to survey the hull and found little discernible damage to the bottom, though noting some small damage to the engines. End of report. Kristof was satisfied with the handling of the incident and sent no further instructions.

He became more and more removed from the day-to-day operation of his fleet as well as his network of connections within the clan. With time and distance, his independent tendencies turned toward isolation.

The decision to build a home for his family on Long Island was a result of Kristof's affinity for the sea, naturally. But it was his attraction to all things modern, especially the newest advances in developing modes of travel, that drew him to this coastal bastion of adventure. In the summer of 1907 he took his wife on the ferry to Patchogue to watch the popular Scooter Race for sailboats in the Great South Bay. They stayed overnight at the Wyandotte Hotel in Bellport, where they could see Fire Island just across the bay. Also home of the America's Cup race, Long Island was clearly the sailing capital of America. And it was there that he saw for himself why Long Island was considered "the automobilist's paradise" with its hundreds of miles of new motor highways. Add to that its expansive railroad system, its thriving ferry service and its forays into engine-powered flight. Kristof felt sure the future was burgeoning here, and he wanted to be a part of it.

It was Maria who first brought home the pamphlet issued by the Passenger Department of the Long Island Railroad titled, "Four Hundred Miles of Shore Line on Ocean, Sound and Bays," reminding its readers it was the only region in the United States where the sea coast runs east to west. What caught her attention was the quote from Whittier that beckoned:

No greener valleys the sun invite
On smoother beaches no sea birds light
No blue waves shatter to foam more white

Her little catalog went on to describe Long Island's famous automobiling, golf links and yachting harbors. She nearly swooned with homesickness for Chios when she read, "On a summer day hundreds of sailboats can be seen skimming over the sparkling surface of the bays." Kristof raised an eyebrow when he read that, but did not exhibit much enthusiasm until he heard about the Scooter Race, when his curiosity spurred plans for a holiday.

Then in October of 1908, he attended the Vanderbilt Auto Race in Westbury where George Robertson's Locomobile beat out Mr. Vanderbilt's Mercedes in a rough and tumble match-up with a wild west, go-for-broke atmosphere that left Kristof electrified. This was excitement, daring and ground-breaking action. Being one of the youngest Greeks ever to master a steam ship and proud of it still, he felt a connection with these powerful men. He enthusiastically joined in the cheering crowd, urging on the formidable competitors. Records were being challenged and broken. Men were participating in manly ventures and Kristof experienced something akin to reverence. For the first time, he felt like an American. He thought surely here he could belong.

By the time the first official air mail flight in the United States took off from Garden City in 1911, Beechwood was already near completion. The property had been selected, in fact, the day Kristof visited the sight of the very first recorded aircraft flight. It had taken place in 1896, thirteen years after he bought his first ship and seven years before the Wright brothers' feat. It was a Lilienthal-type glider that took off from the bluffs of the north shore. As he stood gazing out across the sound, confirming his choice that this majestic and historic vantage point matched the scope of his vision for his new homestead, he wondered what effect the advent of aviation and motor cars would have on the shipping industry. Whatever happened, he had the sense that his decision to settle here, where the risk-takers were racing to meet the future, would prove transformational. He wondered, inevitably, what the clan would think about it. He raised his hand to shield the sun as he surveyed the rolling swells, considering. A soft breeze caressed his face, he inhaled the salty air and dismissed the thought.

His star was still rising and at the age of 50, commissioning the construction of Beechwood, he was ambitiously staking his claim on his piece of the American dream.

*     *     *

Chiron's ambition was as far removed from Kristof's as their personalities were polar opposites, yet their destinies had remained intertwined over the decades and their dedication to each other indisputable.

Kristof often turned to Chiron as a counterpoint for major decisions, yet he spent many an hour attempting to fathom the depths of Chiron's nature. His most trusted confidant was restrained even in the midst of a storm at sea when all hands scuddled around him urgently and the windswept waters engulfed even the heartiest sailors in trepidation. Kristof imagined there was a vaporous mantle enveloping his friend that was illuminated in these fearful moments, and that the aura emanated from his eyes; always fiercely alive, always burning in their attempt to contain the heat of his emotions.

Chiron's fellow shipmates thought of him as a loner and might have employed a cold word to describe him, yet none disputed his devotion to the welfare of his men, his ship and his honor. Dispassionate in all his dealings, professional, fair and unflappable, there was no reason to doubt his seeming lack of vulnerability. He accepted their respect and, over time, their devotion. Stories began to circulate about him. There was even a song that had made the rounds of countless ships crossing the Atlantic and Mediterranean over the years. Sometimes it was accompanied by the sound of a sailor's flute, sometimes just by the slapping of knees and pounding of heels below deck after hours.

> The silent master keeps his watch
> Black eyes extract their tolls
> Though mates beware, he sees them there
> And plumbs their murky souls
>
> He disappears some starless nights
> Beneath the rocking sea
> To counsel Father Neptune's sons
> On how a man should be.
>
> The old man on those sleepless nights
> With black eyes boring holes
> Whispers, whispers wordlessly
> I know your very souls
>
> He'll haul you back from Moby's jaws,
> His hands gripped 'round your neck
> Then set you back to task young man
> Upon his gnarly deck.
>
> Undaunted still he searches
> With his black eyes in control
> There's no need to interrogate
> To spot a tainted soul

Betrayed was he one stormy night
That proved the sailor's last
The morn displayed his punishment
A danglin' from the mast.

Yet still he stands, and keeps his watch
Black eyes with just one goal
To see, to hear, to read your dreams
And claim your very soul.

Chiron himself never heard the song, but Kristof did and sometimes requested it when he was aboard on lonely nights. It was the only sailor's song he ever heard that contained not a single blasphemy.

\*       \*       \*

The two men stood shoulder to shoulder on the dock in easy company, their eyes drawn to the faint beam of Eaton's Neck Lighthouse off to the east. After Chiron had complimented Maria on a fine dinner and acknowledged the championship qualities of Nick's handsome and sturdy features, they had strolled out to the beach to discuss their business. They agreed that when the flagship Constantinas was commissioned sometime that fall of 1912, Chiron would be its master and Kristof would retire from active duty.

Chiron had had his visit with Anna that afternoon in the library and was satisfied that she was content with her position at Beechwood. He had come straight from Maggie's home on the Lower East Side, where he met that young woman for the first time, and carried news to Anna of the robust health of Alexsy and the enthusiasm of his Irish caretaker. Anna inquired whether he had seen her husband. Chiron nodded and replied woodenly that Jasen appeared cooperative. She had not seen him herself for weeks, preferring to stay with Alexsy at Maggie's flat on her Sundays off. That arrangement met with Chiron's approval, and Anna smiled shyly, reassured. Chiron teased her about her rosy cheeks, saying the sea air agreed with her. She had filled out in the last several months and was relaxed in her new surroundings, the strain around her mouth erased and a couple of new smile lines crinkling at the edges of her cornflower eyes, so like her mother's. Relief showed in Chiron's gentle appraisal.

Later that evening the two weather-beaten foreheads of Kristof and Chiron nearly met over the table in the library where the diagrams of the new ship were laid out, held down by paper weights and half-empty glasses. Their shadows loomed up the wall of thick leather volumes behind them and spread baronially across the ceiling as they studied; commenting, debating and scratching notes in the margins of the plans. It was a rare intimacy they shared in these moments of pure leisure, their rumbling voices and occasional laughter reaching the straining ears of Maria down the hall.

After they had parted ways on the island of Chios in 1883, when Chiron returned home for the first time, it was more than a year before they met up again. Chiron was simply waiting on the dock in New York Harbor one afternoon when Kristof disembarked. No explanations were asked or offered; the pleasure of reunion, visual assessment and a hearty handshake sufficed. They had been working together ever since, had amassed their varying fortunes and dispensed of them as they would, independently and privately. Chiron had taken over the duties of the Nichola, investing in it and all of Kristof's ventures, a common practice among members of the Diaspora. They met rarely and almost always on Chiron's terms. Their relationship was unstrained and one of the closest of any within the clan.

*       *       *

# CHAPTER 7

## 1884

Chiron chose to walk the distance from the port of Agios Nikolaos to his village in the south, the same mode of travel he had employed three years before when he departed. He wanted ample time to inhale the full-bodied air of Crete, stir up the Cretan dust with his world-weary boots, and prepare for his sudden reappearance at home. His beard had filled in, although he kept it neatly short. It helped disguise his hollow cheeks and grieving mouth. His long, wavy hair boasted new streaks of bronze glimmering, winking in the sunlight as it tossed about and refused his regular attempts to subdue it with his calloused fingers. His eyes held a slight squint, accented at the edges with fine lines burnished by the wind, cauterized with sea salt. His shoulders were broad, his arms veined and brute, his bold stride barely conforming to terra firma. His spirits were buoyed by the aromatic breeze and the lure of the winding road, gently or steeply rising and falling, twisting to avoid an outcropping of rock, then coming back on itself and meandering anew to match his tempered desire to arrive slowly, eventually, yet to ultimately consummate his journey of long escape.

He had exchanged letters with his mother monthly. She had dutifully reported comments by his father, news of the fishing community and gossip from the village carefully censored. Her graceful hand of tall and narrow letters generously spaced was kindly, cheerful and uncomplaining. His letters were in direct reply to each of her subjects, respectful and intended to appease. His cramped lettering, inevitably marred by blots of ink, a hazard on the rolling sea, was painfully deliberate and tense. He had to stop every so often to shake out his hand, foster circulation and relax his grip. Relief was only achieved once the missive was securely in its envelope, safe from apologetic post scripts. He would invariably sit back, drained, and clasp his upper arms, as if to prevent a shiver of distaste at his own words. Still, he cherished the letters he received from home and kept them safely stowed.

As he approached his village he passed a threesome of boisterous adolescents whom he did not recognize. They didn't seem to notice him and displayed no curiosity, caught up as they were in an uproarious intrigue. He stopped and watched them as they ran along a steep path, pushing and elbowing for ascendancy as they disappeared behind a clump of scrub brush. He regarded their abandon, trying to remember his own days in such company. He closed his eyes momentarily and smiled, fleetingly catching their high spirits and knowing he had had his share.

He encountered no one else other than a sedate mule who twitched an ear and the wagon driver who tipped his hat in passing, and Chiron ambled along for quite a while with only the sweetly familiar countryside for companionship. He halted abruptly when he realized just across the way, within shouting distance, was the home of Corinna's childhood. Of course she didn't live there anymore but his memory placed her forever behind those walls, just out of his reach. The yearning swelled in his throat instantly, as if a day had not passed since he watched for her there, and it seemed as if in truth his entire youth was spent in anticipation of Corinna's presence, rather than racing about heedlessly with other young ruffians.

He grunted with contempt when he realized the reason he was so unprepared for the sight of the Stephanos' house: this was not the direct route home. He had diverged at some point in the last half mile, unwittingly or not, to arrive here unawares. He shook his head, turned around and walked ten paces in the opposite direction before, without pausing, he circled back and continued on a straight line to the gate of the cottage. He pushed it open, knowing just how the latch worked, and walked through boldly, daring himself to be accosted. He passed swiftly to the left of the house and through the hedges to the back. There he stopped while the world suddenly spun around him and he needed to preserve his balance. His eyes focused and unfocused and he rubbed them furiously in their betrayal at this most consequential moment when he couldn't establish whether or not the vision reclining on a chair across the garden could be his Corinna. He was so afraid she might disappear before he could see clearly that he nearly cried out in frustration. He gasped for breath and the sound caught her attention, causing her to shift her glance in his direction. He forced himself to wait for the blood to return to his head and the dizziness to recede. His rucksack fell to the ground of its own accord. Finally, he saw her eyes distinctly, as if he were studying them through the telescope in his bag, as if their hypnotic effect had never been relinquished or ever could be.

She was so still she appeared to be holding her breath. The only sign of emotion came when she parted her suddenly dry lips. She drew him to her as if by command, compelling his feet in her direction, bringing Chiron to the edge of her reclining chair where he saw the tears trembling in her yielding eyelids, determined not to spill over, begging him not to be an apparition.

He went down on one knee and clasped her hand with both of his before he knew he had done it. He was immediately embarrassed and bowed his head, stepping back awkwardly as he pulled himself up. He cleared his throat. He swatted at his pants to brush away dirt that was not there. Finally, he forced himself to stand up straight and to look at her. She was wiping away her mounting tears unabashedly. It was then that her swollen belly, late term, caught his eye.

He stammered, "Corinna." He cleared his hoarse throat again. "I, I did not know." He met her gaze. "Congratulations, I hope you are in good health and, and your child as well." He looked down again at the ground. He suddenly felt as ungainly as the boys he had passed on the hill and wished passionately he were off with them now.

The first shock of his appearance abating, Corinna smiled slowly up at him, unable to take her eyes off his face. When he looked up again, she was regarding him in wonder. After a few moments, a glint of the mischief that he recognized so well shimmered in her eyes, prompting his heart to lurch inside his chest.

"Sit down," she said, and patted the chair next to her. He dutifully sat, perching on the edge of the seat, as if ready to take flight at the slightest provocation or to swoop down and carry her off if the opportunity presented itself. He found himself smiling back at her, realizing his conflicting impulses and assuming she saw them, too.

She tilted her head to one side and surveyed him top to bottom, pausing at his new beard, his trim waist and his sunburnt hands, thick veins accentuated by their constricted grip on his massive thighs.

"You look well," she said in a voice more subdued, more carefully modulated than he remembered. "The sea has made you her own."

"I've just now arrived back home. I haven't stopped at my parents' house even yet, I...I found myself here instead and didn't mean to, to see you here. I mean, I didn't think to find you here. I know you have moved in with your husband, of course." She did not respond, although a shadow briefly passed across her face, and her full lips thinned into a taut line. She looked off into the distance and was silent. He felt he had said something wrong and realized it was improper to mention Felipe, considering his own past with her. He bit his lip in chagrin and looked around for a chance to excuse himself, to escape. Just as he started to rise, she turned back, reached over and put a hand on his arm. A vise could not have had more effect. He sat back in his chair, captive.

"My dear Chiron, did you not correspond with anyone from the village in all of the last three years? Surely you have written to your mamá and her letters have found you from time to time on that vast and wandering seascape, snug inside your elusive watercraft?"

He was trying not to look at her hand that rested still on his forearm, or the belly that took up most of the view, yet her last words stung him as he heard the small crack in her voice, belying her attempt at flippancy. He started to speak but was suddenly drained, overcome by the circumstances that he had not anticipated; not her condition, not this intimate interview, not her startling beauty that left him defenseless.

He looked so vulnerable and young to her, she had to resist reaching up to brush a lock of hair from his brow. Her breath caught in her throat when he looked directly at her. She had so much to say to him, yet she was afraid he might bolt, he seemed so skittish. "Of course," she thought. He felt this meeting was unbefitting. She raised her eyebrows at him. Perhaps he really had not corresponded with his mother. He looked quizzically back at her, feeling as though he had lost the thread of the conversation in his distraction.

"Chiron." She paused. "Chiron, your parents are well and surely anxious for your return. They will be delirious with happiness when you arrive! But have they told you nothing of the events here since you have been gone?"

"My mother has written me regularly and kept me up on village news, at least in general. Not—not in particular, no, not specifically, not really. Why, Corinna? Tell me what you mean. What else is there, is it something besides your baby?"

She closed her eyes for a moment, entangled by more emotions than she could name. "Yes," she breathed before she opened her eyes, "yes there is." She lifted her hand from his arm and he followed its motion. She swung her legs down and sat up straight, facing him. "Please help me up, my Chiron."

He arose like the captain of the ship that he would soon be, and offered his hand to help her to her swollen feet. The baby's birth could not be far off. "Let's take a stroll," she suggested, as if nothing were unusual. They headed toward the back of the property and a view of the sea.

"You must speak, Corinna, I am alarmed and not used to waiting for my lady's leisure. Tell me your news. Please."

Her eyes filled with tears this time that could not be staunched. She watched the whitecaps cavort in the afternoon sun while the tears followed a path down her cheeks unheeded. "Where would I begin?" She addressed the panorama before her. "I believe I will begin with the end. The rest you can infer, if you have not done so yet." She turned to face him then and he saw for the first time the extent of her vulnerability and the fragile bravado that must have been enlisted for his sake. The flecks of gold within her azure irises were magnified by her tears. He ached to enfold her in his arms and hold her so close and so tight as to draw out the pain from her breast into his own. Yet his hands remained uselessly at his sides.

"Five months ago, almost six months now," she ventured and paused. "I guess I have to go back a little further," she amended as she absently placed her hand on her protruding abdomen. "Felipe joined the rebellion a year ago last fall. He was so proud to be in the army and so hopeful of becoming a hero. I believe he felt he had something to prove, something to live up to, something to make me proud of. His father was against it, oh, there were tirades and threats, pleadings and dreadful silences, but Felipe was immune. He marched off in his uniform and seemed happier that day than I had ever seen him, even at our wedding.

"He had been kind and patient. And I in return had been an obedient wife. But the strain of silence and politeness in our home took its toll on him, I have no doubt. I don't remember it much myself, but many months went by before I took notice and by then he was a changed man. He looked...diminished. He seemed like a specter.

There was nothing I could do and I did not really try. I was not as attentive as I might have been and I cannot forgive myself for that. Oh Chiron I was overwrought!" Her eyes pleaded with him to help her to be absolved of her torment while convinced it was impossible, searching his face for a sign that the unhappy choices of the past could be unblamed. For his part, he was equally searching her words for an explanation of the one thing that struck him; she had only spoken about Felipe in the past tense.

"Corinna."

She saw that he could read her still. "Dysentery. Five months ago. He had been home for leave eight weeks before. He had seemed quiet then, yet determined to complete his commission, to fulfill his career as a soldier. We had a pleasant time and his parents relented. There was peace in the family and there was gradual acceptance of our circumstances, for all of us. Time had passed." She paused, searching his face intently.

"I wanted to be a good wife, as good as I was able. When I found there was going to be a baby, I was happy. I looked so forward to the day when I had someone I could love openly, completely, with all my heart!" She swiped at the leftover tears on her cheeks and took a deep breath.

"We had had so much of pain when my father died the year before."

Chiron gasped, shocked and hurt at not having shared in that time of mourning, either.

"I never imagined you did not hear about it, Chiron. I'm sorry." His reaction was so purely abject she was taken with compassion on his behalf.

He reached out impulsively and grasped her arms, pulling her a little closer and holding her a little tighter than necessary. He was struck by all the contingencies he had not considered in those endless hours of unbridled self-pity, indulged as only an exile can justify.

"Corinna, what have you suffered? How is this possible, that I did not know anything of your grief, of your sorrow, or your loneliness? Could you not have written me? Could you not have allowed me to share in your misfortune?"

"Could you not...have inquired?"

His arms convulsed, almost imperceptibly, yet she felt it through to the base of her spine. His heart was pierced by the simple sincerity of her question. He bowed his head then, loosened his grip and let his arms drop to his sides. He stepped back a pace before looking at her.

"I couldn't bear to ask," he confessed. "I was consumed with sorrow, I reveled in it. I was sure it was my only choice, to leave you to your new life, your new husband. I would have been torturing myself by begging for gossip. I could not bear subjecting your name to hearsay, nor to pry rumors from my mother who pitied me enough. I thought it was the only thing I could do for you, to respect your privacy. I thought it every day for three years and not once was it easier to accept."

She did reach up then and gently lift a tendril of unruly hair that had fallen forward, tucking it behind his ear, stroking it to keep it in place. Her hand floated to his temple and caressed it briefly, the tips of her fingers slowly sliding along his hairline down to his bearded jaw where they lingered. Then smiling impishly, she gave a playful tug. Again he felt sixteen, again he was at her mercy. But his hooded eyes were ignited by a tentative spark and his heavy heart was buoyed a little.

"Corinna is that you? What are you doing standing, the doctor said to stay off your feet! Who is that with you, what are you doing over there, daughter?" Her mother was craning her neck to discern who the scraggly stranger could possibly be, standing so close to the girl. Yet she seemed unwilling to step off the stoop to get a closer look, indignant but wary.

Corinna turned immediately to face her mother. Chiron was slower to respond, loath to sever the spell of her touch, her fragrance of lavender and citrus bewitching him as of old. He was compelled to lean in before pulling back.

When he did turn, there was no trace of intimacy in his demeanor and he courteously bowed in Mrs.

Stephanos' direction before offering his arm to Corinna in order to escort her back to her chair.

Their obvious familiarity emboldened Corinna's mother to relinquish the stoop and approach the sitting area. Partway she stopped and peered, squinty-eyed and skeptical. "Chiron? Is that you? Who is that behind such a beard? Could it be you are returned to us at last?" She exclaimed, holding her fingers pressed together before her lips as if in prayer. With effort she began to churn her legs in their direction. Despite being impeded somewhat by the friction of her rubbing thighs she broke into a brisk clip, intent on closer inspection. Her backside followed, taking a somewhat more circuitous route.

"My, my, it is you, our bonny sailor who could perhaps use a little dry dock attention!" She placed her hands on either side of his bristly face and grinned at him in mock disapproval. It was as if he had never been betrayed by her family, as if they had parted on mutually affectionate terms. "Your mamá must be cooking up the prodigal supper, tears of joy flowing into her souvlaki." She patted his cheeks and tsked at him playfully.

"Yes, ma'am, well I'm sure she will be soon enough. I must be on my way, I hope you will pardon me. And Mrs. Stephanos, please accept my deepest condolences at the loss of your husband. I only just now heard the distressing news from Corinna." He bowed again, formally, then turned to Corinna and said hoarsely, "I am very glad to see you in good health. Please extend my greetings to your sisters. Good day." And wheeling about, he strode across the garden, grabbed his backpack as he retraced his steps along the side of the house and crossed to the road beyond.

"He was always such an aloof young man," Corinna's mother declared, watching his straight, muscular back as it receded stiffly, head high, shoulders squared, disappearing abruptly around the corner.

"Do you think he intends to resume his pursuit of you, Corinna, now that you are widowed?" A gleam began to form in the corner of her eye. She looked again toward the side of the cottage where his streaming hair had barely evaporated. She crossed her arms and leaned on one foot, rocking slightly, formulating a scenario to fit her budding notion. Corinna did not respond, nor had she heard her mother speak. Leaning back in her chair, she crossed her own arms and hugged her shoulders close, tucking her chin into her chest.

Chiron arrived at home having strode at such a pace as to deter any intercourse with passing villagers, blind to their various signs of recognition. He did not notice a soul until he was almost run over by a horse-drawn coupe carrying the magistrate's wife. Horses whinnied, harnesses clattered, the startled driver complained and waved his whip while Chiron, stunned at their sudden appearance, stepped out of the way inches before disaster. When they were gone and the dust had settled, he was slightly more windblown and a little nonplussed but hardly impressed. So close to home now, he proceeded along the lane as if he were a fish being reeled in. The first tickle of emotion surfaced when he caught sight of the little whitewashed house with the celestial blue door, patient and unchanged. He covered the last leg of his journey at a trot, until he found himself hesitating at the front door, afraid to burst in, wondering if he should knock or call out first. Hand on the latch, he pushed the door gently and softly called his mother by name.

A gasp and a clatter, followed by quick footsteps, brought her into view. Her expectant face and radiant joy upon seeing it truly was he, suffused him with relief. He grinned at her like he had after his first day at school, when the weight of the big world dropped from his shoulders, her outstretched arms ready to take over the job of protector once again. He shrugged off the tattered rucksack and stepped forward into her flour-dusted arms. Though he was nearly twice her size by now, it was she who held him up and enveloped him in her motherly embrace.

"Lord above!" her voice husky with emotion, "Poseidon has agreed to throw you back after all." They clung to each other and chuckled in unison, delighted to feel the proof of each other's solid form. One last squeeze and they pulled away, holding each other at arm's length and assessing the toll of three years' separation. To him, she had not changed a bit. For her, she was slightly alarmed at the pain that still resided in his eyes, yet quite impressed by his vigorous health, the increased girth of his chest, neck, arms and legs. Her spindly boy had been lost at sea, yet the man who returned to her was surely a force to be reckoned with. She was satisfied. She had imagined much worse.

"Come, come with me into the kitchen where I can see the sunshine on your face," she urged, taking him by the elbow and marching to the back of the house with him at her side. She was a little giddy at such happiness, and her face was out of smiling practice, yet the bounce in her step was filled with pride at the honor of her escort. Within a few short paces they arrived mid-kitchen, nearly bumping up against the old worn table at the center, yet arriving in a shaft of sunlight and turning to face each other once more.

"There now, I can see plainly that all the barbers were sent overboard, but the cook was kept chained to his post well enough." She beamed at him foolishly, drumming her crossed forearms in appreciation of his girth. He laughed aloud, surprised at her easy candor. This was the homecoming he had imagined a hundred times, and better. He had forgotten the feeling of being carefree, and suddenly realized he may have only experienced it here, at home, and long ago. He laughed out loud again, just for the joy of hearing it bounce off these walls.

"There were never such smells as the ones in this kitchen, Mamá, that I will swear, nor could a man keep his mind on his job if there were, for temptation is a dangerous thing to hungry young sailors. You and your mystical spoon would be stopped at the gangway, a guard summoned to escort you beyond the quay, for your spanakópita would be a siren to us doleful jack-tars, ensuring a bad, if blissful end!" His mother beamed at the silken words, not so much for their content as for the speaker who presented them in the flesh instead of through musty, stilted words scrawled on a crumpled missive months out of date.

"You have had a long journey," she said with some irony. "Why don't you get settled in your room and wash up before your babá comes home. He won't be letting you out of his sight for the rest of the evening, Lord knows."

The corner of his bedspread had been folded carefully and turned up just so, in the Greek tradition. When someone went away on a trip, such a precaution ensured their safe return. He smiled and unfolded the corner, smoothing the crease and brushing it down. Then he sat down where the fold had been and as his weight sank heavily into the old bedspring, he breathed a deep sigh. He was drained. He was beginning to feel the full force of his meeting with Corinna. He was affected by his reunion with his mother, understanding only now how much he had missed her. He was worried that his father may wish to rebuke him for his long journey of neglect, knowing still he would never say it aloud. His shoulders ached, his heavy head sagged forward, his hands hung idly between his open knees. He wanted more than anything to lie back and go to sleep. He wished to sleep for a very, very long time.

His father had stopped at the ouzerie at the end of the day, unaware that Chiron awaited him, so mother and son had the leisure to exchange small moments and tease each other into their ease, closing the miles of three years' duration in gentle wafts of conversation amid the evening breezes. Finally, there was a rattle of wrought iron at the door and they both turned, even though they could not see very well into the house from the back patio. Their ears were attuned to his approach and their bright eyes anticipated his response upon discovering them.

At first, Georgi seemed confused by the sight of them. It took longer than they might have expected for him to change from puzzlement to wonder to hope to belief to confirmed belief and finally, exhilaration. He crashed clumsily out the back door, crying, "Yié Mou," My Son, and in three great strides reached Chiron's outstretched arms and clasped him to his chest mightily. Tears pricked the backs of Chiron's eyes, yet he quickly blinked them dry and swallowed against the pressure in his throat that threatened to betray his vincibility.

He noticed that his father had lost some weight and was a little diminished in size, the hint of a stoop stealing into his spine and across his shoulder blades. Yet his full head of hair still disported its salty waves, kept trimmed yet slightly longer than was the custom, for full effect. It was his father's one conceit, and perhaps the reason he was the only one who did not object to Chiron's own untended tresses. They stood admiring each other, assessing, and quietly accepting the changes they perceived.

Babá turned to shepherd Chiron back to his chair and then looked to take the third chair for himself, only to find the dishes Mamá had laden on the table had been too numerous to be accommodated and the excess had spilled over onto the seat of the empty chair beside her son. There were: olives of every dark hue; féta, kasséri and kefalotíri cheeses; wedges of fresh lemon; three partial plates of pítes (pies), one each of meat, vegetables and cheese; a large bowl of piláfi; grilled octopus salad with lemon and olive oil; rolls; a dish of cucumber, tomato and féta salad; the requisite carafes of olive oil and red-wine vinegar and in the center, next to a bottle of retsina, a bottle of Metáxa brandy, customarily reserved for toasting on special occasions. Georgi noted the seven stars on the bottle, indicating the most expensive quality, and looked at his wife, who read his tacit approval and was content. Then she jumped up to rearrange the plates so her husband could sit down.

As the horizon became striated with golds and oranges and the waning moon presented itself off to their right, they conversed in soft tones, his mother's soprano punctuated now and then by his father's gravelly timbre and always, Chiron's low modulation in response. Dishware clinked and scraped, chair legs shifted, laughter erupted and the translucent night listened, making a record of all that transpired and placing it on deposit for future perusal.

Chiron went to bed that night replete. It had been a happy evening. Yet, he had not mentioned his visit with Corinna. It was no longer fitting to discuss everything in his heart with them, nor with anyone. Sometime during his first night home a turning point

146

was marked. As he lay upon his childhood bed, the last of his dependence dissipated with the fading morning stars and was replaced by a labyrinth of untested visions steeped in distant waves and windswept desire.

Sometime after dawn, he slept.

A routine of sorts established itself within days. Try as he might, Chiron could not justify staying away from Corinna. The taboos he had anguished over on his journey home were dissolved by the death of her husband and he ignored the rules of maternal confinement, as his visits were private and discreet. Besides, her mother encouraged him. Her sisters were visibly relieved to see his effect on the young widow, and happy to leave them to the intimacy of the garden for hours on end.

Corinna considered him on that first morning visit. "Even from a distance I can see your mamá has insisted on certain concessions to the house rules of clean living and hygienic comportment. I could swear there isn't a single nest of rodents in your hair today."

"Well, I saved just the one," he declared as he reached behind his ear and presented her with a wiggling finger inside his other palm. She squealed.

"Your mother needs to attend to your manners next, sir. Please tell her I said so."

"Anything you ask, my lady, although I dare say my mother finds me enchanting and wouldn't want me to change a thing."

"Your mother hasn't seen you for a while, it's true. I forgive her."

"I agree, let's give her some time. In the meanwhile, I will occupy myself by enchanting you, although I see that may not require as much effort as my skills might command."

"Your skills shall surely be tried in this instance, sir, as tarnish and rust are gaining on them at quite a pace.

I will, however, grant you a short reprieve, as a man at sea can understandably find himself out of practice."

He was shocked at the suggestion. He took her hand and turned her about to face the view of the ocean beyond the low wall. "That sea? Why, that is where the sharpest cunning is honed daily by the most exacting teachers; wind, waves and waterlogged boots." He nodded sagely at the truth of it.

She giggled and conceded the point. "Come, my Chiron. Tell me. Besides the boots and the rats, what was it like for you out there?" She looked across the glistening water to the horizon that was such a magnet for all ships, her free hand shading her eyes from the sun, not mentioning that this was the question she had asked herself every time she stood before this view, every day since he had departed.

Slowly, over the next days and weeks, he told her. He described only physical conditions at first and she listened keenly, awed by her ignorance of a ship's daily rhythms and routines. Then he told tales of his mates on the ship, with a few alarming episodes of cracking timbers and heroic rescues. He told them in the third person, as if he watched the action from another ship, or from the solitude of his cabin. She knew not to push him, but gradually drew him out, following threads he mentioned until he began to talk about his perceptions, his melancholy, his longing, and haltingly, about her.

She was careful to hide much of her distress when listening to him speak. He was skittish still and he closed up like an oyster more than once when she pried too deeply or reacted too strongly. Yet she knew there would never be another confidant for him and she was convinced their future depended on their acceptance of all they had suffered because of each other. She cried silently in her room many nights, rocking herself in a chair for hours, trying to relieve the aching of the pain he had endured.

Yet he spoke of the sea in such laudatory tones that she was jealous. "Oh, tell me something you hate about the sea," she teased. He was quiet for a long time.

"The sea sucks the truth from wherever you are hiding it." He looked at her and she saw a harrowing glimpse of what that meant for him. She swallowed and could not hold his gaze. She asked him, softly then, what he loved about the sea. He looked past her out to the water below.

"I love that it demands your best. In order to earn a place within its boundless majesty, nothing less will serve." He turned back to her matter-of-factly. Her eyes widened as she realized the weight those words must carry for him. He was still mysterious, would always be, and her heart beat a little faster with the knowledge.

Chiron wondered at the luxury of touching her. He stroked her fingers, holding her hand in both of his; reached for strands of flyaway hair; caressed her ear, lingering at the delicate lobe; and once, ran his fingers down the side of her neck and across her collar bone, stopping at the vee at the base of her throat, exploring it gently in wonder at its vulnerability. He wanted to kiss it. He wanted to protect it. He was enraptured and she thrived under his attention, despite her advancing pregnancy. During their strolls he held her arm in such a manner as to keep their bodies close hip to shoulder as much as possible, the exposed skin of their arms pressing together covertly. As their course turned them away from view, he would press his hand on the base of her spine and guide her by the pressure. When he could time their last walk for when the shadows were their deepest, he might pull her to him briefly and hold

149

her in his arms, discovering the pleasures of her abundant curves and the response of her palpable desire. This was his exaltation and worth to him all the tolls of their separation.

Late one sultry afternoon, as they reached the farthest corner of the enclosed garden, Corinna leaned against a tree with her hands behind her pressing against its trunk and artlessly regarded him through her dark lashes.

"My bonny sailor, whenever are you going to kiss me?"

He started and glanced instantly toward the house as if already guilty of the act. A curtain fluttered, surely. He looked again; nothing. He cut his eyes back to her and laughed. He threw his head back and laughed with hearty abandon.

"I thought you would never ask," he gibed. Then his eyes became serious. He looked at her mouth as if he knew he risked everything and thought he should reconsider. He started to move in, but hesitated. He prolonged the ache, tried to leave the decision in doubt, then gravely gave up the pretense and kissed her with all the longing of these three years. She moaned as she had the first time and clasped her arms around his neck, surrendering to his ardor.

He forgot their surroundings. He forgot the watching windows, the child inside her who wasn't his, the social mores of constant restraint. For the first time forgetting wasn't a discipline. His desire for her wagered this brief indulgence, dispatched every other sensibility and the hunger he felt, so long withheld, overcame all. She, his love, was all.

She sensed the urgency in Chiron's embrace and realized the cost of his restraint these last few weeks. Up to now, he was the one respecting the conventions, attentive to censoring chaperones present or remote.

150

She had taken advantage of his protection. She had indulged her fancy, drinking in his presence, his voice, his beauty, his scent, his adoration of her. He had given her back her youthful gaiety and she had been giddy with the proof that desperate pleas to a god she no longer believed in could be, had truly been, rewarded.

From the time of her marriage, she had been brave in her suffering, determined not to show her resentment towards her parents nor her indifference toward her husband. The toll from the effort, however, was not disguised. Her unaffected enjoyment of all things, her playful temperament, her buoyant spirit had been submerged, locked away where she thought they could never be revived. In their place was stoicism, sobriety and quiet forbearance. Most days she was exhausted by the effort. Most days could hardly be accounted for. A detached look had stolen into her eyes that frightened her sisters. Her father, in the two years before his death, missed his water sprite, and had spent much time alone on his boat in penitence over his decision regarding her marriage.

Now Corinna realized she had been unfair to Chiron. As much as she knew his feelings, she had been caught up in her own. She was careless. She had been taunting him, bedeviling him for days.

She was pinned against the tree. He had whispered an endearment in her ear and now his hands and arms enfolded her ravenously, his weight pressed against her belly. He engulfed her, despite her girth. She was transported by desire. Yet she pulled back. She made a sound of protest in the back of her throat and pushed against his chest. He instantly broke their embrace and she glanced quickly toward the house. He recovered his self-possession, regarding her soberly. He reached out and pulled her to him again, this time pressing the side of her face against his chest, holding it there momentarily by way of apology, his cheek resting on the top of her head. Then he pushed her tenderly away and, cradling her head between his hands, looked down at her and whispered, "I am yours evermore, Corinna, and I will abide by whatever consequences we may face, without regret or guilt. I accept the price of loving you, whatever it may be."

# CHAPTER 8

## 1884

Corinna was moving slowly on Thursday. Her mother hovered, watching her face, careful not to say too much, as Corinna had been short with her for the last week or more and even seemed changed in her attitude toward her, she thought. She blamed Chiron but was careful to hide her resentment, as he needed to be courted by the whole family in the interest of her eldest daughter and by association, the younger two as well. She avoided making eye contact with him and kept a wide berth as often as practicable. But today discretion was thwarted and it was her own anxious attentions that alerted the younger girls, who were then drawn in by the suspense, and by ten o'clock everyone in the household was on edge. Chiron arrived at one.

The hum died out immediately upon his entrance, and what Chiron observed were the three daughters sitting close together, Corinna looking at him imploringly while the other two sat up straight, hands on their knees folded tightly, looking at nothing at all and Mamá hovering over them in a defensive stance, daring someone to object. The outward appearance of quiet took on the buzz of an angry bee stuck inside an overturned glass; a muted vibration from no obvious source but felt by all.

"Am I interrupting something?" was all he could think to say.

"No not at all, Chiron, please come in," said Corinna brightly, then turning to look pointedly at her sisters. She did not, however, rise as she usually did to escort him outside for fresh air and time alone.

The girls excused themselves, making eyes at each other and ducking their heads, obviously chafing at their apparent dismissal. Mamá crossed her arms and claimed her ground, raising her chin at him as if he were the fuse that would likely ignite this firecracker. But resentful as she was of his presence this day, it wasn't seemly to discuss the particulars and she deliberated on how best to extinguish him. Her foot began to tap, and the rocking motion set in. Chiron turned his head and saw the girls lingering just outside the parlor door. He looked back at Corinna who seemed as serene as he had left her last evening, and perhaps more beautiful than ever with color in her cheeks, either because of her family's performance or perhaps from the conversation he had interrupted, but otherwise she appeared as usual. He did notice that the tendrils of hair framing her face were damp, but it was a warm day. There ensued an awkward silence. Corinna cleared her throat.

"Mamá, I am thirsty. Would you mind bringing me a glass of water?" she smiled up at her mother who had no choice but to leave the room at once, which she managed with a flounce of indignance. Her upper arms thwacked and her hips jostled angrily in departure.

"I have a small pain in my back and they are all overreacting. They do not know I have had the pain to no effect for several days," she said demurely. Chiron's forehead was disapproving. "I even had it last week, but it was gone by Friday." He considered that information, knowing she was quite herself last week, hearty and content.

"Today Mamá saw me holding my back when I arose from my chair and they all immediately started to swoon with dramatic solicitude, each of them afraid their own part in the mummery might otherwise be overlooked."

"Corinna, has the midwife been by lately? What does she say about your laying-in?" It was hard not to fall in with the women's wringing of hands. Pacing felt like a good idea, too. Mamá returned, Chiron looked up and relinquished his position to her, feeling out of his depth. A corner of her mouth turned up when she noticed that. A sign of how things ought to be, finally.

"My dear, I think you should go to your room and lie down for a bit today. It is so hot, you know, and you should not exert yourself. Look! Just look, your ankles are swelling up again in this weather. Chiron, perhaps you could help her up from this chair," she added conspiratorially. He half expected her to wink.

"I do not need any help, Mamá! However I do think it is much nicer out under Papoú's old olive tree at the back of the garden. You are right, I will be much more comfortable where it is cooler." Her glance defied a rebuttal. Chiron lurched to take her arm despite her bravado and supported her elbow out of the house along the path to the wall above the sea. A great, heaving sigh followed them from the house. Chiron looked sideways at Corinna and felt a pang of fear in the pit of his belly, mixed with the most soft-hearted compassion he had ever experienced. He realized he was proud of her cool demeanor.

She kept him close by all afternoon, holding his hand, smoothing the hair along his forearm, nuzzling him, even biting him on the neck once or twice and laughing her mocking laugh in the way that bewitched him. Sometimes she was quiet, and looked out absently at the sea, but not for long. He would watch her then silently, etching her silhouette into his memory. When she came out of her reverie he would smile at her, covering the concern that matched her sisters'. They spent the afternoon that way, in their universe of two.

Around dusk, Corinna was growing tired. Emerging restlessly from another reverie, she turned to him. With the earnest tones of an avowal, as if time were getting late and she knew the opportunity might slip by, she spoke.

"I believe I would have succumbed if I had felt a lesser love," she began, feeling her way to her own understanding. "Perhaps I could not have withstood the pain of our separation if you were an ordinary man. I survived, and would have continued to live the life I had committed to, because I had you to live up to. I could not let your worth be diminished by my own weakness. I could not demand less of myself than your noblest expectations. Of all the things I could not bear, I could not bear most to be unworthy of you, my Chiron.

"And it is only now that you are returned that I realize it was you who held me up every day, who was my strength, who was my faith. I had no hope of ever being with you again, and yet you carried me through our separation by the force of your will. I must have known it. Surely I felt it. I stood out here by this wall and I wrapped my arms around myself tightly and I remembered everything I loved about you. I embraced all that we had together, knowing it was rapture, understanding finally it was enough to last exactly one lifetime."

The sun dipped behind a cloud. The breeze quickened. A little flower pot fell over and clinked onto the stone path. A whirlpool of leaves capered past their chairs and dispersed. Chiron's hands enveloped hers protectively, feeling their tremble like the wings of a baby bird. He did not trust his voice to speak. He felt the deep, slow rhythmic pound of his heart as it careened within his chest. He raised her hands to his mouth and kissed the tender pads of her fingers, then took each palm and turned it upward to be kissed, first one, then the other. He looked at her and pulled her right hand to his chest and placed it there, flat against his heart, and held it firmly. Its tempo swelled.

A sprinkle of raindrops wafted across their shoulders, feeling more like mist than rain, but before they could look up, Corinna's mother hallooed from the back door, waving them inside with large, sweeping motions, while the hastening drizzle made its own argument.

Chiron helped her up, using both arms this time, not obscuring their intimacy or considering the observers at all. He put his arm around her protectively and held her hand with his free one. In this gentle embrace, they walked slowly together up the walk to the house.

Corinna stood a moment in the kitchen, surrounded by all of her loved ones, and smiled wearily at Chiron. He pressed her hand and wished her a restful evening. He held her eyes for a long moment. He said his goodbyes to the other women, took up his cap and left for home.

Once he was gone, with the door clicked shut behind him, Corinna's gaze turned to her mother and she stated, "I believe, Mamà, there is water on the floor beneath my skirt."

By midnight her mother was feeling remiss for not having sent word to Chiron. Corinna had insisted he not be called. At first, her mother was excited by the role she played in tending her daughter through early labor, proud that Corinna depended upon her to be at her side for this momentous event, keen to demonstrate the wisdom and experience of her own birthing days.

By the time the midwife arrived, there was bleeding. She, Sophia by name, quickly prescribed cohosh, then raspberry tea. Meanwhile, she made a paste of herbs in preparation for rubbing the uterus to staunch the blood immediately after the birth.

The night pitched and yawed. By daybreak, Corinna and the bed were drenched in sweat and still, the bleeding continued. The baby was born midmorning, and mewled for its mother. The placenta, which had partially blocked the birth canal, now failed to detach properly. The herbs were applied and the uterus was massaged by Sophia in a dauntless effort to stop the hemorrhage, to encourage the uterus to cramp down.

All of the terror the women had hidden for fourteen hours refused submission at last with the sound of Chiron's knock, precisely at eleven o'clock, precisely as scheduled. Only Sophia remained composed. The sisters clung to each other and whimpered. Their mother, with maternal desperation wrought from heartbreak, quickly placed the baby in their care and shooed them from the room whereupon she let a bubble of hysteria escape from her own swollen throat. She quickly covered her mouth, took a deep breath, smoothed her hair, ran her hands down her apron, and went to open the door.

Seeing him stand in the doorway, she gathered the last of her wits and kept her knees from buckling, though they wobbled and she relied on the door for support.

Chiron read everything in her eyes. "Where is she?" He said. She pointed to the bedroom opposite. He ran.

Corinna was weakened by her ordeal but fought against the desire to sleep, instinctively. She was gratified by her baby's cry, relieved to have mustered enough energy to push her baby out, despite having used all her reserves and knowing her strength now was spent. Her purpose was fulfilled and she was content. She was not afraid, nor was she saddened by her condition. Rather, she felt transported by the pure elation of the birth of her daughter. She lay quietly, eyes close, her face beatific in its repose.

When her lover took her hand and whispered her name, she turned to him.

"My Chiron," she whispered. "I've waited for you." He could not tell if she meant now or all this time since he had gone to sea. "I will always wait for you. That…is my vow." She looked at him as if he were truly here to rescue her, and her faith was all she needed. But the light in her eyes changed and he saw that she meant to save him, to be a comfort to him, and he felt a chill of horror. He half rose, leaning over her to kiss her on the lips, then the forehead, where he lingered and unflinchingly stifled a sob. Then he pulled back enough to smile down at her serenely, as if they had awakened here together in this bed and the new day held all the glory and promise of a lifetime to be shared, just the other side of this veil of pain.

"My angel," he whispered back to her. "I will carry your promise branded in my heart all the days of my life, as a token of the faith of our love for each other. It is you who will buoy me in my destiny…in my destiny as the man who lived for the love of Corinna."

She smiled then, and a tear glistened briefly. All of her energy was in her eyes, gold flecks glinting, the fire yet lit. Her adoration and her mischief ignited briefly as the lovers lingered for one last moment in perfect union.

Then she faltered. Her eyes closed involuntarily but she opened them again with effort. She was remembering something, and she looked beseechingly at him, trying to speak. He hushed her and gently stroked her brow.

"My…my Chir…" She was struggling. "My baby…please…take her…my. Love."

"Yes, yes, of course," he promised, knowing nothing about the baby's survival. "Do not trouble yourself, angel, do not fret. I give you my pledge, as in all things."

She believed him, and that was enough. Her fingers convulsed around his in farewell. Then with quiet grace, she allowed her bodily strength to wane.

# CHAPTER 9

## 1946

"Tell me about Thea," Nick had said. The words hung in the air and Chiron seemed to be listening to them still, lost in a thread of his own recollection, pondering the tapestry before him. Nick's eyes followed Chiron's gaze. The maiden was still looking over her shoulder forbiddingly at her lover. The lover still appeared bewildered, yet hopeful there was an explanation he would soon grasp. He still reached for her hand, one breath away.

Nick looked back at Chiron and waited. His pulse quickened, patience a trial as always.

"You remember, I am sure, when your father and I parted ways," Chiron stated matter-of-factly.

"Yes, of course, except my father never talked about it like that. He always talked as if you were still in touch."

"There was no animosity between us and yet, it would have been difficult for us to continue our relationship and impossible to continue our business partnership. We both left the clan at about the same time but for somewhat different reasons. Regardless, the breach was final and mutual."

Nick was alerted. He did not know the friendship of these two most influential men in his life had suffered a rift. His father had never let on. Nick had been so removed from his father's confidence by that time, and so stricken by his own heartache that he would never have suspected the pain of others. Nor cared to hear. He leaned forward, his elbows propped on his knees.

Chiron rose and strode over to the book shelf, where he retrieved the bottle of Remy Martin. Carrying it by its neck, he let it swing by his side, and sauntered back

161

to the sitting area as if the cognac were either second nature or an afterthought, Nick couldn't tell which. He reached for two short glasses from the sideboard and used them to nudge the mugs of ale aside. He tipped the bottle over the rims, pouring three generous fingers in each. When he sat down again he had determined his course, and set about addressing it.

"By that time it was 1932. You were barely twenty. Your father's position in the industry was untenable. He knew he was likely to lose several, if not all, of his ships, that his reputation was severely damaged, I might add irrevocably although he never believed that, and that the clan was well renowned for its acts of retribution. He was under a great deal of stress and at some point, Nicholas, I felt there was a fissure in his sanity. It was small, perhaps, and not always apparent, but it was permanent. The word that came to my mind most often in those days was 'trapped'. Your father looked trapped, and wild-eyed by the prospect. I'm sure he felt guilt about the role I played in the deal as well, which was only partially deserved on his part but inevitable, under the circumstances.

"Then there was you. From the time you were born the focus of everything he did was for the sake of you, his son. He was fiercely determined to provide for you, and equally terrified of failing you. His need to control your surroundings, and his terror of the uncontrollable had been eating away at him for years. He could not experience the joy of fatherhood for the weight of the responsibility of it. I'm afraid he did not give you enough credit for carrying your own weight; as far as I know he never even thought of it. But he would risk everything for you. As he did.

"The Greeks are a superstitious people, as you are well aware. Not only did your father become more religious, seemingly as a shield against evil, by praying voraciously and compulsively, but he also began to follow many of the traditions of his mother and grandmother, including efforts to ward off the evil eye among other things.

"In fact, the decision to break the laws of the clan, though there were many causes over the years, was ultimately enacted because of a táma he had pledged on your behalf. Did your mother ever explain táma to you?"

"I recognize the word, but I'm not sure what it signifies," Nick admitted.

"It is an appeal to a saint that involves both prayer and a vow. The petitioner asks for help in some private matter and then pledges a gift to the church in return. It is often a gift of monetary value." Chiron paused and searched Nick's face, deciding how much of an effect his story might have on Kristof's son. Perhaps it was time for him to buck up, he surmised. He had survived the war, that was a fact. Perhaps it was not too late for him after all.

"Kristof's prayer was that you would follow in his footsteps, taking over his shipping line and marrying into one of the ruling families of the clan in Chios. He had an empire in mind that you and he would rule together. He had even chosen the bride and spoken to her father."

Nick picked up his glass and downed the glowing liquid. This conversation was not going where he had expected it to and he began to realize there were probably other things to dread besides those he had anticipated in coming here. Chiron refilled the glass, and his own.

"There is a saying in Greece. 'Do not make a pledge to a saint or a small child unless you are sure of fulfilling it.' Your father's pledge to the church was exorbitant. And over time, it became apparent to him

163

the only way to pay his táma was to take a risk with his relationship with the clan. Now, his plan did not materialize overnight. He had been scrutinizing his options for years, for years of circumstances where he felt slighted by the clan in their doling out the shares of business opportunities. He felt like the poor relation who is patted on the back and reassured time and again of his importance to the group but who is secretly resented and relegated to the lowest position possible without being blatantly cheated, yet always short-changed. I cannot tell you myself whether or not that was true, but I suspected it on more than one occasion. Your father never doubted the insult and chafed over it with mounting ill will.

"You see, the belief within the clan is that the individual's place is inescapably linked to and subservient to that of the group. One result of that is trust and mutual respect can replace the need for constant monitoring. Contracts are looser, less formal than contracts between non-clan shippers. Make no mistake: trust and loyalty are paramount.

"The clan benefits in every way from the information flow among its members. That is the key to their success. They do not necessarily share all their knowledge with each other, but they rely on each other's individual knowledge to ultimately benefit everyone. The benefit comes from identifying and sharing a wider range of opportunities. Those opportunities are then divided among the members, each in his own turn as the elders see fit. Over time, it is intended to be even-handed and equally rewarding to all. To Kristofer, it was not.

"The rest of the story you can probably figure out for yourself." Nick did not look like he had figured out anything. Chiron continued. "Your father used knowledge that he had himself acquired independently to pursue his own contract without going through the regular clan channels. Already disgruntled, he convinced himself not only that he had no choice, but that his plan was so discreet it would escape notice. He would combine it with another shipment. No one would be the wiser and no one would be hurt. And of course, he would only do it this one time. This time when the profits would go to God. For the sake of his only son. Surely, that was forgivable, he thought. But unpunishable?

"There is another saying we sailors know well. 'No sea is so open as the inexhaustible sea of revenge.'[1] A vendetta against your father and his shipping line was the inevitable result."

Nick was contemplating the chess pieces, trying to discern from this distance whether white or black had the advantage. He did not look at Chiron. His head was just beginning to pound with the implications he had never in all these years considered. He himself was at the heart of his family tragedy and all the blaming he had done over the bitter years pointed back to him in the end, unfeeling and blind. His overbearing father was an ailing, aging man whose devotion to him was not only unearned and unfitting but deleterious. This cruelly passionless, largely absent father had sacrificed his life's labor as well as his posterity, the only two things Nick had thought were of value to him. Shame colored his face and neck and upon swallowing, trickled down into his shirt collar.

Yet still, niggling at him from the base of his skull was another question. What does this have to do with Thea? He wanted to cry out those words in frustration – and by way of evasion. Chiron expected too much of him. Surely he must understand that.

Ice appeared in his newly filled glass, shifting seductively as it settled.

"I was captain of his flagship, the Constantinas. I was also, as you may remember, a part owner. It was my ship that fulfilled the illicit contract."

Nick's heart jack-knifed in his chest. He knew implicitly that Chiron would not have accepted a contract knowing it was unsanctioned. He felt sick and placed the empty glass back on the table before him, pushing it away with his fingertips as far as he could reach, as if distancing himself from its effect amidst these revelations. Chiron watched the movement with interest.

"I understood what had to be done the moment I learned of the infraction." Chiron leaned back in his chair to rest his head against the faded quilt behind him. The tenor of his voice changed a little. It became lower, more resonant. When next he spoke, he was far away.

"I stood that night at the rail, my back to the lights and noises and smells of the docks and the city beyond. We were in Antwerp. I remember clasping the smooth, polished wood behind me with both hands, running my palms back and forth along its gleaming surface, thinking of all the hands that had also rubbed it or leaned on it, rested against it or clung to it over the years, and how dear every length of it was to me. I tried not to look at the moon hanging faithfully over my shoulder, casting its reflection on each beloved object within my view. I saw how the moonlight burnished my ship, highlighting the fealty of all the men I knew who had loved it as I did.

"I closed my eyes and felt the gentle sway beneath my boots and up the muscles of my legs as I absorbed the motion, as attuned to the song of the deep as a babe in the womb."

Chiron paused for a moment, the price of that night's decision visible still in the mask of taut muscles along his jaw, across his cheekbones. Nick waited, rapt, aching.

"The decision to take responsibility for the breach was an easy one for me, and logical. I had failed in my duty to my crew by relinquishing the details of the contract to Kristof, knowing his fragile hold on rationality. The signs were there, had I chosen to scrutinize them. It would be untenable for me to continue in my position as captain regardless, and by taking the brunt of the blame I could perhaps prevent the loss of the entire Moonstar fleet. I had, of course, invested heavily in all your father's vessels over the years.

"I set my plan in motion swiftly. It was quite simple, painless really. I filled out a few falsified papers, I passed them into various grimy hands and I told a couple of deceptive versions of the tale to half a dozen devious ears. I told Kristof of my actions and resigned. He protested, at first. Then he offered me this gatehouse as my sanctuary and I accepted it gratefully."

He paused. "My decision had been made and this arrangement would allow me to live near Thea."

Though he had turned away, Nick could feel Chiron's probing eyes back on him. The muscles of his abdomen had convulsed slightly at the mention of her name. He squared his shoulders then and turned to face his old mentor. His apprehension was confirmed by everything he read in Chiron's gaze.

Nick's expression stirred something familiar in Chiron, an old feeling he'd often experienced in years past that was a mix of pity and sympathy for this bright, lonesome, doleful young man. Yet for the first time he glimpsed something new in Nick's eyes. He glimpsed a determination to face the truth of Chiron's words, and to deal with it. They held each other's gaze for a long time, recognizing a new respect and a glint of hope, each one from the other.

"As you know, that was a full year before your family left Beechwood. It was just long enough for your father and me to formulate a defense against the vengeful actions of the clan, although the prospects were dim at best. Damage control was more the focus, and time was short.

"But it was time enough for me to witness the developing attraction between you and Thea, and bear witness to the pain you would inevitably cause each other.

"After Kristof's shipping line had been ostracized from the clan, he was more determined than ever to make a good match for you. He remained reasonably calm throughout the process of addressing the floundering fortunes of The Moonstar line, but he lost all equanimity when your future was discussed. I began to study everything I could find in my medical books concerning apoplexy, I was that convinced your father would work himself into a stroke over the withdrawn marriage agreement.

"For good or ill, he was insensible to your unfolding love affair with Thea. Even when Maria tried to express her own concerns about the two of you, knowing your father's intentions for your future, he literally did not hear her. Madness was upon him and even I could only hold his attention by addressing direct questions, and repeating myself often. The international influence of the clan membership was astounding and swift. All reputable business dried up within weeks. The next several months were consumed with attempts at combating it, and all the while your father refused to acknowledge the futility."

Nick shook his head in chagrin when he learned his mother had guessed at their affair. She never let on, even in the ensuing years when they lived together in Philadelphia and were each other's only refuge from his father's rants.

"Some of this I knew, Chiron, or at least I guessed at. But I did not concern myself with any suffering my father, or my parents, might have endured— considering my own grief at the time. The Moonstar Line meant little to me; in fact, I placed much of the blame for my own unhappiness on the demands of its business and my father's slavish devotion to it. I never doubted that his plans for me were for his own gain. Even now I am dismayed to hear of his feelings, and slow to recognize them in his behavior toward me. He never...he well, he said it was for my own good but so is spinach. I did not take him at his word. I never did."

"He was not very good with words. But he could choose them well when he needed to. You should have seen him on the bridge during a storm, when the price of inaction is counted in sailor's lives and most words are carried off on the wind. Aye, a man of few words is a valuable thing in a storm, my son."

Nick smiled ruefully, huffing softly through his nose. "I thought of that myself more than once, aboard the Bayou Chico, the freighter I was commissioned on," he mused. "We were attacked by the Krauts twice from the air and once by U-boat. We survived by virtue of a cracker-jack commander and the devil's own luck. Some in our convoy were not so fortunate." It was the first time he had spoken aloud the name of his ship, or any other detail of his service, he realized. He leaned forward again and studied the palms of his hands, inspecting the calluses with his fingertips one after the other, remembering.

He looked up. "Your words are true enough, but come too late. I am a man of thirty-four years, Chiron. And I am arriving late to many things. I am here to begin to make amends, if they may be made. Let me start with you. Please. Can you ever forgive our family? Can you forgive me for what I allowed to happen to my family and yours?"

"Do not look to me for blame or recriminations, Nicholas. I make my own choices and abide by them, and expect others to do the same. I love your father still and will always be in his debt for the life-line he extended me in my most vulnerable days. He was a good man and earned my respect many times over.

"As for the heartbreak that Thea has suffered, I admit I have suffered from it as well. So have you and you have paid a price. You were in love. It would be feigned virtue for me to lay blame where love is concerned. We all fall victim to that siren. And yet. And yet there is no more exalted way to spill your life's blood.

"If you survive," he smiled wryly, "you may earn your portion of the elixir of the gods. Or," he shrugged, "the unabating thirsts of Hades. How you face it is your choice. Either way, you do not escape the struggle." He turned his open hands palms-up and held them in supplication, leaving the outcome in doubt. But his eyes spoke otherwise. His black eyes told the tale of internal violence and infinite trial.

Chiron looked down then, clearing his throat, seeing something deep within the earth below the stone floor. He leaned forward again, clasping his hands, and scrutinized Kristof's son. "The last six months of that year your father spent retrenching, salvaging what he could. He sold all his vessels except the Constantinas, the pride of his fleet. He took a beating but to his credit, never uttered a word of grievance once he set upon his course. He was feverish in his myopic determination to recover his reputation and rebuild his fleet without relying on anyone. I admired him for his fortitude, even knowing it was self-deceptive and ill-fated. He had to sell Beechwood, which might have broken his heart if he had allowed even a moment's reflection or sentiment into his deliberate triage of amputations. He believed his best course of action was to return to his earliest triumph, with the oil traders of Philadelphia. That was where he had gone as a young man the first time he dared to venture outside of the clan mold, fairly bursting onto a new industry and betraying the early tendencies of an independent temperament. Only at that time, because of his great success, no one took offense.

"But by this time the transcontinental oil trade had moved to New York harbor and I think he knew it full well. He needed to pull out and lick his wounds but New York City was no place to hide, so he convinced himself his remaining connections in Philadelphia would prove viable enough for the time being. I wish he had been right."

Nick snorted drunkenly, contemptuously at the understatement. Chiron noted his changing mood, saw the sneer forming under the surface of his stiffly polite countenance.

Chiron glowered at the young man before him. "Being consumed by attempts to resuscitate his foundering empire, he did not realize what advantage you were taking of my Thea."

Nick blinked and sat up as if his commanding officer had just walked into the room. His visceral reaction preceded his comprehension by some seconds; he might have risen and saluted if he had been capable. Once he grasped the words and their intent, he cut his eyes to their voice and pain swept his brow, quickly extinguishing the artificial light in his eyes. He held his breath, preparing for the next blow.

"Despite the love you claim you felt for her you were blind to the pain you were causing. She adored you so and dreaded her inevitable rejection."

"Never! I would never have rejected her! I would have stood by her, Chiron, you must know that. I tried everything. I never forgave my father for taking me away. Tell me you remember all that. I thought you believed in me." He felt that old tug in the pit of his bowels and the beginnings of the nausea that always followed. He remembered now why the war had provided him a source of relief, with its everyday life-and-death distractions. Blindly he reached up and pulled at his hair with both hands, beads of sweat suddenly rivulets down the sides of his hairline. He began to rock back and forward in small, tight motions, mourning the events as if the torment were fresh and as yet unbearable. This is why he had stayed away. This is why he had stayed away. He rocked in silence, stifling a moan. Chiron remained composed.

"After you left, after your family was gone from Beechwood, we stayed here alone for a while. A pall befell the house, the grounds, even the shoreline and the water beyond. Those were dark days. She was stunned and my impotence to affect her fate was paralyzing. But we had little enough time to dwell on the circumstances, as the Bayards were arriving soon."

Nick sat motionless, fingers still entwined in his hair, elbows on his knees, eyes studying the whorling pattern of the rag rug beneath his feet.

"I took her back to the city to live with her brother Alexsy and his wife, Adicia. They had a toddler, a son named Perry. Soon they had a new baby as well, Todd. As quickly as I felt I could, I prevailed upon her to return to Beechwood. She seemed to want to be here too, here more than anywhere, I suppose. I'm not sure it was a good idea, even now. My mind was beclouded by my desire to have her near, to protect her like I had failed to do once before." There was the smallest catch in his voice when he said that.

"But I had resolved to stay here myself in retirement, once your father determined to leave. 'This house is more yours than mine by rights' he had said and though it wasn't true, I believe he meant it, fraught with guilt as he was.

"Perhaps I chose to hide here myself, or perhaps I was weary of burdens I had carried and thought to lay them at the feet of my tapestry and find respite." He picked up the Remy Martin and regarded it. He gestured with it toward the tapestry above him, as a delayed afterthought, not looking up himself, though Nick's eyes followed the motion and he wondered idly again what meaning the scene before him held for Chiron. The two men sat silently for awhile. A clock chimed the quarter hour, though neither of them heard.

"I came along with the house, the Bayards were told. We all did: Thea, Maggie, Clement, Clarisse. And life went on. We fell into our old routines, for the most part. Hephron and Adrianne were quite accommodating and gracious. By the time the twins were born, we had grown fond of our new family and were captivated by the babies. Thea, however, was changed. She rarely spoke. She kept to herself. She developed a kind of a tic where her left hand would jump up a few inches as if startled. I thought she wasn't aware of it until I noticed whenever she sat down she would place her right hand over it as if to keep it still. She became thin and I thought it was from mourning. Her hair became dull. Her eyes..." Here Chiron passed his hand over his own eyes, then looked across at Nick, as if just now realizing he was speaking aloud. Nick looked up. He knew everything else had been prologue and now was the time. He fought the desire to interrupt, to stop Chiron before he delivered his depth charge. He felt abruptly sober.

"Shortness of breath was the symptom that finally caught my attention." It was evident he was remembering a scene or scenes. He paused and Nick realized Chiron was not going to tell him any details. He was still protecting her and Nick couldn't blame him.

"I took her into town to see the doctor, a real doctor. We spent half a day having tests done. I insisted on repeating more than one of them, several in fact, to the doctor's exasperation. But I knew, had diagnosed it myself from my own examination. The symptoms were clear, though I couldn't admit it.

"She has congenital heart disease." He spoke the words aloud for the second time, the first being when he had explained it to Alexsy, more than ten years ago.

Nick swallowed. "How serious. Is it?"

"Nicholas. She has done well. But a person with this disease, the narrowing of the aorta, does not get better. She will die from it. It is fatal."

Only his lips trembled and he did not trust himself to speak. He continued to be riveted to Chiron's face, waiting for the 'but' or the 'except' or the 'maybe' and quaking with the knowledge he would not hear them.

Finally, he risked his voice. "What are you doing for her?"

Chiron was a little surprised, expecting many other questions before that one. "We are treating her high blood pressure, for one thing. I also have a few remedies to relieve leg cramps, dizziness, headaches, that sort of thing. She is as comfortable as possible and she gets all the rest she needs. She only works as much as she feels like she can, and that only because she insists. The best medicine for her is the children, that is

174

what she tells us. Some days are quite good. She seems content, Nicholas."

If only Nick did not know Chiron so well, he could avoid the implication in his eyes and tone. "Will you forbid me to see her?" There was a measure of relief in being blunt.

Again Chiron was impressed by Nick's unexpectedly direct question. He contemplated the answer, not deciding what he would say but considering the repercussions after he said it. Just as he began to speak, a vision of Corinna passed before his eyes. He sighed.

"This is not my decision to make. I do not presume to hold her life or her heart in my hands, nor can any man, unless she herself chooses to offer them. You said you want to make amends. Whatever you decide, Nicholas, do not be guided by your desire to relieve your conscience. That is between you and God, regardless. As for Thea, she has a short time left. This time her life-blood is at stake. Remember that."

Chiron rose, pushing off his thighs with his still-powerful hands, and reached for the quilt on the back of his chair. He handed it to Nick and said, not unkindly, "Sleep here. You will never find your car in the darkness." He turned and headed for the stairs, not waiting to see if Nick took the advice.

# CHAPTER 10

## 1946

It was daylight by 5:30 these mornings, which did not escape the notice of Herman, vigilant even in slumber. His first thought this morning was of the shadow he had seen from the back hallway window last night. He lay on his back, pulling his fingers through the knotted fringes of his Ba, contemplating the list of suspects he had reason to, well, suspect.

He went through the names slowly, carefully scrutinizing each of their movements the last time he saw them.

Clement and Clarisse went home yesterday at their usual time, around five o'clock. He had seen them walking down the drive side by side, like two old soldiers exactly out of synch. They each marched in perfect time; outside foot, inside foot, outside foot, inside foot so their heads nearly knocked together on the inside steps, and they veered away from each other so far on the outside steps as to be in danger of toppling over into their own side of the woods, yet angling in again just in the nick of time on the very next step. They had been married so long they were more like twins than husband and wife. Herman chuckled at that, until he realized it could be him and Iris someday and he sobered up quick enough. He coughed and cleared his throat. Definitely nothing suspicious there, check them off the list. He made a clicking sound with his tongue as a note of finality.

Dad. Ho-ho, no, not him! He was the grumpy man roused out of bed to search the basement for that dammed scrap of dirty rag that someday would find itself unfindable for good if he had anything to say about it, stubbing his damned toe on a broken cement step, hobbling and muttering clear back up the staircase. Big check off the list for him, tchkt, tchkt.

Mom. Obviously not. She was also part of the search party, the one who actually found the Ba. Tchkt. With his forefinger, he made a big check mark in the air.

Todd, Iris. No and no. In bed. Double check for them, and no help one bit in the investigation, either.

Maggie. Maggie Ole Girl. Now there's a sneaky one. She could turn up anywhere. Snooping is her middle name, especially if she's in his room, poking her nose in his stuff. Suspicious, definitely. Investigate.

Chiron. Hardly likely. If Chiron were sneaking around, no one would be likely to know about it. Let's see, the last time they had seen Chiron was after the storm two days ago when he told them the story about the lead bullets from the Aprocolis. The Adropolis. The day Nick came for a visit.

Hmmm: Nick. The last time anyone saw that character was when he said goodbye and went over to the gatehouse to visit Chiron, as a matter of fact. Now there's a slippery kind of Joe. Keep an eye on him. Slippery as an eel, he'd say. He stroked his chin sagely with his thumb and forefinger. Yes. Investigate. As for Chiron, he shrugged; an all-clear check for him, tchkt.

Now who did he forget? Ah, Thea, his Sweet Thea. Golly, she was the only one around here who was nice to him. She could never be up to no good. She never ventured far enough away, anyhow. If it were Thea roaming around at night, he'd be out there in a flash to make sure she was all right. Bring her a shawl or something. She had been a resident of Beechwood their whole lives. She didn't carry much power but she held them each in the palm of her hand with her

177

kindnesses. She came with the estate, something no one ever thought to question. Like Maggie and Chiron but different. She was the universal safe haven who loved them unconditionally and never tried to make them improve themselves. She was gentle and doe-eyed, perhaps a little fragile to be trifled with by insensitive rowdies like them, but they never noticed. They each visited her room daily, unmindful of the disruption, confident of her smile and quiet solicitude. Thea was gentle. Thea was safe. She kept their secrets and dried their tears, read them stories and forgave every selfishness. If they'd thought of it, they would have realized she never asked a thing of them in return. Okay, check her off the list, too. Tchkt.

That left his main suspect: an Intruder. Someone was sneaking around here and he could prove it. Being trained as he was in surveillance, he had seen that other shadow from the lookout up in the gatehouse when the rest of them had only noticed the dumb ole owl who flies around all the time practically invisible. He alone, Herman, had the sly eye and cunning wit to catch wind of the undercover movements of a professional outlaw. And why not? It's a wonder it's taken till now for the criminal element to discover this place, ripe for the picking as they say. He shook his head in professional disgust. No one else takes these things seriously, why does he have to save all their hides single-handed? He heaved a sigh at the fate of it, and shivered just a little from the perilous thrill. He threw back the covers and was out of bed in a thrice.

An early breakfast and the threesome was bounding off toward the beach with Poseidon at their heels. Like Herman, Todd had awakened with plans churning in his head. He had found an old yellow rubber ball that he thought Poseidon would like to play with. Then, as he sat in his bed bouncing it around the room at

178

challenging angles, off various objects that reverberated throughout the entire house when properly struck (with the only rule that he had to catch the ball without falling off the bed) he remembered Poseidon's ocean diving exhibition. Maybe it was a good day to explore the full potential of Poseidon's diving skills, he mused. This time he would use a brightly colored, buoyant, unsentimental quarry like a ball. He tossed it up and down a couple of feet above his head, weighing it thoughtfully each time it landed in his palm. He would train the dog to hunt and retrieve it from the water on command, and surprise Hephron with his cleverness. He dressed quickly and ran down the stairs to enlist the twins.

Things might have gotten off to a smoother start if they had explained the plan to the puppy before he spotted a crab in the sand and pounced on it. In the end, the only one who actually witnessed the crab attack was the raven, whose full attention was riveted on the dog and his prey. The three kids were scuffling over the loose ball, each convinced he or she should be the first one to throw it into the surf and furious that the other two were being so selfish about it. It was clear the winner would be the one in possession of the ball and grabbing it out of each others' hands was fair play or not, depending upon one's status at the moment.

The puppy squealed out in pain and they looked up to see the intrepid crab being whipped left and right, left and right, drops of water and blood going one way, claws and shell flinging the other. In desperation, Poseidon finally trapped the body of the crab on the sand with his paws and pulled back his head with a howl, ripping himself free of the attacker and running off into the scrub brush whining and shaking his wobbly head. The raven lifted off casually from the dock post and swooped down. Older and wiser, he carried off the crab without incident.

For a moment the children were glued to their spots in dismay, the ball forgotten and rolling to a stop at the edge of the water line. Then they erupted into cries of sympathy and charged across the deep sand, arms and legs akimbo. Mired in slow motion at first, they eventually gained ground and raced to catch the poor little pup before he ran off and got himself lost or his nose fell off or worse.

By the time they emerged from the pine trees and underbrush, they could see that Chiron had scooped the pup into his arms and was carrying him off to his infirmary. The children instantly broke stride in their relief, knocking into one another blindly and stumbling to a walk, catching their breath while scrutinizing the trustful wagging tail that poked out from under Chiron's protective arm. Within seconds of assessing the rescue scene, however, their curiosity over the gory injury spurred them on for a first-hand glimpse.

Their boisterous arrival was met with a growl and a snap, by which they were quite crestfallen. Even as they rocked on their heels in surprised rejection Chiron shooed them away, and the trio soon lagged behind, feet scuffling, heads bowed. Before they reached the gatehouse, however, all was forgiven and Chiron had to wait outside his own doorway until they arranged themselves out of his way to allow room for passage inside.

Chiron had Todd fetch an old towel from his storage room and placed the pup on top of it gently, there on his workbench in a shaft of sunlight. The dog allowed the exam with quiet resignation, worn out by the episode and reassured by Chiron's cool ministrations. The children kept their distance, kneeling with hands on knees, mouths more or less withholding comment, eyes missing nothing. A few deft strokes with a half-concealed instrument, one yelp of pain, a dollop of menthol-scented unguent and Chiron pronounced him on the mend. The convalescent was carried to the greenhouse for a prescribed rest, no visitors allowed.

The children followed Chiron back to his office where he lowered himself into the cracked leather chair behind his desk and settled into his usual pose. They took their places before him accordingly. They were most anxious to fill him in on the attack of the crab, who had grown in stature considerably over the last hour. He listened with fingers entwined upon his desk blotter, looking studiously from one twin to the other. When they wound down, he turned his eyes to Todd, who was struck by the somber cast in his gaze and the dark crescents underneath.

"Did you notice what happened to the crab after Poseidon threw it off?"

Todd answered readily, "Yes, a crow swept down and flew off with the crab in its beak."

"It was a raven. Ravens are in the crow family and are very similar. They are larger and if you look closely you will see their beaks are rounded while the crow's is straight. Their tail feathers and wings are more pointed than a crow's, whose feathers are square-cut.

"Ravens are worthy of careful observation. They are among the most clever and advanced of all birds. They are circumpolar, which means they live in every part of the world from the North Pole to the South. They can adapt to any conditions, from frozen tundras to tropical forests. The only place where they don't live, in fact, is New Zealand.

"Their society is highly developed. They live up to twenty-nine years and they mate for life. They congregate together for roosting at night, though they may hunt as much as thirty miles from their roost. They are the very largest of songbirds and have up to a hundred vocalizations, different sounds they make to communicate with one another.

"When one bird finds a source of food, he shares it with the rest of his group, which in turn helps to increase the food supply for everyone. They never fight amongst themselves over food and have great respect for each other's rights, regardless of social standing. But they are territorial. A group of ravens, in fact, is called a murder." He paused for the expected sounds of disbelief. "They will eat almost anything, including carrion, and often work together as a team in the hunt. When I was not much older than you, I witnessed two ravens sitting in the upper branches of an acacia tree studying a hawk nearby with a fresh kill. Upon some invisible signal, one of the ravens flew in a wide arc into position behind the hawk, snuck up on it and boldly pulled its tail feathers with his beak. When the surprised hawk turned to see what was the matter, the other raven swooped in and grabbed the prey, flying off with it before the hawk could react." The children's eyebrows raised and Herman giggled.

"Down by The Point," he motioned with his head in the direction of the light house, "I saw half a dozen crows go after a Great Egret, teasing it and chasing it until it dropped its prey. While it was flapping its wings at its attackers, one of the crows quickly grabbed the food and carried it off. A family of ravens has even been known to overcome a weakened fawn by continuously attacking it and attaching themselves to its back with their talons and beaks, pulling and tearing at its hide until its strength is sapped and it falls to the ground, defeated." With frowns and clucks of sympathy, the raven's stock visibly plummeted.

"As for their cunning, I have read accounts of ravens who follow hunters and wait until they hide their catch, sometimes in snow up to three feet deep and then, after the hunters leave, dig it up themselves and steal it. Or ravens that follow fishermen who drop their lines in frozen fishing holes and then leave them there unattended. When a fish has been caught on the line and before the fisherman returns, the raven walks boldly up to the hole in the ice, takes a hold of the fishing line with its beak, pulls it up a few inches, steps on it firmly with both feet, then pulls up a few more inches with its beak and steps on that new length, repeating the process over and over, until the entire line is out of the water and the fish is landed." Skeptical guffaws erupted all around.

"They are clever and they have outwitted more than mere puppies many a time. There is even a story about a raven in Australia who waited regularly for a particular farmer to drive up to his gate. When his vehicle approached, the raven would fly along behind and then wait on a nearby fence rail while the driver stopped, opened the door, got out and walked over to the gate to open it. The raven would then dart into the car, turn off the engine with his beak and flit right out again. The confounded farmer watched it happen time and again. It seemed to be a game. It seemed to the farmer the raven was having fun and was not too impressed by the farmer's smarts, either." With howls of laughter and swatted thighs, the bird's prestige rebounded dramatically.

Chiron rubbed his nose and waited for his audience to settle. "In Norse mythology, there were two ravens named Thought and Memory. Their job was to fly across the world each day and return to the god Odin each evening to deliver a report of all they had learned." Something about that sounded familiar to the twins, but the connection eluded them.   Todd was reminded of something else.

"Chiron, I thought it was owls that are the wisest birds, the best hunters," he ventured.  His own heart soared every time Webster ventured within view and he had spent many hours peering into the night sky for a glimpse of this mysterious alter ego.

"Ah, the owl.  You ask a good question, Theodore." Chiron often called him by his formal name during study sessions.  "You may be interested to know a group of owls is called a parliament and they also hunt mostly away from their roost.  The owl in fact is the only real enemy of the raven.  It is susceptible to ravens in a group, the same as any other bird of prey, including eagles and turkey vultures.  Not only do ravens trick such birds, they band together in large numbers to dive-bomb them, making lots of noise and driving them from their territory. However, a lone owl, with its night-time stealth and hunting skills, can easily kill a raven in the dark."

As if in afterthought he added, "Beware, my children, of enemies who operate in the dark."

Herman sat up straight, eyes widening at the warning.  His heart gave a double-thump and he squinted at Chiron, peering closely to see if he had missed something.

"What enemies in the dark?  Did you see enemies in the dark, Chiron?  Around here?"

Chiron regarded Herman with sharp eyes.  He realized he had been half speaking to himself at that point, but was taken by Herman's charged response. Slowly, he leaned back into his chair, which creaked with the weight of his consideration.  He looked intently from one child to the next, as if making a fresh assessment of their demeanor, searching for a flicker of something nameless yet vital.  For their part, they barely breathed, aware that Chiron's focus had shifted suddenly from his story to them and despite having no idea why or what was now expected of them, they each experienced a palpable desire to measure up. Each one looked at him directly, refusing to blink or even move, basking in Chiron's scrutiny regardless of the motivation. He closed his eyes briefly, but not before a spark appeared that reflected the recesses of his ancient aspirations. Todd thought for a second that Chiron was going to smile.

"No, Herman, of course not. I merely point out different methods by which species operate in order to survive in their world as best they can. We need to take note of such methods and then choose our own path. There is something to be learned from every creature in this vast and mystical landscape. It is up to you to be observant, and thoughtful in your observation. It is up to you to be an adventurer of the mind.

"You may acquire the patience and cunning of the raven, the independence of the owl, the curiosity of the pup, or the tenacity of the crab. With such skills as those, you may respond to life's great call of adventure.

"You must be watchful. You must be prepared. You will find your quest. It may be the quest of your own choosing or tests and trials that are thrust upon you by the hands of others. But when you recognize it, you may have the opportunity to transform the world."

His words were met with silence, but he could almost hear the roiling of their thoughts, as they teemed with the romance of the hero path as he had described it, themselves in the title role. They were suddenly flush with the burning determination to prove their mettle, to suffer their setbacks, to overcome their obstacles, to prevail, to prevail, and bring back the elixir to Chiron himself.

You may have the opportunity to transform the world.

Herman's mouth hung open. No one had ever taken him seriously before, not about anything. Could it be that Chiron saw his true, noble character when he probed Herman's mind with his fiery eyes? Was it possible that Herman could play the role of Thought or Memory in Chiron's kingdom? He took a deep breath and straightened up slowly at that possibility, as if to fill the physical space worthy of such expectations. At the last second, with no hint of irony, he dropped his arms limply by his sides and simply bowed his head at Chiron's personage, acknowledging his new stature in both their eyes and accepting the responsibilities the role implied. Then he covered his mouth with both hands and smiled as wide as the Little Midshipman's outstretched arms.

Todd was studying the maps behind Chiron's head, considering them for the first time as other than the habitual backdrop of the larger-than-life sea captain before him.

Three glorious interpretations of the earth covered the long wall, three points in maritime history. Each rendering emphasized the vast swaths of open sea that enveloped and dominated the patchworks of terra firma. The land masses, struggling to keep afloat, braced for preservation along their jagged shorelines, enduring the relentless assault of the ocean's perpetual rhythms. Todd felt the power of the moon's pull on their coastlines as if he were being sucked by the watery tentacles himself. He swayed on his feet and had to reach for the desk to steady himself. He was left lightheaded, a swelling in his chest. He was suddenly finding it difficult to swallow, his body responding to a call his mind could not yet grasp.

The knuckles of Iris' fingers were white as she clenched the edge of the desk, her soaring heart searching for its true purpose, her feminine handicaps unchained by Chiron's words. He had looked at her often as he spoke; she was an equal in his eyes. Chiron believed that girls could be heroes, too, and he saw one in her, she just knew it. Suddenly, she smiled her saucy smile at him and scurried around the side of the desk to throw her arms around his neck and lavish upon him her biggest bear hug. He held her to his chest for a moment, and reveled in the gentle, sweet fragrance of her baby-fine hair.

He set her back on the floor next to him and said to them gruffly, "The path to glory does not pass by the greenhouse today, mind you. Now off." And with his hand he motioned them to the door.

They regrouped outside, intoxicated by their new stature, bound by the benediction of their master, flush with geniality for each other, of one mind without having discussed a word.

"The first thing we need to do is make a pact," Todd announced and was rewarded with eager nods. "If we are to be effective in our mission, we must be united, strong, and devoted to our cause. First and foremost, we must be trustworthy and disciplined." More nods. "We must forswear our enemies and we must be willing to prove our loyalty to each other at all times." That seemed to cover it.

"All for one and one for all!" exclaimed Herman, arm raised, fist beating the air in emphasis.

Todd gave him a deflating glare. His arm wavered, then fell slowly to his side.

"We are not the Musketeers, Herman. This is not child's play or didn't Chiron make that clear enough?" How quickly he was reminded of the twins' youth and the challenges they would present. He paused, contemplating whether or not it was worth continuing at all.

"All right," he said finally. "Your youth and inexperience are just handicaps we will have to live with. Now try to listen and do your best to pull your weight. And what about you," he pointed abruptly at Iris, "Ole Mother of Drowning Dolls, are you brave enough to take a blood oath? Are you? We may as well find out now what we are made of. Right here and now. Iris: declare."

Iris stepped forward, face still aglow with Chiron's faith. "I am ready, Theodore," she said solemnly.

Todd looked down at her appraisingly. "Okay. Good. And don't ever call me Theodore again.

"Now Herman. Are you ready for the call? Are you as brave as a sissy girl?" Cries of protest and Todd raised his hand at Iris, "Sorry, sorry, I didn't mean that, it just slipped out. Never mind. Relax. Herman! I'm talking to you!" Herman was laughing and rocking back and forth on his heels, relieved to have the focus away from the subject of his own bravery regarding physical blood-letting. He quickly swallowed the last laugh.

"Yes, sir!" He saluted.

"Oh geez. Could you stop playing games, Herman? This is serious stuff. And this is your last warning. Either you're with us one hundred percent or you're an outlier."

"I am not a liar!" He objected heatedly.

Todd appealed to the heavens with his eyes. "No one is calling you a liar, idiot. Now are you in or are you out?"

"I'm in," he stated tersely, swallowing a comment about idiots.

"All right. Good. Now here's the plan. Iris. Go get a pencil and some paper—no, make that a pen. A pen and paper. Herman. Go into the boat house and get that old flag hanging up on a nail by the dinghy. Then both of you. Meet me by the crossing of the 'T'Iris and You're Afraidies' in ten minutes. Hurry! We don't have much time before your mom or Maggie comes looking for us." Mute for once with excitement, the twins turned immediately and set off at a lope to fulfill their duties, exuding obedience.

Todd set off for the kitchen to find a paring knife. Halfway out the door again he paused, as if listening to something no one else could hear. He turned back and ran to his room where he opened his top drawer, picked out what he was looking for, regarded it briefly and stuffed it into his pocket, then left the room on cat feet, the abandoned drawer yawning wide.

They met back at the T'I & A, from now on known as their base. A little breathless, the twins awaited Todd's proclamation. He stood, tall and sober, on the largest rock at the brook crossing, and somberly contemplated the trickling water at his feet. Herman cleared his throat. Todd did not seem to hear. When he looked up, he regarded not his companions, but the trees and sky that shifted and swayed within the open space before him.

He turned to Iris and held out his hands, urging her to do his bidding. She tried to guess his meaning, nervous in case she were not keeping up properly with the demands of the initiation process, when he looked pointedly at the objects she held in her hands and motioned for her to pass them over. She jumped to attention and quickly handed him the pen and paper, only slightly wrinkled by then.

Todd sat down and studied the empty page for a moment. Then he began to write, laboriously at first and then rapidly as he tried to keep up with his own thoughts before they escaped him. When he was done, he took a moment to reread what he had written and was satisfied. He placed the paper and pen carefully on a dry rock, placing a stone on top to make sure they did not get away. He stood up again, and seemed taller, broader than he had just a few moments ago.

"There is a sacred oath we must swear to uphold from this day forward. It is a vow that we will respect at peril of death or torture, and be true to it from hence, um, from here on out, to whatever far corners of the world our quest shall take us. We shall never waver in our loyalty to the cause or our purpose in fighting for it. We shall never betray our trust or reveal our purpose to our enemy or anyone outside of our sacred circle. Upon pain of banishment! Forever and ever and ever, amen." He had raised his arms when he threatened banishment, and now he lowered them with dignity and deigned to acknowledge his subjects. Their mouths were round O's of wonder, like bewildered little strawberry-blond raven chicks, he couldn't help thinking.

Slightly deflated, he shuffled his feet for better positioning on his rock and mustered the deepest voice he could manage. "Raise your arms, with your fists clenched together like William Campion at the Equitable Life Assurance fire! This is our signal!" He was gratified at their perfect imitation of Maggie's description of the hands frozen to the window bars. Then he motioned for them to place their fists each on top of the other in a straight line of six strong fists as a show of unity and tribute. He nodded in approval.

"We shall never forget. We shall invoke his good memory in every deed we perform. We shall be respectful of his bravery and we shall practice his endurance in all challenges." They fell out of formation and the twins waited expectantly for the next pronouncement.

Todd did not reach for the paper where the oath was written, he had no need to read from it. "Now repeat after me: I hereby solemnly swear."

"I hereby solemnly swear." Voices raised in harmony.

"That I will perform my duties as a dedicated servant."

"That I will perform my duties as a dedicated servant."

"....To uphold the goals and ideals of a righteous world where good will prevail and our enemies will fear to tread! So help me God."

"To withhold our enemies and rightly fear no dreads! So help me God!!" They chimed like they had rehearsed it for days. They were so pleased at their performance that Todd did not have the heart to make them go over it again. He grimaced with fortitude. Then without warning, he pulled out the knife.

He brandished it before himself, turning it this way and that, pretending not to hear their intakes of breath, not to see Iris step back, or Herman pull Ba out of his pocket and hold it against his pale cheek.

The knife and his eyes glinted menacingly at each other, the grim smile on Todd's face more unnerving than the sharp blade in his hand. He looked over at the twins and said, "Sit," swishing the point of the knife toward the rock next to his. They obediently sat.

"Now is the time for the ceremonial washing of the feet. Place your feet in the sacred 'T'Iris and You're Afraidies' and scrub them clean." He sat down himself, carefully placing the knife on his side of the rock out of their line of sight, and reached down to demonstrate the ritual. They watched. Herman contemplated his Ba, then reluctantly tucked it into his pocket. He and Iris both reached down and began to rub their toes and heels and ankles. The cold water felt good and numbed their feet just a little.

Then they watched silently as Todd placed the knife reverently in the brook as well and rubbed it gingerly, to keep from slicing his fingers. He lifted it up dramatically in a cascade of water and held it gleaming and dripping at arm's length before him.

"Who's first?" he asked with exaggerated foreboding. When he looked over at the twins, he felt a pang of sympathy for the fear they were palpably trying to hide. "Ah. It should be I! As the leader of the quest, I should be the first initiated. Do either of you object? Feel free to speak up, now." Heads shook vigorously, no.

"Fine. Then we shall begin. It has been made clear to me in a vision that we should have a true hero as our figurehead, as our spiritual leader and guide through all our trials and triumphs. And it came to me that the perfect choice for such a leader would have to be a god, a true god, for nothing less would be worthy of the honor. And the god I choose," here he lifted his right leg out of the water and rested the ankle across his left knee, so the sole of his dripping foot faced Herman and Iris, at a level with their faces, "is Achilles! The greatest of Greek warriors and the bravest of them all!"

He peered curiously over his foot to examine his heel. He ran his finger along the calluses at its base. He tested the blade of the knife with his thumb like he'd seen in the movies.

"Achilles' one weakness, as you know, was his heel. So it is natural that we would make our blood pledge at that same point of weakness, as a reminder of our determination to overcome all of our own weaknesses.

"First, we make a cut." He made a motion to do so, but his hand wavered oh so slightly. He lowered the knife and continued.

"Then with our blood we will sign our sacred oath, thereby pledging our words of honor for all eternity." He tapped the knife thoughtfully on the rock beside him as he considered.

"Then we will walk a ceremonial walk from here to the sea, the home of the great sea god, Poseidon. To the waterfront, over by the dock," he added for clarity. He raised the blade to his heel again and paused. Dramatically he flourished it upwards.

"There we will cleanse our wounds and our souls with the eternal healing powers of the ocean!" He lowered the knife again reluctantly, fresh out of proclamations. He looked down once more at his foot. A solemn shadow gathered across his brow. With no more hesitation, he flicked the point of the knife along his skin, slitting a notch at the back of his heel where blood gradually began to bead up and seep. It was a perfect execution.

He studied the effect for awhile, then glanced up to see the twins intently watching his face for signs of pain or regret, probably both. He smiled at them reassuringly.

"Who's next?" An eternity passed while they each waited for the other one to volunteer. Remembering how Chiron always waited patiently for him to make up his own mind about things, Todd exercised patience. The silence went on for so long the twins became hopeful he was going to let the subject go and they started to relax, look around, inspect imaginary scabs, whistle a little tune.

"Aaah! What's that in Iris' hair?" Todd cried out suddenly. She squealed and shook her head, flicking her hair and swatting the air. Herman hopped up on his knees and leaned over to get a better view. Todd grabbed her foot and sliced.

"There," he smiled with satisfaction. "Look at this girl. Not even a whimper. You are a brave warrior, Iris, I must admit I wasn't convinced of it until now." He fashioned a grin of appreciation and awe. She stared back at him blankly, hands still raised, fingers still splayed, strands of hairs still floating around her head. She lowered her arms slowly and bent over her knees to regard the knife's workmanship. Blood. It was done. She was a warrior, Todd had said it, and here was the proof of it. She sat up then, her spine long and regal, a look of wonder on her face. She turned a sublime glance of satisfaction in Herman's direction. It was met with abject envy, his face betraying the overriding emotion he hopelessly felt: trapped. His eyes darted from one of them to the other, hating them, knowing the only way to make the situation worse was for him to run away, which was also the only thing he could think to do.

"I have an idea," Todd said in a conciliatory tone. "I have read where many soldiers, when put in danger, make use of their own secret talismans, which protect them, keep them from harm and allow them to perform their duties without fear or pain. How does that sound, kid?" He slapped him on the back jovially. Herman swallowed and nodded tentatively, still trying to formulate an escape plan.

"Give me your Ba. Come now, we just pledged our oaths to each other. From now on you can trust me in all things. Hand over the Ba."

Todd received the Ba gingerly between thumb and forefinger, trying not to disclose his disgust at the gray wad with dangling tentacles. He quickly dunked it in the stream.

"Hey, wait!"

He snatched it away from Herman's reach. "You do have to start to trust me, Kid. Watch me carefully, you have nothing to fear." And he yanked at the Ba with the fingers of both hands, stretching and pulling until it formed something like a length of knotted string with patches of fabric randomly intact. He made a show of wringing it out.

"Now, place your foot in the water again. There. Hold it in for a minute or so. See? This is not so bad, is it? Now keep still while I tie your talisman around your ankle for the fullest protection possible. Hold on there, sailor! No reason to jump ship! This will just take a second." He tested the tightness of the tourniquet by trying to fit his finger under it. It was good and tight and the circulation was surely being squeezed off. He patted the ankle and while his left hand was ceremoniously lifting the foot out of the water, he reached into his pocket and slipped out the knife. It was over before Herman had a good idea of the intent. The cut was deeper than the others, Todd had moved a little too urgently and sacrificed finesse, but the blood was gratifying to all concerned and dripped languidly onto the rock while Todd untied the knotted knots.

He held the dripping Ba before him, bowing chivalrously as he passed it back to its newly puff-chested owner. It was hard to say who was more proud, the inductee or the convincer of the inductee. Either way, there was a measure of relief all around.

Todd wiped his hands on his shorts and retrieved the paper, the official record of the sworn oath, lacking only the bloody signatures. They looked around for a flatter rock and settled for a stump off a ways from the T'I & Y. That was about the time they heard the first call from Maggie, but it was faint enough they felt comfortable ignoring it. It did remind them that time was short, though, so they hastily set about their gory business. Todd had a time of it convincing blood out of his own wound and had to dig the point of the knife in just a tad to get satisfactory results. He clumsily mashed his heel onto the bottom of the page, already crumpled, some of the words bleeding as well, from sympathy or dampness, lending their own drama to the promise they bespoke. Now the twins were eager to participate and shoved each other like un-sworn children in order to be next until Todd rapped his knuckles on both their noggins in order to restore the peace. He was beginning to question the value of banding for all eternity with infantile halfwits.

Perhaps the twins sensed his distain because they suddenly discovered restraint and remembered their status as brave soldiers ready to die for their cause. Herman gallantly gestured for Iris to be next, which was a good thing because the oozing from her cut was also slowing and mustered only a smudge of red for its pledge. Then Herman placed his bloody foot on the paper and was gratified to observe a few dramatic crimson drops trailing off the edge.

Todd blew on the signatures and waved the paper in the air to accelerate the drying, not sure what to do with it now that it was so sacred. He couldn't roll it up and store it in a log or something, knowing the smell of blood would lure unwanted snooping from the local residents. He shrugged his shoulders and announced, "Off to the ocean for the ceremonial cleansing! Follow me!" He ran in that direction, letting the oath flap in the breeze behind him, dripping and drying as he flew.

Except for a few surprised yowls, two to be exact, from the sting of the sea salt, the cleansing ceremony lacked drama and Todd did his best to build it up symbolically in their minds, but he was losing his audience, who were examining their wounds and rocking back and forth on the sand holding their feet as close to their eyes as they could manage, peering, prodding, brushing sand away, reinspecting.

Todd stood staring out to sea. Hands on hips (paper blowing gently at his side), shoulders thrown back, chin jutting genteelly before him, he looked the true part of a young god. He envisioned the hero path, repeating Chiron's words in his mind, feeling called to service, yet unsure of his rightful purpose and wondering if he would recognize it when it beckoned.

It was Maggie who beckoned. There she stood, undetected, legs splayed in the sand, fists mashed into her soft hips, cap askew, a strand of hair defying pins as usual. An unwitting imitation of Todd's stance, she made a poor picture of an authority figure indeed, but nevertheless managed to get her charges shuffling along in the direction of the house with her animated patter.

"Herman, are you limping?" She asked suspiciously.

"No, and I'm not bleeding at all," he added for emphasis.

"Oh, good heavens what's happened now?" She stopped abruptly and Iris, close behind, rammed into her buttocks with a woof. Maggie hardly seemed to notice, concentrating on Herman's foot. Iris bounced backwards and rubbed her nose. Todd snorted, barely suppressing an outright guffaw, a relief from all the tension of the last hour.

"Show me right now young brigand, you are not tracking blood across my clean floors." The parade arranged itself around the squealer, who reluctantly raised his foot for inspection.

"Well Little Jimmy Dickens, what have you done?" Dismayed at the preponderance of blood, she nimbly lifted him up and hauled him all the way back to the house, one ankle propped deftly over her forearm to keep the blood away from their clothing. She put him down gingerly just outside the screen door and looked around. That's when Todd remembered one other object of his planned ceremony. He reached into his back pocket and pulled out the clean, white handkerchief he had taken from his drawer, the second symbol from the Equitable Fire, and before she could stop him, had wrapped it around the wounded, bloody heel. He was becoming adept at swift movements.

"Now who do you think is going to get that blood out of your white handkerchief, Dr. Todd? Go on now, shoo. You and Iris get ready for your lessons. Good thing your mama is running late or she'd have our hides. You stay put, young man, we're cleaning out this cut but good and I don't want to hear a peep out of you." Todd and Iris headed off to sounds of protestation from the invalid. Well, he asked for it, telling her about the blood and all.

While they waited for Herman, and as yet Adrianne, Todd remembered the other part of the ceremony they hadn't performed. "The flag! Our symbolic flag has to be raised and its position on the flagpole has to have secret meanings that only we can understand. We have to find a time to raise it properly and learn our signals. We will meet tonight, right when it starts to get dark. We will sneak down to our base and perform our final ritual. Then we will be ready."

Iris peered up at Todd, who seemed to have grown in stature as the day wore on. "I just have one question," she ventured. He looked at her and waited.

"What exactly did we take an oath to do, anyway?"

Todd opened his mouth to answer, but nothing came out. He looked a little quizzical, a little stumped, frankly. As he tried to formulate a concrete answer from all the mumbo jumbo of the day's declarations, Herman piped up from behind them.

198

"I know," he announced quietly. "I know what our mission is." They turned and regarded him cynically. "Our mission is to track down the Intruder. You know, hunt for the Shadow."

Todd and Iris blinked at him. They looked at each other, then back. Encouraged, Herman leaned forward and whispered theatrically, "I saw it again last night after everyone was in bed. Out back at the edge of the garden." He waited for that to sink in. "It was real. And it was sinister." He wasn't sure what that word meant but he had heard it the other day on his favorite radio series, and it had given him the chills. Then, to seal the deal and to stave off skepticism or worse still, laughter, he added, "It will just be a test, of course, our first test." And he gave them a wink. Todd wasn't the only one who had grown in wisdom and guile that day.

# CHAPTER 11

## 1946

In 1911 Kristof bought a Mercer Raceabout Type 35R, a two-seated speedster that could hit 90mph. It was a four-cylinder T-head engine named for Mercer County, NJ, where it was built in a vacant brewery in the town of Hamilton. In 1917, he bought a 22/72 Touring car. By 1927 it was a Packard Roadster. In 1932, he drove off with his family to Philadelphia in his farewell exhibition of indulgence, the DeLuxe Eight 904 sedan limousine. He loved his cars almost as much as he loved his ships. They were an extension of himself; powerful, modern and imposing, and they kept the private man well-insulated, as he preferred.

Nick mulled over this parade of vehicles in his father's life; reined in, rarely tested, the growl of their engines more promising than fulfilling, his father's silent absorption as he drove, surging and holding back at once, frustrating both driver and passenger. This as he sat in his own jalopy, engine flooded and obstinate among the weeds where he had pulled over to gather his wits. He felt as though he tripped on his past with every step since his visit to Beechwood. If the past had weighed on his mind all these years and throughout the war, now it was oppressively front and center. He couldn't seem to retain a grasp on the present; it seemed so ephemeral. Only the past held substance and tenor. He shook his head, trying to clear the muddle, trying to throw off the groggy lassitude of sadness that felt like a physical weight engulfing his brain. The hangover had worn off, but not the bleary confusion that had nothing to do with the cognac he had consumed.

He despised himself for a further sign of weakness, that his conversation with Chiron hadn't galvanized him, but cowered him instead. He gripped the steering wheel and shook it until his body rocked and the sun glinted across the shivering windshield. He stopped in frustration and hit the steering wheel with the heel of his hand, fed up with self-loathing. Here he sat, mortified to admit he had driven back up the old road behind the estate, bereft and impotent and pitiable. He felt sucked in, a pawn in the saga of Beechwood.

A picture of long ago came to his mind. It was a chilly day, breezy on the bay. Chiron's cutter stood moored at the dock, swaying unevenly in the choppy waves, unresistant and unconcerned by the changeable weather. Nick was standing alongside dutifully, awaiting instruction as Chiron's assistant. Flapping his arms around his torso to keep warm inside his flimsy jacket, he contemplated telling Chiron about his nightmare. He risked sounding juvenile and was afraid of appearing weak, yet yearned to relieve the sense of foreboding that had followed him doggedly ever since he awoke.

When Chiron emerged from the cabin, something in his eyes seemed sympathetic, open to confidence, and Nick took courage. Chiron passed him the winch handle, stripped by overuse and slated for repair in the boathouse later. Accepting it with both hands, Nick blurted out his thoughts.

"I dreamt last night there was a fire. I watched it helplessly from somewhere far off and then when it was over, I came to look. Your boat had sunk, I couldn't tell if it was the Corinna," he indicated the cutter, "but when I looked down I saw that my hands were filled with ashes. Then, as I watched, something in the ashes began to move and that's when I woke up, terrified by the impossible stirring I felt in my hands."

Chiron shifted his feet with the rolling tide and motioned towards the boathouse. "I'll meet you inside," he said, turning back to the hatch dismissively. He arrived thirty minutes later carrying the leftovers of a roll of sand-painted canvas over his shoulder. He and Nick had glued wide strips of it onto the deck to help prevent slippage.

Nick, meanwhile, had built a welcome fire. The great fireplace was set into the corner of the large, high-ceilinged, rough-beamed room that housed the relics, supplies, tools and workspace for Kristof's and Chiron's extensive collection of seacraft. On either side of the fireplace were wide windows that let in the best light. That coupled with the comfort of the fire, whose warmth filled that quadrant cozily but quickly thinned to wafts of tepid vapors just a few yards out, the area was given over to the big work table as the prime space for drafting, repairs, projects and general congregating—or fiddling around, as Maria liked to say.

When Chiron entered, Nick looked over at him shyly.

"Ah, the best first mates can read a captain's mind!" Chiron proclaimed heartily, admiring the blaze over his shoulder as he tilted the roll of canvas into the recess of a storage cabinet. Nick flushed with pleasure.

Chiron stood before the fire with his arms outstretched, basking in the warmth and reflecting its glow off the ends of his unruly, graying hair, his flexed fingertips, the pewter buttons on his shirt and even the broad expanse of his gleaming forehead. Nick relaxed and sat down on one of the old wicker chairs stored here long summers ago and since forgotten by the main house. The faded cushion emitted a musty smell as he settled into it, a comforting smell that invoked countless childhood remembrances and set off a singular flare of contentment in his chest.

"Fire is transforming."[1]  Chiron spoke to the fireplace. Nick swung his attention to the speaker, not sure which fire he meant.

"Nicholas, you say you watched from afar, that you were an observer during your nightmare."

"Yes," was the muted response.

"Did you take any action yourself?  Did you speak?"

He shook his head, no.

"You said you were helpless.  What else did you feel?"

"I felt," thinking aloud, Nick screwed up his face because the word that came to mind didn't seem to apply to the situation.  "I felt ashamed.  And then, of course, I was scared, just really scared.  It was creepy. It was eerie in a way I never felt before."

Chiron, as always, accepted his words without judgment. He seemed to validate Nick's impressions.

"Dreams have the power to alter the life of the dreamer.  They are like myths that belong only to you.[1] They tell a story of conflict, repressed, that only you have experienced.  They symbolize your energies, they project your wishes, they predict your destiny, and will serve you whether you unravel them or not."  He paused there and was silent for a long time, long enough for Nick to think he was finished with his analysis and had drifted off into his own private musings. When he next spoke, his voice was carefully modulated and sounded to Nick like resignation, like regret.

"I think this dream is a premonition, Nicholas.  I can't tell you much more than that.  But I think it's something that hasn't happened yet."  He caught the intake of breath and the waggle of anxious eyebrows.

"Don't concern yourself, son, dreams are not literal. Think of this as a hint, a clue, a game you can puzzle out when you are lying in bed at night. Let me know when you formulate a theory, I am intrigued by your dream messengers. They seem determined and intuitive! Those are admirable traits to have within you, and not to be feared."

He turned, his coal eyes having absorbed the light of the fire, the glow now aimed at Nick's immortal core. "Remember, all the gods of all the myths are within you. They can be unruly, even brutal. But they are exalted. Learn to recognize them, accept them and embrace them for yourself. Then they will be able to guide you."

He paused and Nick found himself clinging to the arms of the chair, digging at the pattern of the wicker with his fingernails.

"The fire of the gods is unquenchable. But when it is within you, it is your energy.[1] Yours. Trust that, and don't hold back." Nick gulped, then smiled bravely, to show he was equal to the demands of gods.

Though Chiron had his quarters in the gatehouse even then, he was not at Beechwood often, nor for extended periods. He came between voyages and then spent nearly all his time on his boat, often went missing for days but would be sure to return with a small gift for Thea, for Maria and for him, Nicholas, his devoted admirer.

To this day Nick hadn't come up with the first idea of what that dream might have meant. It hadn't been long after, in fact, that he simply shrugged it off, convinced that Chiron was trying to cajole him out of his fears with his claim of powerful gods in his dream mind. After that he avoided thinking about it at all, which to an adolescent was the very solution.

But now, as he shifted uncomfortably behind the steering wheel and leaned forward to peel the back of his damp shirt from the seat back, he thought maybe it was time to reconsider the gods within him. Maybe he was ready, about ready to reexamine what Chiron had said.

He sat in his car all morning and well past noon. He had long since opened the doors to admit whatever meager breeze might cross the narrow lane and now shared his vehicle with what was surely more than one cricket, a cornered bumble bee and a spider generating an ambitious cobweb between the driver's side-view mirror and the window vent. These haphazard occupants had passed the day together affably enough within their two-door universe.

When he swung the doors closed and walked away, he did not check to see the damage incurred by the taut foundation of the spider's web, though he had followed its construction intently enough.

He headed straight toward the beach a quarter mile away and then cut left along the sand to the boathouse. His approach was obscured by the pines and ignored by the plovers scurrying along the water's edge. He lifted the wrought iron latch, noting its well-oiled sheen. He pushed the flimsy door inward, exposing startled dust particles and the sawdust scent of decades of nautical pursuits.

He stood for a moment inhaling the memories, hefting the breadth and height of the real-life space with his eyes, savoring the smell of long forgotten boathouse exertions that yet permeated the heavy air. He sauntered among the dry dock vessels, running his hand along their hulls, craning to see above the sides for a glimpse of the polished decks, the upholstered seats, the bronze cleats and pulleys, the winking glass of the cabins, the shadows of past voyages. He admired the exposed keel of each sailing craft, made of lead and contributing up to half of the total weight of the boat. On the catboats and the cruisers, the very ones on which he learned to sail, the white spruce masts rose majestically to the rafters, lacking only wind and a mainsail to lift them off, to escape the confines of their indoor purgatory.

He remembered standing just here when he overheard his father say to someone, a dinner guest perhaps, "If they acted above board, that would change everything. That's all I ask." Nick had been struck by the tremble of frustration in his father's voice. Days later, while they trolled the sound in their old fishing boat together, he asked his father about it.

"Above board? What does that mean?" His father repeated congenially. "Well, in the old days pirate ships gained close proximity to merchant ships by hiding most of their crew below decks, giving a false sense of security to the crews of the ships they wished to overcome. Appearing non-threatening, the captain would allow the pirate ship to approach, treating it as a fellow commercial vessel in distress. The result was usually disastrous for the faithful captain.

"So back in those days, an honest ship that openly displayed its crew on deck was said to be 'above board.'"

Nick shook his head remembering that day, how he had expected Kristof to ask why he wanted to know, how the silence that ensued had seemed hollow, like a missed opportunity, a deflating omission. He turned his head to look for that old trawling boat, wondering where it might have ended up. What he saw outlined by the dimming light of the salt-streaked windowpanes across the room stopped his heart cold. His hand fell slowly from the keel he had been caressing. He could not command his senses, he could not even draw a breath.

She was there, or a mirage of her was there, a few strides away, her piercing blue eyes beholding him, bewitching him, stabbing him to the quick. He turned back to face the streamlined hull, a resting place for his forehead.

"You do not wish to know me, then." She ventured softly. He pressed against the mahogany so hard he thought he might shift the boat in its frame. He squeezed his eyes as tightly as they would go, in hopes of erasing that voice, dispersing its sylphlike embodiment just beyond his reach, knowing he could not withstand its scorn. Then, otherwise paralyzed, his eyes flew open with the fear that she may in fact have disappeared in the interim, not sure how long he had remained insensible. Gently, gingerly, he placed his hands on either side of the hull before him and pushed himself off. Straight-armed, he focused his eyes on the wood and resisted an urge to scrape off a particle of algae that had somehow escaped detection. He bowed his head and chuckled self-mockingly, then lowered his arms and turned to view Thea in full; enchanting, graceful, beloved as ever.

He grinned sheepishly then, reaching up to pat the boat beside him, tapping it nervously while he formulated a response that would not result in scaring her off. His mind would not cooperate, it was no judge of propriety at the moment but his heart succumbed to impulse and he felt himself striding boldly to stand before her. Unhesitating, he grabbed her hand with both of his, clasping it, engulfing it and expressing his joy at holding it, all that in one spontaneous motion. Her surprise reflected in her eyes as pleasure and she smiled at him openly. Tears sprung to his eyes when he saw that and he dropped her hand, swiping at his tears apologetically. "I'm sorry! I'm sorry, you are just so beautiful and…real. And you didn't run away from me, I thought you would run away from me if I ever came near you again. I thought I'd wreck any chance I had of getting close to you so long as you knew I was coming. And look what happened! I turned and you were here and I... I'm the one who would have run off if my legs had been able to carry me. I was that afraid of ruining the fantasy of your forgiveness. That afraid." He wanted to reach out again to touch her, lost in the awe of her presence, her solid form, her material proof of his desperate prayers.

"It was you who closed the windows in the kitchen the other day before the storm, wasn't it?" she inquired simply.

He blushed, discovered. He wondered if someone else had guessed and told her, or if she had seen him that day after all. His coloring, his silence was admission enough.

"I knew it was you. I knew somehow you were home. The air was crackling when I awoke from my nap and I felt your nearness as if you'd announced it. At first I imagined I had been dreaming. But then I knew it was you, you had come back after all this time, even though we feared so that you had been lost in the war." Both anguish and relief played across her features. She cocked her head then and inspected the toll the years had taken, assessing which parts were due to the havoc of the war, which parts indicated other, personal scars. Mostly, she wanted to glean what was left of the young man who had been capable of imparting such happiness at one time, when time and happiness had coexisted. She pressed her hand to her breastbone, as if to contain the turmoil within, the turmoil that did not show on her face except in the slight flush across her cheekbones.

When she noted the discomfort her scrutiny was causing him, she caught his eye and smiled indulgently, "I have seen you look worse, Nicholas, surely you remember that. And I might even detect an improvement or two if you would stand still long enough." He stopped swaying from one foot to the other then, slowly unfolded his arms, unclenched his jaw and withstood her gaze humbly. He couldn't help relishing her small compliment. She saw through him and laughed lightly. Perhaps he hadn't changed so much, his boyish transparency irresistible still.

Arms hanging limply at his sides, he allowed himself to cautiously assess her appearance, hoping rashly to be encouraged by evidence of good health.

Thin, yes. She had always been slight. Pale, somewhat, but color marked her cheekbones disarmingly. Eyes bright, a little tired maybe. Nothing had happened in the interim years to dampen her undeniable beauty or grace. He was both relieved and captivated by her delicate appeal. He refused to feel hopeless or discouraged by Chiron's report. Chiron was too close to her. If Chiron had a weakness surely Thea was it. He promised himself he would keep that in mind. For now, the tension having abated just enough to allow other emotions to unravel within him, he noticed butterflies, old-fashioned butterflies, making him feel giddy, luring him into the simple joy of seeing her, his heart's muse, within arm's length, only one weary, aching, arm's length away.

"Please tell me how you are feeling," he was shocked to hear himself say. He had never been forthright in his life and wasn't sure why he was starting now, but a sensation was beginning to grow in his chest or his gut or his dream mind that it was time to act decisively, trusting the gods of his war years, his tortured years of self-doubt, his young gods who had surely acquired some wisdom and confidence in all that stolen time. And he wasn't willing to fall back on restraint any more. Of all the things he dreaded, perhaps what he dreaded most was the aftermath of self-recrimination that followed every exercise in timidity, every missed chance to inject honest gusto into some experience he never truly had. At this moment, he wanted to throw off that mantle with a reckless flourish of defiant resolve, flinging his restraint from across his shoulder blades dramatically and permanently. Thea watched as he rotated those very shoulders back until they were squared, making him a little taller, as he lifted his chin slightly and the shadow in his eyes began to move off, emitting a lightness she had not observed before. It was alluring, that stance. It was enough to make her forget whatever reservations she had carried with her into the boathouse after following him from a safe distance, cutting through the scrub, peeking in a side window for the guilty enjoyment of observing him undetected and allotting herself a few moments of pure indulgence. With reservations, surely. But the privilege of seeing him alive and unharmed was immeasurable.

"Well, I am here," she allowed. "I walked here from the house. That is an extended distance for me these days, I admit it, but I feel fine. I am guessing Chiron filled you in on his concerns for me." She looked at Nick as if accusing him of being in cahoots with her godfather. "You know how he is, so serious about everything. You remember." She smiled confidentially. She could chide as well as Chiron could and who was he going to believe after all, she seemed to be asking. Then with a gleam in her eye, she held her arms out like a ballerina and pointed her right foot on the floor in front of her. She paused, giving him time to step back a ways, then raised her leg high, luffing her cotton skirt into the air as she twirled about on her left foot, all the way around. She lowered her right leg slowly, gracefully, then her arms, the flexed wrists and dainty fingers floating to her sides at the last.

He bowed to her and held out his hand, "May I have this dance, mademoiselle?" he offered.

She laughed and placed the hand he requested against her breastbone again, shaking her head ruefully. "I'm afraid that was my dance, kind sir, you will have to be quicker to offer next time." He colored again, feeling naïve at believing her show of vitality. This time he reached out and took her free hand in his and said, "Come sit down on the bench over here by the window. The sun is behind a cloud and I don't want to lose sight of you again so soon." She let him pull her, and believed she did feel better already.

Once they were seated, however, an uncomfortable silence set in that became more strained with each unspoken breath. He had let go of her hand, letting his own rest awkwardly near her knee, then felt even more awkward about moving it away, so it lay there belly-up like a beached fish that held their gaze until he felt compelled to speak just to get her attention away from it.

"I met the children, you know, I met your nephew Todd, he's a corker, and polite, he's very polite, too. They gave me a tour of the new ice skating rink."

It took her a moment to react, she seemed lost in thought, but she looked up at him quizzically. He laughed abruptly to break the tension and stuffed his hand in his pocket.

"Well okay, they took me to see the twin brooks that have a very sophisticated name that I cannot pronounce and showed me the plans to dam it up in time for a winter wonderland of frozen delights. They had me quite convinced they could do it and a little jealous that

I wasn't asked to help." He tried to read her features. "I haven't given up on wrangling an invitation from them yet." That got a smile, small but a beginning.

Nick jabbered on, his nervous energy compelling him to talk, saying anything that might get her to warm up again. He was frustrated at having let their easy banter slip away, he could not bear the strain much longer. He felt she was about to fly off.

His eyes flitted around the room, his mouth gone dry. Desperation was billowing in his chest when he glimpsed an object lying on the ledge of the mantelpiece. It struck him, stopping his chatter mid-sentence. Thea followed his gaze. He stood up at once, sure he was mistaken. It seemed impossible, but there it was. He looked down at Thea, his nerves melting, a sheepish grin stealing over his face. He ducked his head self-consciously and stepped over to the fireplace to claim its artifact. Carrying it reverently with both hands he sat down again, offering it to her with shy anticipation.

It was a doorknob. It was simple brass, unpolished yet gleaming softly in the waning afternoon light, heavy in the tender hands that presented it. If there had been any other sound in the vast boat house he would not have heard her slow intake of breath. She looked up at him, speechless, blushing and grinning at him with her eyes. Their discomfort dissolved as they were captivated by the rush of memories and shared secrets from their true-life idyll, the proof of it lying here between them, the undeniable proof.

In no time they fell into their easy posture of old. They recounted the hours of privacy afforded them by this dear doorknob, the exhilaration of escaping from prying eyes, the thrill of being alone. It had been idyllic, hadn't it? In those days, they had rashly proclaimed their willingness to bear any punishment as the price of their eternal love.

The doorknob fitted onto the spindle in the storage room door, across the room opposite the fireplace. They had sneaked in the boat house one dreary afternoon in late fall under the pretense of looking for a lost rain jacket when they heard footsteps approach and in their guilt, frantically searched for a hiding place. Nick grabbed hold of the doorknob of the storeroom, stripping it from its threading, rendering the hiding place inaccessible and leaving them helplessly exposed when Clarence walked in. Nick thrust the knob behind his back and the two of them sidled out with varying degrees of embarrassment and high-pitched inquiries about the missing jacket. They were very lucky it was Clarence who discovered them.

In the long days before they schemed another chance to be alone, Nick consumed hours of contemplation over that doorknob, which began to take on a romantic symbolism burnished by time and yearning. He stopped mid-yearn one day, catching the knob like a baseball in his palm, struck with a plan. Surely the doorknob was fixable. And at the same time, if a missing knob could keep them from getting into the storeroom, it could keep everyone else out! He immediately darted from his room and raced to the boat house where he scoured the area for a hiding place for his new key of deception. A scuttle built low into the wall nearby proved ideal, its dark recesses casting no hint of its clandestine employment. From there, it was easy enough to thread the doorknob onto the spindle for access to the storeroom, then unscrew it and carry it with them into their sanctuary, closing the door and sealing off the world from their trysts. It was sublime.

What lack of blame or distrust Thea showed toward Nick that afternoon over a decade later was remarkable by any measure. Artless or remiss, perhaps it portrayed too transparently the level of sophistication her sheltered world afforded.

They touched, his hand tracing her hairline, her hand caressing his arm, their limbs intertwining easily, luxuriantly. They marveled at the boon of second chances, at the lifting of their grief, the grief they hadn't even known if the other one shared. The blessing of relief was beyond expression.

Mostly, they rejoiced at the possibility of making up for all the pain they had inflicted or endured. They believed at that moment even that was possible. The shadows deepened around them, the slant of daylight bathing only the rafters by then, but they did not notice. They felt, they heeded, they sensed, they beheld each other like lovers do; kinetically, acutely, exclusively.

The door banged open against the wall adjacent, stopping the hearts of even the mice beneath the floorboards.

"Maggie, turn on the lights! It's in here, I know it is!" Herman demanded, his impatience undisguised. A brief shuffle and the overhead lights blinked on brazenly. A short interlude ensued where four pairs of dilated irises adjusted themselves to the sudden brightness. All four sets were anxious, two at being discovered, two because of what was yet undiscovered.

"It's gotta be in here somewhere, Maggie, there's nowhere else to look! And I was here this afternoon, I had it then, I'm sure of it. It was still wet from the initiation ceremony and all tangled, practically in shreds, gee. Look in that storage locker, will ya? I'll go over…"

He gasped and fell back a step. "Whoa, Nelly!"

He was instantly on the defensive. "Hey. What are you doing here, huh? What are you doing here with our Thea? Huh?" His little hands formed fists and he adjusted his stance to balance his weight for assault. Then he heard a soft hum and a whimper off to his left. He looked over to see Maggie with her hand across her mouth, her arms trembling, tears rising in her lower eyelids. He paused. He looked where she was looking, at Mr. Nick. He looked back at her dumfounded. What was going on here and how does Maggie know anything about this sucker? He had forgotten his professional opinion that she was his mother. Then Nick was standing, smiling like a fool, reaching his arms out, wait a minute, and striding over to Maggie like she was something precious and hey, he's not going to grab her, oh no, wait, what's he doing hugging her? And she's hugging him back, is she crazy?

"What's going on here?" he demanded petulantly, taking a tentative step forward. No one heard him. They were looking at each other now and if the light weren't shining at such a funny angle Herman would have sworn Nick had tears in his eyes as well. The world was going mad. Just as he started to suspect Nick had something to do with the disappearance of his Ba, his nemesis spoke.

"Maggie, my darling Maggie I have missed you so! You beautiful old girl! Give me another hug. I thought you would have changed at least a little bit by now!" He actually beamed at her, obviously confident she would be thrilled to hear his phony compliments. Herman's mouth fell open and his eyes bugged out when that proved exactly right. She giggled! With delight!

"Oh, you go on you scoundrel," only she didn't sound like she meant it. "I wouldn't forgive you for a minute except I'm so overjoyed to see your wicked hide all in one piece. I despaired of that I surely did." Even though she was scowling, her eyes smiled like a young girl. What kind of a spell does this fellow cast, anyway? And why do the women always fall for it? He remembered Iris acting coy and even his mother falling for all those slimy manners.

"I have so much to make up for, Maggie. I hope you will be among the first ones to forgive me." Without letting go of her, Nick glanced over at Thea and Herman noticed instantly the sudden change in Maggie's countenance. She had followed Nick's glance. It didn't take much for her to figure out the entire situation, including the deep circles under her girl's eyes. She stiffened noticeably, drawn back to the reality of Nick's reappearance. He felt the change under his hands as he held her arms and he glanced back at her curiously.

"What's wrong?" He studied her wooden features, so recently forgiving. "Ah. I see. I can tell where your loyalties lie these days, my old nurse, and I can't say as I blame you." He released his grasp. "Try not to worry too much, darling, I will do everything in my power not to inflict any more harm on those you love. And if I fail in any way, I know I will have you to set me straight." He smiled sadly.

"Yes, Mr. Nick," she said formally, "you are right about that." She turned to Thea then. "Thea, my dear, it's almost dark. We should get back to the house before it gets pitch black out there. If you guide me and my poor old eyes, I will hold your arm and Herman can follow. Come now, Herman, open the door for us, do as I say, there's a good sailor." And she set about prattling their way out of the boathouse and up the path, deaf to Herman's protestations about the missing Ba and blind to the forlorn man she left standing under the ceiling light's glare.

# CHAPTER 12

## 1946

Heph looked up from his morning paper as Adrianne walked into the breakfast room. She was wearing a blue-checked sun dress with white piping at the waistline, across the sweetheart neckline and along the halter straps as well, tied neatly behind her well-bronzed neck. Her hair was swept into a bun, allowing only the shortest tendrils to linger between her skin and any cooling breeze. Baby blue skimmers covered her unstockinged feet, and were immediately sloughed off upon sitting. She set her cup and saucer on the table and reached for the sugar bowl, shaking her head.

"I know you told me this is the best way to break Herman's dependence on that dreadful blanket scrap, but it's about to drive me to distraction, his obsession with finding it. Tell me the truth now, Heph, you didn't take it yourself, did you? Because I'm about to hire my own private detective to track it down and end this torture."

"Oh for heaven's sake," the newspaper rustled impatiently, "you know I'm way too cowardly a father to do something smart like that. I'm afraid it's genuinely missing and good luck in your search but that detective's fee is coming out of the new dryer fund, so help me."

Adrianne sighed and blew a straggling wisp of hair from her face. "We've truly looked in every crevice in this house and unearthed every lost item since before the twins were born but not a hint of that Ba. Someone's got to deal with him, I'm convinced this time it's really gone."

"Why not send him to Thea?" Heph's eyebrow cocked cleverly. "She seems to have a calming effect on even that devious rascal."

"O-oh," Adrianne's eyes widened meaningfully. "I knew there was something else I had to tell you. I swear I am getting nothing done at all around here and can't concentrate on a thing." The newspaper knew enough to lower itself to lap level. "Thea came to me last night and asked me something I didn't know how to answer. I told her I would speak to you about it. She told me she had run into our friend Nick Karras." She stopped, perplexed. She turned her body to face Heph squarely. "I think we missed something somewhere."

"Besides the Ba? In one of those crevices?" He smiled innocently.

She frowned and closed her eyes in forbearance. "You will be officially in charge of the Ba search in short order if you don't mind yourself," she warned. "I think we missed a big chapter of the Karras family mystery if the heightened state of Thea's nerves is any indication." That meaningful gaze again.

"What is it?" he asked soberly enough.

"She asked me if we would mind if he came here to visit her from time to time."

He decided a pause was called for here. He paused. He considered. He took a big breath and blew it out. He waited. Then he looked at his wife with a mischievous glint in his eye.

"That poor, battered veteran of the second world war had something more in mind than just inspecting the new owners of his childhood home after all then, I would guess."

She was taken aback, at first affronted by his teasing inference. Her face showed its disapproval. Then, as he remained silent, she examined the situation again and gradually found herself biting her lip to keep from smiling. She chuckled. She sat back in her chair and let her arms dangle by her sides, relieved.

"Sometimes you are right, my sweet, romantic husband. I guess there's really nothing underhanded going on. She did come right out and ask me. I just worry so about her health. I feel overly protective of our Thea, we all do, even you. But I guess maybe a little happiness wouldn't be such a dangerous thing, at least not for her, I hope. But if you had seen her! Her color was high, she was breathing a little faster, at first I thought she was taking ill." She felt compelled to justify her concerns. Heph did not respond.

Adrianne stood up from the table. "I will tell her it's fine with us. I'll tell her right now. In the meantime, I'm sending Herman in here to you." And she disappeared around the corner before he could formulate a protest.

That very evening, Herman stood dolefully looking out the window toward the ocean, vaguely suspicious that his Ba was at the bottom of it somewhere, when Heph and Poseidon ambled across the garden below. He watched them idly, wondering not for the first time if Poseidon had in fact done the same thing with his Ba that he had done with that silly doll. Then he jerked to attention. The garden! How could he have forgotten to search the garden? Geez Louise, that's the ticket. He pushed off the window sill and with rising hopes, trotted down the stairs.

The garden was grand, the plan intricate, the inspiration Maria and Chiron. It had originally been designed by a notable landscaper from New York when the house was built, but the result was stiffly traditional and uninspired. Maria replanted gradually, often assisted by Chiron, reshaping as they went and instilling an eye for color, shape and whimsy that belied their reserved demeanors. Viewed now from the terrace at the back of the house, the overall design was a large scalloped shell shape with ridges and borders of low boxwood, as well as sections of moonshell and nautilus designs, each spiraling in rich lanes of greens, blues and purples, with occasional yellows and pinks. Near the top of the scallop was a pool of water choked with water lilies, fecund and alluring. A smaller version of the scallop surrounded this pool, the space filled in by a collection of thousands of shells from around the world; a source of great curiosity, speculation and untiring inspection by children and adults alike.

Within the boxwood borders were such favorites of Chiron's as white turtle-heads, Turk's cap lilies in yellow, blue boneset, wild crane's bill with their lavender and purple flowers, anemones, wild comfrey to attract butterflies, jacks-in-the-pulpit and evening primrose, which opened at dusk and closed again everyday by noon. Tufts of purple love grass intermingled at the ends of rows like exclamations. Filling in everywhere else was wild ginger, a spongy, soft ground cover.

Along the bottom of the shell facing the ocean front beyond, planted a terraced level lower, was Maria's rose garden in variations of color from white to ivory to pink to red to deepest burgundy and back again. She chose the Alba Maxima with its double blooms of aging white, the cabbage rose, the repeating noisettes and her favorite, the Dupruy Jamain, the huge double roses of deep cerise-red.

Many of the peonies across the top of the garden, planted in a wide, graceful swath of scallops, had begun to fade. A row of their petals dropped in a concurrent path along the grass below. The earliest of the vibrant pinks and soft whites of just a few days ago were showing signs of browning and drooping with encroaching exhaustion.

Outside the shell on either side were shrubs of mountain laurel, swamp azalea and maple leaf viburnum. Beyond those were the ferns that edged the pines and disappeared into the wooded sections taking their own paths. Their carefully planned randomness included the grey-green marginal wood ferns, maidenhair ferns with their delicate black stems and lady ferns, whose red stems sported lacy fronds of green.

The fiery reds and oranges missing from the formal garden were rampant along the patio, lush with orange trumpet vines entangling the arbors, red azaleas, now finished, and a strikingly unusual wine-colored hydrangea that flourished under Chiron's care.

Herman passed by these rousing displays unseeing, focused on the garden paths that veered toward the left and disappeared into the pines on that side. He had taken that route to the boathouse to get the flags Todd had requisitioned for their initiation ceremony.

A quick perusal of the garden proved unsatisfactory, so he bent over to rifle through the plantings with his hands, peering intently through the growing dusk, even kicking at some overhanging leaves to uncover camouflage, finally getting on all fours to scour inch by inch, expecting any moment to spot a shred of faded cloth peeping from under a leaf, just the tiniest hint of the hiding place his Ba had found, a corner even, that he could snatch from concealment triumphantly and never, ever, ever let out of his sight again. He made his way well into the trees, which had been searched twice yesterday, and all the way back again to the fountain before admitting defeat. Still on his knees despite the jagged, broken shells and sharp edges, he sank onto his haunches, his shoulders slumped, his head hung low, his hands resting on his thighs helplessly, palms turned up. A tear fell into one, then the other. There was nowhere left to look and that was the truth of it. His cherub lips trembled, afraid he could not bear the pain of such loss.

First he heard a rustle, followed by a low utterance and a soft, answering giggle. He sucked in his breath and leapt up instantly, afraid of being seen like this, caught crying like a baby. He scurried to the edge of the garden and rolled under the stone bench placed in the outside curve of the great scallop. His heart raced as he maneuvered to get a view of the approaching voices without giving away his presence. He didn't have to wait long. A pair of men's canvas shoes and a pair of sandals approached, close to each other and in step together. Pants and a skirt. Arm linked in arm. Faces now exposed clearly and unmistakably in the moonlight. When he recognized Thea and Nick in cahoots not three yards away from his hiding spot, his head shot up in dismay and smacked sharply against the seat of the bench above. He groaned loudly, wincing and clamping his hand over his mouth, frozen with the fear of discovery. He held his breath until he realized their voices had continued without pause, whereupon he dared to reposition himself for a better view of his quarry. He was mystified by their lack of awareness of their surroundings. They'd never get a job in his agency, for one thing.

Emboldened by his apparent invisibility, he leaned an ear out from under the bench and tuned in to their subdued remarks, still rubbing the top of his throbbing head.

Thea was pointing upwards. "The crescent moon is my favorite," Herman heard her say. Gazing languidly, she sighed. "Its beauty is refined, yet ephemeral. She is only showing a small measure of herself, hiding the rest behind a shadow. It makes her mysterious. She appears delicate to the world while keeping the bulk of her strength hidden quietly from view."

Nick considered the moon's discretion for a moment, then chuckled self-deprecatingly. "Do you mean to suggest that moon up there is not my own? Do you claim it for yourself as well?" He shook his head and laughed, realizing somehow he was only half kidding.

He smiled ruefully then and said, "As far back as I can remember, even when I was a kid, there have always been two things that were...so beautiful to me I couldn't bear to look at them for more than a few moments at a time. I look, yet before long I feel that I can't withstand another second of such anguish. And I look away. I have to look away." He paused humbly.

"What is it? What has such an effect on you?" she asked, but her eyes turned back to the sky.

He was fingering one of the flowers. He looked up and replied quietly, "The moon." He considered it for a few seconds, head angled to one side as if acknowledging an old conspirator who often liked to tease him. Then he looked down before adding, "And these. Peonies."

He cupped a dark-rimmed peony of softest pastel in his rough, thick palm. "Always, my mother's peonies." He regarded it, then glanced off to the side. Finally, he spoke again.

"And neither one approaches the sweet ache I feel whenever I look at you." He turned then to face her.

She did not move. His words vibrated within her breast, above the sound of her heartthrob. The air was still, the heavens were calm, gravity bound her feet by earthly decree and yet she soared, weightless, untethered from other restraints of purpose or place. She was freed from the boundaries of time; time

223

allotted, time stolen, time squandered or begged. It was the moment of purest joy that captured every moment before and the promise of every moment yet to come. The past and present met here, in this instant and reconciled their purpose to whatever end God deemed fitting. It no longer mattered what God deemed, she wanted for nothing.

Her eyes shone as she looked up at him. There was neither artifice nor restraint in her regard. He saw the purity of love she had carried through all the years of her abandonment, and none of the resentment or pain he had dreaded. He closed his own eyes against the torment of this understanding, and his old fears began to churn, rising biliously, coming dangerously close to overwhelming him. But this time his fierce desire to fulfill a vow of restitution he had pledged to pursue at any cost galvanized him and he opened his eyes to face her once again, passion and tenderness mixed in his gaze. His face conveyed his earnest intent, his lips parted with longing. Desire pumped through his long-dormant body. He closed his eyes once more just briefly in relief at finally feeling his own feelings, and submitting to his vulnerability before her. This was the sweetest emotion of all, and the first time he had ever felt it.

He kissed her. He held her in his arms and wondered at the years he had languished without this exquisite joy and why he had idly allowed it to elude him. He vowed not to let it slip away. He knew there was no price he wouldn't pay for this privilege and he had an idea of what that price might be. He wrapped his arms more tightly round her until he could feel her pulse and match his own to its rhythm. Then he bent forward and lifted her off the ground, with one arm firmly behind her shoulders, the other under her knees, and carried her over to the bench, mercifully the bench on the opposite side of the garden from where Herman lay snoring gently.

For several long, luxurious moments she leaned against his chest, his arm protectively around her. She shivered once and he wrapped his other arm across her body, rubbing her skin to warm it. It was a balmy night and redolent with the fragrance of countless blossoms.

"When your father took you away, did you resist? Did you try to talk him out of leaving, did you talk to him about us? Or did you want to escape the scandal of having been caught with a servant of your family's household? I've always been so ashamed of making you feel that way, of embarrassing your family like that." She kept her face low, half buried in his shirt front.

He stiffened and she cringed, the old feelings of disgrace closing around her throat once again. She wanted to bite back the words, deafen them, erase them and leave the subject alone forever, what did it matter now anyway. How many nights she had played out the storyline where he escaped his father and returned to Beechwood to steal her away to marry her and live contentedly, even in poverty, where they could have been happy together and no one would have judged them or shunned them or kept them apart. For a long time she believed it would happen that way, which was why she fought Chiron and stayed longer at Beechwood than she might have before moving in with her brother. She was so sure all she had to do was wait for him and ever since had wondered what she could have done to force his return. To this day she yearned for the answer to that question. But even now, she was met only with silence. She sagged a little in his arms and closed her eyes, though she could not bear to pull away from his embrace.

He expelled a great breath of air. She thought he was exasperated. He leaned his cheek against the top of her head, and squeezed her closer, but did not speak. A long, suspended moment passed. Night had indeed fallen, the garden was in darkness. But when she opened her eyes at last, Thea could see the light from the back hall windows still illuminating the patio serenely.

"If I had known you thought I ran away from you, I would have gone mad. I was sent away almost immediately after arriving in Philadelphia as the greenest useless sailor on my father's ship, the Leonardas, which embarked for Chios and returned weeks later without me. If I were not the owner's son I would have been strung from the masthead for repeated drunkenness, although there was no alcohol allowed aboard any of my father's vessels and I don't remember much about the voyage myself. I was ultimately transported to Lassithi Province in Crete, where I was met in port by my grandmother and some burly male cousins who seemed primed to run after me the moment I might take a fancy to being alone. They were my constant, lively companions and probably would have been good company if I had been sensible to their attendance. I did take to the local ouzerie, which was surely a relief to them and the most common destination for our endless idle evenings. During the day, I helped them build a new fishing boat where my knowledge and skill astounded them, low as their expectations were. I was there for five months, during which the only development seemed to be the deepening of the creases in my grandmother's forehead when she looked at me. I didn't learn much Greek and no one bothered to speak English to me, or maybe they did but I don't remember it. I was the burden that sometimes ate their food, but I paid well. I bought their ouzo night after night certainly. Ever since that time I gag when I smell anise in any form, licorice candy or anything like it. And when I think of my Yiayiá and her tired kindnesses, I blush with shame. I was upright and occasionally responsive, but in truth I was blacked out senseless in every meaningful way."

Nick placed his hand under her chin and lifted it gently. She met his gaze, pain flickering in her eyes as she searched his imploringly. "For the first time," he began, "and long, long overdue, I want you to know how sorry I am for all you suffered. I would not have blamed you, how could I? I knew you would not refuse me anything, and I, I know I took advantage of that. I was so wrong and so foolish and I risked your entire life's happiness. But I meant to marry you, you cannot ever doubt that. That's the way I justified my actions. Our actions. I knew there would never be another woman for me and I convinced myself it was about fairness and devotion and the bond that love-making seals, those are all the things I told myself and none of them was valid. Not for the price, none of it. I'm so, so sorry, my angel, I'm so sorry." He stroked her hair, caressing the ends tenderly, reveling in the privilege of doing so.

He followed the curve of a curl as it lay along her shoulder. "Fairness?" she asked. "You mean because of your father?"

"It was all he talked about when I was with him, that cousin's daughter he had betrothed to me without my knowledge. We nearly came to blows over it, at least I did. I tried to minimize its importance when I told you about it, but it was deadly serious. It was my father's last grasp at using me to make up for all his lost dreams and he was sure it was foolproof. The one place he would tolerate no resistance was from his own son. He didn't even take me seriously when I protested. He was so preoccupied in those days, so obsessed with survival, I guess, he hardly even registered my presence. I was one of the tools he needed to save his fortune. He was desperate. So was I.

"Huh," he blurted with sudden clarity. "I never noticed before how alike we were that way. I thought we were polar opposites. I hated him. And I never forgave him. But the truth is, I treated you the same way he treated me. I took from you what I needed and never considered what it might do to you. I loved you and I assumed you saw things my way. Just like my father. The same kind of love as my father's kind. The same." He looked at her with sudden self-loathing. She shook her head and smiled gently, denying his words. She placed her hand on this cheek and leaned in, kissing him reassuringly. She felt his anger dissolve a little and she kissed him again.

She glanced away, her eye catching a distant glint of silver as it skipped across the bay. "Do you remember the day you found me kneeling under the beech tree out front? I had my back to the house and you frightened me when you approached. Do you remember that?"

He shifted his weight and leaned his arm against the back of the bench, concentrating. He looked off into the darkness, breathing in deeply. First he nodded slightly, then definitively. "Yes. Yes, I do. You were…it looked like you were praying or something out there under that tree and I startled you, wasn't that it?"

"That was it, yes. And yes, I was praying. I thought you heard my prayer. You walked away so abruptly I thought you heard my prayer and decided right then you had had enough. That you wanted to escape from my desperation, my pleadings, my prayers. I had become a burden and an embarrassment and you had been caught up in something that had gotten quite out of hand, a man with your potential, your future, your family. You didn't intend to mislead me but here it was, and it was time to end it for good. I never saw you alone again after that, not once. I was frantic at losing you and blamed myself for scaring you off. I tortured myself for years over what you would have said to me if you had not overheard me praying."

"Jesus." He let go of her then. He sat forward impulsively, hands clasped between his knees, as if in supplication himself after all these years. Abruptly, he stood up and strode a few paces. He stopped, pausing by the pool. The shimmer of moonlight angling across its surface leap-frogged up to highlight a lock of his hair, drawing Thea's eye, and her compassion.

He took a few more steps and stumbled, kicking a few shells as he went. One of them struck Herman square on the nose. The sleeping detective grunted and stirred. By the time he gathered his senses, aided by a strong urge to empty his bladder, he understood a quick exit was in order and rolled silently out from under the bench, stood up on the spongy ground beside the path and padded silently toward the kitchen door far away from the brooding lovers. The next morning he had no idea how he'd gotten back to his room.

Nick had already turned back toward Thea, consumed by their discourse and his sudden understanding of what he must say next. This time he kneeled before her, taking her hands in his, capturing them in an ardent grip and generally alarming her with his sudden movements.

"Thea, you must listen to me. Nothing is the same as it was back then. You don't have anything to worry about concerning me, concerning us anymore. I'm not the same man, I will not ever hurt you again and I will never abandon you, never, if you will forgive me and promise me you won't give up." He faltered with those last words and could not hold her gaze. He looked down at his knees then, as if realizing he was kneeling before her unknowingly and stood up, self-consciously shaking out his pants legs. He felt her eyes on him.

"Give up what, Nicholas? Do you mean give up on my health? That is not such a simple request my dear dreamer. Even for you, that is a tall order. Everything has changed, nothing could be truer than that, but do you really understand what it means? And do you want to go through the heartache of losing me all over again, Nick? Because that's the way it will be, there's no escaping the inevitable, plain and simple. You and I, we are not to be granted the singular privilege of fulfilled dreams." She heard herself say those words, realizing they sounded harsher than she had intended. She stopped then and looked at him, holding her breath, feeling a little faint.

All thoughts of restraint evaporated. Nick was having none of it. "We can't be resigned like that, Thea! We can't accept a fate that has not been handed us yet! Don't despair, do not ever let me hear you—no, I mean, don't even imagine defeat, we don't have to accept it, we don't. Look, look here," and he pointed toward the sky. When he followed his aim, he saw that the moon had shifted behind the outstretched limbs of the chestnut tree and he pulled her up, drawing her across the garden for a full, resplendent, star-encrusted vision of her crescent moon.

"You have to have trust, Thea, you do. It's something Chiron told me. 'The moon sheds its shadow the way the snake sheds its skin,' he said. 'It's the power of life to throw off death.'"[1] Nick turned away from the night sky and faced her, clasping her shoulders fervently. "It's the power of love to overcome death," he proclaimed and let the words resonate unto the heavens.

# CHAPTER 13

## 1946

"Herman, where have you been?" His mother demanded, partly exasperated and partly confused, as two Rob Roys ago was the last time she wondered about that and she wasn't sure exactly how much time had elapsed or if she had been told the answer at the time. Herman ignored her and headed for the bathroom. She watched him go by and then stood outside the door until he emerged. She harangued him up the stairs about wandering about at night but when she finally petered out all she could discern was a cryptic, sleepy response.

It sounded almost as if he had said, "I'm searching for exquisite amguish."

"What?"

"My mission. My mission is.....exquisite ank...wish." He always was a mumbler.

They passed Iris and Todd racing down the hall, one in a flowing robe with the belt trailing behind and the other wielding a telescope and camera.

"Hey, Herman, where were you? You missed the action! A lot of good you are to us, criminy." They did not wait for an answer or seem to notice Adrianne.

Long after they'd disappeared around the corner she called, "To bed this minute, all of you! One more sound and you will be reading an extra New York Times article for me tomorrow!" That usually had an effect.

Herman continued sleepwalking into his room. He did not notice his mother following behind, peeling off his clothes, stuffing his arms into his pajama top, turning off his lamp or closing his door as she left. But he did reach under his pillow for his Ba, whimpering just a little when he remembered why it wasn't there.

The next morning Iris was up early, dressed in a crisp peach summer frock with matching peach and yellow ribbon in her hair, decidedly unlike her usual tomboy attire, because she knew the Daughters of The Skating Club were coming over, which included Miss Lynn, who always noticed what she wore. She was careful to spread her napkin all the way across her lap and to lean forward while she ate to avoid the merest hint of a crumb or stain on her adorable dress. She even sat still while Maggie adjusted her ribbon and smoothed a few tangles from her wayward tresses. Then she stood up from the table and curtsied at Maggie, for the sheer enjoyment of displaying the full spread of her tulip-embroidered hemline and skidded off to find a good vantage point to watch for the ladies' arrival.

By the time they arrived three hours later, she had raced up and down the beach with Poseidon, who barked at the waves and tried to keep them on shore by pouncing and snapping at their foam; played two games of badminton with Todd, circled Chiron half a dozen times as he traipsed around the estate on his rounds, slurped water from the garden hose and picked a couple dozen anemones for the meeting. When she heard the honking staccato that Miss Anita always used announcing her arrival, she charged around the side of the house to burst upon the driveway in total dishevelment.

She counted seven automobiles. She knew immediately the Mercedes belonging to Miss Susie was missing, she was always last to arrive. And Miss Carol's car was in the shop, she heard that at the club yesterday, so Miss Charlene probably brought her. Just then, Miss Lynn alighted from her Oldsmobile and Iris

232

clapped her hands, admiring the perfect slant of her turquoise hat and the ivory gloves that matched exactly the shoes and belt of the tailored shirt dress. It seemed to Iris that she even matched her car, two-toned and gleaming.

"Why look at the lovely Iris waiting here to greet us!" Miss Lynn exclaimed, as if the two of them had emerged out of the same band box. Iris smoothed her hands across the front of her frock. Then, reminded of the lovely border, grasped a fold in either hand and spread it wide.

"Tulips are my favorite! You are a breath of springtime air on this muggy day, young lady," and Miss Lynn passed into the shade of the overhang, not pausing to knock, gliding smoothly into the cool recesses of the shaded house.

Iris swatted at a pesky fly and stood alone, wondering if she should wait here for the last guest or go inside and try to swipe a lemon bar before Maggie set them out. She could really use some iced tea as well, it had been a long morning.

"Now don't you go in there and interrupt those ladies like you did last time, you hear me, rascal?" Maggie warned as she handed Iris a flaky square topped with tart lemon filling. "Scoot, now, take this outside and don't go feeding it to that scoundrel of a puppy I saw skulking around out back." She watched as Iris, scowling and shuffling, huffed out the screen door. "I'm not wasting my good baking on that little thief now, you hear?"

Iris never could figure out what was so riotous about the Skating Club. They were always laughing, for hours on end, yet she could never quite catch the jokes. Her mother did not seem to laugh so much around them, her own family, not as far as Iris could tell. And what was the point of that ole club anyhow? She certainly had never seen any skating going on that's for sure. Who's ice skating in June, besides? Maybe they could call it the Daughters of the Iced-Tea Drinkers, that would be more like it. Maybe they would think that was funny! She sat outside on the terrace sulking, feeding the dog bits of crust, though careful to be positioned within earshot of the ladies' meeting just on the other side of the veranda's glass doors.

Poseidon had climbed up onto her lap and was licking crumbs from the table when Miss Sandy emerged from the sacred meeting grounds, propping the doors wide to admit the fresh breeze that had mercifully sprung up. Seeing Iris and the new puppy, she strolled out for a chat.

Miss Sandy was always friendly and jingled with bracelets on both wrists. She let Iris inspect them sometimes, separating out the bangles from the chains, pointing out the new charms from exotic places like Sacramento and New Orleans.

"Why is it called the Skating Club?" Iris asked sulkily. "You don't even skate."

Sandy chuckled. "Oh we skate all right. Usually on very thin ice." She glanced over to see that Adrianne was within earshot. "We're quite accomplished skaters as a matter of fact. All but Carol, there," she said a bit louder, craning her neck to see behind Adrianne, "who never learned to ride a bicycle and never strapped on a pair of skates in her life. But look at those pink cheeks of hers. She's the picture of health, I have no idea why. Carol, what makes you so robust?" She called out.

Iris looked at her. "So why is it called the Skating Club then?"

"Well," Miss Sandy said conspiratorially, "it's actually called the DSC. It's just outsiders who think it's the Skating Club."

"The DSC?"

234

"The Daughters of the Skating Club." Well, Iris knew that. "We gave it that name because of your mother, in fact." She winked at Iris. "She being a southerner of high social standing, you know, she has spent her entire life trying to become a member of the DAR, but they won't let her in no way so we decided to make her feel special. With the name of our club, I mean."

Adrianne interjected from the doorway where she had not missed a word of the conversation, "Sandy, that's my Aunt Alise who wants to be in the DAR and you know it."

"The DAR?" Iris was beginning to question whether they were making this up as they went along.

"Daughters-of-the-American-Revolution," Sandy pronounced each syllable slowly and distinctly. "Your mother has tried and tried to convince those high-falutin' women that her confederate ancestors are linked directly to the fathers of this, our great nation, but she just can't seem to make it stick." She looked over disappointedly at Adrianne.

"My Aunt Alise can't make it stick. I probably could, though, if I pursued it myself, you know."

"So." Sandy looked back at Iris. "We are the Daughters of the Skating Club, which is just about as prestigious as the DAR anyway, only much more exclusive. Although we did have to admit your mother or she would have fallen all to pieces."

Adrianne called out loudly, "Iris, Honey, don't forget who's the storyteller in this fictitious history lesson, you hear?"

"Who wants to know about the Skating Club?" Miss Winnie emerged from the dimness of the house, smiling indulgently and ready to tell her tale. She carried her drink with her, a tall glass covered in beads of condensation, the iced tea spoon clinking against the rim, the color of the tea open to speculation.

"We have to talk seriously about the recipe for this Cougat Congo, Adrianne darling," she saluted her hostess with her glass as she passed through the doorway. "Didn't I ever tell you about my introduction to the Skating Club in Oyster Bay, Iris?" And she sat down at the table with Miss Sandy and her new quarry. It was among her favorite stories, after all.

"I was a little bitty thing, much younger than you. My father let me ride in his automobile there with him one afternoon. The ride itself was exciting enough to be memorable, we bounced and jounced and smiled and waved at people the whole way. And even though I had to stay in the car and didn't get to even peek inside the lodge, to this day I think my perfect ladylike behavior on that trip is what my father remembered when he decided to take me to the grandest event of my life the very next fall, the National Red Cross Pageant of 1917 in Huntington. For that reason if no other, I remember distinctly my visit to the Skating Club.

"We went through a gate and down a long, winding drive, down to the pond, a very large pond I could hardly see the other side of, it was so wide, frozen over and zigzagged with blade marks, and we stopped in front of a lodge alongside a dozen or so other cars. And that, my dear Iris, is when I learned the truth about the Skating Club, and the reason we chose their name for our own club, the reason you are about to find out yourself right here today." Winnie nodded at her, acknowledging the import of her coming disclosure.

"You see, even though the owner of the pond was a serious skater and even though members did skate there in the winter, the real purpose of the club was for hunting and shooting." She clapped her hands on her thighs, as if she had announced a shocking state of affairs. Iris looked at her, trying to figure out what was sinister about a hunting club.

"It was a men's club in truth, not a skating club at all. It was not what it seemed." She looked thoroughly disenchanted by her father and his cronies. She shook her head. Iris looked over at Miss Sandy, who was enjoying the story immensely, even though she had obviously heard it before.

"Ergo," Miss Sandy said, "thanks to Miss Winnie, we are the Daughters of the Skating Club. And perhaps not entirely what we seem, either." She was looking at Winnie when she said it, her eyes glinting with mischief. Iris looked from one to the other, verifying what she had always suspected: she was never going to understand what grown-ups were talking about. Really, she wasn't sure she even wanted to.

She made a motion to stand up, assuming the story was over, when Sandy patted her on the knee, effectively pinning her to her chair. "Now Winnie, my dear, you must tell our future Petite Daughter the story of the pageant. No young lady of Long Island has completed her education until she has heard about that historic event." Miss Sandy was always teasing, so it was hard to tell if she was being serious even when she sounded like she was being serious. This was one of those times.

"Well," it was clear Miss Winnie did not require much prodding on the subject, "like I said it was the grandest event of my life and I was younger than you, only six years old. No one knows how to entertain on the same scale today as they did back then when I was a girl. There were five thousand patrons of the arts at the National Red Cross Pageant of 1917, and they paid up to two hundred and fifty dollars each for the privilege."

She paused a moment to let those formidable numbers sink in. "It was held at Rosemary Farm, the great estate of the Conklin family. The beautiful lawns seemed to spread out for miles, and people were milling about everywhere, dressed in their finery, carrying parasols, conversing, laughing, greeting friends they hadn't seen in ages, making new friends, tittering with excitement over the big event, proud to be seen, proud to be making history on that glorious day. There were only a few children present, mind you, and they were very well-mannered and proper, every one of them. Well, at least as long as any grown-ups were looking." She blushed at some memory, then took up the story again with gusto.

"When the time came for the big event, somehow everyone knew to take their places around the little man-made lake surrounding the island where the pageant would be held. The crowd suddenly became hushed with anticipation. Every face was rapt with expectation, every guest present tingled from the excitement in the air. And then the music began.

"It started with the first public concert ever performed by John Phillip Sousa and his 250-piece Enlisted Marine Band. They performed at the beginning and again at the end of the spectacle. They inspired the patriotism of every spectator there with their rousing marching music. Toes were tapping, arms were waving, the grown-ups were smiling, the children were trying so hard to keep from jumping up from their seats. The enthusiasm was near fever pitch by the time Ethel Barrymore took the stage!

"Yes, it's true, Ethel Barrymore! There was a cast of over one hundred players, including Ethel's brother John Barrymore, Clifton Webb, Tyrone Power and oh I don't know how many other famous stage stars of the day. The most beautiful ladies, including Miss

Barrymore of course, played the parts of the Court of Truth, Liberty and Justice. There were maidens dancing before the great altar, kings and bishops processing in royal processions, gilded banners being unfurled and then furled again to reveal new spectacles, including a real barge on the water, oh such sights as I have never witnessed since. And at the end, after the fears and terrors of all the world's countries were presented to the audience with great drama and their cases pleaded with heartfelt pathos, a trumpet blared that brought everyone to attention and there, at the forefront of all the citizens of the world, America herself ceremoniously pledged her sword to her allies. And a new day had dawned." She paused theatrically, then sighed with rapture. "And then John Phillip Sousa's band performed again and we all sat stock still this time, spellbound, exhilarated and floating with patriotism, patriotism that carried us home on a cloud of euphoria that lifts us over and over to this day, each time we remember that afternoon of glory." Her voice had risen with the story, as had her chin and her gaze, rising toward the heavens and proclaiming with emotion the dramatic events of nearly thirty years before. Those passions would never fade for Miss Winnie, Iris could tell, and she liked her all the more for it.

"That was a good story, Miss Winnie, I'm glad you told me about the Red Cross Pageant. And the Skating Club as well." Iris turned to Miss Sandy. "I kind of get it now, I guess." And before anyone could detain her again, she jumped up and headed for the house to see if there was any more iced tea left in the pitcher.

Both ladies opened their mouths to comment, but Iris had already vanished and before them suddenly stood Herman, looking distinctively odd. They turned their attentions to him. He was staring bug-eyed at the puppy, who was obviously very happy to see him, wagging his tail, rump and midsection following suit so that his back legs had to shift left right, left right, in order to keep up. After a few long seconds, during which Sandy and Winnie watched his fixed expression curiously and waited for him to come around enough to acknowledge them, his face went slack, and he slumped, sighing with obvious disillusionment.

It sounded to them like, "Not even the puppy," was what he mumbled. Poseidon watched Herman retreat, his tail wagging much slower now, his head cocked in confusion. When it was clear his companion was leaving without him, he lowered his head, sniffed the ground and trotted along behind, keeping a discreet yet loyal distance.

Sandy and Winnie looked at each other. "You know Adrianne and Heph practice very liberal child-raising methods," one of them whispered to the other.

"How true," the other one agreed as they regarded each other with eyebrows raised.

Who would have guessed Herman was a romantic. While Poseidon, now bounding all around him, barked encouragingly and even brought him the old yellow ball (how had that escaped the surf?), Herman moped throughout the property in search of the same rapturous response to some object of beauty that would match Nick's description of the moon and peonies. It was the last thing he had heard from under the bench before succumbing to his drowsy repose. It was as if he had been enchanted by Nick's words, and so close to slumber when he heard them that they were etched in his mind irrevocably, nor could they be ignored. He was dragging after a full day of searching and his eyes were dried out, practically shriveled up by their efforts at staring hard enough. He was determined to discover sufficient passion for something in this world as to find it unendurable.   And then, in the ultimate test of an undercover agent's endurance, overcome it.   That was the plan.   The problem was, as far as he could see it, there was too much regular stuff around here for a man of his sensitivities to be overwhelmed by any of them. But he wasn't a quitter, not him, and so he persevered. It's just possible that his Ba might turn up in the search, of course; boy that would be enough to bring a tear to a kid's eye.   And so he persevered some more.

Iris carried her iced tea glass with a spoon in it just like Miss Winnie and had tilted the bottom up while sticking her tongue as far inside as it could reach, holding onto the spoon with her free hand and letting the ice tumble onto her upper lip, trying to lick the last grains of sugar still clinging to the sides.   This totally absorbing activity prevented proper navigation and ended with a jolt at the telephone table in the hall.   She nearly dropped the glass, yet recovered in time to hear something clunk onto the floor and skip out of sight. She quickly placed the glass on the table and bent down to search.   Peeking out from a crevice between the floorboards and the baseboard was her mother's daisy-enamel earring.   As usual, she had removed it to answer the telephone and must have forgotten it after she hung up.   Iris checked it carefully and was relieved to see it was not chipped or damaged by its fall.   She picked up her glass and moved to replace it with the earring when the words on a piece of paper caught her eye.   Cougat Congo it said, and she read as best she could what was listed below.

¾ jigger white rum
¼ jigger grenadine
Juice of ½ fresh lime
1 teaspoon of sugar
Dash of absinthe
Iced and well-shaken

241

Slowly, she raised her glass to eye level, scrutinized it gravely and gulped. Something Miss Sandy had said about the club was in the back of her mind, but she couldn't put her finger on it.

*     *     *

Not far off, but far outside Iris' current sphere of awareness, Todd was glowering with frustration.

"Herman, where have you been?" he barked and Herman jumped. "How are we going to train for our duties if no one is ever around to participate? How are we ever going to know our signals during a borough alarm if we are not even in communication with each other?" He was exasperated by the lonely duties of a captain and gratified at least to have found someone to reprimand.

"How should I know?" Todd was not the only one whose patience had worn thin. Herman picked up the ball casually and threw it into the surf. Todd immediately looked at Poseidon and sure enough, his ears were pricked, his body tense, his eyes alert.

Finally, a chance for Todd to be commander. He snapped his fingers, calling the pup's name at the same time.

"Poseidon!" When the dog reluctantly shifted his eyes to Todd, Todd swept his arm wide in the direction of the ball and bid him, "Retrieve!"

Poseidon did not have to be bidden twice. He tore off at top speed and dove into the water at belly depth, disappearing altogether, then emerging sideways right alongside the ball, mouth open to snag it in one motion and turn quickly, paddling back to shore with alacrity. The boys watched him approach, eyes shining just like the first time and whooped with delight as the retriever padded proudly up the sand to his masters, dropping the ball at their feet.

No Borough Alarms were practiced that day, or the next, when Iris had rejoined the team and training was in full force. By the end of the weekend, Poseidon was diving to the bottom and bringing up such treasures as a dog bone, a Coca Cola bottle, an unsolicited bucket that had been missing since May and, as a test for Herman's sake, a scrap of cloth.

The children considered it part of their quest, and honed their training skills without the help of adults. The only supervision was in the form of the raven, who observed keenly and cawed occasionally by way of comment.

# CHAPTER 14

## 1946

"Have you ever heard of Psamathe, moon of Neptune?" Chiron asked Thea, pronouncing the name SAM-a-thee. They were sitting together on the bench behind his gatehouse, resting in the shade and listening to the intermittent ack-ack of a red-breasted nuthatch perched nearby. More quiet than usual, Chiron could sense a resignation about her today, a melancholy. He glanced down at her hand resting on the bench and wanted to cover it with his own, but refrained.

She turned her head to look at him, smiling gently. "No," she responded, knowing he did not ask questions idly.

"Psamathe is an unusual moon. She was apparently broken off from her other half, named Neso, which also orbits Neptune. It takes approximately twenty-five years for them to make one complete orbit around the planet. But Psamathe travels in a counter-revolutionary direction from the orbits of the other moons, so twice every quarter century her path meets up with Neso's."

He paused for awhile, letting Thea envision Psamathe and Neso in their orbits. "Once the two moons were broken apart, they would never have encountered each other again if Psamathe had traveled in the usual fashion. If she were a customary moon, they would have pursued each other endlessly, futilely, through all time."

"When I wonder at the trials the gods place before us, I am awed by our willingness to adapt to whatever obstacles fate has assigned. I marvel at the spirit's ability to endure despite its torment, and am struck by its ability to remain ever hopeful; grasping whatever happiness it is afforded, even when it is brief. Even when it is fragmented.

He was looking up at the sky. "By accepting that fate is cosmic and we are a part of its vast greatness, I must, therefore, be willing to accept its rules. I must be willing to abide by them, follow them the only way I know how, and find contentment."

Chiron looked down again to see that she had closed her hand loosely into a fist and he smiled. Now he reached down and covered it in his own furrowed grasp and squeezed it reassuringly. Her eyes glistened as she looked up at him.

Then they both turned to see the plumpest little red bird take flight off the tip of the branch before them, leaving the twigs all around bouncing and shivering in its wake. They chuckled at the sight and lapsed back into silence. She slid her fingers between his and they sat watching together for the nuthatch's return.

\*         \*         \*

"I had thought to be done with death for a while," Nick said over his shoulder by way of explanation when he realized Todd was standing behind him and probably had been for some time. He was drunk and glad of it. He turned back to his view of the Long Island Sound, seeing the Atlantic Ocean beyond, seeing the years he had spent on her roiling surface, attempting to glide through all those days of the war, where there were only storms. He covered his face with his hands, elbows propped on his knees, pants legs drenched, his fanny feeling the cool dampness of the night through the sand on the dune he had lurched upon in the dark over an hour ago. He could not imagine how Todd had found him and wished that he would leave him, walk away and be done. He could not attempt small talk, he could not feel sympathy or camaraderie or brotherly love tonight. It was self-pity he required, long overdue and patently well-earned.

It had been a golden-honey month. He had discovered the raptures of the innocent, the reckless exuberance of the guiltless and the vulnerability of the foolish, rashly embracing each facet of unearned happiness and brashly evading the piper he couldn't pay. But today he woke up on the other side of the veil and the shock vibrated in his breast until it shattered each illusion of happiness and well-being he had embraced. He loved Thea. These last weeks, that was all and enough. Today it was his hell. Today he saw tomorrow and all of his tomorrows and he knew; the price of happiness is eternal and unremitting. The only naked fact he still managed to avoid was this: tomorrow is arrived. He held to the wisp of faith that though she would not live forever, they still had time owed them. He denied the hints that contradicted this maxim.

Today he was himself, the Nick of old, the kid who was torn from Beechwood, the kid who was banished to Greece, the one who rode the war on a Merchant Marine ship that forfeited a multitude of worthy men. Today he was bereft and he was not up to the occasion. Today he needed to be fortified and he had managed that to a near-satisfying degree, despite remaining conscious.

When Todd had approached, guided by Nick's own slurring baritone, he was reciting a poem he had invoked a hundred times since his discharge. It was his tribute to his fallen mates, the only one he could think to offer in his self-imposed exile.

Reserve, I pray, one lusty cheer
For men whose names you never hear.

Who win no stripes and wear no braid,
But face Great Dangers Unafraid.
Who go wherever ships are sent;
Whose breast no medals ornament
Whose deeds no scrolls of honor stress
But who are heros none the less.
Who sail the ocean's vast expanse
Nor hesitate to take their chance
Against the swift torpedo's blast
Nor know which trip will be their last.
Who take both peace and war in stride
Who, when torpedos strike go overside
Perchance to be the lucky men
Who live to sail the seas again.
I give you then, each gallant crew,
Of liner, freighter, tanker too,
Out-bound I know not where or when.
The men who man our Merchant Fleet
Whose bones lie in the ocean deep!
Unknown, unheard of and unsung,
God keep you now, your task is done![3]

He jerked his flask high, a toast to the abiding stars, and laughed loudly, a hollow sound and bitter.

"I have learned two things, my friend Todd-o," he bellowed. "Two things more than I expected to learn." Silence, drawn out. Todd leaned toward his companion, ear first, to catch whatever words might escape Nick's rumination.

"First," Todd jumped at the suddenness of his hoarse voice. "The war is never over. For a soldier, for a sailor, for an officer alive or dead, the war is never over. That's a fact. And second," here he turned with pointed finger at Todd's retreating nose, "whatever leave you are given from the duty of repaying your sins, it is temporary and short-lived. And it applies to everything, every damn thing." He lapsed back into heavy silence and seemed to forget Todd was there.

Todd took the break in soliloquy as a chance to arrange himself on the dune next to Nick, settling into the sand and facing the same black seascape that was more imagined than visible this cloudy evening. He was content to sit in silence for quite a while. Then, on impulse he began a poem of his own, a poem recited to him since infancy by Chiron himself.

> Some time at eve when tide is low,
> I shall slip my moorings and sail away.
>
> With no response to the friendly hail
> Of kindred craft in the busy bay.
> In the silent hush of the twilight pale.
> When the night troops down to embrace the day,
> And the voices call, and in the waters flow.
> Some time at even when the tide is low.
> I slip my moorings and sail away.
>
> Through the purple shadows that darkly trail
> O'er the ebbing tide of the Unknown Sea.
> I shall fare me away, with a dip of a sail
> And a ripple of waters to tell the tale
> Of a lonely voyager, sailing away
> To the Mystic Isles where at anchor lay
> The crafts of those who have sailed before
> O'er the Unknown Sea to the Unseen Shore.
>
> A few who have watched me sail away
> Will miss my craft from the busy Bay:
> Some friendly barks that were anchored near.
> Some loving soul that my heart held dear.
> In silent sorrow will drop a tear.
> But I shall have peacefully furled my sail

In moorings sheltered from storm and gale
And greeted the friends who sailed before
O'er the Unknown Sea to the Unseen Shore.[4]

Todd, as he got older, had surmised that Chiron wanted to prepare him for his passing. After all, he was ageless and getting more so. He had been a grown man already in the previous century! But Chiron had in fact wanted to prepare Todd for any inevitabilities of life, and help him to view them as the natural course of things. It remained to be seen if he succeeded by any measure.

Nick's astonishment grew from the first lines and by the time Todd was finished, the bottle had clinked to the sand against a shell, forgotten, and the drunkenness it had imbued was somewhat dissipated, at least flattened out a little.

"The soul is a circle,[1] Chiron says," Todd mused. "What does he mean by that?"

"Hell if I know," was the response. Nick grabbed the bottle by the neck and struck it against the shell a few times, agitated. There was something niggling at the back of his brain and he continued to bang the bottle rhythmically, as it seemed to help jar his thinking processes.

Midair once, he paused. Holding the bottle aloft like a club, he turned thoughtfully to Todd. Intently regarding the young boy by his side, not even in his teens he realized, he slowly lowered his truncheon to the sand, disposing of it.

"Does Chiron provide you with study sessions in his gatehouse?" He watched Todd's face closely.

Not sure about the tone of Nick's voice, Todd replied in kind. "Yes, often. Why do you ask?"

Nick snorted unintentionally. Hearing himself, he shrugged at his own obvious resentment. He peered again at Todd, eyeing him archly, nearly sneering. "I can only hope he found a better apprentice in you. I was just a practice round, and not a very gratifying one, not for either of us. It's a wonder he was willing to go at it again."

Todd was leaning away, avoiding the sour smell of Nick's person and the aggressive demeanor that seem to be magnified by his close proximity. He had the sensation he got when he was near a strange dog. He knew he should be afraid, but he wasn't.

"Mr. Nick, I don't know what you're talking about, but Chiron is good to me. You might say he's my best friend. He's taken care of me for as long as I can remember, considering my father is dead, considering my mother can hardly manage to take care of me with her hands full and all. Maybe you don't know him like I do but if you did, you wouldn't say things like that. Chiron never gives up on anything. If you know him at all, you know that."

Nick's throat suddenly felt as if hot wax were dripping down its length and he felt his face flush with the shame of being reprimanded by a kid. Some kind of a kid, this. Wise. Almost fearless, even. He forgot himself then and concentrated on the lad who could put him in his place and not inflame resentment on the part of a drunken man quick to anger at any assault to his ego. He scooted away a little to get a clearer view of his successor, his heir presumptive to Chiron's vault of mystical knowledge. He tucked in his chin and squinted, trying to focus.

What he saw was an angular face with high cheekbones, determined jaw, deep blue eyes emphasized by strong, arched eyebrows and a few locks of wavy black hair sweeping the high forehead. The eyes faced scrutiny without flinching, forthright and alert. The two disciples squared off for a moment, stubborn specimens of Greek training. Nick was the first to break the tension.

"Your mother," he said. "You mentioned she has her hands full. What did you mean by that?"

It was Todd's turn to color. He turned back to face the water, hesitating to answer. "I was just mentioning that my mother has all she can do to handle my brother, Perry." He stole a glimpse at Nick without turning his head in his direction. "My brother Perry is almost a year older than me and has no interest is coming here to stay at Beechwood. He has his own crowd in the city and would be bored to death here in what he calls the middle of nowhere. But my mom, she does her best. It's just not easy keeping him in line, not one bit easy, believe you me." He stopped. He did not intend to complain any further about his own family, gee.

Nick leaned back and rested on one hand, placing the other one on his bended knee, casually assessing this rogue interloper. The tension was gone from his face and he was beginning to enjoy the mild breeze off the water and the regular slap of the placid waves. They both looked behind them reflexively when they heard the familiar hoot of the owl far off and moving. Nick glanced then at Todd, a glimmer of pleasure in his eyes.

"You are a fine example of the kind of companion I would wish for Chiron. His greatest joy is in sharing his knowledge with a quick mind like his own." Todd was not sure at all he had heard correctly.

Nick laughed out loud appreciatively. "Tell me something, my friend, tell me why the horses on Chiron's chessboard are cross-eyed. I've been trying to figure it out my whole life."

*     *     *

251

For nearly a year now, since Chiron had been charging her with the responsibility of delivering Thea's medicine, Iris had been imagining herself someday as a nurse. It was a romantic notion, noble and worthy. She thought about this destiny today as she carried the packet protectively to Thea's quarters behind the kitchen. She had told no one of her plans, not even her sworn comrades of the quest. Especially not them. Being the only information she had ever succeeded in keeping to herself long term, in fact, it made her feel powerful and her secret somehow portentous.

She presented the dose to Thea formally with both hands, proud of her service and reliability.

"Why thank you, my dove," Thea crooned as always. She lay upon her coverlet this morning fully dressed rather early in the day, an encouraging sign according to Iris' medical assessment. Having completed her duty, she plopped herself onto the edge of the bed, unaware of the wince it wrung from the patient. She was primed for a chat.

"What exactly are Chios Tears, anyway, Thea?" She probably needed to know these things, things like what medicines she's doling out to her patients and stuff.

"My medicine? Ah. Chiron calls it Chios Tears, doesn't he. Its base is mastic, really. The mastic comes from the Greek island of Chios. In order to collect the mastic from the trees, they score the trunk until the resin, the mastic, weeps from the gashes. It seems as if the mastic tree is crying tears of regret, they say."

Iris wondered if maybe she should write that down. She was thrilled to know the secret behind the name of a very special medicine and she looked tenderly upon her patient. Before she knew it, she was lying on the bed next to her and her patient was gently stroking her hair. They cuddled like that for a while, until Iris heard

Maggie call and she bounded from the room. Her special touch, allowing Thea to hold her close and inhale her sunshine fragrance for a time, boded well for her future career.

Thea studied the half-closed door long after Iris had disappeared through it, contemplating how much she loved these children, realizing they would miss her, at least for a little while. It was one of her great heartaches, that she would inflict pain into their childhood yet she could not see her way to warn them or to say goodbye. She was a coward after all. Yet her timid heart was known to them and she counted on their forgiveness someday. She also counted on Chiron to be true to his word and watch over their free-spirited assault on life; rambunctious, headstrong and fearless as ever. She pictured them in their usual state, forever trailing little tornadoes of energy in their wake, zigzagging every inch of the estate, every room of the house, criss-crossing, banding together and churning up a mighty dust storm, then separating and continuing unflaggingly on their own paths of exuberance all the long day and into the night, leaving a vaporous plume that engraved itself on the memory book of the universe. It warmed her through as always, bringing a smile of gentle amusement to her lips. She thought especially of Todd and her heart shivered a little with renewed grief, convulsing at once with hurt and hope. She lay that way for a while, savoring, praying, then drifted into a wounded sleep.

That afternoon, not long after lunch, she was sitting up with her back against the headboard propped by pillows, tucked in with sheet, coverlet and heirloom throw and a shawl around her shoulders. The day had turned dismal and cool, the first break in the heat in weeks and welcome. Rain assaulted the windowpane in sudden intervals like handfuls of rice, fierce and invasive. Nick sat on the chair pulled up close, artificial cheer masking his headache and remorse over last night's wretched indulgence. He was lifting Thea's hand to kiss her fingertips when Maggie strode in.

"Ah, here comes the Goddess Komodia!" he announced gaily, his eyes dancing in his valiant attempt at merriment. Thea smiled appreciatively. Maggie did not.

"Aw, come on Maggie, Komodia is the goddess of happiness and amusement, you have to make a better of show of it than this!" He saw then the bouquet of the last of the peonies, the ones from the hothouse that Chiron coaxed to a late season, that Maggie held in her hands. The voluptuous petals drooped languidly over her hands, top-heavy and wistful. She looked up at Nick then and carefully drew one peony from the bunch, holding it out to him dispassionately.

"Do you know about peonies, Mr. Nick?" she asked coolly.

"Well, I know that they are beautiful, beautiful beyond description, but no, no, I'm not much of a gardener, Maggie, you know that," he smiled hesitantly as he accepted the blossom, curious at her tone.

"I don't mean the growing of them. I mean the legend. The myth."

"Why no, Maggie," somewhat surprised that the peonies he worshipped had a legend, he nevertheless winked at Thea, adding jovially, "Would you like to tell me?"

"I'm just giving this peony to you, young man. If you know the legend, that's telling enough."

"Why…thank you, Maggie. I'll be sure to look it up."

She turned her back to them and arranged the flowers in the vase on the bureau. They watched her in silence, Nick absently twirling his peony between thumb and fingers, shaking loose a few soft petals that drifted to the rug unheeded.

When she had departed, Nick smiled sheepishly at Thea, contemplated his flower for another moment, then carefully placed it on the bedside table close by.

He became serious then, as if Maggie had flipped a switch on the mood in the room. He knew he would not be sitting here in an unmarried woman's bedroom, alone with her, in any but the most dreaded of circumstances. As modern as the Bayards were, they would not have condoned such an improper private visit in their home. It was obvious how Maggie felt about it even now. Emotion started to well up in Nick's chest as he began to speak. "I have so many regrets about my past behavior, my darling angel, more than I can number. Sometimes I am desperate to escape from the guilt of it. I keep trying to change the outcome, make new decisions, see the signs I missed, speak up for myself, speak up in defense of you, stand by you. Mostly that. Stand by you. Again and again I make amends. I fix up the broken hearts, I patch the cracks in the hollow promises of that hot summer. I plant my feet with steely grit and I refuse to be bullied. I'm wise, I'm unyielding. I'm what you really thought I was."

His eyes were filled with such sadness as he looked at her that she reached up to touch his face, stroking it with her thumb, tousling with a decision about what to say to him now, now that there was no need for holding back. She searched his face one last time, then, satisfied, began to speak.

"Please don't have any regrets, Nicholas, I don't," she began. "With the way things turned out, now, now that I have you back and know that my faith in our love for each other was valid and true all this time, despite everything, despite my lapses into doubt and denial, despite missing you every single day as much at the end as from the first, I am glad for what we had and what we share together now. I want, it's time, I..."

He clasped her hand and held it to his cheek, closing his eyes, thinking both how cold her hand was and how much he desired her touch, wanting to pull her toward him, to hold her, to protect her, to make love to her one more time. He suppressed a groan and ignored the pain in his own breast, unwilling to name his true fear, refusing to give in to it while he was in her presence. He wouldn't allow her to die with the old Nick lingering still; it was all he could offer her. Yet he heard himself speak impulsively, to keep her from upsetting herself any further and to channel their conversation away from their mutual pain.

He forced a rueful laugh as he lowered her hand and regarded it, studying its delicate beauty, tracing the blue veins showing palely through her translucent skin. "Do you remember that iron box we found in the boathouse, the one we decided to use for our love notes, our treasures, I think you called them our ode to eternal love, wasn't that it?" He smiled indulgently.

She looked askance, "No, that was what you called it. I, a true disciple of Chiron, called it our poem of metaphysical essence. I even thought I knew what that meant at the time," she laughed, feeling lighter. His eyes gleamed appreciatively and he nodded his head, remembering, and tingled with the fleeting elation of being there again, hearing those words the way she said them those Walt Whitman days of exalter.

"We were going to save them weren't we, for something important, something eternal, I hardly even remember what they were, the things we cherished so much." He instantly regretted those hasty words and bit his tongue when he saw her face change before him. He knew what she would say before she did.

"I remember. I know everything in that box." He closed his eyes, remembering them every bit as well as she did.

"I have taken them out and examined them a thousand times over the years, careful not to damage the memories, careful not to disturb their fate," she added. He looked up then, obviously confused, more than a little concerned.

"You have the box? How did you find it? Did Chiron bring it to you?" That was not possible, that could not be possible. Fear began to bubble in his throat, how did she find that box?

"The box? No, the box is gone, long gone. I meant in my imagination, Nicholas, my daydreams. Now I'm embarrassed to have admitted it! Do you worry that I am foolish after all?" She put her free hand on his, though her eyes were clearly expecting indulgence.

His relief was immeasurable. He berated himself for impulsively speaking about the box at all, he never meant to do it but for the quick fix of changing the subject.

"How I wish we still had it. It was meant to be passed on. I was so happy thinking its contents would be preserved and cherished, and recorded for all time; like we said—like a poem, a poem of such essence, Nicky…" Her voice faded to a whisper.

She gripped his hand with strength he did not know she had and he reached over with his free hand to wipe away her tears. His confidence flagging, he remembered his handkerchief and quickly pulled it out to offer her, launching into a romanticized version of the rescue of the men from the Equitable Life Assurance fire. He described the handkerchief waving bravely from the icy basement window, and his father's insistence that Nick always carry his own white handkerchief, just in case of emergencies.

"Finally, I understand what he meant," he said. "It was worth carrying one around with me all these years just for an occasion such as this," he deadpanned. "Even if I caused it myself." He succeeded in getting a smile out of her, a laugh, and soon he had cajoled her out of her gloom. They moved on to pleasant subjects. In a matter of moments they were intimately conversing again in lovers' shorthand, touching, kissing, teasing, unaware of the passing of the afternoon, or the passing of their allotment of time together. Their portion of the elixir of the gods.

They parted, she with the purest, most promising smile that ever sang of love's devotion and he with a gallant bow from the doorway and a private signal with his hand cupped over his intrepid heart as his eyes pierced hers, shooting a pang of thrill straight through her. For a breathless moment he lingered, then softly took his leave.

He slipped out the side door and retraced his steps across the lawn, under the beech tree, past the clothesline, through the gate and along to the back road where he had become accustomed to leaving his car. He did not realize he was drenched to the bone from the downpour until he was closed inside, had started the engine and saw that he'd need the windshield wipers and the defrost vent before he could see a thing.

# CHAPTER 15

## 1946

Thea, a little drowsy, fluttered her eyes at Maggie's approach then frowned in concentration, trying to remember the question she had been waiting to ask her. As Maggie fussed about the room, shifting objects, adjusting, smoothing, Thea's forehead cleared with remembering.

"Maggie, tell me what you meant when you asked Nick about the myth of the peonies." It was Nick's curiosity more than anything that prompted her question.

Maggie stopped mid-fluff, and did not meet Thea's gaze. She vigorously brushed some lint from the chair seat, started to sit in it, then changed her mind and retreated to the curtains at the window, pulling them together against the evening shadows to come. After she adjusted the folds in the fabric just so, she lifted a corner and spoke to the undulating panes beyond.

"Poene was one of those Greek goddesses. She was the Goddess of Retaliation." Her voice carried the deep impression that title had made on her.

"Mrs. Maria described her to me a long time ago, out back in the garden one day. She told me the Goddess of Justice sent Poene to punish those responsible for the death of Psamathe, a blameless mortal woman. Poene was powerful. And she took her revenge on those who harmed...helpless mortals. Like you." The last more of a whisper, escaped, unintended.

Maggie stopped, eyes widening, on hearing the promise of doom in her own words, and unsure herself now of their import. She had spoken to Nick more in pique than premeditation, wanting to chase him away from Thea and the harm she was sure he was causing.

She had been quite pleased with her insinuation at the time, and was gratified by the veiled threat she had conveyed. And she had gotten his attention, too, she reminded herself, curbing that surefire cocky air of his for once. Her chin jutted out with grim satisfaction, remembering.

But now she imagined herself alarming Thea and fairly trembled at the thought, suddenly out of her depth and unable to extricate herself from this, her own vengeful act. She lowered her head and her shoulders sagged.

"Shame on me," was all she could think.

When she finally managed to peer meekly over her shoulder toward the bed, she saw Thea holding the peony Nick had left on the bedside table, twirling it gently as she had seen him do, smiling a private smile that belied Maggie's explanation and in fact, indicated she had forgotten that Maggie was still there.

Maggie slipped out then, her last glimpse indelibly of Thea serene and softly lit from within.

The next morning it was Adrianne who found her, a pale supplicant in sweet repose. When she opened the bedroom door a curtain fluttered and she caught her breath before she knew why. She could not say how long she stood in the doorway, watching the dust particles floating in the air, illuminated by a crack of sunlight diffusing the space around the bed, the quiet sense of powerful grace permeating the world of one life relinquished, gently, embraced in the rapture of wisdom and acceptance.

*     *     *

What followed was a time of confused memories, foggy actions, tearful inactions, passing specters, wordless hugging, whispered reassurances, occasional wails from varying distances at unpredictable times of the day or night. Passing; mainly family members crossing paths, interacting without eye contact or with the intensity of locked, questioning gazes, explanations unasked, careful attention to kindnesses given and received. Decisions made themselves and someone acted on them. The children sat in puddles of sadness or played boisterously not quite out of earshot, then broke into pieces before the slightest frustration. They realized their great desire of having no bedtime, then wandered forlornly to bed anyway, sometimes tucked in, sometimes forgotten, sometimes suffocated with tender affection.

Nick was ever-present but no one remembered conversing with him. He sat by himself, mostly. If everyone present had been asked where he was, they would each have described a different place on the estate where they had seen him, yet none would have been able to say just where he'd been since. They did not know where he went at night and would have been perplexed to hear he retreated each evening, after the moon had set, into the storage room of the boat house, the one with the missing doorknob.

Maggie did not appear for two days. When Adrianne finally went looking for her, she was struck dumb by the sight, not of her puffy face or the ruffled nightgown floor to neck, but by the head of abundant white hair cascading across her shoulders and down her back, unclasped and unprotected by her fleet of hairpins and unruly cap.

Friends, a few business associates, the Daughters of the Skating Club, arrived and left, filling every counter and side table with aromatic dishes of sweet bounty, overflowing with steaming sustenance, where words felt less than apt. It seemed there was always someone at the kitchen sink in an apron and high heels, washing or drying dishes, others in pearls boiling water for tea, slicing generous servings of dessert onto fine china, pouring more coffee, conversing in low tones with those carrying in or carrying out the trays of refreshments, erupting occasionally in small ripples of laughter, opening and closing drawers and cabinets to avoid asking questions of the residents (to the consternation of Clarisse who would have preferred to do it herself) and from time to time calling for a passing man to take out the garbage.

Adrianne was surprised that these visitors readily accepted that Thea, an employee by definition, had been so beloved by the Bayards as to leave them bereft with such a hole in their family. Perhaps they had similar affections within their own households, or perhaps they had a fondness for Thea themselves after all this time. She mulled over the probable reasons for their kind attentions a few times between bouts of mourning, wondering why it seemed so confusing. Her hands fluttered in her lap sometimes as she sat, prompting her to try to remember what she should be doing.

In the end, Chiron saw to most of the arrangements, led the private procession to the cemetery, bowed his head and squeezed his eyes tightly behind his weathered hand. By the time the prayers over Thea were concluded he had vanished, the space where he had stood bearing flattened footprints steeped in dew.

A few weeks into August a modified routine had been reestablished, a refuge for exhausted emotions in activities rote from repetition and normalcy. The children were immensely relieved to be transported to the yacht club and left to the attention of the young instructors absorbed in their own dramas and mercifully neglectful of the Bayards' burden.

Nick had had ample time to consult the cognac Chiron had left behind in his desertion of the mourning household and was seriously considering sobriety on the day he emerged from his crypt to join the early morning beach scavengers. Instead, he found Chiron poking the toe of his boot at a pile of gelatinous substance strewn in heavy globs along the waterline. He wasn't sure which was the more surprising sight; the globs or the man.

As he approached, Chiron turned to him with deep regret in his eyes and said, "I was hoping these eggs would arrive this year, but they are too late to be of use after all."

"These," Nick stopped to clear his throat. "These piles of gooey mess are eggs?" Was all he could think to say.

Chiron nodded. "They are bluefish eggs and have a valuable medicinal effect. I had great hopes I could use them for Thea's condition. I was convinced of it, in fact. But they wash up on this shore rarely, and I find it somehow much worse that they are available too late than if they had never arrived here at all." He sighed heavily and Nick realized he had never heard that sound from him before. It increased the ache in his chest, hearing it now. He could not bear Chiron's pain on top of his own and he blinked back a tear with determination, swallowing its rising whimper.

The men stood side by side, alone and motionless, until even the plovers felt safe scurrying around them fore and aft. The wind blowing their hair, bathing their weary thoughts in sea-salt air, their shadows disappearing and reemerging with the passing clouds, their ears deaf to the caress of the gusting breeze, their thoughts crossed the boundaries of speech and were remarkably intermixed.

"What are you doing here?" Todd's voice was small and tentative. The men turned toward each other to look behind them where Todd stood several paces off, not wanting to intrude. Chiron gave him a gentle smile of encouragement, and motioned with his head for him to join them. Todd placed himself between those two pillars and mutely studied a cresting wave not far from shore. He stepped into a deposit of fish eggs with his bare feet, which wriggled their toes as if independent from his body and reveled in the squish.

"The ocean heals all wounds," Chiron's voice resonated above the surf.

A moment later he spoke again, more reserved. "And love bears all things. That is the pain of being truly alive."[1]

Nick reached across and put his arm around Todd's shoulders. They were broader than they had been a few months ago, the bones straining against new muscle, their girth outpacing his weight gain, angular and vulnerable.

Todd took a breath, blew it out, decided to ask his question. "That poem, at the funeral. What does it mean, 'crossing the bar'?"

The two men glanced at each other, Chiron's eyes indicating Nick should respond.

"You know what a sandbar is," he began. "They can come and go near the shoreline but most rivers and bays develop them across their entrances. In order for ships to make it out to sea, they must cross the bar. Sailors know that once they do, they are leaving the safety of the harbor and passing into the unknown.

"Mariners compare that to dying; crossing into the unknown...from the unknown sea to the unseen shore," he added. His arm slipped from Todd's shoulders and he looked down in time to see the recognition those words evinced on his companion's young face, from

264

the night they had met on the drunken beach. Nick watched as the bony shoulders rose and fell in understanding.

Todd's eyes searched the ocean from horizon to horizon and back to the beach where a seagull pecked a writhing crab the size of his thumb. "Some things never heal. Sometimes life is just Hell." He looked quickly out the corner of his eye at Chiron to see if his use of a swear word had shocked him. It felt good to be brazen for once, to be shocking.

"The worst of Hell is the absence of love,"[1] was the unhesitating rejoinder.

At that, Chiron placed his hand on Todd's head, pressing back enough to command eye contact for a brief moment. Then, softly ruffling the curls with his gnarled fingers, he turned and strode away. The acolytes followed a few paces behind.

Chiron walked on toward his own house while the other two continued along the path through the garden. Nick had spent these weeks of Chiron's absence performing Chiron's duties and knew he would no longer be required at Beechwood, nor able to justify his presence. He decided he would return tomorrow to thank the Bayards for their hospitality and speak aloud his bottled-up thoughts before parting, he owed them that. But for now he wanted to go back to his cottage and clean up, gather his thoughts, gather himself, remove himself from here at least bodily and distance himself from some of the opportunities for self-pity. Maybe his chest would loosen up enough for a full breath of air, if he drove fast enough and far enough away.

When they arrived at the back path that turned off toward the clothesline and the lane beyond where his car awaited, Nick paused to say goodbye to Todd. Todd looked up at him then, the tears streaming down his face unchecked, uncontrollable, his eyes begging for solace. Nick reached out instinctively and enveloped him in his arms mightily, fiercely. He held him close for as long as the sobs lasted, held him against his chest, the anguished sounds muffled by his embrace, absorbing the pain and racking expression of incomprehensible loss.

## Crossing the bar
## by Alfred Tennyson

Sunset and evening star
And one clear call for me!
And may there be no moaning of the bar
When I put out to sea,
But such a tide as moving seems asleep,
Too full for sound and foam,
When that which drew from out the boundless deep
Turns again home.
Twilight and evening bell,
And after that the dark!
And may there be no sadness of farewell,
When I embark;
For tho' from out our bourne of Time and Place
The flood may bear me far
I hope to see my Pilot face to face
When I have cross'd the bar.

# CHAPTER 16

## 1946

Adrianne sat by the telephone table, swinging her crossed leg and idly fingering the gold earring she had removed so she could cradle the phone to her ear. She had just hung up with her friend, Lucy, who jarred her into realizing how far off track she had allowed her sadness to take her. She needed to buck up and today, not when she felt up to it. She heard a buzzing in her head, like the warning she imagined might precede the rumble of an avalanche, a warning that may come too late but requires instant action regardless.

It was nearly time for the new school year to begin and nothing had been done to replace Thea or provide for Todd, who always went home at the end of the summer. Todd, who was here because of his relationship to Thea; something they practically forgot as he melded with the family so seamlessly each year. If his mother had called about him, no one had informed Adrianne. She sat dazed for several minutes more, concentrating on her befuddlement more than the problem until she hit upon a course of action: find Heph.

She closed her eyes and shook her head to clear it, then quickly reclipped the earring and arose from her stupor. She looked around her, gauging the time of day in relation to Heph's likely whereabouts, and pointed herself toward the greenhouse. It was Saturday afternoon. They should be back by now from their hunt, he and his curly-coated protégé.

An observer outside the greenhouse windows, such as Maggie for example, would have witnessed shrugging shoulders, pacing and hand wringing, which graduated into sweeping arm motions, nose-to-nose declarations and fists planted firmly on hips, all while Poseidon frolicked around the edges of the fray, stopping occasionally to voice his own opinion, then leaping right back into the action. Generally at an impasse, the dance erupted once or twice in a repeat performance and ended with Adrianne's arms locked across her chest, the toes of one foot tapping masterfully. Maggie smiled a little at that, knowing what would come next. She didn't have too long to wait before Heph heaved a great sigh, lifted his arms wide in surrender and mouthed what she could imagine were the words, "All Right. Go Ahead." Maggie chuckled and walked away. She had no idea her household was about to be turned as askew as a certain dust mite protector she could name.

Adrianne lost no time in making her arrangements and was quite pleased with the plan she had been struck with, achieving all of her goals in one fell swoop. It was settled. Todd's mother, Adicia, would give notice at her present job and move to Beechwood in a couple of weeks with Todd's older brother, Perry. Best of all, Todd would become a permanent fixture so further loss to the family had been averted. She knew Chiron would be grateful. After all, Thea's family was all he had of relatives in this world.

Chiron regarded her with one raised eyebrow when she divulged her scheme to him the next afternoon. He did not speak. He did not thank her. She waited, sure she had given him a jolt, letting him take in the surprise before expressing his appreciation.

"I believe you have met them, Adicia and her son Perry?" he asked matter-of-factly.

"Oh yes, lots of times, well, once or twice when we drove Todd home with all his gear from the summer, on our way to visit Heph's mother in Rhinebeck. We were always caught up in our goodbyes and the twins were quite overwrought by the separation, but we had a chance to chat with Adicia, she was perfectly polite about thanking us, if a little reserved. I think she's somewhat shy, who could blame her, poor thing. As for Perry, no, I don't think we got a glimpse of him either of those times but for the sake of keeping Todd here with us, another boy prowling around with the gang we have already could hardly have much effect! I understand he's a year older than Todd, that makes him about thirteen, doesn't it?" She smiled sweetly at Chiron to show she was not prejudiced about young hoodlums, if that was his concern. His face did still look rather stern.

"Maybe he could be of help to you?" she suggested.

"We shall see." he said. Then he studied Adrianne and relented a little. "Adicia is a very good cook, you will like that. Let me know if you need my assistance with anything, in the meantime." He turned before she could respond and headed toward the boathouse.

When they arrived, delivered by Heph and Poseidon, there was a general uproar of greetings and it was already clear Perry and Poseidon had become good buddies. When he looked up from stroking the pup's broad head, Perry spied Maggie standing off to the side, hands clasped across her abdomen, making no effort to approach the greeting party.

Perry straightened up slowly, a cheeky smile crossing his face. "Hi, Tex!" he called out smartly, "Did you ever get them cowboy boots?"

Everyone paused mid-action and looked over at Maggie, who colored and set her mouth just so.

"Cowboy boots! Ho ho, Maggie doesn't wear cowboy boots! Do you, Maggie? Um, Tex!" Herman bowled over with that one.

Adicia was busy getting a bag from the back of the car and did not appear to notice the exchange.

Adrianne looked from her to Heph, then chose to reprimand Herman for his rudeness and ended the topic there, so no one got to find out how Maggie was connected to the State of Texas. Or how Perry could possibly have known about it.

Adicia and Perry turned simultaneously to see Chiron approach from the direction of the old copper beech. The other eyes followed their gaze. Chiron stopped on the gravel, facing the new arrivals. He nodded to Adicia formally. She returned the greeting, then her eyes faltered and she looked down. Chiron took a few steps and reached his hand out to Perry, who took it with some surprise, and relief. Chiron clasped his hand for a moment and they regarded each other.

"Welcome, son." he asserted. "Be sure to take advantage of the opportunities here."

Perry nodded tentatively once, then again with eagerness. Chiron let go of his hand, bowed again to Adicia and excused himself. Adrianne bit her lower lip as he walked away. A honey bee buzzed loopily among the bystanders and the birds resumed their song.

Once they were settled in, Adicia in Thea's room and Perry with Todd, Adrianne found the first opportunity to say, "I'm sorry you could not come out here for the funeral, Adicia. It was lovely and you would have been comforted to see it."

"Yes," Adicia acknowledged. "I wished very much I could have come, but I took sick and couldn't make the trip. It was a shame, it was."

Adrianne nodded and waited for a moment, then realized there was nothing more to be said. "Well now. Let's see. How about if I show you around the kitchen and we get started, hmm?" And she led the way down the hall into Adicia's new base of operation.

Heph invited the kids to bring Perry down to the dock for an initiation sail, a quick trip on the Sound in his 52′ cruiser, Beecham. Built in 1945, at his own shipyard to his individual specifications, she had a two-cabin layout. Forward was the main salon with two pilot berths and two settees. There was a private cabin aft, a stateroom with a small double and a single berth and a rear entrance from housing on the deck that prevented spray from getting in. It was designed mainly for day sailing and overnight cruising. The sheets were set to the cockpit for single handling. With speed in mind, Beecham's bow was high with sheers dropping fairly low at mid-ship and rising again for an artful stern. No eye could miss her sleek grace and balanced proportions. No kid could resist the lure of her gleaming mahogany deck, winking bronze winches and cleats or the slap of the halyard against the mast, its sail fairly begging to be raised.

Just as Perry stuck out his foot to step onto the gunwale, Iris quickly called out, "Permission to come aboard, sir."

"Permission granted," came the baritone reply. Iris risked a peek at Perry just before hopping on board. He pulled back and watched as Todd repeated the formality, then did the same, muffling the words in some embarrassment, but earning a slap on the back from the captain for his courtesy. It was the last contribution to the conversation he made until he was back on the dock some two hours later. He watched alertly from his position of least interference on the bow, legs crossed beneath his life preserver, back straight and stiff, wind whipping his dark hair across his eyes as he swiveled his head at each maneuver, trying to follow the choreography of the three sailors in precise coordination around him. If he was frightened he did not let on, but his inability to relax gave away his discomfort, and advertised this outing as his maiden voyage.

When they had reached the farthest point in their trip, Heph turned head to wind and the sailboat stalled. The breeze was mild here and the view of the Sound was glorious.

He never resisted this elation of escape, beckoned by the throb of the sea and sky. Invariably urged to follow wherever the water would lure him, he was a disciple of her undulating seduction. It was, he knew, this captivation that ultimately freed him to remain grounded for all the other demands of his life.

He refilled his barrel chest with fine salt spray and bared his teeth into the glare, crinkled eyes ablaze.

"What are you looking at, Daddy?" Iris inquired, head cocked with anticipation.

He looked down, startled. He smiled at her, or at himself, and had a ready answer.

"Look over there," he indicated with his chin. "As far as you can see. Just about eight miles off shore, it is. That's where the USS San Diego sank in World War I. 1918. Sank in minutes after hitting a German mine." He looked down at their faces and saw that they were primed for more.

"The ship's main mission was to escort convoys through the first leg of their submarine-infested journey across the Atlantic. Mid-morning on July 8, they suffered an explosion on their port side. They assumed it must have been a German sub and quickly manned their battle stations. They fired their guns non-stop at anything that might be a periscope or any other indication of a submarine until their port side listed so badly it was swamped and their starboard side was shooting at the clouds. By the time the captain ordered them to abandon ship and the last man was off, only twenty-eight minutes had elapsed. He had been steering towards shore as fast as he could on his starboard engines, hoping to delay the sinking of his ship long enough to reach more shallow, salvageable depths. When it was over, there were six men dead and six more wounded. She was the only major warship to be lost by the United States in the first world war. And as far as I know, she lies there still."

"No one has searched her? No one has raised her or tried?" Todd was aghast. He pictured himself taking on the task one day, see if he didn't. To be abandoned like that, forever, after such service to her country, it was inexcusable.

"She keeps her secrets for sure, and perhaps she prefers it that way. You never know," Heph replied, thinking of it that way himself for the first time. Todd stared at the horizon, skeptical, brooding. Heph prepared to gybe, called a warning as the boom swung about, and was soon running with the wind toward home.

As they approached the dock, with the sun setting starboard, they could distinguish Herman poking truculently with a stick at something in the sand. Then bending over from the waist, hands on hips, rear end aimed high and petulant, he peered intently at whatever it was he had unearthed. It was clear before long, even at a distance, that the specimen was another disappointment and they watched as he turned to flaunt his disdain when the cruiser caught his eye. He raised his hand to shade his eyes and as he confirmed their identity, splayed his feet wide and raised his chin in obvious indignation. Heph sighed, recognizing the stance as well as anyone.

"Hey, if you snooze you miss the cruise, Bud. You know that," Heph tried to sound conciliatory as he made a final knot at the dock post, tugged it once more and dropped onto the sand. He reached out to tousle Herman's hair but the little martyr ducked and backed away, no dice.

"I wouldn't have to be so vigilant around here if anyone ever told me what was going on. A real gas. I can't be everywhere you know, I have stuff to take care of. Couldn't someone have come looking for me?" His voice cracked and Heph realized he was dangerously close to shedding an embarrassing tear in front of the new guy. Heph looked over and sure enough, now that he had manipulated himself out of the life preserver, Perry was watching Herman closely and there was a gleam in his eye. Herman was aware of it, too.

Perry, his dark blue eyes nearly purple with intensity, pointedly turned his attention toward Iris, who was just about to leap down off the dock into the sand. He held out his hand and said, "Here, Iris, let me help you."

She was clearly torn between the insult of seeming to need help and the allure of gallantry by this dark newcomer that no one had ever deigned to show her before. She hesitated, but his hand remained steady, expectant. She took it.

She flounced down with both feet, hardly lady-like by any measure, but turned to him and said, "Thank you" with aplomb. Herman watched, mouth agape. She sashayed just a little as she passed him and he raised his eyes to the heavens.

Heph approached, put his arm across Herman's shoulder and leaned over to speak confidentially in his ear as they walked back toward the house.

"Were you looking for your Ba, son?" he asked not unsympathetically.

Herman didn't respond immediately and Heph assumed he was still feeling resentful about the missed sail.    He squeezed Herman's shoulder gently, reassuringly, whereupon he thought he heard the rasp of a response, "Yeah, sort of."

Finding the Ba was always a hoped-for by-product of Herman's activities no matter what he was doing. But for now, his obsession with extreme anguish overrode most other ambitions day and night, it seemed.    He was hounded by the belief that if he couldn't experience supreme emotions, he couldn't hope to rise above the average joe; a state abhorrent to the mind of a master spy or master of anything. He was getting worried, his confidence wearing thin. He had already worn out the theory that his tastes were so very refined by nature that it would be nearly impossible to surpass his own expectations; that opinion only held water for so long before even Herman had to admit it was rather unrealistic.    But he was nothing if not determined and it was a shame he didn't appreciate that trait for the true value it held in a man of high ambitions. His hands formed fists of frustration and he broke away from his dad, running the rest of the way to the house, passing even Perry in his pent up need to escape himself.

With no time for anyone in the house to get used to the new configuration, all focus by necessity turned to school and routine.    Adrianne soon devised and implemented a regimen for the children; the goal being homework, punctuality, neatness, chores and a big breakfast enforced in that order. Like soldiers all of the same rank, the treatment was simple and uniform, and optimistic at best.

The boats were hauled out one by one for winterizing, the off-shore breezes turned chill,  the puppy doubled again in stature, Adicia claimed her dominance in the kitchen wing of the house, Maggie fumed off and on daily from intrusions on her authority, the children scuffled with growing rancor and summer hobbled away.

One raw October afternoon, when the sun had abandoned its post and thickening clouds were vanguard to a biting wind, Maggie glimpsed Chiron enveloped deep within his garden. He was staking lengths of canvas gingerly around various plants, their long-expired blooms leaving her at a loss as to their identities. She put on her sweater and ventured out.

They chatted at first about the weather and the plants, then fell silent. Maggie clutched her sweater close around her middle, crossing her arms for added warmth, then cleared her throat.

"Did you recommend Thea's sister-in-law for the job here as cook, Chiron?" she began, careful to suppress any note of accusation in her voice. Chiron finished tying the knot in his twine and then straightened his bent-over shoulders, supporting his back as he rose. He studied Maggie for a moment, contemplating all her question implied.

"No, I did not," he answered kindly.

"Why are they here?" Her voice was plaintive, confused and still filled with the sadness of loss. The familiar glimmer of mischief had not yet returned to her eyes, he noticed.

They talked together for awhile, progressing eventually from one bush to the next, she offering a hand from time to time with his ministrations, he removing his scarf and wrapping it around her neck despite her objections.

"There were two crucial times that I was away at sea with Kristof Karras that I should have been here, that I should have been watching out for the well-being of Thea's family." He picked up the next stake and leaned on it as he looked off into the distance. "I had promised her grandmother I would always look after her family as if it were my own.

"Perhaps of all the failures of my life, these were the two most unforgiveable. Perhaps another guardian would have addressed impending developments with more foresight than I possessed. Perhaps I underestimated the temptations of the hearts I purported to safeguard.

"Bah." He waved a hand with contempt. "Whatever the reasons, I regret it still.

"Anna, your friend Anna, Thea's mother, was living with a distant cousin of her mother's family when she was old enough to find work. I was, as I said, months away at sea and sending regular envelopes to the States to support her, but she was sent nevertheless to earn an income." He gritted his teeth with the resentment that still invoked. "Her job took her along the docks, where she met Jasen Nikandros, who pursued her and won her consent as well as the approval of her cousin, who knew his family. His family was also from Crete and the connection carried weight. He, however, was a drunk and an ingrate. And he beat his wife."

Maggie covered her mouth, ashamed, feeling the guilt herself, as she had more than suspected the abuse.

"I warned him twice. The second chance was given as a gift to his wife, whom I could rarely refuse. Not long after the third time, when Thea was an infant, Jasen washed up quayside and saved someone else the trouble." He looked at Maggie then and she did not move a muscle.

Chiron's hand passed before his face and he turned back to his burlap. As he shook out the next piece of burlap, he resumed. "Anna raised her children herself after that, as you well know. I was an uncle to them, but not much in attendance when they were young. They did not want for much, and yet it was an arduous

278

life, and lonely. Alexsy was small for his age, agile and wily, but underweight and easily led. He ran with a rough crowd, learned some back alley skills and married the sister of one of his hooligan pals. Adicia was younger and admired him, as he was one of the few who acknowledged her at all. Once he was a father, he got himself a job in the kitchen of a Greek restaurant on the Lower East Side. His past was not so easily shrugged off, however. I tell you this, Maggie, in as few words as possible, and still with the bitterness on my tongue.

"Alexsy was accused of murder and spent his last days in jail, unconscious from his own injuries in the fight and unable to mount a defense. The story I eventually unraveled portrayed him as innocent, accosted in the alley behind the restaurant after closing one night. He had a knife and defended himself with it, but was beaten senseless despite his efforts and died several weeks later of his injuries. After being charged with murder.

"A man can convince himself he is righteous, that he follows the path of the gods, that he is devoted to his family and his duty. It does not make him heroic or even worthy. The hero path is sometimes an illusion. Despite my having spent my life trying to prove otherwise.

"I have one last intention, Maggie." He abandoned all pretense of work. "To shepherd these children. So when they find themselves at The Threshold, when they must face the abyss, they realize they have the power to prevail.

"That they can be the ones to return with the elixir.

"And that they don't need to travel the path alone."

# CHAPTER 17

## 1947

"Oh, who closed the linen closet this time?" Maggie threw her hands up in the air then scurried to the storage chest down the hall to find the little gismo that pried open the lock if you put it in just so and jiggled it just right. The key had been missing for months now, no one could say since when but heaven knows no one had had a new one made, either. It surely was a nuisance, especially on a day like this when dozens of people would descend upon them within a couple of hours and the napkins were sitting on a shelf deep inside that closet. As she jiggled and pried and tugged on the knob, she could smell the faint fragrance of lavender soap from behind the door, the only thing liable to escape its confines, apparently. Lordy, who could keep up with the goings on around here. Christmas barely over, and here we are dragging it all out again with a snowstorm threatening and the children all with colds. She jumped as the doorbell rang.

"Now who is it?" she demanded of the ceiling with exasperation. "No one could be this early." But it was the back door and it was Beth, coming with the tray of hors d'oeuvres she had promised. Before anyone else abandoned whatever preparations they were in the middle of making, Iris reached the door and swung it wide.

"Hi, Miss Beth," she said, heaving a great sigh, exuding self-pity from every pore. There could have been any number of lamentable causes; small, legitimate or imagined or perhaps it was merely the sniffles, hard to tell, but she wasn't going to get by Beth without an explanation.

"What's happened now, young lady? I know you're a party girl, I thought you would be modeling your best new dress for me and here you are looking fit to be tied. And not even a lacy pair of socks to show off, this must be serious. Come on now, tell me what's wrong." They walked together into the pantry, where Beth could put down her dish, slough off her coat and give her full attention to the situation.

Iris' lower lip was quivering under the scrutiny, so Beth glanced around, heard noises nearby and whispered, "Let's go into the library where no doubt there's a roaring fire to sit by. We can talk then without being interrupted, I'll bet." Iris could not resist such a rush of kindness, something she felt quite lacking around here lately. She meekly led the way down the hall to the library and plopped her fanny onto the velvet bench before the fire, quickly scooting over to make room for Miss Beth and looking up expectantly, patting the space next to her by way of invitation.

"All right, my girl, I'm all ears."

Suddenly embarrassed, Iris looked over at the fire. He legs began to swing rhythmically against the seat. Beth rested her hands upon her knees, patiently.

"It's that ole Perry, that's what. He's mean as a snake. And he gets the others to gang up against me, me against the boys it's so unfair. I know, I know, I'm used to it, but now it's worse and I just can't stand it anymore!" The tears began to flow. Perry had played up to her at first, giving the snub to Herman. But now he'd turned on her and she couldn't imagine what she'd done to deserve it. Try as she might.

"We were practicing the Borough Alarms…"

"The what?"

Perhaps Iris did not hear the question. "We're always training for our quest and I'm pretty good at some of the challenges, too, I can run faster than Poseidon, practickly! But now with that ole Perry butting in all the time, they keep giving me the challenges that no one could do. Today they wanted me to get buried under the snow—by them, of course—and then prove I could escape! I almost did it, too, but once they started piling snow on my head and I got some up my nose, I just burst out bawling and they about laughed their fool heads off, calling me a weak-kneed girl and saying maybe this should be a boys-only kind of training program. After my blood oath and all! Perry didn't give no blood oath I can tell you that, who's the real coward, huh?" She stopped for breath and crossed her arms.

Beth seemed a little perplexed and decided to just stick with the main idea. "Well now." She paused until a glimmer of firelight flared in her eyes. She turned and faced Iris squarely. She put her hand gently under the freckled little chin, and waited until she had the full attention of the pouting face.

"There was a woman who lived out in Setauket during the Revolutionary War named Ann Smith Strong. Her spy name was Nancy." Iris blinked theatrically.

"She was part of the spy chain that kept George Washington informed about the movements of the British troops around the coast of Long Island. The British were always on the lookout for what they called American saboteurs. One of her jobs was to give the signal to the local patriots announcing the arrival and hiding place of a local scout who came to report on British movement. He had to sail secretively in and out of various hidden coves to avoid detection. Nancy, free to move about among the British soldiers, being a woman and discreet, was able to keep a close watch on his comings and goings.

"Back in those days, most women wore red petticoats." Those words elicited an admiring reaction. "So when Nancy hung a black petticoat on her clothes line, it meant the patriot had come ashore. Each of the hiding places for his boat had been assigned a number, so she let on which place he had chosen by the number of handkerchiefs she hung next to the petticoat. It was a simple plan, and brilliant. And unlike many of her male counterparts, including her own husband, she was never caught."

Beth studied her companion, whose legs had mercifully stopped pumping, and said, "Don't let anyone…" Footsteps clicked in the hallway, coming in their direction. "Well, Hon, just remember, it's the women who prove their bravery by using their brains."

It was a rousing party after all, and Iris danced with both Miss Kathleen's and Miss Lucy's husbands, showing off her sateen skirt to its fullest when she realized if she flounced just right, it ballooned up all around magnificently.

She sighed with contentment as she viewed herself from all angles one more time in the hall mirror upstairs, after she and the boys had curtsied and bowed and been banished from the party like always, only this time she didn't care because she just didn't care, that's all. Finian's Rainbow had recently opened on Broadway and someone mentioned how remarkably like the young leading lady Iris looked tonight. She smiled at her reflection, to get a glimpse of what the grown-ups thought was so enchanting, when Perry's shadow crossed the mirror behind her and he emerged in fact around the corner. She whirled about, not even for the sake of her skirt's effect, to witness his surprise at finding her there. He grinned a crooked grin at her, as if they shared a secret she must have forgotten, and spun around to go the other way, knocking his shoulder against the corner and swaying across the hallway like a, like a, sailor.

It was Herman who stood scowling before Chiron's desk two weeks later, waiting for him to get back from his rounds. Church had dragged on beyond endurance, they had been fed that rotten tomato soup for lunch that was practically worse than sitting in Sunday School every week, and he had just now been released from his penance for the disruption in the pews that was not his fault at all and it was practically going to be dark soon, golly.

He fiddled absently with the Little Midshipman on Chiron's desk, manipulating the sextant in its hand so the index bar shifted to the widest point at one end of the arc then slid smoothly back to the other end, again and again, picturing how he could use it for some future celestial navigation.

He was quite chagrined and a little miffed when Chiron's footsteps sounded not from outside but from up the stairs in his private quarters. He squinted his eyes in the direction of the footsteps, taking the mislocation personally. But when Chiron's broad face emerged from the shadows of the staircase, he was so delighted he found himself racing across the width of the guardhouse to meet him. Then he side-stepped all the way back, accompanying Chiron, bouncing and sliding to the rhythm of his ebullient greeting.

Once Chiron was seated in his ancient, cracked-leather chair, he said to his guest, "I'm sorry, Herman, I did not hear you knock," to which his guest colored judiciously.

"I'm here to report the first signs of spring!" He rushed to fill the silence.

"Herman, it's January."

Well that was a fact only an amateur would fall for, his look distinctly indicated. "I saw a huge flock of robins out front. Like about ten or twenty dozen of them! They were everywhere, Chiron. They swooped up and around in waves, across the lawn, into the field and then back again, landing in the big tree then the grass then the rooftop chimneys, whole platoons of them. A couple even flew in a circle around my head! That sure seems like a sign to me, what do you think about that?" He thrust out his chest as if it were red-breasted.

"It sounds like quite a sight to see," Chiron admitted.

"So are we going to be able to take the boats out of dry dock soon, what do you think?"

"I think you can expect a big snowstorm in the next few days and the robins will be gone. In the winter, when it's not mating season and they don't require their own territory, they tend to travel in large flocks. But they don't like snow. It's a dry winter that brings them here together, not an early spring, I'm afraid."

Herman glowered, fairly growling at that news. "I don't like big flocks myself," he decided suddenly, the first hint of the reason for his visit, Chiron surmised.

"Big flocks or new birds in the flock?" he asked casually. Herman looked at him.

"Aw gee, Chiron, things used to be swell around here, we were a band of marauders, just like Maggie said. We had adventures and, and plans and real live loyalty for each other and stuff. Why does someone have to come along and ruin it?"

Chiron did not choose to respond.

"He is, Perry I mean, he is always lording it over us all the time. He thinks he's the only one who can tell us what to do, even Todd, and boy does he let us have it if we don't do it his way. And, and if we tell on him as well, aw gee." He hit the desk with the heel of his hand

and turned away, resting his behind against the edge of the desktop and hunching his shoulders in defeat.

Then he whipped back around and continued, "And boy is he hard-boiled. He's not afraid of anything, he's crazy, that's what I think. He's crazy," he tapered off. He studied Chiron closely to see how he was reacting.

"Perry is a pale criminal," Chiron stated. Herman reacted with amazement. Even he did not call Perry a criminal.

"He has the courage of the knife, but not of the blood."[1]

"Huh?"

"Herman, remember those words and use your powers of observation. You will soon learn what they mean and you will decide then how to handle yourself. You are not quite ten years old, but you have the resources to deal with Perry on your own. I have faith that it won't take you very long, either."

Herman took a step back and looked over Chiron's head at the map on the wall behind him, in contemplation. Concentrating mightily, he mouthed the words of courage and blood, committing them to memory. Chiron was satisfied.

Adrianne was opening and closing drawers. The final place she could think to search was the telephone table, knowing her penchant for taking off her earring and leaving it there while she talked. She even crouched down to peer into the crack where the baseboard had separated from the floor. Nothing. She sank into the nearest chair in consternation; those were her best gold earrings and she really had no one to blame but herself.

The children were just finishing lunch, still rosy-cheeked after valiant efforts to navigate their home-grown ice rink, diligently planned, eagerly anticipated for months and executed as promised but something short of satisfactory, nonetheless. Branches, leaves, old snow and other debris broke up the frozen surface, which remained mottled and uneven despite repeated efforts to spread fresh water and refreeze the surface. Despite endless buckets of water hauled from far upstream, poured strategically, spread carefully with various under-qualified implements such as mops and snow shovels, and infinite patience for freezing time between layers, well, infinite impatience in some cases, it just wasn't enough. So today they decided it didn't look so bad after all and in no time had strapped on skates by rink's edge, resulting in wet fannies all around, and launched. It was frozen solid, that was the good news. But no one got a single good glide or avoided a flat-out sprawl from momentum stopped dead every few strokes. Still, Herman's bruised chin was the worst of it, and even now they were devising new solutions for their future official hockey arena. This was a quest, for sure, Todd pointed out, and excellent training for solving the impossible in the face of the unfathomable forces of nature. Perry snorted at that, but refrained from comment. He was starting to be intrigued by the idea of a quest and with no one around to impress with his disdain for such childish ideas, scorned it less and less.

Maggie wandered in just as Iris was leaving the table.

"Whoa, little swashbuckler! Go back and clear your place. You know better than that, now go on."

Adicia stepped forward. "I have told you so more than once, Iris, and push your chair in as well." She grabbed the napkin by Iris' plate and made a swipe at her mouth, then glanced at Maggie to make sure the effort had been noticed. Maggie looked away. She followed Iris across the kitchen to the back hallway where the snow pants were strewn and leaking puddles.

Iris looked up at her quizzically. Maggie started to speak, then closed her mouth and exhaled. She looked over her shoulder, turned back and began again.

"Whenever you leave a room, my girl, always turn round and check it first." She was not quite sure that was exactly what she meant to say, and Iris thought it rather strange advice, even coming from Maggie. But she was too busy to chance prolonged discussion so she nodded agreeably and snatched up her hat. Maggie watched her dress, the uneasy feeling that was niggling at her too obscure to unravel or attribute.

"Last night I got up for a drink of water," Perry gulped his milk. "I saw someone outside, slinking along on cat's feet. I don't think he was from around here. He was way too shifty-looking. Then I heard an owl hooting off somewhere out by the boat house and I saw him turn to look, too, all jumpy-like."

Todd and Herman exchanged looks.

"Then what?" Todd asked softly.

Perry shrugged. "Then nothin'. I was tired. I went back to bed."

"Sounds like we're back on the Shadow Hunt. Sounds like the intruder has returned," Todd suggested to Herman, winking.

Perry was impressed. He hadn't expected his story to rate credibility, much less fit into a scenario already in progress. He awaited further developments.

"About time you believed me." Herman did not always appreciate sarcasm. "This investigation has been on the back burner is all, but I knew the heat would get turned up sooner or later, I've just been biding my time."

"Yeah, like that night when Iris and I had the binoculars and discovered your intruders out by the garden smooching, Nick and Thea. Hoo boy! Where were you then, sitting somewhere on your back burner? You missed everything."

Perry leaned forward discreetly, careful not to distract them.

"Oh no, I'm not the one who missed something that night, tough guy. I am always on duty. In fact, you missed one very important shadow that night, I see. I am surprised and disappointed in you. You are too easily satisfied, Watson, my dear. Yes, very disappointing, indeed."

Todd raised his eyebrows and snorted. Perry's eyes followed the sound. Aware suddenly that Perry was watching, Todd leaned over and whacked Herman on the back and guffawed.

"That's a good one, Old Man! You're a regular comedian!"

"I heard every word they said. I was there. And I learned a lot." He peered meaningfully at Todd from under his shaggy locks, but inside he winced once more at the memory of his missing Ba, exquisite anguish and his eternal sentence of longing as a result. He tried not to show the agony it invoked. After all, he wanted to be a tough guy, too.

"And they were not the intruders," he added unequivocally.

Perry heard the rap of a wooden spoon over by the sink. "Aw no, Ma, you're not going to make me eat that are you?" Lunch was over and he didn't want a scene, but he had known all day what was coming. Maggie came back in time to witness the procedure the second time it was performed by Adicia's expert hands. She lifted the other half of the pomegranate, scored the hard rind five or six times, then holding it over a bowl, rapped the shell with the spoon. The seeds ejected from the casing and gathered congenially in the bottom of the dish, impeccably cooperative. There was a small gasp of admiration from Maggie's open mouth.

Adicia picked up that bowl as well as another filled with raspberries and carried them over to Perry's place at the table. She set them down, took a step back, clasped one wrist against her belly and settled in to observe.

Perry made no move to eat. He looked down at his hands in his lap, as if they refused to perform. Adicia cleared her throat. Only Todd knew what this was about.

"I was always glad my birthday was in the summer, when I was here" he declared. "Those things could kill a body."

Perry scowled at his brother. Sympathy did not sit well with a doomed man.

"You mind your manners, young man," Adicia warned.

"I love raspberries!" Herman offered.

"I scoured every last market in town for those raspberries this time of year, they're Perry's favorite."

At Adicia's tone, Maggie bristled.

"Go ahead, son, I am waiting," his mother directed.

Perry dug in and crammed a fistful of pomegranate seeds into his reluctant mouth.

Herman furrowed his brow in confusion. "Did you say it was his birthday or something? Perry, is it your birthday today?"

"It's his birthday all right, he's fourteen years old today."

Herman was flabbergasted that this was the first they had heard of it. Maggie ruminated.

"Pomegranates are popular fruit in Greece. Among other things, they are a symbol of good luck. We always serve them for birthdays in my family. And raspberries are my boy's favorite. I got them special."

"Here," Perry pushed the bowl of raspberries towards the middle of the table, then forced another fistful of pomegranate seeds between his lips. "Want some?" He spewed.

Before Herman could make a grab, Adicia held out her hand imperiously. "Eat them, Perry. You eat every one of them. I got them special."

Herman's hand retreated and disappeared under the table. He eyed Adicia warily.

Perry was looking apoplectic; red-faced, cheeks bulging, red juice dripping down his chin. Todd suffered for him, silently submissive, impotent.

Maggie glared until Adicia felt compelled to look over at her accusing eyes. She turned then and walked back into the kitchen, Maggie at her heels.

Before Maggie, nearly sputtering, could formulate a commentary, Adicia turned to her from the sink.

The two women faced each other, taking their measure like wrestlers on the mat. Then, voice wavering, Adicia uttered, "Sometimes you love your children more than you can afford to." Her narrow lips pressed together defensively, emphasizing the lines around her mouth. She picked up the spoon and turned to wash it.

Maggie's opened mouth was becoming a habitual response around Adicia. She stood back and pondered her antagonist for a moment, bemused.

"Adicia," she kept her voice carefully modulated. "We don't want no trouble here."

Adicia put down her dish cloth, placed her hands on the edge of the sink and spoke with her back to Maggie.

"Life is trouble. Only death is no trouble."[1] She picked up the dish cloth and thwacked it against the edge of the counter. And Maggie's objection found no voice.

Adrianne entered from the other side of the house and saw the boys at the table.

"Have you boys seen my gold earring, by chance? It looks like this." She held out the remaining earring for their inspection. They all peered obediently into her palm. They all shook their heads, not me. Only Herman raised an eyebrow of suspicion, but kept his counsel, for once. He did not want to comment in front of Perry.

"Well, let me know. They were my favorites." She passed across the kitchen to where Maggie and Adicia were, even though they had already been queried. If she felt the tension between them, she didn't let on. Only Maggie seemed uncomfortable and Adrianne was gone before noticing her high flush.

When spring did finally arrive, Adicia was the first one to avail herself of the one outdoor pursuit that held any allure. She was apparently an avid fisherman, although she hadn't shown any such inclination when she first arrived last fall, when the weather was equally enticing. Preferring to perch on an old camping chair she found in the boat house, she set herself each morning after breakfast at the edge of the western dock and dangled her line over the side. Then she sat back to bask in the warming sun as if she had achieved her purpose and any actual catching of fish would be an unwelcome, if sometimes unavoidable, side effect. The twins had the opposite view. They noted that she seemed superstitious about her methods, as they often saw her leaning over the water with a long stick, as if she were prodding the water in a proscribed manner as ritual to lure prey. When they laughed about it one day, Perry and Todd both cut them to the quick, making it clear that criticism of Adicia would not be tolerated.

On the weekends the children often spent their mornings at the beach with Poseidon, who no longer required training in the retrieval of submerged treasures, but who loved the game so much that he hounded them with choice objects for throwing until their arms wore out. In between throws, they practiced challenges intended to prepare them for battle mode; skill sets they never tired of honing; tests of bravery, endurance and memory as infinite as Poseidon's diving obsession.

This week's plan required all the nautical flags from the storage closet. They included most letters of the alphabet, all the numbers except 3, 7 and 8, plus the code flag, three answering pennants and the Abandon All Races flag, which was highly prized just for its dire potential. Some had an easier time decoding the color patterns than others, and Perry refused to participate at all beyond the letter P and one or two others, but Todd studied diligently and could identify them like flash cards by the third try. Iris was just a few missteps behind. It was decided that not everyone needed to know how to send and read messages, just those who could be spared from more crucial endeavors.

After the flags had been placed around the estate, in a scavenger hunt sort of way, the twins stood at attention before their captain. Perry held the stopwatch.

"Is this a Borough Alarm, sir?" Herman inquired.

"Not everything is a Borough Alarm, Herman. How many times do I have to tell you that? A Borough Alarm is the highest level of alert possible. And it would not involve a stop watch, sheesh. Any more dumb questions?"

"No, sir!" Herman was unabashed.

"Now! Raise your fists!" Everyone gathered close, Perry deftly shoving the stop watch into his pocket first, and stuck out their fists, one on top of the other in their ritual salute.

"To William Campion and the Equitable Fire!" they proclaimed in unison. Then the timekeeper resumed his post and they were off.

The raven kept a record of much of the activity surrounding the dock, with one eye on the dog in case he provided another morsel she could wrest from him, the other often trained on Adicia, with a suggestion of distaste in her haughty avian posture. Today she flapped her wings noisily, cawed a promise to return and swooped off toward something that caught her attention down the beach.

Finally Herman's day of days arrived. The boats were set in the water and bobbed gaily with the promise of new adventure upon his vast high seas.

Just before Decoration Day, Adrianne kept the children with her in town while she ran her errands. They were vexed by the tedium, choosing to remain in the car as a protest to the chafe of her apron strings. The promise of an ice cream was only an inducement to Herman and even he was not particularly gracious about it. Adrianne was remarkably tolerant of their bad temperaments and still quite cheerful after cajoling them into double cones after all as she herded them back into the car with their sticky fingers and chocolate-stained shirts. By then it was early afternoon. She looked pointedly at her watch and smiled up at them, announcing it was time to go home. She ignored their performance of it's-about-time eye rolling and exaggerated moans of relief, drawn out though it was. Eventually the car ride home turned quiet, while various degrees of resentment were examined and confirmed in each of their minds, dark clouds consuming most of the back seat.

When she skidded to a stop on the gravel just beyond the newly flowing fountain in front of the house, she announced that Heph was looking for them and shooed them off toward the beach. It was then the older boys got an inkling that something was up.

They were truculent at first, determined not to show any eagerness to follow Adrianne's orders, but curiosity impinged upon their resentment and soon their pace turned brisk. The twins sensed the sudden change in the air and perked up instantly. Within seconds they were all racing down the path, jostling and angling for the first glimpse of what could be something big; the black clouds being left to disperse by themselves in the car.

It was Todd who gleaned the significance of what they saw when they arrived, breathless and quizzical, at the water's edge. At the third dock, the farthest east, were two identical cat boats, painted navy blue. Sails unfurled, bronze trim eagerly signaling the sunlight's invitation, lines straining impatiently against their confinement, they implored their new owners to climb aboard, climb aboard, come test the farthest limits of our streamlined prowess.

Heph was beaming, watching them as they admired the steam-bent white oak frames with Atlantic white cedar planking, the timeless lines and powerful hulls of the Beetle Cats. He knew these little boats, 12′4″ long, wide-beamed at 6′, could be ferocious when the winds picked up, yet their value was in their simplicity, ease of handling, shallow draft and overall stability. They were unsinkable and with their gaff rigging, if the tiller were released, the boat would more or less head into the wind and practically stop. It was a good choice for these young racers, yet still impressive to their aspiring eyes. Todd and Perry knew instinctively these beauties were meant for them.

Speechlessly admiring, standing arm in arm, the boys hesitated to approach their craft, in case they proved to be an illusion. No one urged them on; this show of reverence seemed appropriate to the occasion. Looking at the first boat, Todd's eye caught a movement at the top of the mast. The crow was perched there, claiming her right to a vessel's highest vantage point, the position named for her species in fact, and her privilege of overseeing the scenery below. They eyed each other with mutual recognition, she and Todd. He nodded to her in deference.

"I know what we will name our boats." he said. Perry looked at him askance, the younger brother taking such liberty.

"Chiron told us a Norse myth about a king whose messengers were two crows: Thought and Memory. They traveled the world and reported back to him everything they learned.

"Thought or Memory. Take your pick." He offered his hand to Perry, who regarded it, thinking, then grasped it and shook heartily.

"Thought and Memory it is," he affirmed. Afterthought and Short Memory might have served better, as it turned out.

# CHAPTER 18

## 1947

The Bayard family was late for church on Sunday, so they found themselves seated just a few rows from the back of the church, close enough to hear the whispering of the choir members who stood just inside the nave awaiting their signal to begin the procession.

Iris distinctly heard Miss Carol trying to distract Miss Charlene.

"Surely you are aware that everyone knows you are not that tall and by wearing those high heels you aren't going to fool anyone. In fact you will probably fall down flat and turn us all into a line of blue bowling pins sprawled all the way up the aisle."

"You are not that much taller than I am, who do you thing you're fooling?" Charlene was used to Carol's idea of small talk.

"And do you see me wearing stilettos to church? Mark my words, you're going to take a fall."

They continued in like manner, their voices too low to distinguish but punctuated regularly by muffled laughter.

Adrianne whispered to no one in particular, "I swear they have so much fun in that choir it's a sin. They almost make me wish I could carry a tune."

"Not all of them can," Heph turned a leering eye toward Carol.

From the back of the choir, the whole congregation could hear a "Hush!" Iris recognized the voice of Mr. Roy, Miss Charlene's husband.

As always, Herman watched for another member of the Daughters of the Skating Club, Miss Susie; he thought she was dreamy. She was the choir leader and whenever she sang a solo, he blushed as if she were singing it just to him.

The blue gowns eventually proceeded, voices raised on some invisible cue. Just as they reached the steps leading to the chancel, Miss Charlene's ankle bent to the side and she stumbled slightly, bumping against Miss Carol. There was no way to tell if she did it intentionally but Iris had her guess.

Once again, that was the end of the good part as far as the twins were concerned. The rest of the service involved more self-discipline than they could muster and never ended well. Sometimes Mr. Roy signaled to them from the choir and made them giggle, but this week they were too far back. An eon went by, and Iris did manage to get Herman in trouble as usual, even with the distance of two parents between them. What was the point of even trying to be religious? It never paid off, at least not for him.

Scuffling around aimlessly outside after the service, straining against the four in hand knot at his neck, shirttails freed in the hopes of luring fresh air up his sticky, itchy back, waiting for his parents to finish gabbing with the minister and their friends, Herman wandered toward the shade of the old elm tree near the parking lot. As he stood studying an earthworm from this morning's shower valiantly writhing toward the edge of the blistering sidewalk to the grass beyond, and frankly betting against its chances, he heard light footsteps approaching. Without looking up, he could tell it was Miss Lynn; he would know her perfume anywhere.

"There you are, my buddy Herman! I was looking for you; I knew you'd be wandering around here somewhere."

He smiled up at her and turned in her direction, the worm show being pretty much over by then, anyway. "Hi, Miss Lynn," he said with Sunday School polish.

"Did you ever find your Ba, Hon?" She inquired gently, reluctant to reopen old wounds.

"Nah," he responded casually. Then he looked up at her guiltily. "I'm sorry I lost the blanket you knitted for me, it was swell. I mean it, it was the best. Even though I did sort of wear out it, by the end."

She laughed at the understatement. "Well how about if I made you a new one, just like the old one? That's why I came looking for you, to see if you would like me to do that. I'd be glad to."

Alas, the poor jaded kid knew such a tempting idea would not change anything. Ba was not replaceable, and the knowledge made him want to fling himself down on the scorching sidewalk with the earthworm. It was that hopeless. Suddenly he knew it absolutely. He looked at Lynn forlornly, not sure how to respond. Reading his answer on his face, she reached out to pat him on the shoulder. "Don't worry..." she began.

"Miss Lynn! Miss Lynn!" Iris skipped over brightly and waited to be greeted. After a few ritual exchanges between fashion mavens, Iris turned so she stood just alongside Miss Lynn, facing the same direction, in order for all observers to see clearly they were both dressed in yellow.

Adrianne and Heph strolled over with Miss Anita, who practically rounded out the whole club membership for the day, at least the Protestant members, except for Miss Kathleen who was a Catholic and besides, she was off in Arizona for a golf tournament. But she was the one who had grown up in Hell's Kitchen, so Herman never minded talking to her. Even if she was awfully lady-like, considering.

299

Now Anita put her arm around Herman's shoulder and leaned over as if she were about to conspire with him.

"You ought to have a chat with Miss Anita, Herman, her little brother just entered the Merchant Marine Academy," his mother nodded significantly.

"You don't have to invoke my brother, he's got nothing on Herman here and besides, I can beat him in a fight any time." She winked at her co-conspirator.

Herman said, "Maybe you should go to the Merchant Marine Academy."

Anita laughed heartily. "Now there's an idea, Herman, that might solve a lot of my problems." They started off together. "Let me show you how I always got my brother in a headlock."

On the drive home, Herman thought he saw Nick's coupe pass them going the other direction, but he glimpsed it a little late and could not identify the driver. He became slightly alarmed that he also could not read the license plate, what if his eyes were going bad from all that staring and stuff? He turned back around and whopped the back of his head against the upholstery a few times, wondering what else could go wrong. He just whop didn't whop feel whop so good.

The next day Hephron was searching for his gold stick pin, the one with the diamond in the middle. He wanted to wear it to a dinner engagement where he was giving a speech to a group of yacht enthusiasts, several of them clients. The design was an intricately-carved shield, made of eighteen-carat gold and a gift from his grandfather. The detailed description he insisted on giving to everyone did not increase the incidence, however, of its whereabouts being recalled by any of them. A week later Maggie noticed the antique bottle on the shelf in the corner of the living room was missing its silver fleur-de-lys stopper. The next day

Clement approached Adrianne to report on the stained glass window he had been repairing in the plow shed. He said he'd be darned if one of the panes wasn't missing, the one with the teardrops of amber in it. Now the household was spooked, the locks on the doors gained new respect and the children galvanized for assault. No one made any more jokes about the Shadow Hunt. With school out for the summer, it became nearly a full time pursuit, practically a quest.

"Why don't you try making phanouropita?" Adicia suggested at breakfast. "It's a cake you bake in honor of St. Phanourios, the patron saint of lost articles. I can help you."

That suggestion was met with a rousing endorsement, more for its call to action than anything. The morning wore away amidst clouds of flour across shafts of kitchen sunlight and cake batter on the linoleum for Poseidon to dispatch.

When they ceremoniously presented a thick slice of cake to Chiron, he asked them if they had said a prayer to St. Phanourios as well as his mother, as per the tradition. They quickly formulated a prayer over Chiron's portion, and for extra measure the older boys genuflected and made the sign of the cross. The twins imitated them, somewhat irreverently in their Protestant ignorance, but with enthusiasm.

"And now you must share it with at least seven people, but you cannot tell them what you are trying to find." They stood mulling over that development, at a loss, counting and figuring and counting again.

"Did we by any chance tell you what we are looking for, Chiron?" Iris asked hopefully.

In the end, Poseidon got a piece of cake and the rest of the recipients, including Clement and Clarisse, pled ignorance regarding what the children could possibly have lost and so their mission was ultimately accomplished. By that time the day was nearly spent. If Adicia had told them all this project entailed they may have given it a pass. But as it was, they took Chiron's binoculars upstairs to the gatehouse hallway and stationed themselves on the window seat to await developments.

In contradiction to the skeptics among them, it was not long before a suspect presented himself. The buzzer at the gate sounded and Chiron allowed the dubious caller to gain entrance. Herman made a mental note to check the expected visitor clipboard in the alcove later, being as he would not leave his post now for love nor lettuce, convinced these other three comedians were just here for back-up; this surveillance called for a pro with a track record.

They watched as the delivery man pulled around to the side, got out of his truck and rang the kitchen doorbell. They held their breath as they waited until Adicia appeared at the door and accepted the small package. When the delivery man held out the clipboard for her to sign, she dropped the package into her apron pocket to free her hands, and gave him her signature. She nodded and said a few words before turning back into the house. The delivery man disappeared in front of his truck and they all rose up on their knees, craning their necks for maximal visibility. Heartbeats passed, enough to suggest several scenarios to at least one eager scout, primed and ready to spring. Where did he sneak off to, huh? He could have gone anywhere, he better not try coming in here he'd be in for a surprise then, and mighty sorry, too, I'll give him one right in the kisser, see if I won't. But what if he steals something right from under our noses this time like, like, Poseidon or something while we're just sitting up here gabbing? Shouldn't we go down there now? Shhh! He's going to hear you. Shush yourself, this is giving me the heebie jeebies. We may have to bump him off. What if he takes a powder and we're watching this truck he left right there in the driveway acting like a decoy, blocking everything he does, didya think of that? I say it's time we call a spade a spade, or a spade a Borough Alarm, gee.

The sound of a smack achieved a measure of silence.

Maybe he had stopped to tie his shoe or something, but there he came, around the front of the truck to the driver's side door, casual as a jaybird. They couldn't see anything suspicious bulging in his pockets, under his shirt or clasped in his hands. Drat. They all umphed down onto the cushion, deflated. They didn't even watch as he turned the truck round deftly and drove right under their window on his way out. As a final insult, his truck backfired and they all jumped a foot in the air.

That night they played Easy Money on the library floor and didn't do any night prowling as they had planned. It was no use, anyway.

But that night, not for the first time, the long shadow of their old friend Nick crossed the garden path.

Well, what harm could it do, coming here? He knew nowhere else to go. He was foundering. He was forfeit. He had descended into the belly of the whale.

In the darkness and hopelessness of his solitude he was worn down, insides writhing, desperate to conjure the formula of escape. The magic incantation. The key that unlocks something like solace. His center, he thought, the center Chiron told him every man had to find within himself. He pined for that quiet center from which all purposeful action stems. It was his singular focus now, the only desire he could muster nearly a year after her death. Yet he felt naked, spent; far worse than his night prowlings here a year ago. More an actor than ever.

It was no more than a battle-worn survivor's instinct to retreat to Beechwood. It was as close to the location of a center as he could imagine. Imagination was not his strong point. Strong points were not his strong point. Salvation was an illusive bugger. He tripped and went down hard on the shells at the fountain, cutting his knees and his cheek, wiping the blood with his scraped palm, smearing it, tasting it, laughing soundlessly, shoulders contracting with each spasm, finally coming to rest against his ears, chin sunken into his collar.

The heels of his shoes were worn down at the outer edges as if he had been traipsing aimlessly in that very pair every day for a year, which he probably had but couldn't be sure. His pants were a little baggy in the seat. His handkerchief, relatively clean but unironed, poked limply out of his back pocket, stuffed there some time ago and forgotten. His hair was shaggy, curlier than it seemed when trimmed. A lock of hair had fallen across his forehead, making him appear vulnerable yet dashing, despite his neglect. It helped disguise the weary grief in his eyes.

He had spent this year amassing his father's papers, studying his affairs, wrapping up agreements with the military over the one vessel his father had leased them in anticipation of the war. He had proven to be a good manager and was planning to invest in another shipment bound for Europe next month. Kristof had been more prudent during his financial collapse than Nick could have imagined, and displayed more foresight than even Chiron would have given him credit for. There was a family business to be salvaged and Nick had discovered an affinity for the challenge.

But it was a lonely endeavor, requiring minimal contact with business associates or government agencies and no employees or interaction with the public necessary at all.

One by one the lights of the house went dark and still Nick did not move. When the last lamp was extinguished he looked up, suddenly feeling his solitude surge in a torrent through his veins, as if its goal were to excise every drop of blood from his system, allowing it to escape, to drain from the shell of a body that no longer nourished it, no longer tended its welfare. He peered into the murk below him for signs of the thickening pool. He was light-headed. He was muddled. He closed his eyes and dreamt.

There were people all around him, dark shadows, different sizes, familiar yet indistinguishable. The farthest of them carried a torch and as they approached him, the bearer passed the torch to another, who accepted it and glided through the throng until he found his own intended recipient and handed the torch off in turn. He watched the fire pass from person to person with a growing desire to feel the warmth of its glow for himself but it eluded him time and again, coming close but veering just as he reached out, receding, then flaring temptingly once more, nearly searing his fingers this time yet again unattainable. Soon it was handed off to a shadow just the other side of him and the throng departed the way they'd arrived, in a choreographed mass of dark bodies that ebbed and swelled and sang like the ringing in his ears, until only the song was left, lingering in the night breeze as a reminder of what he had forgone.

When he opened his eyes and looked into the infernal pulsing sky, he had a notion that the tenor of the shadows had been prescient. They were...he thought about how they were. They were steadfast.

305

Faithful. Open. With a show of deference they had handed off the fire, by which each of them had been burned, and yet the next disciple invariably accepted the torch with relish. They accepted the torch as if it made them come alive. He felt their impulse to life, then, their attraction to the light.[1]

In this last year, Nick had learned that loss is relentless. Love can no more be restricted to the living than it can be banished beyond the grave. No barrier can resist love, no resolve can withstand it. No pain can destroy it. No tears can dilute it. Love is impervious to every weapon. Time does not diminish its power. Torment does not deter it. Heartbreak can coexist with love in direct proportion to the greatness that love has achieved. Courage, the more the better, serves only for the sake of appearances; it does nothing to assuage the haunting ache of sorrow. Love does not release its hold, and as much as the bearer may rent his soul with the desperation of eternal suffering, it is the love itself that no power in heaven could induce him to relinquish. It is the paradox of loss. It is inexorable.

And yet. And yet. "It is exalted." He said the words aloud, each syllable reverberating within his chest. He heard them echo off the fountain, felt them bathe his fevered head in cool relief, the breeze offering the kindest of ministrations. He took note of each sensation as if his salvation depended upon it.

Maybe all he could do was lean toward the light. He arched forward then, face raised to the heavens as if basking in its divine glow. He looked up and, as a star with a surfeit of high-spirits flared above him, he responded to its shimmer with an echoing thrill in his core that commanded no remorse, nor guilt, nor fear as the price of its exuberance. He began to tremble at the barest inkling of promise, the faintest ember of hope. He pressed the fingers of his hands against his sternum, encouraging the flint of desire to fan the ember within his nascent, gaping center.

*     *     *

The four kids were a little boisterous the next day, the older two feeling somewhat foolish about their spying debacle of yesterday, the twins sensitive to their bravado and eager to demonstrate some of their own. They wandered around, exchanging barbs mostly, tiring of each other, snappish. Heph had instructed Todd and Perry to practice the skill of reefing their sails, a method of tying the sails to reduce the area exposed to the wind, highly effective in blustery weather and especially valuable on a beetle cat. They eventually drifted over to the beach and began to address the task. It was a little tricky and even though they had performed it well enough with Heph standing by, they were somewhat clumsy and tentative on their own. And they did not care to suffer any little barnacles clinging to their sides. Herman and Iris found themselves forbidden to step within a league of Perry and Todd's dock, whatever that meant, and after gazing balefully from afar for an interminable amount of time, they drifted over to where Chiron was working on his own vessel, preparing to depart.

He was replacing a couple of the chafe guards on his cutter by the time they arrived. As they stood and observed with unusual restraint, something caught Herman's curiosity and he inched closer until he was right off Chiron's shoulder. He saw that it was a spider, crawling over and under the wisps of Chiron's iron-grey hair, as if considering the location from all angles for its suitability as a possible habitat. Herman was tempted to warn Chiron of his approaching demise,

307

but could not resist seeing the developments for himself.

He popped up straight when Chiron spoke. Without interrupting his task, he asked, "I understand you are looking for unbearable beauty, Herman, yes?"

Herman looked quizzical at first, then it dawned on him what Chiron meant. Appalled, he looked at that head of thinning hair before him, and stated with distaste, "Well, I wouldn't be searching for it there." Chiron sat back on his haunches, looked over at Herman's expression and roared with laughter. He was still chuckling as Herman raced across the sand toward the path and out of sight.

It was Iris who pointed out the spider, which was soon dispersed, landing on a coiled line by the halyard cleat and departing with Chiron soon after to parts unknown.

That afternoon they were cooling off in the water, the kids and the dog. Adicia had been fishing but she was gone. The raven watched from her usual post, without comment today. Todd wondered, not for the first time, where her nest was, knowing neither crows nor owls ever hunted near their roosts. She preened at his musings, then settled in for events to unfold.

Clouds enveloped the sun and the wind picked up. Iris, feeling goose bumps, hopped over the rippling waves to the beach, where she spotted Nick coming down the path. Her face lit up and she forgot all about the chill.

Today Nick was in new pants, a crisp white shirt with sleeves rolled up and collar open, squeaky tan boat shoes and a fresh haircut, making him a little less debonair in the wavy hair category but still quite fetching for any young ladies who may cross his path, or leap into his arms soaking wet and exuberant. He swung Iris around, as was only right for the occasion.

Soon the boys were ambling down the beach, Poseidon at their heels barking, Herman somehow part of the crew again and the first to arrive. Even Perry was glad for the distraction and only a little stand-offish around this visitor who had been seen evenings from time to time with Heph and Adrianne out on the patio, subdued but always kind to Maggie's marauders.

It wasn't long before they were all sprawled out on the sand, Nick leaning back on his hands, disheveled again, sandy, but relaxed and smiling at the competing storylines, impressed by the sailing adventures, duly concerned about the shadow hunt and inquisitive regarding the training challenges he hadn't heard about before. He quickly became Poseidon's diving partner, throwing the rubber painted dolly that had replaced Iris' treasure as his favorite quarry. It sank nicely, held up well to teeth marks, and reflected off the bottom of the sandy depths with its white body and yellow-painted hair.

Inevitably, Nick's arm wore out long before Poseidon's enthusiasm waned. He picked up the doll and wagged it before Poseidon's snout, giving him fair warning.

"This is the last throw, old buddy, you're a better man than I. Are you ready? Come on now, boy, this is it!" and he flung his arm behind him, then heaved with all his strength. They all stopped and watched as the doll arced above the surf, rotating slowly, performing cartwheels for the spectators, one in particular whose mesmerized tail was wagging high and slow. A streak of sunlight peeked out to glint off the doll's wheeling limbs, then they watched as it descended and was swallowed whole by the water gods out near the dock. The raven squawked, impressed. The dog splattered them all with a shower of sand in his lurch from a stock-still take-off position, eyes agleam, tongue flopping out the side of his mouth, dragged backward by the force of the breeze and his own exertion. He leapt over the first wave without touching a drop, then landed with panache in the surf as if the size of the splash was a goal in itself. He swum mightily, muscles rippling beneath his glistening coat, eyes unblinking and riveted, ears pricked; youth, joy, intensity uniting in one athletic discipline of divine purpose. He slipped beneath the surface directly above the doll's splash.

The spectators all cheered and resettled themselves in the sand, brushing off the residue of Poseidon's sandstorm, watching just beneath the surface for those eyes that always appeared first, riding a wave and emerging just after the crest. The sun was gone again, this time behind a grayer cloud of menace, eliciting a chill among the observers, a hunching of shoulders, a touch of concern. Iris brushed the hair from her face and pulled her towel closer around her. Perry cleared his throat. Herman looked at Nick. Todd stood up. A moment passed. Then slowly they all stood up. The kids gravitated toward the water's edge, until they were submerged up to their knees. Still, they waited. It wasn't until the raven flapped her wings and hopped to a closer post that they were able to break the spell of impotent dread. The kids all started talking at once, one of them moaning, building up to a panic. Only Nick remained still. Without looking away, he said, "Iris. Go to the boathouse and get a snorkel and diving mask. Now. Go now." She started, then stopped, turned, decided to do as she was told and took off.

"Herman. Go with her. Go, I said!" He ran.

As soon as they were gone, Nick turned to Perry.

"Give me your knife," he stated, and held out his hand. Perry hesitated only a moment, wondering how Nick knew he had a pocketknife. Then he handed it over and watched as Nick pulled his shirt over his head, kicking his shoes off, halfway in the surf already. He did not wait for the mask. He swam directly in the path Poseidon had taken. When he dove under, not two feet from the dock, Todd and Perry clambered into the water behind him and swam with all their might.

It took four trips to the surface to cut through the collar that was snagged on the bottom of the protective fencing below the dock. The shifting sands must have exposed a prong and Poseidon got too close, then was unable to tear loose. The first time down the boys saw the situation and were convinced Nick would get him free. The second time down they were getting in the way and Nick had to call them off with bursting lungs at the surface. The third trip under the boys were distracted by something else they both clearly observed dangling alongside the dock, a couple of feet from the bottom. When they broke for air, they looked at each other, then quickly resumed the rescue and dove again. That time they came up with Nick and choked on the sobs that had begun before they could gasp air. They clasped each other and bawled, barely strong enough by then to kick their way back, as one, to the shore. Nick stood in waist-deep water, cradling the body of Poseidon, gently keeping his head above the water, guiding him to shore and then lifting him up and walking with him toward the greenhouse, where he knew Hephron would want him to be. The twins reached hysteria way before that and with a quaking glance over his shoulder, Perry herded them along for Todd to attend and turned back to the water for one more trip to the dock.

There was a vigil over Poseidon's body, there in the greenhouse, everyone in attendance except for Chiron, who had sailed, and Heph, whom each mourner counted on to take over whenever he finally arrived. No one was prone to action before then. Iris kept her face pressed against Maggie's blouse front, her back to the deceased. Maggie kept her arms wound tightly around her girl, rocking gently, her cheek resting on the crown of Iris' head, and it was hard to tell who relied on whom the most. Adrianne had covered Poseidon with his favorite blanket, but Herman didn't like the effect and before long reached over to fold the blanket back, uncovering his face, tucking the excess gently, smoothly around his neck. A prolonged silence ensued, broken occasionally by a cough, a scooted change of position, a sniffle, a moan, a pat on the shoulder, a heaving sigh from every breast.

Adicia, Clement and Clarisse sat on the bench against the wall just behind and to the side of the group, dutiful and subdued.

Herman snuffled deeply, wiping his nose with the back of his wrist. Absently, Nick reached into his shirt pocket, vaguely wondering when he had gotten dressed, and pulled out his white handkerchief. He pushed it in Herman's direction, wordlessly encouraging him to take it. Herman reached out for it and then without thinking, instead of using it to blow his nose, held it against his cheek with both hands and closed his eyes. Nick smiled sadly.

"I can imagine at a time like this you could really use your Ba," he said softly. Caught off guard, Herman's eyes flew open and he quickly balled up the handkerchief in both hands and placed them firmly in his lap.

"It was just an ole talisman, is all," he mumbled, eyes averted.

"Talisman?"

"Yeah, like that ole silver hair clasp Chiron keeps in his pocket all the time."

Nick had not known about that.

Eventually, muted whispers between Perry and Todd took on a hissing tone and became heated. By the time they attracted Adrianne's attention, Perry had grabbed Todd's arm and was glaring at him, matching the deadly anger in Todd's own flattened eyes. Just as Adrianne was gearing up to say something, they all stopped and turned at the sound of gravel crunching on the drive. Even Iris ventured a peek. A breath of relief escaped from Adrianne's throat.

Perry gave a shake to Todd's arm, whispering, "I mean it," and stood up. He strode to the rear of the greenhouse and turned to stand in the shadows facing the door, arms crossed, awaiting Heph's entrance. No one else breathed.

As Heph walked toward the back door of the house, Adrianne started, realizing he had no reason to think they were waiting for him. At that, Clement rose up from his chair with a quick movement and waved her off.

"I will go, Mrs. Bayard, you stay right where you are now, don't you worry." He pushed against the screen door firmly and then let it slam behind him.

Todd followed right behind, shouldering the door and bounding off in the direction of the plow shed. Perry pushed his backside off the wall and circled the mourners, hastening to intercept his brother. The rest watched without comment, assuming sorrow had gotten the best of both boys. Nick spoke reassuringly to the twins and stood up himself as Heph approached.

In the dark of the plow shed, amidst the owl droppings, moldering hay and rusty equipment, Todd faced Perry; legs wide, fists clenched, chest out, daring him to come closer. His cheeks were still wet and streaked with tears, his mouth still quivering with grief.

"Look, I don't want to hurt you, Toddo," Perry ventured. Todd gave him a look of reckless disgust and rolled his eyes, snorting derisively, then bored in again on his adversary with a gleam of bloodlust in his gaze.

"We have to talk about this," Perry added.

"What's there to talk about? You saw it, you saw the proof. What are we supposed to do, cover up for her?"

Perry's eyes widened at the stupidity of the question. "Of course we are, Bud, what do you think? She's our mother."

"She stole all that stuff. She! She's the intruder for crissake, Perry, our own mother!" He was pale and looked as if he might throw up. Or cry. Again.

There was silence as they each stood their ground and continued to trade glares, when Perry saw that his younger brother was beginning to crumple with the shame of their discovery, compounded by his horror over Poseidon. It was too much for one kid. It was overwhelming. Not until then did Perry begin to feel a little queasy himself.

The object hanging from a string tied to the fishing post, the fishing post where Adicia sat poking her stick and dangling her pole every day, was a jar that even in the murky water showed clearly enough a diamond stick pin, a key and a collection of other gleaming stuff. When Perry swam back and hauled it out of the water, he identified the fleur-de-lys stopper, the gold earring, the piece of amber from the stained-glass pane and something else, a fancy navigation set that matched the one Heph had chosen from a mail-order catalog.

So they had seen the intruder after all, that day when they watched the delivery man hand Adicia a box. A box she had casually slipped into her apron.

Perry was ashamed to feel the prick of tears behind his own eyes. It was the closest Todd came to getting a licking, then, that moment. He was primed to lash out, even stepped forward to grab Todd, but that was when the fight died in his brother's eyes. He watched as Todd faltered. As he deflated before him.

Perry stepped forward, then. He put all of his own struggle with impotence and sorrow into the violent shove he dealt Todd. Todd, surprised, fell back hard, landing breathless and akimbo on a bale of hay with a grunt but no protest. As Perry stood over his brother, Todd made no move to protect himself, instead remaining a target with arms and legs spread wide, eyes round and hollow.

Perry leaned in closely, poked Todd's bare chest with a long finger and threatened hoarsely, "Don't you ever, ever dare tell a living soul about any of this. Do I make myself clear, boyo?" He was vibrating from the effort.

"All right. All right. I promise," came the rasping response. Perry kicked a harmless pile of hay in Todd's direction and turned to stomp out of the shed. Just by the door, he was stopped in his tracks by a different tone, a new, hardened tone of voice coming from the haystack.

"But you better make sure she never takes anything else ever again. Never."

Perry hesitated, but did not turn his head. He walked out, leaving behind a different young man from the one he had followed in.

# CHAPTER 19

## 1947

The day after they buried Poseidon, Herman followed Perry out behind the plow shed and into the overgrown field that extended nearly to the edge of the property. Perry stopped halfway across the meadow and turned toward Herman, who was keeping stride several paces behind. Herman pulled up immediately, fully expecting a reprimand for being a nuisance, again. Instead he was quite surprised when Perry offered,

"Whatcha walking so far behind me for? A man can't have a conversation with his back to a body."

Herman's forehead cleared instantly and his eyes lit up with gratitude. He galloped forward and stood expectantly before this agreeable version of Perry, bouncing gently on the balls of his feet, ready for anything, anything.

Perry turned and languidly stretched himself out in the long grass, lying on his side with his back to the sun, resting nonchalantly on one elbow. Herman looked for a smooth spot and plopped himself down. Perry pulled on a piece of grass a foot long or so with seeds bursting from the top, inspected it soberly and stuck it in the side of his mouth, brandishing it there to good effect. Herman watched, hands absently snatching clumps of clover and tossing the shreds in the breeze. Chin down and observing through his eyelashes, Perry appeared pointedly at ease and unhurried, as if this had been his destination all along.

The silence lasted as long as Herman could stand it. He fairly burst with all the things he wasn't saying.

"I remember the first day you came," he began, finally. Perry looked at him as if he'd forgotten he was there.

"I was kinda scared of you." He forced a little laugh. "But not any more though, now it's like you've always been here. You and Adicia, too." Perry cut his eyes at him then, and the truth about Herman's being over his fear felt a little premature.

"I been wanting to ask you something ever since that day." He peered furtively to see if Perry would tense up again, but observing no sign of that changeable temperament he took a breath and continued.

"When Maggie came out to meet you, out in the drive by the car that day, you called her Tex! You asked her about her cowboy boots!"

Perry looked at him, some vague amusement crossing his face as he decided whether to swat this gnat after all or indulge him. Finally he sighed, the desire to belittle subsiding for once and he found himself responding affably.

"Ever since me and Todd could remember, Chiron was kind of a regular visitor to our place, our apartment over on the Lower East Side. Down by the bridge, near Fulton Market. He always came on a Sunday and sat on the sofa in the front room. They talked in low voices, him and my mom, but he never stayed long. He asked me stuff, questions about friends and school work, and minding my mother, that sort of ossified crap, you know how it is." Herman nodded eagerly, feeling very chummy and swell all of a sudden. He was on his knees by this time, leaning forward eagerly.

"I always hung around until I was sure he had slipped the envelope over to my mom, which he always did, then I was quick to take a powder, you betcha, my job was done." Herman was a little confused by that but wise enough to reserve his questions and allow Perry to tell his story.

317

"But this one time, not too long after Todd had come home after the summer, I got curious. I was hanging around at the corner when I spotted Chiron leaving and I decided to follow him. He walked about two blocks and then he paused in front of a park bench where this dame was sitting all prim and proper, resting her hands in her lap, some dumb flower hat on her head. I laughed out loud when she turned to look up at him; there was a long-stem daisy or something wagging off the side of that hat, boing boing next to her ear, she looked ducky that one." His eyes gleamed with derision even then. "I had to quick jump behind a trash can so they wouldn't see it was me having a belly laugh."

Herman smiled politely at the joke.

"Then I peeked out and he was offering her his arm! She stood up and took it and they marched down the street together thick as thieves."

Now that got Herman's attention. He sat back on his haunches, mouth open wide. Frankly, he began to suspect Perry was pulling his leg, no wonder he was acting all nice and all, stringing him along. There was no way Chiron ever walked off down the street with no lady, not Chiron!

"What are you looking at me so funny for, Boyo? Who do you think that dame was anyhow? Huh? Think, Idgit! It was your Maggie, ole Tex herself!"

Herman leapt to his feet and ran at Perry full force, head down, plowing into his stomach like a bull and pummeling his ribs with his little fists. Perry rose up and backed away but Herman stayed right with him, never flagging, face red, grunting with every swing. Perry laughed with delight, throwing his head back and letting loose his enjoyment, then gently pulling Herman's arms out to the sides, which resulted in Herman's legs assuming responsibility over the assault, kicking and kicking again in a frenzy of retaliation. While Perry finally held Herman at arm's length, rendering him impotent yet still flailing, he eventually wound down. Then he looked up at his adversary with Plan B. He hawked, filling his mouth with phlegm and lifting his chin to let loose. One warning look from Perry, though, and he involuntarily swallowed the missile.

"Are you about done yet, son?" Perry inquired. He put his face, rather bravely, down close to Herman's. "No one's insulting your precious Maggie! Not with such a ferocious protector as you around!" Herman screwed up his face and squinted to show he wasn't buying that line, boyo. He was still catching his breath, but the hair on his arms wasn't standing up anymore and the world wasn't black like it was a minute ago.

"Now." Perry thought it was safe to let go of the little menace but held his own arms straight out in front of him, palms first, just in case. "Now," he repeated in a calming voice. "Do you want to hear the rest of the story? Hmm? Ready?" He lowered his arms slowly, motioning for Herman to be seated, and he sat himself, crossing his legs and generally showing that he was ready to play nice. Herman stepped back, one giant step, but sat down and said nothing; a big concession, that.

Perry took a theatrical sigh, "Phew!" And grinned congenially at his companion, not quite able to hide a new respect in his eyes, for his toothless gnat had shown some venom.

"So like I say, I followed them until they got down to Water Street. There's a saloon-restaurant place down by the river called The Empire House and they turned in there, Chiron pointing it out to Maggie and leading her in. I snuck up and peeked in the doorway, but even out in the street I could hear the country-western music, must have been a special event or something cuz I never heard anything sounding like that coming from there before. Anyhow, right as I come up a man in a cowboy outfit leaned over and spoke into a microphone, real slow-like, with a countrified voice saying, 'My next song is by Tex Williams. It's called Shame on You.'" Perry tried to imitate the drawl. "Now, that made me laugh! I covered my mouth with my hand but there was no use, with so much hooting and stomping going on in that saloon and all. I looked over at Maggie and there she was just beaming from ear to ear, and clapping her hands together like a little kid, daisy wagging one beat behind the music. She didn't seem to mind the smell of beer and sweat none, not as far as I could tell. I couldn't really hear what she was saying but her eyes got real wide and she tugged on Chiron's sleeve to get his attention. Then she pointed to that cowboy's boots and it seemed like she was calling out, "Now I'd like a pair a' them!" I about laughed till my sides split. But about that time Chiron looked over at the door and I figured I'd spent my nickel and I slid on out of there."

He looked at Herman expectantly. Somewhere in the middle of the tale Herman had found his own piece of foot-long grass and now it stuck out the side of his mouth, held there by pursing his lips tightly around it on the one side, which required much of his concentration. But he had to admit that something of the tale rang true, knowing himself about Maggie's penchant for hillbilly music from the radio in her room. It always sounded fuzzy and shrill to him, as the station was from somewhere far away, somewhere with a different audience than the New York stations attracted, somewhere you could usually get reception only in the middle of the night, nights when Herman had bad dreams and found his way to Maggie's room. He eyed

Perry, the eye on the same side as the piece of grass squinting slightly.

Everyone belonged to one of two camps over the next few weeks, though the membership varied from one camp to the other on any given day. There were the ones who grieved openly for Poseidon and the ones who were adamantly cheerful in order to bolster the ones who couldn't contain their grief. Everyone, it should be noted, took their turn in each den of lament, neither one less taxing than the other, both impinging on the untimely lessons learned when Thea died the summer before. A second death resurrects the first, clawing at heartstrings tenuous and strained.

When the date of the big sailboat race at the yacht club arrived, everyone tried to join the cheerful camp and at least the excitement of the day was real, undeniably. Todd and Perry had both qualified for the finals, by skill or by luck or a measure of each. Regardless, the brothers were both in the race, and rivalry would have its day.

The weather was glorious and Hephron said a prayer of thanks for that. The breeze was steady, out of the southeast, and the few billowy clouds above flounced across the sky harmlessly. The sailors checked their lines, rechecked their knots, cinched their mae wests securely, peered out at the horizon as if reading the sea and trolling its surface for secret advantage, then strutted about with what bravado they could muster among their supremely confident opponents.

"How come it's always boys in the sailboat races, Daddy? I don't see how that's fair. What makes that fair?" This sort of question was occurring to Iris more and more these days and she was beginning to feel an uprising, or at least the seeds of a cause, forming within her breast.

Heph was trying to instill one last piece of advice in the boys' minds.

"Remember, there is rarely one thing by itself that will maximize your speed. It's more likely to be several small maneuvers together that make the difference." They looked at him blankly.

It was too late for esoteric generalities and they knew it if he didn't. Sucking air through his teeth, he thumped them both on the back and said, "Don't worry about a thing, I'm sure you're ready.

"Just remember everything we discussed.

"But mostly just go with the feel of the boat.

"Trust! Trust your instincts."

He was backing away all the while, throwing them an oversized salute. "I'm sure you'll do great!"

"You look great! You look ready! Bon voyage!" Now that was a stupid thing to say. Maybe they didn't hear that last part, they were upwind of him for one thing and he was retreating quickly, nervous and fretful and in the way. He stopped at a distance and cupped his hand over his brow, watching intently, his heart rate slightly elevated.

"Huh, Daddy? How come?" Iris hadn't left his side and yanked now on his belt loop.

"Hmm? Girls?" Slowly, he lowered his hand and looked down at his daughter. "Don't be silly, Iris, girls can sail. Why, I'm sure you'll be a fine sailor and give these chumps a run for their money some day. You're just a little young for that yet, is all." She glowered at him.

"Did you ever hear of Hope Goddard Iselin?" Iris shook her head mutely.

"Well, you should look her up in the library. She is in the America's Cup Hall of Fame. She was the first woman to compete for the Cup and she was on the team that won it in 1895, 1899 and 1903. Now that's what

322

girls can do." And he turned away from the shore to head to higher ground leaving Iris in the sand, rocking on her heels.

He joined Maggie, who would not have missed this for anything. She had brought one of the sailing flags, the solid red one with the vee-shaped cutout that stood for the letter B for Beechwood. She waved it enthusiastically, as if she were the one on the deck of a ship bidding her fair racers farewell. Adrianne was out on the dock with the parents of some of the other sailors, chatting with Nancy (of the DSC), whose son was the usual favorite.

When the warning flag had been posted and the boats maneuvered for position near the start line, the chattering on shore died down and every observer shifted to face the same direction, expectant and tense. The horn sounded and the cheering rose instantly, as if the point of the horn had been to activate the crowd. The boats passed the starting mark cleanly and headed into the wind. Todd took one deep breath, gritted his teeth and craned forward, muscles taut, expectant. His boat, Thought, was distinctive because of its black sail, the one gift he had requested for his thirteenth birthday a month earlier. Perry's vessel, Memory, was the other blue hull on the water.

Perry believed his only chance to beat his brother was to pass him early on. Todd, the student of discipline, focused on his own race. At the second mark, Perry came up on the port side of the black-sailed Thought and completed a tack clear ahead, forcing Thought toward an overlap, squeezing him between Perry's own boat and the mark. If Todd overlapped Perry's Memory at that point, even unintentionally, it would give Perry the right of way. So, following protocol, Todd requested room. Perry denied it. Then

Perry tacked starboard, cut off his brother and forced him into touching the mark.

By Todd's accounting, Perry had been obliged to keep clear on two counts: one; Todd had never actually overlapped Memory so Perry never established the right of way and two; Memory was the outside boat, which in fact required him to keep clear of Todd. It would be up to the judges to make the distinction and award any penalty, under the rules of the club, but Perry wasn't thinking about the fine points of the rules. He was only thinking about Todd.

While Todd performed the penalty for touching the mark, which in this case was to make a complete 360-degree turn on the spot, including one tack and one jibe, Perry sailed ahead. Todd was incensed. His face was mottled with emotion and he thought his head might burst wide open with the enormity of the insult. His own brother forced him into a penalty! His shame at Perry's action took away all his concentration, erased all focus on his strategy, denied every rational thought and left him with one goal: murder.

On shore, Adrianne was making deep fingernail marks in her crossed arms. Heph had whipped off his hat and was beating it against his thigh. Maggie was mute with shared disgust at the Perry she knew so well.

"Maggie," Heph said, replacing his hat with resignation, "I think someone's going to walk the plank today."

"I believe you're right, Mr. Bayard," was the sighing rejoinder.

The twins continued to jump and cheer, seeing Perry pull ahead, a winner being irresistible, after all.

Halfway through the course near the windward mark, Perry ran wide. While he rushed to correct his error, Nancy's son slipped by starboard cleanly, effortlessly. That rattled him. He shook his head to clear it, flinging water from his hair, stinging his eyes. He wasted precious seconds in confusion. He was consumed to distraction with the fear of Todd's closing the gap, possibly even coming astern at this moment. He was going to lose. Bile rose in his throat and he swallowed hard. He licked his lips, tasting the sea, grateful for the salt that masked the bitter acid of his dread. As his sail began to luff, the sound of the flapping sheet caught his attention, and abruptly he remembered what to do. He pulled the tiller with his right hand and as the boom swung across, he hauled in the sheet until it was taut. He ventured to wipe his burning eyes in relief, when he was paralyzed by the sound of the voice directly off his right shoulder. It was cool and measured and lethal.

"You figured you had to cheat to win this race, didn't you, big brother? Jesus. You truly are your mother's son, now aren't you?"

Perry roared over the side of his craft and landed on Todd, forcing him backwards, cracking his head on the gunwale, digging his kneecap into his groin, bruising the back of his other knee as it thwacked against the seat. The breath was knocked out of Todd, who struggled frantically for air, shocked by the helpless sensation. Perry, finding no resistance, began to pummel his brother; face, arms, chest, neck, it was all a blur, saliva spattering from his raging mouth, sea water mixed with tears distilling the spew. All the while Todd was gasping, finally managing to draw a little air. He tried to turn his shoulder to relieve the weight of his brother on his pelvis and avoid some of the blows to his face, but his weight was thrown back behind the seat, his head crammed against the tiller, his legs pinned, useless. He eventually forced his arms between his own and Perry's chest. Then, heaving with all this strength, he reared up and to his side, taking Perry with him. They both rose up, wrapped in each other's grip, twisting and grunting and rocking the boat. Perry kicked. Todd howled. Todd lunged at Perry, heedless of the consequences and they both toppled over the side.

Under water, their fury showed no sign of abatement. They could have drowned each other for spite. But their flotation devices soon forced them to the surface and they each sucked for air. Perry pounced on Todd, forcing him back under the water. Todd ducked his chin, effectively breaking Perry's grasp and moved down and away, out of Perry's reach, and out of his sight. Perry was left on the surface with no adversary to fight. Todd circled around, sculling madly to stay below the surface despite his mae west, then used the momentum of the buoying jacket to shoot out of the water and grab Perry from behind.

The battle off shore hardly eclipsed the reaction on land, officials tweeting whistles, running back and forth along the shoreline opposite the thrashing duo, parents milling, calling out warnings to their own children out on the course, men racing to launch a rescue boat, lifeguards in the surf, children squealing, flags being raised that no one obeyed, the sun blinding the observers with reflected rays glinting constantly on the choppy surface, appearing and disappearing amidst the passing clouds, confusing everyone's retinas, adding to the feeling of a movie set gone awry.

The other young sailors were the most composed members of the cast. Some saw the disruption as a chance to pull ahead and vie for the finish line, which they accomplished gracefully and silently, somehow above the fray. Most slowed their boats and floated so they could watch, avidly anticipating disaster and thinking this was the best race ever.

By the time the boys were hauled out of the water, spent and bedraggled, the crowd was sated and the denouement played out in pockets of family units, huddled officials, lifeguards whispering to teenaged girls behind cupped hands, feminine giggles stifled or not, everyone reaching for a jacket or a towel, the sun suddenly fraught with clouds.

The show was over.

Herman stood alone in the sand, his mouth covered with both of his hands to hide the delight he could not disguise, his eyes dancing with pride at his relationship to these infamous buccaneers. His little shoulders shivered from the chill but he was warm inside with the glow of reflected adventure. He was still watching the boys, who displayed nothing resembling his own high spirits, as they apologized to the race officials and the owner of the club. Heph stood nearby, sober and resolute. When they were done, he added his own regrets and the men shook hands stiffly. Their beetle cats remained tied to buoys beyond the dock and would be retrieved another day. As they trudged back across the empty beach, they met up with Herman. Heph, silencing him with a glance, turned him around and herded him along firmly, father and son trailing the two young men in custody.

It was a sign either of the enormity of the boys' infraction or that he himself was beginning at last to emerge from solitude, that Nick heard about the fight soon after it occurred and drove over to check on the state of morale at Beechwood.

The first person he saw was Maggie by the clothesline, who shook her head ruefully at him and reached out to place her hand on his arm.

"You surely are a sight for sore eyes, Mr. Nick," she declared.

"I heard you've had an eventful day."

327

"Well, some of my boys did and that's the truth."

He covered the speckled, veined hand in his own reassuring grasp, and turned to walk with her arm in arm down the path toward the garden. Hanging nightgowns and undergarments fluttered disquietly behind them, their damp lavender scent swirling faintly in pursuit.

"Those boys were out for blood, I never saw anything like it," she said, shaking her head, clearly mystified by such animosity. "What could have got into them?"

"Well, I imagine things build up sometimes between brothers," he offered. "You never know when the dam is going to break."

"I expect you're right. But what a shameful sight they made, just the same." They walked along in silence until they stood at the top of the steps bordering the rose bushes and regarded the Sound at a distance, just visible beyond the pines.

"Well, I feel sorry for them, having to face the wrath of Maggie McGinley!" he declared.

"Those boys are carrying a burden, is all I can say, and it probably goes way back, way back before they came here to live with us," she mused. "But what it was that set them off today, I just can't figure. They were like to kill each other out there on the water." She raised her chin in that direction. Then she shook her head again, racking her brain, examining the events of the last few days and weeks since Poseidon died. The answer eluded her.

"I'd say if anyone can puzzle it out, you can, Maggie Old Girl. After all, you always saw straight through me, now didn't you?"

She feigned surprise, or so he assumed. She said, "Me? Why no, I never thought of such a thing, Mr. Nick."

"Oh no? How about the peony? The myth and the prediction about the peony."

"Oh, that." She colored a little, remembering her heated words, her bitter resentment. The corners of her mouth turned up slightly, though, gratified that he hadn't forgotten the sting of her disapproval.

"'Shaw. That was back when I thought it was because of you Thea was dying. I'm sorry about that, Nicky, surely I am. I know different now." She looked up at him, her first baby, with her head cocked to the side and placed the palms of her hands gently just below his shoulders, then stood on her tip-toes and kissed him on the cheek. He felt the impossible softness of her wrinkled skin and inhaled the memory of a thousand childhood embraces. She lowered her heels and smiled up at him, with all the forgiveness of a besotted parent, and he felt its measure as only an unconditionally-loved son can feel it.

They stood for a while arm in arm and watched a lone fishing boat chug for home after a long, tiring day at sea.

Chiron and Todd sat at the chess table late in the afternoon. There was a fire, despite the humidity. Chiron's bones rationed their warmth less and less efficiently these days.

Todd's concentration was spotty, he wasn't very invested in their match. With the loss of his second horse in as many moves, Todd slouched back in his chair and addressed his opponent.

"Remember the question you asked me once, the one about the paradox of Theseus?"

"Yes," the old man answered, "the paradox of replacing the components of his ship. When, over time, all of the parts of the ship have been replaced, the question is whether or not it is still the same ship.

"You have made up your mind about that?"

Todd nodded. Then his face darkened and he straightened upright. He looked searingly at Chiron and with a hissing whisper he declared, "I know the answer. The answer is yes." The last word was practically spit out.

Now Chiron leaned back, and folded his hands over his middle. "I see. And what is the reasoning behind your conclusion? I am intrigued by your certainty."

The smoldering anger in Todd's eyes had hardly receded since the race. "Yes, the answer is yes, it is still the same boat because you can only change the outside, the physical parts. The soul never changes, no matter what you do..." His voice faded; he was confirming the proof in his head, reaffirming his fury, his shame.

Elbows propped on the armrests, Chiron tapped the finger pads of one hand against the corresponding pads of the other, rhythmically, deliberately, choosing his words with care, contemplating Todd's resentment and hurt.

"That is a fair conclusion and well stated, though there are many who would refute it."

"Some things just are, Chiron. Some things you can't do anything about. And the only way to deal with them is to leave them alone. Walk away. Give it up. Some battles aren't worth fighting, some planks aren't worth trying to replace."

"And Perry is one of those."

"Yes. Him and my m~, my ~

"It's just childish," Todd's voice caught, "and futile and pointless. All of it. The race. The quest. The hero path."

Chiron's hands stopped mid-motion. Slowly, he placed them in his lap.

They sat awhile in silence, listening to the declaration Todd had aimed at his confessor's heart. It filled the room before long, throbbing amidst Chiron's aching empathy, Todd's blinding torment. Neither one dared speak too soon. Both sensed the import of the moment and felt a yearning for a kinder god of enlightenment.

A log snapped and crumbled, flicking sparks at odd angles. One fell on the hearth and surged brightly redder before fading to dust.

Chiron cleared his throat. He indicated the room around them, or perhaps the world at large, the universe, the heavens, Hades. Hard to tell.

"It is as it has to be, my boy. You live the life you must live. And to do that, you must participate in the game."[1]

He shifted in his seat.

"Perry is standing on a whale, fishing for minnows.[1] Where do you stand, my son?"

# CHAPTER 20

## 1947

Adrianne was hurrying Herman along, urging him to climb in the car quickly so they wouldn't be late for his appointment with the dentist. She opened the back door for him, but when she turned to let him in, he was no longer there. She looked around in confusion.

"Mom," she heard her name called softly, reverently, as if they were in church. Still, she didn't see him.

"Mama, come here," the same tone, the awe in his voice unmistakable, almost a sob. She followed the sound with her eyes and glimpsed the soles of his shoes poking out from under the lowest branch of the beech tree, the one that almost touched the ground before swooping back up again; his bright crepe soles standing out against the purple shadows of the leaves around them. She bent over, squinting. She walked toward him, still bent and peering, seeing the disembodied feet motionless, rapt. When she reached him, she saw he was stretched out on his knees, his bottom end the highest point, his chin nearly touching the grass, his elbows supporting his arms, which were trembling. She looked back at the car, sighed once and lowered herself to crawl in. At first she couldn't tell what he was looking at so she leaned around to get a view of his face. Tears brimmed in his eyes, his long lashes wet and shining.

"It's the most beautiful thing I've ever seen," he whispered, his voice quavering.

Intrigued, she scoured the area for the source of such praise, until she spotted an object lying several feet away on a small pile of leaves, camouflaged by shadows, resting at an angle under the cradling limb that had hosted it.

It was a bird's nest. It was an empty robin's nest, abandoned or dislodged, empty except for a few downy feathers. Then her eyes widened and she let out a small gasp, because woven unmistakably through the sticks and reeds and dross of the estate were the faded strips of Herman's Ba.

He reached out gingerly and touched the nest with his fingers. He stroked the remnants of his blanket tenderly, tenderly.

Presently, he pulled back and rested his chin on his hands. He looked and looked at the nest until his font of tears had spilled over into the earth beneath him. Then he closed his eyes, a smile on his lips, and the untroubled forehead of a pilgrim who had known all along his was a worthy journey.

Adrianne reached in and gently scooped the nest into her palm. They sat together, the two of them, embraced by the sanctum of their tree, contemplating their discovery, reveling in quiet examination, engrossed by the sublime harmony of nature.

"Do you realize what this is, Herman?" Adrianne said finally. He looked at her quizzically, at the superfluous question.

She held the nest out to him. "Sugar, you have discovered the reincarnation of beauty." Her statement hung in the air like the notes of a birdsong.

He looked at her and beamed. He accepted his treasure with grace and a nod.

Then softly, he stated, "This is what he meant, Mom. This is what Nick was talking about that night out in the garden. That night I waited so long under the bench and he talked about unbearable beauty. He was talking to Thea, Mom. And suddenly I understood about devotion and quests and following the path of the best within us. I knew I had to find it for myself or I would never find out anything at all.

"And now I know it's real. The feeling; it's real." He looked up at his mother with wonder. "I was searching for my Ba that night, remember? And look here." He indicated the nest. "It was my Ba! It was my Ba all along." He giggled. Then he threw his head back and laughed with joy, and relief and a new sense of himself.

*　　*　　*

Maggie stepped onto the pier as if she were about to cross a tight rope, arms spread wide, feet placed carefully one in the front of the other. She had always been uncomfortable near the water, never having learned to swim. But she had spied a pile or two of discarded clothing out on the Adirondack chairs at the end of the dock, wet towels, a snorkel if that's what those contraptions are called, and whatnot. When will those children listen? She doesn't ask much, all she asks is that they carry their wet things back to the house, whoa, loose board someone's going to break their neck and drown out here, it's really not asking too much for a little effort on the part of people who get waited on hand and foot without a single word of complaint day after day and all day long in the summer.

One of those mounds turned out to be Perry. He was slumped over and studying the water morosely, arms hanging limply between his legs. He had a stick, like he was going to stir the water the way Adicia had so often done.

"Oh Lordy! I nearly tipped right off the dock into the drink, young brigand! Where did you come from?" She pressed her hand against her fluttering heart.

His look indicated he was not about to answer that question. She began to collect her laundry. Articles too close to the edge she nudged with her toe before bending over to snatch and drag them to safety, listing mightily away from the deep. At last she scanned the area, reached over and pulled a wadded t-shirt from behind Perry's fanny, then plopped her armload in the middle of the dock and sat herself in the chair next to his.

"Is this a private fight or can anyone join in?" She tilted her head genially in his direction.

"Where's your sailing-partner-in-crime today? I used to hardly ever see the two of you but when you were joined at the hip."

"He's not my partner," was the begrudging response. "Or my friend or my anything." He turned his face so she would be addressing the back of his head. The breeze lifted the dark curls off his neck, and she resisted the temptation to reach out and smooth them into place with her fingers.

"You know," she began, "Your grandmother Anna, my dear friend Anna, told me something once that I won't soon forget." She paused and regarded him, trying to determine if he was listening. "She said, 'Show me your friend and I will show you who you are.'

"I was proud to hear she believed that because I knew I could count myself as a friend in her eyes. She was a wonderful woman, your Grandma Anna, she surely was. And wise."

He relented a little and turned back enough to study the stick in his hands, tapping it broodingly against the edge of the dock.

"You also have such things to be proud of. Both of you grandsons. And it's my privilege to be around to witness them for myself. Sometimes I like to think I watch over you for her, and for Thea. Maybe between the three of us marauders, we can make them smile down at us from time to time, what do you think? I like to imagine that, sometimes. It feels a little bit like sunshine on my old worn-out bones, it does."

The only response was from a disgruntled seagull as it veered east with an empty beak, followed by the smell of dead fish wafting dockside. After a moment she slapped her knees and used the force of her arms against them to help her bulk rise up from the chair. "Now don't you forget about the big soiree tonight, there's lots to be done up at the house before sundown, Cap'n. I could use some help around here and about time. See if you can scare up them other fugitives for your old Maggie, as well." She threaded her way back down the pier to solid ground, damp laundry as ballast.

*     *     *

Perry decided to stop in at the boat house to see if any of the others were there. He turned his head at the sound of a hinge squeaking off to his left and saw it was Chiron, just closing the storage locker door. It was enough time to glimpse the jar, still filled with stolen articles, sitting on the top shelf, the rope yet tied around it. He looked sharply at Chiron, who was watching him closely.

Without thinking, not meaning to expose his feelings or his secret, he blurted out forcefully, "How could she do it, Chiron? How could she betray us like that?"

"So you did find out. I wasn't sure."

"And you knew? You knew she was a thief?"

"I only suspected. And then I guessed the tension between you and Todd might have something to do with your mother.

336

"I'm sorry this happened, my boy. This has been unsettling and bewildering, I know."

Perry felt his chest constrict. His eyes welled up and his throat tightened with the effort not to cry. His shoulders heaved a couple of times and he turned away, knowing if Chiron approached him or tried to comfort him in any way, he would lose his composure entirely and he couldn't bear for Chiron to see that. He fingered a loose splinter in the door frame that faced him and tried to swallow his turmoil.

His wide, angular shoulders shivered sporadically like the withers of a yearling, vulnerable and young, so young. The shoulder blades stood out sharply against his thin shirt, the long muscles of his back barely foretelling the power they promised someday to wield. His bent head betrayed the weariness of a spirit hard-shelled and neglected and lonesome. Chiron contemplated this great-grandchild of Corinna, and he mourned a little more for what he missed and what he would miss. His own shoulders were heavy today, his gait somber, the light in his sore eyes occluded.

After what seemed like a very long silence broken only by squeaking floor boards as Perry occasionally shifted his weight, Chiron took a deep breath and straightened up to full height, noble head erect, the crinkles round his eyes deepening with the recollection of an ancient tale.

"Many centuries ago there was a samurai warrior who was renowned for his strength and bravery. He knew no fear, avoided no danger, left no battlefield before the last man. He had suffered many wounds, lost horses and swords by the dozen, watched comrades killed and maimed by the thousand, killing and maiming hundreds among his enemies himself, and never once wavering in his duty or his loyalty to his emperor. He was the most respected warrior in all of Japan."

Perry stood quietly, his arms hanging at his sides, his posture expectant.

"One day, as he sat after a meal in his encampment, an unfamiliar soldier approached him brazenly. The younger samurai was clearly angry, filled with bravado and foolish. But his resentment, whatever its source, was great and his nerve admirable. He approached the revered samurai and without a word, he spit in the face of the most formidable warrior in the empire."

Perry turned around.

"What do you think our samurai did?"

"He decimated him."

"Think again."

"He decapitated him. And paraded his head on a spear throughout the empire."

"He did nothing. He did not even move."

Perry looked for the trick.

"When his followers clamored around him and asked him why he didn't take his revenge, terrified that he would appear cowardly and lose respect, lose his authority, this most powerful of samurais responded coolly,

'One must never fight in anger, only in honor.'"[1]

Chiron turned to the workbench nearby and began to tinker with a navigational instrument. Perry waited. When it was clear Chiron was finished with his story, Perry took a stroll along the row of boats, just three or four in the boat house this time of year, running his hand along their sleek hulls, thinking, reflecting, stewing over the story's significance. He circled around at last to the opposite side of Chiron's bench and placed the palms of his hands on the battered surface. Chiron looked up at him, and reacted to the spark he saw in Perry's eyes.

"I've been very angry."

Chiron lifted his head slightly.

"But I did not steal from the Bayards."

Chiron shook his head in agreement.

"Todd.  Todd and I did nothing wrong."  He swallowed.  "There's nothing we can do about what happened.  Except return the objects."  His eyes went involuntarily to the locker across the room.  Then his face turned red and he looked away.

"I don't think she—I don't think my mother will do it again."

"No, I don't suppose she will.  Not now."

"How will I ever face them?  How can I explain?"

Chiron noted the use of the pronoun, singular.

"With honor and dignity."  It was as Perry expected.

*     *     *

By the time Perry tracked down Todd dusk was not far off.  He was up on the landing, in the wide, inviting window seat next to Chiron's private quarters, peering intently through the binoculars as of old.  He did not even hear Perry's tread up the staircase.

"You hid out cleverly enough to avoid Maggie's chore list, didn't ya, Fella?"

Todd jumped but did not remove the binoculars until he was good and ready and then slowly, as if he were still focusing on a thought-provoking scene far beyond the windowpane.

"What's out there that's so important anymore?  I thought we caught the intruder or did you forget?"  He wanted to make amends, but his pride wouldn't back down enough to risk seeming apologetic.  After all, they had been in this together at first, and Perry would have stuck together with Todd through anything.  It was Todd who was disloyal. Todd who was tearing the family apart.

"I was watching for Ole Webster. I'm pretty sure I spotted him out beyond the back road a little while ago. I was trying to figure out where he goes off to at night.

"Do you know the difference between the owl, the raven and our mother?" he added.

"Be careful, son. I'm warning you. You watch your mouth."

"Owls, ravens, crows, they never hunt near their own roost. Did you know that?" He said it mildly, as if it were a curious thing, this trait of predator birds.

Perry felt his temper rise in this throat. He took one step toward the window. He practically choked on the effort it took to stop his forward motion, to unclench his fists, to slow his heartbeat. His ears hurt from the pressure of clenched muscles and held breath. Todd never moved, not a finger, not a blink. The sun went behind a cloud and the room dimmed. The clock ticked at the bottom of the stairway. Then they both heard something else. Off in the distance, the owl hooted. Distinctly, it hooted off beyond the driveway, towards the main road, the opposite direction of what they would have guessed. Todd's demeanor changed instantly and his shining eyes acknowledged the thrill of that call, the romance of its mystery. His tension dissolved like the concoctions of Chiron's pestle.

Perry turned and stormed down the stairs, and out of the gatehouse.

*     *     *

Nick was among the first guests to arrive at the party, his eyes overly bright, his cheer somewhat forced, if anyone had scrupled to notice. He and Heph and two hunting buddies opened the bar for business and demonstrated their prowess for appreciating Heph's Highland Park single malt.

The band was just striking up and the rooms beginning to swing when Nick slipped out the terrace door and headed for Chiron's quarters. He was not deterred by the unanswered knock at the door, he didn't require Chiron's presence or even desire it for his mission. He disposed of his glass on the coffee table and approached the fireplace. He stood before it for a few seconds, as if unexpectedly jarred by the memories it provoked. Then he recalled his purpose, ducked his head and entered the fireplace as if it had invited him in. He had to bend over, to be sure, but not all that much and he didn't have far to go, just over to the left, where he reached up by memory and quickly located the object he desired. He clasped it with his left hand, twisted and yanked expertly, then caught the box with his right hand as it was released from its resting place.

All of this Todd observed keenly, having come down the steps to answer the door knocker and been taken aback as he watched Nick stride into the fireplace as if he were a Christmas elf.

He was still hovering at the corner when Nick emerged, sprinkled with soot, and carried his plunder to the couch for inspection. He was struck by the thought that the strongbox Nick held must have been tempered by a thousand fires.

As Nick brushed off the top of the box, Chiron strode into the house and, reflexively, Todd melted into the shadows of the staircase behind the wall.

There was silence. Chiron's footsteps had stopped soon after he entered. Then, a few more brushing motions. Silence, Todd waiting for Chiron to reprimand Nick for getting ashes on his carpet. He imagined Chiron assessing Nick, that way he had of seeing whatever you had carefully hidden even from

341

yourself. Soon, he heard the creak of old hinges and the sound of rummaging. There was some clattering, some chinking and a rustle of paper, letters, perhaps. Objects were being shuffled, lifted, possibly inspected and replaced.

Something scraped along the bottom of the box and a few seconds later Chiron commented, "I added that. It is an old coin from Crete. Gold." A pause, then the coin clanking back into the box. Soon, something metal seemingly dragged along the edge of the box. Pause. "The pendant is a rare violet, pear-shaped sapphire from Ceylon, nearly the size of a robin's egg, wouldn't you say? On an antique gold chain, a gift to Maria from your father, naturally. She asked me to keep it for when you returned, thinking someday it would go to her grandchild." Another long pause, as Todd pictured the stone catching shards of spare light in the gloam of living room, twisting slowly on its chain, inspected with wonder by its holder. The chain jangled as it piled up on itself, back in the box, he assumed.

"I can translate the journal for you, if you wish. Thea's grandmother, Corinna, kept a detailed record of her youth. You might find it riveting."

"Thea's grandmother? I thought you got this from my father, from the Karras family. You gave me this journal, Chiron, I remember distinctly. Why would you have Thea's family journal?" He sounded more suspicious than curious.

There was no answer, but Nick seemed to have forgotten the question.

"Where is the shell?" he demanded.

"I don't know anything about a shell." More rummaging, a grunt.

The crinkle of paper was unmistakable, just a sheet or two at most. It was followed by steps, must have been Chiron's steps approaching and finding a seat in his favorite chair. He settled himself in, too far away though for both of them to be reading at the same time. It must have been a rather lengthy letter, or he must have read it more than once, for Nick took his sweet time studying it.

When he was done, his tone had changed. The insolence was gone and in its place a sadness that ached in Todd's own heart to hear.

"I don't remember it this way. This isn't what I remember my father saying at all. I only thought of him as angry and disgusted by my being caught with Thea. I thought he hated me. I was convinced he abhorred her. I don't remember his feeling passion or...devotion like this, I don't. Chiron." Todd suddenly felt sorry for Nick and didn't know why. He didn't know anything, he realized, and chafed at his self-imposed exclusion. That he was eavesdropping had not yet occurred to him.

He was struck by a new sound. Almost like a blubber. Nick was not himself, hadn't been from the beginning. He had the feeling Chiron knew it, too.

"Oh, what the hell." His voice transformed again, hostile, bitter. "The letters are gone, the love letters Thea held such store by. I destroyed those myself, Jesus. I don't know why I had to see all this stuff again, it doesn't change anything. What good does it do, it's just wallowing in death and sorrow. Stone cold sorrow."

Something must have struck a chord in Chiron then, because there was a tinge of sharpness in his voice, like impatience with a pup who doesn't realize the damage chewing on the furniture is doing, but is plenty old enough to stop doing it.

"You're drunk, Nick. Be careful of creating new regrets out of old ones."

343

"All right. Then explain this to me." Soft sounds of the chain being lifted again. "Why have I never seen this rarified, valuable family heirloom necklace before, but my mother gave it to you to keep to pass on to her future grandchild? Come on, now, explain that."

"Maria knew more than you might guess. She knew about you and Thea long before your father did, and she stayed out of it. After you left for Greece, she worried that they had made a mistake in sending you."

A rude noise was the only rejoinder.

Chiron spoke firmly then, pointedly. "She was afraid that Thea might be pregnant." Another sarcastic response, unintelligible to Todd.

"She was pregnant, Nicholas."

Luckily the sharp intake of air by Todd was matched by the reaction from Nick. Todd was paralyzed with shock, and confusion. He was afraid to breathe. He strained for sound, tried to pierce the wood paneling with his eyes for a clue to what was happening beyond the wall. Soon enough he heard the crash of the metal box and the clatter of spilled objects rolling onto the floor, as Nick must have stood up abruptly, blindly. The footfalls striding from the room could only be his. Halfway, they stopped and a thin voice declared, stricken, "But there was no baby."

And the voice and the steps retreated, and were gone.

One sound lingered; it must have been the gold coin, rolling across the uneven floor to career into the hearthstone and wobble until it, too, fell silent.

Todd dropped his head in his hands, his fingers grabbing his hair, eyes closed, agitation swirling around him, pulling his mind in directions it was not prepared to go. He was breathing hard, trying to focus, yet hoping he wouldn't. He did not know how long he remained there, unconcerned about Chiron coming around the corner to discover him, unable to name his impressions, or form any conclusions from the scene he had overheard. Occasional shifting sounds suggested Chiron remained in his easy chair, but that was all Todd concluded.

When he was finally ready to think again, perhaps go back up the stairs and feign sleep in the window seat, something like that, there was another knock at the door. Before Chiron moved to answer, the door creaked open a few inches and a familiar feminine voice called out, "Anybody home? Chiron, may I come in?" With only the shortest of hesitations, Chiron answered kindly, "Of course, Iris, of course."

She sashayed into the living room and quickly turned on the nearest lamp, the better to show Chiron her party dress.

"Those blue and white strips are lovely, my dear, you are quite lady-like tonight."

"Why, thank you, kind sir!" She beamed in response, swaying a little with pleasure. "I just wanted to peek in to see how you are doing while the band is taking a breather. I have been dancing with strangers tonight, Chiron, I feel so exotic!" Her cheeks were flushed, to be sure. He raised an eyebrow at her new vocabulary.

"Come here by me, little one, let me get a close look at you on this star-crossed night." He took her hand when she arrived at his knee and studied her freckled face, her long neck, her graceful posture, her promise of elegance and stature. She smiled trustingly down at him, waiting.

"There is something I have been saving to tell you, Iris, and I think this might be just the right time to do it," he began.

"It is a great secret; a great ritual prayer that can never be written or its power is lost. It can therefore only be passed on by word of mouth, from a man to a woman (or in this case a young lady), and from a woman to a man. It is called ksemátiasma. Now listen carefully, for its power is in its secrecy and it can only be told once, when the bearer is old, because its power is then passed on to the receiver, for the duration of her life, until it is her time to pass it along."

Iris' eyes were round with excitement and honor. She thrilled at the idea of being chosen by Chiron. She understood it must be a portentous secret, and she must accept it accordingly. A secret! Thoughts of dancing and music evaporated; for this, this was a special night.

Chiron motioned for her to lean down, so he could whisper in her ear. She quickly brushed her hair out of the way and bent slightly to his level, obedient, hoping to be able to hear him above the beating of her heart.

To her he disclosed his confidence, syllable by syllable, slowly, melodically, fervently, his Greek accent heavier than usual. She nodded once or twice and when he was done, she put her arms around his neck and hugged him for all she was worth.

"I love you, my Chiron," she said, knowing it was enough, knowing it was all, and then she kissed him on the cheek. She poured out her heart and her gratitude in the smile she threw at him and then walked away, trancelike, gliding. The door clicked softly closed behind her.

The room would have long been pitch dark by the time Chiron arose, if Iris had not turned on the lamp. He took his time getting out of his chair, feeling the weight of his bulk, the weight of his memories, as he lifted and straightened and gathered himself. He squared his shoulders, confirming they were prepared to wield any burden still. After all, they guarded unassailably within his breast the mastery of all heaven and hell within us.

He looked around the open rooms before him, his eye stopping momentarily at the Little Midshipman on his desk, moving on to the three maps of the old and older world, then slowly crossing the expanse, noting each and every familiar treasure, gazing last upon his tapestry, the one that cost him half a year's salary. His eyes embraced it, glimmering. On his way out, he paused to run his hand along its surface, fingering once more the hem of the lady's gown and struck by a new glint in her eyes from that angle, as if all this time she had just been testing his mettle.

# CHAPTER 21

## 1947

The engine was flooded and he worked the choke. From time to time he pulled out his flask and drank deeply, then resumed his attempts to start the maligned jalopy. On some level he knew he had to wait it out, the flooding, and during those lulls he contemplated the strongbox and his conversation with Chiron. His brow was furrowed with confusion and sadness, though he couldn't articulate its origin. Something was missing, a puzzle piece or a contradiction in something Chiron had said. He shook his head, sure it was Chiron and not himself who misunderstood. He tipped the flask again and was grateful for the burning liquid that coated his throat, and lingered. At last he gave up, tossed the bottle on the seat beside him and climbed out. He had to go back. Some kind of business was left unfinished and he was feeling the insult of it.

Todd, for his part, had waited long minutes of tenuous silence before venturing off his step, rounding the corner and emerging onto the scene of so much incitement this fathomless night. Spotting the coin on the hearth, his eye followed its imagined path, across the floor to where, strewn about the rug and across the table, he recognized the objects he imagined as Nick had inspected them. There were other items that had given no rise to comment, like a silver medal of St. Nicholas on a chain and a sextant, heavy, hefty, old, an exquisite artifact of bronze or brass, he didn't know, intricately inscribed with measurements and symbols and bearing several adjunct pieces that swiveled and turned and instructed with celestial precision. Hughes & Son, London 1880 was etched below the eye piece.

He replaced it gently in the box, as his eye fell on the letter from Nick's father. He reached for it, hesitated, then found both pages in his hands and himself sitting on the chair Nick had occupied as he read it there less than an hour ago.

For my son, Nicholas,

You have been the focus of every goal I have strived for in the last thirty years. I made my pledge to you, yet unborn, every time my ship left port, every time I crossed the bar, every time I scanned the night sky for a sign of safe voyage. It was in your name then, under the guise of the patron saint of the seas, and it is in my heart forever, every dream, every hope, every happiness—in the knowledge that you are here—that I continue to devote my life. You are my past, my present days, and all the potential of our shared future. I did not guess that my love for you would emanate from my faith in myself, that I would relinquish the best in me on your behalf and feel the richer for it, despite my own diminishment. I give that piece of me freely, joyfully, gratefully, that it may help you to be a better man than I could hope to become, strive as I might. You are the better version, the greater hope. You are the potential that your father cannot fulfill on his own. Together we will forge our family's destiny, and I will ensure you are not held back by any earthly means, by no man, no scheming woman or beast or force of nature, so help me God. Joy has replaced all other emotions, and I will face Hades and hellfire if need be, to defend the privilege of having such a son.

I have been encouraged as of late by your neglect of a certain companion, your adventures with young ladies of more appropriate lineage, and gratified to note your casual unattachment to any of them. It bodes well for the future I have devised, the future that will graft our family to its roots, its legacy, its vast empire that rules the seas from Chios to Istanbul to London to Philadelphia, that is your birthright. I write you now as I embark on one last mission to reestablish your birthright, whereupon I plan to pave the way to introduce you and forge the basis for all future bonds within our clan, as is our privilege and our duty. I swear to you, my legacy, my darling, I will clear the way for your future, and the Karras & Son Moon Star Line will dominate the shipping lanes of the world for generations to come.

Your servant, Kristofer Karras

The date after the name was illegible, and just as well. Todd was unnerved by the rambling letter, threatened by the malignant passion decrying love and family loyalty. He hastily folded it and placed it under the sextant in the bottom of the box, then crawled around gathering all the other objects he saw, placing them in the box as well. He closed the top forcefully.

He was fretful, anxious to remove all traces of this menacing collection of haunted memories. He faced the fireplace, estimating just where Nick had dislodged his strongbox, when the door swung opened and the owner of the box himself lurched in.

Todd jerked his head around to see who had caught him and was mortified to see it was the worst person possible. His watery bones refused to gel, nor would they allow him to leak mercifully into the floor, so he stood unbreathing, awaiting the wrath of justified doom. And he was not disappointed.

"What are you doing with that box?" The voice was deadly angry, quaking with fury at Todd's obvious prying and possession of his most secret belongings. It would be hard to say who felt more exposed at that moment. But the separate responses of guilt and resentment could not have been more extreme. Nick covered the distance across the room in a few strides and grabbed for the box. In the violence of that motion, Todd was suddenly struck by the absolute certainty that somehow, he had a right to an explanation, and he held on to the strongbox stubbornly. Neither of them noticed that a third party had entered the scene, and set irrevocably in motion all that would follow.

"Nicholas, stop!" Chiron's voice boomed above the rushing blood in their ears. Todd's neck snapped back as he clutched the box to his chest and Nick pulled on it.

"Stop, you'll hurt him! Nick, listen to me! For God's sake, Nick, Todd is your son!

"He is your son," he repeated. And so it was imparted.

Nick yanked the box from Todd's suddenly slack hands, then swerved violently toward Chiron's voice.

"What?" He slurred as he swung around, accidentally knocking into Chiron, who staggered and fell from the force of the impact. His head struck the poker by the fireplace, and instantly his body went slack. He lay motionless at their feet.

Whether it was from dread or clarity, neither of them moved to verify the outcome of his fall. There was a palpable shift in the universe and they both indisputably felt it. Being stunned merely demonstrated the occasional mercy of the gods.

The sound of their tandem panting throbbed across the room, swallowed by the sympathy of the objects displayed there, absorbed by the smoke-stained walls enveloping them, the surrogate ears of accumulated wisdom, the recorders of earnest reflection, the private sanctuary echoing decades of study and contemplation. The air still beat with endeavor, struggle, conflict, consultation, travail, reassurance, resolution, promise.

At this moment when they were each alone for the first time in their lives, they were most poignantly aware of the comfort that enveloped them here, within the steadfast gate house, the haven that was Chiron. Their heads were bowed, their breathing ragged, their hearts full to bursting.

The twins and Perry walked in as Nick roared in primal anguish. Todd was on the floor next to Chiron's body, clutching his vest cloth, his head buried in Chiron's chest, his own chest heaving with muffled sobs of desolation. The other children rushed forward, then pulled back in horror. There was an outpouring of overlapping questions that went unnoticed, keeping their hopes alive that this was not after all another tragedy they could not face. But when Herman declared he was leaving for help, Todd roused himself with alarm, and rose up to see that he and Nick were no longer alone.

The confusion and wailing despair that soon followed was edged with hysteria and required every skill of persuasion Todd had acquired during this year of mission training to keep them from abandoning the last grasp on their wits.

In the chaos, Nick escaped. Seeing the children so distraught, it struck him, what he had done. He had staggered out the door, mad with remorse. Todd, hyper-charged from the tension, sensed his absence almost immediately.

"Iris! Iris!" He shook her arm until she looked at him. "Go. Follow Nick. Don't let him get away and don't leave his side. Make sure he doesn't speak to anyone. Hurry!" She closed her mouth, swiped her arm across her runny nose, sniffed loudly and swallowed. Then she turned and did as she was bid. He saw in her eyes that she understood. And he was palpably grateful she did not ask any questions.

Perry and Herman watched this exchange and became quiet themselves. Perry visibly bucked up, pressing the heels of his hands against his brow momentarily, closing his eyes and squeezing out the last of his tears. Then he dropped his arms to his side and regarded Todd, shaking slightly but restrained, careful to keep his body turned away from Chiron's.

Herman watched Todd as if he were a life raft. He had begun to worry that this scene would fall upon his own shoulders and knew his scrawny frame was not up to the task. Fear was spread across his face, little boy fear from the darkest recesses of his nightmares.

Todd tried to gather his wits. His gaze darted around until he noticed the chess table had been upset in the melee and on the floor peering dispassionately at him with its blue porcelain eye was the onyx horse. Calm, yet piercing. And suddenly he could hear distinctly Chiron's words.

"Ótan mbis sto horó prépi na horépsis. When you get into the dance, you must dance."[2]

He knew, then, what he must do. He knew he had to try to save Nick. His father. The jolt of that realization, like an electrical pulse that surged through his weary body, caused his head and limbs to visibly twitch. He looked at Perry.

"Before long, Nick will sober up and confess. Believe me, it was an accident. He didn't even realize Chiron was there when he turned. We have to figure out a way to keep Nick out of this. To keep him from being charged with murder." His eyes pleaded with the boy who was not his brother after all.

"But Chiron is dead," from Herman, in agony.

A vivid memory surfaced in Todd's mind then, the poem Chiron had told him again and again throughout his childhood. Death and the unknown sea, the unseen shore.

"He always wanted to be buried at sea," was all he could think to say.

Perry responded after only a moment's hesitation, "The USS San Diego."

The boys looked at him; Herman with confusion, Todd with dawning appreciation.

"It sank off the coast."

"And has never been disturbed."

Todd checked his premises one more time, then finally stated his intentions. He looked at Herman, knowing Perry was already with him. "We have to make it look like it never happened. It's just a matter of convincing Nick, is all. Maybe he's drunk enough. He might be. We have to formulate a plan."

Perry brushed his floppy curls from his forehead and licked his lips. "He could show up again at any minute and go report the whole thing. How are we going to get rid of the...get rid of the body and make sure Nick doesn't call the cops in the meantime?"

The churning silence that followed threatened to outlast Nick's stupor. Todd realized he was up against time and the need to establish a logical scenario that would not only prevent Nick from becoming a suspect but avoid any chance the four of them, the witnesses, would be asked any dangerous questions. The twins could never withstand a strenuous interrogation. None of them could corroborate a lie without ultimately stumbling on a stray detail no one could anticipate. The plan must be simple, clean and most of all finite.

Random thoughts flickered through his head. First: establish that the twins were at the party when the incident occurred. Second: the only way to protect Nick was to keep him out of it somehow, ignorant of the plan and their manipulation of the facts. How to do that? Third: no one, including Chiron, must be blamed for anything in the end. Finally: Chiron's

354

disappearance must remain mysterious, and personal. This much he knew. Now he just had to make it stick.

Finally, Todd spoke.

"Can you hit someone without really injuring him, just make him black out for a while? That's all we need. Considering all the fights you've been in, I mean, it seems natural that it would be you who would do it."

Even though he had pretty much avoided all those fights, disappearing when the attention was elsewhere and then chiming in just when the gang reassembled after all the gore had been spilled, Perry hardly hesitated, "Sure, I can do it."

Herman picked up the poker that had killed his hero, his oracle, and studied it.

"Here, use this," he said. His detective instincts were beginning to wise up although he was far too shaken to truly decipher Todd's plan.

Todd watched him. "After we make sure Nick is out cold and out of our way—out of harm's way—for the time being, then we will put Chiron in his skiff. I can manage to tow it behind the dingy. That way it'll look like he took off again, this time in his skiff but otherwise, just like he always does.

"I'll tow it out into the sound and sink it." He looked around for confirmation and received tepid but growing nods as the boys digested the idea. "No one will ever know why this time he never came back." A tear slipped out then, but he flicked it away.

"What will we tell Nick?" Perry challenged him.

"That's where you come in, you and the poker." Todd faced Perry with warmth. "We'll tell him Chiron hit him, thought he killed him and horrified by what he had done, he ran away. You know, the Shadow, the Intruder, all that stuff. It makes sense, it's all we kids talked about for months, everybody heard us. Chiron included. He saw a man in the dark in his home with his box of heirlooms and attacked him before he could.....harm me, who had come downstairs from the lookout and saw everything."

The silence that met this explanation was quaking with sadness, intrigue and admiration.

"Let's go find Iris."

They crept out the door, peering first into the palpitating dark beyond, then softly calling her name. They were wondering which direction they should take when she answered close by, behind the gate house on the little patio where Chiron and Thea liked to sit and watch the nuthatches.

Overhead the fractured clouds were sullen and on the move.

They saw Iris and Nick in the dim light thrown by the gate house windows. Nick was doubled over on his knees in the gravel, his head in his hands, his hands resting on the gravel in supplication or in an attempt to prevent his eyes from seeing what had transpired. Iris was patting his shoulder, rubbing his back, trying to soothe and calm this adult who might have comforted her in her heartbreak, but remained insensate and helpless under her ministrations. She looked up as they approached.

Todd motioned to Perry to go ahead, hit Nick. Perry regarded Todd with round, haunted eyes, trapped and frozen. He hesitated, his face turning white as he attempted to gather courage, mortified by his inaction.

Herman studied him.

"So tell me something, Perry," he stated softly, yet clear as a bell, "are you a pale criminal after all? Or do you have the courage of the blood?"

Perry's eyes darted to the source of such an accusation. He thought. He scrutinized Herman, and thought some more.

Nick began to rise. Perry swiftly raised the poker and brought it down. Nick wobbled, then slowly collapsed. A precipitous, terrified check verified he was still breathing.

Todd turned to Herman. "Go to the greenhouse and get a wheelbarrow. Perry. Find a lantern. And a...shroud. Something to wrap him in. Something to...bury him in. Please." His voice broke.

"Iris," he croaked and cleared his throat roughly, "Guard Nick. Don't let anyone near here or in the gate house. I will prepare the skiff. We'll meet back here as soon as we can.

"Wait. Wait. Herman!" Todd rose to full height and faced his young disciple and first mate. "Herman, what is this? This time, now, what is this, Herman?"

There was a pause as everyone felt the magnitude of the question. Then Herman, in a tremulous voice, barely audible but growing in conviction stated with pride and awe, "This is a Borough Alarm, sir."

"Yes, son, it is that." They gathered round quickly, making the sign of the fists, one on top of the other, in honor of William Campion and the Equitable Life Assurance Fire of 1912. "Now go!"

Perry and Herman tore off, galvanized and anxious to prove worthy of everything Chiron ever taught them, everything that ever meant anything in their short, wisdom-infused young lives.

Todd turned toward the boathouse, slower, subdued by the weight of his intentions, drained by his show of certitude and leadership. He was stopped by Iris' gentle call.

"Todd, hold on a minute."

She had been trying to take in the plan as it was unfolding, her eyes flicking from face to face, gleaning their intentions after the shock of Perry's attack on Nick. Still, in her relief at their arrival, she was ready to acquiesce to anything, just to bask in their unity and confidence. But now she had a contribution of her own and she knew it was something they had overlooked.

Todd was quite taken aback when he turned to observe her lifting her skirt and methodically pulling off her petticoat. She stepped out of it and proudly held it out to him, arm outstretched. "You see this? This petticoat? I'll hang it on the lamp post outside the boat house if it's all clear for you to come ashore. I'll leave the light on so you can see it. If you don't see it there, wait. When the coast is clear, I will give you the signal, and you can come in. Understood...sir?"

He grinned then, proud and relieved to have a thinking ally. "Aye-aye," he winked, and saluted her.

He had turned and taken two steps when she pounced on him from behind, wrapping her arms around him, squeezing for all she was worth. He waited until she had her fill, then they both proceeded, in opposite directions, to face their burdens.

Iris sat by Nick's inert form and waited, jumping at every crack, crunch, groaning tree limb in the gloom, imagining lurking spies who somehow suspected foul play, desperately trying to formulate believable explanations and marketable deterrents. Then she heard a voice, she was sure of it. It must have been one of the guests, one she didn't know.

"Yes sir, I know it's late," she heard the frustration in Herman's attempt to be polite.

"Well then, young man, whatcha doin' with that wheelbarrow this time of night? I do believe your mother is wondering where you are. Let's just put that aside there and I'll walk with you back to the house." His voice sounded tipsy, his offer of escort ironic. Iris, rushing to the scene, pictured him flopped in the wheelbarrow and hauled off by Herman if she didn't get there quick enough.

"Herman, there you are. It's about time! Dad said to hurry up and get done, so we can go to bed, gee! I'm tired, it's getting late."

"And what are you doing here, young lady, don't you know what time it is?" The stranger's sing-song voice admonished.

Coming along the path, perhaps drawn by the voices of the children, Iris spied Miss Winnie and Miss Charlene. Quickly, she blurted out the only thing she could think of and she made sure to say it loudly.

"It's all about patriotism, sir! America pledges her sword to her allies and proclaims, 'I am the Truth, when Liberty and Justice call!'" And she climbed up into the wheelbarrow where she stood with her sword arm raised.

"Why, it's the Red Cross Pageant!" Miss Winnie exclaimed. "Iris, my child, you remember!"

"Of course I do, Miss Winnie, and Herman here and me, we have a real important cause to attend to but this gentleman thinks we ought to be in our beds at this hour. Patriots like us!" She placed her hands emphatically on her hips and puckered her lips in a moue of disdain.

Miss Winnie looked disapprovingly at the unknown guest and Miss Charlene deftly put her arm through his, turned him around and said, "Now Bill, if Iris Bayard has important business to attend, I assure you we had better leave her to it. So. What have you done with your delightful wife? Let's go see if we can locate her." And off they strolled, after an affectionate pat on Iris' arm by her devoted Miss Winnie.

Herman raised his eyebrows at his sister. "Nice work, Watson," he allowed.

They shoved off, each pushing one handle of their wheelbarrow cum patriotic soapbox cum funeral bier.

359

When they pivoted it warily through the gatehouse door, they were relieved to see Todd and Perry already there. An old swath of canvas lay on the floor by Chiron and they were attempting to lift him onto it. It proved less a matter of strength than maneuverability, grip and emotional fortitude. Neither one heard the twins' arrival. Iris stood motionless at the edge of the room and began to shake. Her focus and forbearance were beginning to crack, and leak. She felt a moan rising in her throat and tried valiantly to subdue it, knowing it was the crack that would crumble her entire seawall of willpower if she succumbed. Just as she felt herself being swept away by grief, Herman hauled off and whacked her across the back, most likely in an effort to ward off his own meltdown and she choked on her sob, but swallowed it after all.

"They look like they need a hand," he bid her, "let's get this over with."

Between the four of them, inch by inch, tugging and pulling the canvas several times to reposition and even it out, they settled Chiron on his shroud. The older boys began to fold it over to cover the body of he who was the single greatest influence on their lives, past, present and future, and too preoccupied not acknowledging that fact to think of anything else. Then Herman remembered something.

"Stop! I need one more minute with Chiron!"

Todd looked at him with pity in his swollen eyes. "Herman, we're running out of time. I'm so very sorry, I know how you feel, but we can't afford to lose even one extra minute."

"No, I mean yes, you must!" He held his arms out imploringly, then seeing that they did not understand, turned quickly and grabbed the poker that he had brought in with the wheelbarrow.

"Fingerprints." At that point he didn't care if they knew what he meant or not. First, he wiped it clean of Nick's and Perry's fingerprints, using his shirttail. Then he kneeled down beside his Chiron and gently, if awkwardly, pressed the lifeless fingers around the poker, creating proof that it had been Chiron who had wielded the poker after all.

The other three respectfully held their tongues, watched and waited. Herman was methodical but mindful of the clock in the passageway ticking loudly, marking his progress. When he was satisfied, he carefully smudged the part of the poker he himself had touched, then holding it by his shirttail, laid it nearby at what might appear to be a reckless angle.

Utterly spent, he rose from his knees with effort and silently, solemnly stumbled away, straight toward the door without looking back once, though hesitating at the last and slumping against the door frame momentarily, trembling, then continuing headlong out of the gatehouse, aiming somewhere, perhaps for the patio to wait with Nick.

The ones left behind made quick work of wrapping the body and tying it with cord, Perry insisting on checking the knots, Todd sweating now profusely with nerves frayed near to snapping. They managed to lift him into the wheelbarrow, attempted to make him comfortable, then pushed off, getting stuck in the doorway and nearing panic before shoving perhaps a little too forcefully but no longer mindful of anything except the likelihood of getting caught.

As they passed outside onto the stoop, Iris paused, something tickling the back of her memory. She looked over her shoulder and then she remembered what Maggie had said.

"Whenever you leave a room, my girl, always turn round and check it first." She ran back inside and across to the hearth. After studying the scene, she fetched a towel, wet it and vigorously washed away the patch of drying blood. Then she scuffed it underfoot with some ashes from the fireplace. Satisfied, she picked up the towel to leave, but on her way out veered over to Chiron's desk and grabbed the Little Midshipman in her free hand. Clutching it fiercely, she raced out to catch up with the funeral procession.

Before crossing the path she carefully scrutinized the laughter in the distance and verified it was not approaching, then sped up to the boys and stuffed the towel and figurine into Chiron's shroud. She patted them gently, to make sure they were snugly tucked in the crook of his arm. Not until then did she attempt to catch her breath, ragged and whimpering.

The sand was a problem, they hadn't figured on that, but they tugged and pulled and wobbled across, half blinded by tears and the horror of their own actions, but steely with the determination to literally plow through and get Chiron safely off shore. Perry realized that lifting from the front eased up on the wheel and allowed them to carry the cart more easily than they had lifted the body. Herman showed up just as they got bogged in the wet sand of the water line and made the difference in surmounting the final few yards to the waiting skiff. It was a rather unceremonious pouring of the shrouded body into the little boat, but it sufficed and again they rearranged him as best they could for comfort and dignity. They stood around the boat then, in homage; speechless, spent, honored by the responsibility conferred on them, effusing love and devotion with every heaving breath; naively hopeful of some kind of redemption after this ghastly tragedy that would take a lifetime of questions, a lifetime of brooding scrutiny and contemplation to decipher.

Todd took a step back, partly pushed by an aggressive wave. The breeze had stiffened and the sliver of new moon was obliterated, leaving only the glow of their eyes apparent, and the glint off the gunwale of Chiron's rocking coffin. They looked about them, blinking, remembering they must not be seen, startled back into the present of unfinished business. Wordlessly, Todd checked the tow and climbed into the dingy. As he positioned the oars to row out a ways before starting the motor, the others lined up the skiff with the direction of the lead boat and mouthed their private farewells, a wail escaping from one of them sounding faraway, eerie, non-human. Perry reached in his pocket and pulled out a white flag, one he had found in his search for the sheet of canvas, and passed it over to Todd.

"I'll be watching for you. Fly this if all goes well. Fly it for Mission Accomplished," a reference to a World War II fighter plane documentary they had seen together in the movie theater years ago, when they were still kids. One last glance prompted him to add, "Hey. You can do this."

Then he shoved Todd off as the twins pushed the skiff. They ran with it in the surf until they lost their balance and tumbled underwater, reluctant to surface, terrified to face the world beyond this without their anchor.

Todd realized quickly he could not row for long, the wind becoming a factor and the waves gaining in heft. He strained against the current, then used it to float around the far dock where the Corinna rolled rhythmically and bumped against its mooring, nodding deferentially to the skiff. He glimpsed the wistful shimmer of barnacles on the dock posts just under the surface of the water, exposed, immersed, exposed again.

Impulsively, he turned and reached for the cord to start the motor. He didn't care anymore who heard him. He would disappear into the murk soon enough, and he could no longer bear his thoughts matching the repetitive cadence of the ocean's perpetual breathing. In, out. In, out. He could feel it growing in urgency. He pulled the cord.

It was slow going, but he felt better under the power of the little outboard, the sputtering, acrid fumes from the engine pervasive and reassuring. He aimed northeast, keeping his eye on the lighthouse starboard, and the familiar landmarks of his neighbors' houselights. Enfolded in utter darkness now, caressed by salt spray, lulled by the thrum of the engine as it surged and purred with the waves, he felt calmer. Chiron remained his unfailing companion and it was their privilege to take this last journey together, together. He was no longer fearful, and suffered no further doubts about his decision. He wondered for a moment if he would ever feel more at home in his life than he did right this minute, out here on this expanse of water, untethered to the world yet tied securely to the only father he had ever known. No son was ever more blessed, that he understood irrefutably. He smiled into the wind, squinting against the sting of the salt, breathing deeply of the burgeoning marine life all around him, sensing its beckoning embrace, its excitement over Chiron.

Poseidon had waited a long time for this catch, Todd considered wryly. He supposed it was his due. They had ridden the waves together, the sea god and the oracle, for parts of two centuries, and criss-crossed the oceans of the world in every configuration of weather, temperament, whim and eye of the storm from proud ship to grand ship to hand-built sailing vessel, through decades of upheaval, hope, desolation and redemption;

all the while the pair remaining synchronized, matching pulse to matching pulse. Theirs had been a partnership of trust, courage, respect and sun-drenched glory, epic in its breadth and mastery.

Todd peered into the water and wanted nothing more than to sleep there himself. Time passed, time he could not account for, and he was lulled. When he glanced up, he had passed the lighthouse and did not recognize the lights onshore. They seemed farther away than they should be. He felt a spatter of drops that were not salted. He felt a trickle of fear at the base of his spine as the breeze swirled around him. A wave swept over the bow and startled him. He turned abruptly to make sure the skiff had not swamped. Not without his say-so. Not without saying goodbye. It rocked precipitously, taking on water, but proved seaworthy enough and soon settled again. Todd breathed deeply with relief. It was time to perform his duty.

He looked up into the dark sky, swathed in cloud cover. "All the gods are within you," Chiron had said. "Take them into yourself."[1] He knew he had reached the point of no return when he made the decision to cover up Chiron's death. But to invite the gods into himself seemed risky, presumptuous. And yet, he had crossed a precipice, this he understood, and the rules had changed. He had been changed.

As he gazed, a hole opened in the sky and he detected the outline of the new moon. He was reminded of an evening like this when Chiron had indicated the moon's new cycle to him saying, "The phases of the moon, that wax and wane with unfailing regularity, represent the power of life to throw off death, and come to new life."[1]

He considered that edict for a while, rocking in his little boat that idled patiently, awaiting his comprehension. This new life, he thought. This new life that Chiron gave his own life up for. He glanced over his shoulder mournfully. It has to do with Nick. It is a chance for Nick to redeem himself. To reclaim his life. To take up where Chiron left off. For himself and for Todd. For his family and the future of those Chiron loved. This had been Chiron's intention all along. This was his plan and they had all played their part in it. They trained for a year. They suffered bereavement. They tested their limits. They leaned on him, depended on him, hounded him, turned to him for every little thing, used him up. And he knew that they would.

Todd was on his knees then, pulling the tow rope until the skiff came alongside and he could bury his face in the shroud of his most adored companion, his protector, his teacher, his first and always father. His heart broke wide open there on the watery bier, and all the love a child ever had the capacity to express poured itself into the shroud, to be buried and dissolved in a sea of fidelity on this tempestuous, overwrought, electrifying night.

When he was depleted, when he was so weak with grief that he was in danger of sinking along with the ship, he gathered himself enough, shivering from head to toe, and rose up enough to reach for the knot of the rope tow in order to untie it. His fingers were stiff and uncooperative. They slipped again and again, refusing to grip. Finally, he used his teeth and pulled until his jaw ached, until the fibers of the rope had slit his tongue, until it acquiesced, loosening just a little, making Todd work with all his strength to accomplish what his natural inclination refuted with every ounce of his will.

With the knot unraveled, he turned the skiff sideways and gently pulled it toward himself. Clasping the gunwale, he carefully tipped the edge into the water, letting the sea pour in, gradually filling the vessel, weighing it down, enveloping its occupant, its valiant, honored disciple; bathing him, sanctifying him, preparing him for the gods.

"Love is the burning point of life."[1]  It was Chiron's voice he heard, distinctive and compelling.  Its deep and confident resonance soothed him and bolstered him up.  Todd bent to kiss him, and rested his cheek against the shroud, until the water rose to engulf it.  He sat up and watched through his tears as the skiff slowly, gracefully lowered into the sea.  It was all in slow motion and gentle.  Then a rogue wave broke from nowhere over the stern, encompassing the entire craft and when it subsided, the skiff had vanished.  Todd wiped his eyes feverishly and finally seeing, gasped.

He was racked with new sobs from a depth he did not know he had, and frantically swirled his hands, his arms up to his shoulders, in the water behind the dinghy.  He wanted him back, he had to get him back just for a moment, just one more moment, this was not endurable, not out here like this all alone, not without Chiron, he couldn't bear to live anymore, not without Chiron, oh God what had he been thinking.  Was it too late to go in after him?  Just one quick dive, just below the surface, he had to be there still, so close, he must be there still.  He was quaking with regret and terror.  He was turning himself inside out with bereavement and would soon be shredded beyond healing from the pain.

Another wave swelled ominously beneath the dinghy and he was forced to cling to the motor to avoid going overboard.  His head cleared a little from the scare, jarred enough to be reminded of his promise.  And his training.  He sat back and grabbed the edges of the beam with his fingers gripping tightly.  He looked around him, seeing little but feeling the hulking shadows of greedy, unsated sea demons lurking on all sides within tentacle-reach of his lonely vessel. Childish. Lonely. Finally he pried his hands from the seat and addressed the motor. As he got it going and took the tiller to bring his boat about, the lighthouse caught his eye off to port, and he took heart. It was then that he noticed the breeze had quieted somewhat and above, the clouds had thinned. He spotted Sagittarius in the southern sky and studied it. Sagittarius, the king of the centaurs. His reward for surrendering his immortality had been to become a constellation. There, standing guard, to reign in the heavens for all time.

As he approached home, Todd reached in his pocket and pulled out the white flag. He had no mast, so when he recognized the pattern of lights that meant Beechwood, he aimed his little boat straight toward shore, stood up with feet propped wide and waved it for all he was worth. Just as he glimpsed the dock and the Corinna placidly moored there, he remembered to look for Iris' signal. There. There gently billowing as it dangled from the designated lamp post was her lacy petticoat, translucent and reassuring, beckoning him ashore.

He killed the motor and glided along the middle dock, swinging himself up from a post and tying up quickly. As he crossed the walkway and jumped to the sand he spotted a figure emerging from the west end of the shoreline, camouflaged by the shadows of the scrub pines. Perry looked a little seedy, rumpled, sand caked along his jaw line where he must have lain on the beach, waiting. He approached cautiously, uncertain of what he would find of Todd, what toll his journey may have claimed.

Reaching Todd he paused, refraining from any overt show of emotion as he waited patiently for him to speak. It took Todd some time to find his voice, feeling overcome at seeing Perry there, safe, vigilant, obviously worried yet unspeakably relieved. He handed him the flag and as their eyes met, he nodded his thanks, and his reassurance.

The twins were fresh-scrubbed and slick-haired, wearing their pajamas and robes. They sat on chairs on either side of Nick, who was sitting up, rubbing the back of his neck, grunting, mumbling and peering at Herman suspiciously when the boys arrived. He moved stiffly and reacted slowly when they erupted in joyful whoops as Todd crossed the patio. They knocked over their chairs as they leapt to greet him, exuberant despite their sober intentions, relief from the responsibility of a petulant drunk immeasurable.

Fear that Todd would disappear with Chiron, though never admitted, had seemed more and more likely as the night wore on, their faith waning with every interminable delay of his return. Here in the flesh, though, it seemed a preposterous idea, that Todd could ever desert them. Their worry allayed, they laughed as they hugged him, clutching tighter than they meant to, breathing in his vitality, his solidness, his burgeoning self-possession. And he hugged them back. As he stood in the dim light, surrounded by his steadfast mates, he looked across the flagstones to where Nick sat, elbow propped on one bent knee, studying him. Their eyes met, the eyes that resembled each other's strikingly, if anyone besides Thea had thought to notice.

Herman saw the exchange of glances. "We told Nick he was wrong, Todd. He thought he hit Chiron but he's wrong, he got it backwards. Chiron thought he was the Intruder, the Shadow, and Chiron hit him with the poker. We reminded him of all the missing stuff around here. And Chiron must have been upset when he saw it was Nick he hit, because he left, he disappeared. But no one ever worries about him, so relax. Right? Right Todd?"

Nick looked at each of them one at a time. When his eyes rested once again on Todd, he started to speak, then thought better of it and decided what he had to say to him must wait until later. Instead, he smiled sardonically up at the group of Maggie's marauders and chuckled.

"So," he observed. "My lifeboats came after all."

"Your what?" Perry thought he misunderstood.

"My lifeboats. My father worried my whole life that when I needed it most, I wouldn't have any lifeboat on board to save me. And here you were all the time." He shook his head in wonder.

They righted the chairs and gathered around Nick, drawn by his open demeanor. He was examining his hands, noting what looked like soot and dirt, maybe ashes. Ashes. His memory was jarred by an old thought. He couldn't remember. Ashes in his hands. A dream. Something. Fire is transforming. Yes. Fire and ashes and a boat.

Herman pulled out the handkerchief Nick had given to him when he lost his Ba, and offered it to clean himself up with. He scrutinized Herman, considering the likelihood he may have long underestimated this young man, since the day at the twin rivers and the water in his shoe. The corner of one side of his mouth turned upward as he accepted it gratefully and wiped.

The elation of reunion wore off quickly and the letdown that followed, combined with exhaustion and lowered defenses, hit them hard. Their ebullience drained away, taking their color with it, sapping their energy, extinguishing their bravado, threatening to turn to mass keening of cosmic magnitude. Nick, sensing the dramatic downturn of spirits, picked himself up and took charge of the twins, breaking up the group dynamics that he could only fathom, and effecting a short goodnight. One arm around the shoulder of each woeful sibling, he herded them tenderly across the deserted pathway and veranda to the back door, left standing ajar since their sneaking escape after bedtime. With hushed encouragement and pats on the back, he urged them inside. As he walked away he overheard Herman, addressing his sister.

"Our quest. Do you think Chiron knew what it was all along?"

Nick wasn't close enough to see her eyes fill with tears and watch as one escaped to roll down her cheek, following a trail from freckle to freckle, searing her skin as it fell.

Todd and Perry walked arm in arm along the same path, steeped in shadows and night echoes. As they crossed the garden, Perry looked at the fresh mound of dirt in the shell collection by the lily pond. A couple of hours earlier he had stolen the gold coin from the strongbox and buried it there. He wasn't the first to appeal to the gods in such a manner, Thea having rendered the very shell that Nick had been asking about earlier this evening, herself prayerful and yearning as ever Perry had been. They desired nothing more than a claim, a stake in Beechwood, a chance to be a part of its legacy; its roots, its permanence, its clan.

Todd broke into Perry's reverie saying, "Let's sleep in the plow shed tonight. Let's lie awake and wait there until Ole Webster comes home. He'll eventually come home, he always does. And I want to be there this time to see him."

They slipped by Maggie's room, the soft light of her lamp in the window caressing their skin as they passed, the muffled refrains of a country ballad floating on the air.

For their support and expertise, I extend my sincerest gratitude to:

Eva Branton and Father Jim Moulketis for their knowledge of Greek traditions. I also relied on the book, *Greek Traditions and Customs in America,* byMarilyn Rouvelas.

Laura Schramm, Dan Ladd and the boating staff of Avery's Flathead Lake Lodge, Montana, for their expertise in sailing.

Lucy Bermingham for her research and guiding tour of the Lower East Side.

The members of my book group of nearly two decades, aka the Daughters of the Skating Club, who read the early manuscript and offered their usual shrewd, artful insight and encouragement.

Patrick, Peter, Elizabeth, Cooper, Colby, Matthew and Joseph, my indomitable children. I picture them all body-surfing at the Jersey Shore: my enchanting mermaid daughter among her divine sea brothers; brilliant, exuberant, vital. They are my life's inspiration and I hope they know it.

The only two people I allowed to read my book as I was writing it; my oldest son, Patrick, and my husband, Bob. I chose Bob because I needed a cheerleader. He loved every word, as I knew he would, and never had a single criticism. He cried and laughed and told me it was as good as Jack

Kerouac (his favorite author). He even thinks he means it. I can say categorically that besides all of his other virtues, he is way kinder and smarter than I am. And as anyone who knows him would agree, well along the path of a truly heroic spirit.

Lastly, my son Patrick, who edited the first half of the book for me, because I knew he would take it entirely on its own merit, and use his extensive knowledge, love of reading and flawless honesty to comment and criticize, but still allow me to write my own story. He also explained the monomyth to me and introduced me to my muse, Joseph Campbell, whose ideas I used in every facet of my story.

The day I finished Chapter 14 was the last day I saw my son, Patrick. He died suddenly of a heart attack at the age of 33. Our lives ground to a halt, in a stunning instant. It was months later that I realized Chapter 14 ends on the day Thea dies of heart failure. That was a distressing discovery for me and in our unbearable heartbreak, I struggled with the coincidence of it. Now I wonder if it had been my tale telling itself from somewhere spiritual I could not fathom. Almost a year later, when I began writing again, I felt the story take on a sense of death's redemption, perhaps a story I had become more qualified to tell. For me and for THE SEXTANT, it's all mixed together; what's real and what's truth and what's mystical.

# NOTES

[1] "Joseph Campbell and the Power of Myth with Bill Moyers," televised interviews, 1988.

[2] Father Jim Moulketis, St. Nicholas Greek Orthodox Church, Wyckoff, NJ.

[3] "A Toast to the Merchant Mariner," Anonymous, USMMC, Polaris Magazine, July 1943.

[4] "The Last Voyage," by Lizzie Clark Hardy, USMAA Memorial Service, May 2000.